onyx

FELICE PICANO

alyson books
los angeles | new york

Manufactured in the United States of America.

This hardcover edition is published by Alyson Publications,
P.O. Box 4371, Los Angeles, CA 90078-4371.

First edition: May 2001

01 02 03 04 05 a 10 9 8 7 6 5 4 3 2 1

ISBN: 1-55583-640-2

Library of Congress Cataloging-in-Publication Data
  Picano, Felice, 1944–
    Onyx / Felice Picano.—1st ed.
    ISBN 1-55583-640-2
    1. Gay men—Fiction. I. Title.
  PS 3566.I25 O59 2001
    813'.54—DC21   00-053597

Credits
Portions of this book appeared previously in somewhat different
form in various periodicals and anthologies as follows: Chapter
Two as "A Married Man" in the anthology *New York Sex*, Painted Leaf
Press, and as "Onyx" in Genre and the anthology *Best Gay Erotica 2001*,
Cleis press; Chapter Six as "Jesse: November 1992" in *Rebel Yell*,
Haworth Press; Chapter Eight as "Chinese Violin" in *Harrington Gay
Men's Fiction Quarterly*, Haworth Press.

To Edmund White

Leben ohne Liebe kannst du nicht.
—Marlene Dietrich

...Till the bridge you will need be form'd, till the ductile anchor hold,
Till the gossamer thread you fling catch somewhere,
O my soul.
—Walt Whitman, *A Noiseless, Patient Spider*

MIKE

OCTOBER 1992

one

A stark, golden shaft of 7:15 A.M. October sunlight gleamed through a minute slit formed by two unevenly closed slats in a vertical blind, sparkling in the otherwise darkened bedroom. Light épéed across the tousled, multileveled linen of the double bed upon which one male form slept, torso twisted, arms and legs extended, bent to configure a flawed letter X, nearly a swastika. Light spilled off the ivory comforter's tufted edge, briefly spangling the carpet, inducing its royal blue and pale tan pattern to dance. Light ascended across a second quilt, up to a second, flimsier, more temporary bed, and there illuminated three-and-one-fourth-inch band across the face of a second sleeping male. Briefly the sunlight hid behind an interrupting cloud, and the somnolent, apparently annoyed face relaxed. The cloud passed, the sunbeam returned with renewed brightness, and a pair of chocolate-brown eyes opened enough to be offended, shut again. The thickly curled, dark blond head turned and nestled too late into the blurred security of a crush of down pillow.

Minutes later this second man got out of bed, stood up, and approached the other, still sleeping, shallowly breathing male. He half crouched, half crawled onto the larger bed to make contact with the pale, sweat-wetted forehead. He sighed, got off the bed, padded into the nearby bath, where he passed water, stretched, yawned, muttered a word that sounded like "Fer-ber." He turned on the shower. When it was steaming, he closed the connecting door.

When he stepped out again, the sunlight had widened from a fencing sword's narrow edge into a Saracen blade, obliquely slicing his well-shaped lower torso, now partly swaddled in a damp towel, and redefining the figure still upon the bed, which had solved its algebra and reconfigured into a nearly perfect letter I.

"Don't get up," the standing man said. "Don't wake up yet."

He drew the quilt, sheets, and pillows off the smaller bed with a practiced toreador flourish, his body, packaged in its tiny towel, looking to the man in bed, awake despite the other's entreaties, like the icon on some Minoan mural. He swung fluffed linen gracefully up and atop a maple blanket chest, bent to metallically close the bed, launching it into a cranny behind the chest where it was effectively hidden.

"You know it takes forever to get up, Ray," the man on the bed said, his face hidden in darkness. He hoped it came out as fact, not a whine. "Open the blinds."

"You sleep OK, Jess?" Ray asked without looking back from the tall window casement where he slowly rotated the vertical blinds. The room became lambent by degree.

In profile, Ray now looked Egyptian: a courtier painted amid enigmatic hieroglyphs, overseer perhaps of some grand Nilotic project, sleek and sturdy, strong, faultless save for the hard-on, the eternal hard-on the tight white towel every morning revealed to still be there; the hard-on once familiar and desired, now unceasing, slow to go away. His fault, his undoing—lack of doing—Jesse knew.

"I'm getting up now," Jesse announced, lifting the covers off himself. Perspiration had matted the cotton T-shirt to his chest. No surprise: He was sleeping right through the night sweats these days, too exhausted to be appalled as he'd been not that long ago. Ray dropped his towel and bent to step into his underwear.

"Oh, my God!" Jesse cried. Ray spun around, alarmed, one foot into the Calvins, the other dangling aloft. "Is that...could that possibly be," Jesse began, "a blemish? An imperfection on your otherwise perfect buttock?"

A foxy smile replaced Ray's frown of alarm as he continued to dress. "Don't start about my imperfections, Buster, or you'll be sorry. C'mon up, if you're getting up."

Jesse fumbled into a kneeling position on the bed and Ray pulled off the sopping T-shirt and drew down the now overlarge cotton shorts.

"Unhand me, vile seducer!" Jesse falsettoed. "Bodice ripper!"

"Quiet, or I'll rip something else." Ray tossed the clothing across the room, and came in closer, popping open a sealed plastic bag of fresh towels and underwear. He playfully toweled dry Jesse's hair, discarded that towel, shook out a scented towelette and used it to wash Jesse's face and upper chest.

"I expect the bath of ass's milk is ready," Jesse said. "They'd better be Phoenician. I'm bored with the old Babylonian ones. Stop, you're tickling me."

"We're in luck. No new rashes or bumps or dots today!" Ray announced, kissing Jesse's clean, medical-scented shoulder. "Genitals now."

"Please, sir! Not my private parts! Anything but my private parts!" And as Ray used a second towelette to wash Jesse's lower body: "Lord, How long must this abuse go on?"

"Some folks pay a hundred bucks an hour for this abuse. All the way up, now." He lifted Jesse to stand on the bed. A third towelette was shaken out and applied to Jesse's legs and feet. "OK. All clean now."

"Remember when I had muscles?" Jesse said in a changed tone of voice.

"In your imagination you had muscles. Oh, wait. It's coming back to me. In the summer of '82. Yes. Now I recall. I couldn't wait for them to go away." Ray kissed one scarred, disinfectant-smelling kneecap, and pulled the new pair of cotton shorts over the still-firm legs, up the slender hips, thanking God that emaciation hadn't set in, and might not for a while. The new T-shirt went over the shoulders. A fourth towelette rubbed the hair clean. Was there ever a man so lovely?

"That's it, chum! Maid's work's over," Ray announced, lifting Jesse from the bed to the floor. The body, which had once weighed the same as Ray's, seemed lighter every day, as if the shell remained perfect, but as Jesse slept, night by night, the stuffing seeped out. He suddenly noticed Jesse was shorter by maybe an inch. They'd always been the same height, looked straight into each other's eyes.

"Kiss me," Jesse demanded.

He bussed Jesse's lips, wiping off the kiss with the edge of the last towelette.

"No. Really kiss me. French kiss. Hard! Deep!"

"C'mon, Jess. You know we can't do that."

"Please, Ray. I'll gargle with the poison crap that snotface gave me."

They kissed, mouths open, tongues probing, bodies pressed together until Jesse felt he was leaving the ground. Ray pulled away first, bussed and licked Jesse's disinfected neck and shoulders and chest, knowing he'd have to towelette them again. He kept it up until it was too much, and Jesse couldn't help but flinch and draw back.

"Sorry." Ray withdrew another towelette to recleanse what he'd just kissed. "Go rinse and gargle now. Doctor's orders."

"I wanted it," Jesse said. "I did want it."

"Me too, Buster Brown. Me too."

"I can tell. You're toting a major woody."

Ray hefted it in both hands. "A bone crusher!" he said, making a grim face. "A diamond cutter! A tree limb! A Sequoia! A…"

"Jeez, I'm sorry I mentioned it," Jesse kvetched, then went into the bathroom to gargle. He hadn't gotten hard, of course. He couldn't remember the last time he'd gotten hard. Last month? The month before? He was chafed from where Ray had kissed him, despite the disinfectant; he'd need hydrocortisone cream.

That done, he called out, "Who's Fer-ber?" as he came into the bedroom. No answer, Ray was already upstairs.

Alone, Jesse sat on the bed and slowly, with effort, pulled on the socks, slacks, shirt, tie, and shoes that Ray had laid out for him, knowing the suit jacket was already upstairs, brought up and placed by Ray across a breakfast chair back. Even before he was done, Jesse sighed, exhausted, and fell back onto the bed and thought, just a snooze, a minute. No, I can't, I'm going to wrinkle everything. He raised himself with effort to a sitting position, stood, wavered on his feet. "I had muscles more than one summer, didn't I?" he asked his reflection in the mirror. He steeled himself for the walk upstairs: "It's your own fault," he soliloquized. "*You* were the one who wanted to stay at work as long as possible! Nobody's making you do it." Having said that, he was unaccountably happy. He smiled at his ability to still find pleasure, and approached the staircase with more energy than before, almost a strut.

A complete array of breakfast smells greeted him. The little table nook window, however, was raised for him to sit by so he wouldn't become nauseated by the odors, which happened more and more. Seated and looking outside, Jesse faced the corner of Joralemon and Clinton Streets from his second-floor vantage point. Mrs. Schnell, in her oldest son's mottled green-and-gray Vietnam flak jacket, walked her ancient chows—her diurnal alibi for peeking into every unshuttered, unshaded window. Mr. Nissen across the street sprayed and wiped the tinted windshield of his matte-gold Lexus sedan. Passing behind him was the lesbian couple Jesse and Ray had met at a Manhattan fund-raiser. Both were clad in dark suits with lighter coats and carried stout leather briefcases. What were their names? Forgotten. Autos slowly cruised looking for that rarity—an unmetered parking space: Brooklyn Heights was waking up.

"Who's Fer-ber?" Jesse asked. "You said the name. Edna Ferber?"

"No. A Belgian pianist," Ray said, feeding Jesse his mug of herbal tea and British cereal Weetabix. "I can't find him in the Schwann catalogue. Not in the *Dictionary of Performing Artists*. Not even in the *New Grove*."

Jesse's herbal tea tasted odd today. Of orrisroot. Was orrisroot in it?

"So how do you know the name?" Jesse asked.

"Sarah Fishko played a record a few weeks ago on the radio. Faure's *Theme and Variations*, a few of his barcaroles, some nocturnes. I had a cassette in the Revox, so I taped it. I only half listened because I was busy back-billing invoices, but it sounded pretty good. I listened later on. He's the best Faure pianist …and I'd never even heard of him."

That was quite an admission. "Better than Tagliaferro? Jesse asked. "Better than Marguerite Long?"

You sweetheart, Ray thought, *to remember those names. To ask me. To be interested.* "There's so little from Long or Tagliaferro. If not better, 'as good.'"

"And you want what?" Jesse asked. "To put Ferber on CD?"

Ray operated a record company out of the office on the lower floor of the townhouse: Klavier Stuecke Records, a one-and-a-half-man operation. (A college student from nearby Long Island University helped two afternoons a week as packer for heavier shipping.) It was a private label specializing in pianists and occasionally harpsichordists and organists. Piano recording had been a hobby for a decade when Ray was an A&R man for EMI's International and Classical Divisions, working in Manhattan. That job had helped Ray develop the connections he'd needed to start up his own company, from LP pressing plants to young illustrators willing to do cover art.

When compact discs debuted, then flourished, a ravenous demand for product arose, and some of it was for older stuff, especially pianists of the past: Moritz Rosenthal, Harold Bauer, Michelangeli, Cortot, Rosa Lhevinne, Egon Petri. Ray used his savings to transfer old music to the new format, placed discreet ads in music magazines, sent out review copies, and pushed discs to local record stores and chains, in person or by phone. And when EMI shut down their mid Manhattan recording studio, offering Ray a choice of London or Los Angeles or a separation package, he opted for the money and came home from work to stay. He upgraded his computer system and became so profitable his accountant recommended incorporation. He'd added Jesse to the company roster so Jesse would have more than just the medical coverage from his job at Casper, Vine and Markham, the ad agency where he was a senior vice president in copywriting. The previous year, two of Klavier Stuecke's CDs received awards. One, the resurrection of a poorly recorded Italian pressing of a 1935 performance of Vladimir Horowitz playing the Brahms First Piano Concerto with Arturo Toscanini conducting the New York Philharmonic—a milestone previously thought undocumented or lost—had become a bit of a classical best-seller.

"I'd love to put out a Ferber CD," Ray said. "If I can find a reliable source. The tape I took off the radio's not good enough. It's clear, but the upper register's clattery. Miked too close, typical of the mid '50s in Europe. And there are shifts in the aural surround from piece to piece. The recording was probably done over time with different microphone setups, maybe in several studios."

One reason for Klavier Stuecke's success was how good—yet free of gimmickry—Ray made the pianists sound. Not long ago an international recording giant had approached him with a substantial offer for the rights to his "process." As there was no process, only Ray's "aural vision," he'd said no. Instead they'd tried a disc-by-disc option. The recording giant gave him a test, a record of a dozen Domenico Scarlatti sonatas: Wanda Landowska on the eve of the German invasion of Paris in 1940 playing a double keyboard Pleyel-reconstructed harpsichord. In the background of the delicate Italo-Iberian keyboard tracery, one could make out the distinct, muffled booms of Panzer cannon. Ray's pal Liesl had once told him about Bertrand Russell meeting Landowska on the Bois de Boulogne in 1915, walking arm in arm with a man and a woman. "This is my husband," the Polish virtuoso said, "and this is my wife." Ray was so thrilled with the historicity of the recorded pieces, he'd left in every military boom. The client wanted them out. They'd argued. The project had been aborted.

"Why not call up Fishko and ask where she got her record?" Jesse asked.

"She left the station. Her dad got ill or something, and she won't take messages from strangers. I tried the show's producer and the other DJs, who all told me she brings in her own records. One promised to get my message to her. So far, no dice. You going to eat that?" Ray pointed to the cereal Jesse had been poking with a spoon.

Jesse's appetite was poor to begin with, and the tea hadn't helped. They were saved from a potential debate by the phone ringing. Ray picked it up. After three exchanges of barely a word each, Jesse figured it was one of the kids, Chris or Sable. He drew a question mark in the air.

"Dan didn't hit your mom or anything like that, did he?" Ray said. It had to be Sable, Ray's sister's youngest child. Dan was the latest of Kathy's 15-year-younger live-in boyfriends. Jesse already knew this conversation. He poured more herbal tea. "If Dan comes anywhere near you or Chris…" Ray threatened into the receiver. "I know he hasn't. I'm saying if he does, OK? Sure, I'll talk to her. Today. I promise. Want to say hello to your Queer Uncle Jesse?" As he handed the phone to Jesse across the table, palm of the hand over the receiver, he said, "I'll kill the bastard!"

"Can I rape him first?" Jesse asked. "C'mon, lighten up." Then into the phone, "Iz thiz Mizz Sable, hun-eee?"

Nine-year-old giggling on the other end. "Yesss."

"Why don't you and your beautiful brother come for dinner tonight?" The latter said to embarrass Chris, surely listening on another line. Jesse looked to Ray, who shrugged "Why not?" The kids lived five blocks away and came to eat twice a week as it was, sleeping over on holidays and occasional weekends and always when Kathy was "breaking in" a new lover.

"What's for dinner?" Sable asked.

"Whatz thiz shit? Mizz Sable, the girl who'll eat anything, and I do mean *anything*, including frog stew and roadkill cookies, asking whatz for dinner. Whadafuck?"

She giggled again, loving his cursing. "I'll come. We'll both come," she added, meaning Chris was there and was behind or at least supporting the call. "What'll we tell Mom?"

"Leave a note for when she gets home from work, saying you're here." He looked to Ray, who nodded yes. Neither wanted to deal with Ray's sister until she'd either straightened out her affairs or gotten rid of Dan. This was their agreed way of dealing with it. "Tell Chris I've got two new porno tapes!"

Chris was 13 and making a big deal out of being suddenly sexual. Now he got on the phone. "You know I'm not allowed to look at those things," he complained in his raw-squawky voice.

"Sure, you can, kid. This one is called *Debbie Does the Carnegie Deli*. Fifteen sexy yet weird foodstuffs. And the other one is titled *Miss Otis Regrets*."

"Uncle Jesse?"

"You mean Queer Uncle Jesse, don't you?"

"Right, and Uncle Ray? Thanks, huh?"

"You'll pay, kid. And pay. Probably in trade."

"I don't even know what that means."

"Yeah, right!" Jesse said, and they both laughed.

"Be here at 4:15 on the dot!" Before Dan or Kathy got in. After he hung up, Jesse said, "Well, at least we've got them trained."

"You've got them trained," Ray said. "They adore you."

"Gay couples are suing every day to adopt kids. And we've got two without even asking." Jesse took Ray's hand. "Lucky us!"

Ray was moping. "We aren't all that lucky."

"Yes, we are, Mr. Stupid, Ugly, Brutal, and Poor. Lucky, lucky, lucky us."

They tightened their grip on each other's hand and looked at each other across the table, until Ray released a half sigh, half laugh, rebonding, solidifying as they'd done every morning of their 16 years together.

As they pulled apart, Ray said, "And now for the really bad news. Your mother called yesterday, while you were in the midst of your beauty sleep. Foolish me picked up."

"*Eeewwww!*"

"You still haven't told her, have you?" Ray asked.

"I believe this is the point in the movie where I start screaming hysterically."

"You've *got* to tell her! Everyone agrees. J.K., Liesl, Gene, your shrink, your 18 doctors, the social workers, even Kathy! You've got to tell her *now*. Now, while you're still healthy," Ray repeated his weekly litany.

"I know. I know. I know."

"If I end up having to tell your mother, I swear to God, Jess, no matter what condition you're in, I'm going to stomp into the intensive care ward and finish you off. Strangle you with your IV tubes. Smother you. Understand?"

"But Ray, she's such an astonishing bitch that—"

"That's why you have to do it now."

"She'll...she'll..."

"She'll what? Disinherit you? Tell you to leave me? Make our lives hell? She's done all that already. What more can she do? Follow your corpse into the ground and harass you in the afterlife? Promise me you'll tell her next time you speak."

"You don't know what it's like."

"I've been son-in-law to the Mother From Hell for 16 years. I know. Do it now! While you're still strong. While you're still in good health."

"I will...when you go out and get laid," Jesse countered.

"I get laid every day. While you're off at work I trawl the streets of the

Heights, dragging in delivery boys and meter readers, sanitation workers, anyone vaguely hot. I'm known to the neighbors as the Slut of Joralemon Alley. You've seen the Dimitris avoid me when we walk together? It's a wonder the company hasn't gone under by now."

Stalemate.

"I'll tell her," Jesse promised. As usual. Meaning it as he said it. As usual.

"Get ready," Ray suggested. "I'll warm up the car. Don't say no. I'm driving you to the eye doctor in Chelsea."

"OK. We are lucky, though, aren't we?"

"Sixteen times blessed."

"And I did have muscles, once."

"Prove it!"

"There are photos," Jesse threatened. "I'll find them. You'll see."

While Jesse brushed his teeth, Ray arranged his attaché and wallet on the breakfast table next to the suit jacket and scarf where Jesse could easily locate everything. There were no indications yet of memory loss or dementia and Ray wanted to forestall them as long as possible.

He pulled on a windbreaker and bounced downstairs to the bedroom and office. When they'd first visited from central Illinois, Ray's parents had unceasingly marveled over the perversity of having the master bedroom downstairs while the guest room was upstairs next to the living quarters. This, despite Ray's nonstop elucidation: The two-story apartment had been a pediatrician's, featuring street-level waiting room, office, and examination rooms he and Jesse had converted to lodge Klavier Stuecke Records (an office and storage area) and their good-size bed and dressing rooms.

Immediately outside the office door was an abbreviated concrete driveway, sole direct access from their duplex to the set-back garage.

Lying in wait so close to the office street door that Ray all but stumbled over the body was Otto, their caramel-colored Persian cat. Three months earlier, following the detection of a feline infection, Jesse's doctors had declared the cat verboten. Otto carried too many germs and bacteria that were all too instantly conveyed to Jesse, who lacked means to fend them off. Ray had been forced to board the cat with Ann and Jim Dimitri, their neighbors on the other side of the driveway. The narcissistic Persian instinctively knew where to position himself to be attainable to the greatest number of admirers, and the prime site in the Dimitris' turned out to be a bay window facing Ray and Jesse's breakfast nook. In this way, Otto and Jesse might at least glimpse each other on a daily basis.

Despite this consolation, Otto persisted in feeling his banishment to be uncalled for. Today, yet again, the cat stubbornly attempted to slide in through the ajar office doorway. Ray held him back by his darker colored, pushed-in face, then lifted the sweet, soft body and firmly ejected the cat, who turned back to glare as he sauntered away. Otto, Ray knew, would engineer his way inside one way or another by the end of the day. Ray would find the cat stretched upon a pile of manila envelopes or bivouacked across floorboards at the most trafficked point in the office. Not a huge concern, as long as he kept Otto out of the bedroom, made sure the corridor door was shut so Otto couldn't wander, and washed his hands compulsively.

Ray started up the car and drove around to the front. Jesse was perched halfway up the flight of stone steps. The car, a Buick Regal, was a gift from Ray's parents. It had belonged to Ray's mother and was in pristine condition, silver-blue outside, navy leather inside, only five years old. When Harve and Mona Henriques had visited and noticed the unused garage, they offered the car to Jesse and Ray. After all, Mona was retired and they had the Chrysler van; that was enough for them now. Ray protested until Jesse calculated that if they kept the car registered and insured from Ray's parents' home, the upkeep would cost less than their three-times-a-year car rentals. The Buick, big and plush the way a mother's car ought to be, was quite unlike the tiny, spartan Tercel that Ray had driven throughout college; he'd now grown accustomed to the larger car's cushy, imprecise steering and vague braking, and clement weekends he and Jesse sometimes drove to Westchester or the North Shore. Naturally, they could use it to drive to the Fire Island ferry too. But they went there so seldom now.

Jesse stared up at something—a bird?—in the upper branches of one of the gingko trees that ornamented the street. From this angle, and in this illumination, his golden eyes appeared virtually transparent: a special effect that had never ceased to thrill Ray. With his attaché leaned against his side and his mahogany cowlick sticking up, with his suit jacket one size too large for him, Jesse looked like a cute boy on his way to school; someone 11, 12 at most. Seeing his partner so childlike, so defenseless, so distracted, Ray began to grasp the colossal loss headed his way. He had to look away, down at paper trash whirling slowly in the middle of the street before he could gain control of his voice to call Jesse to the car.

"Buckle up, Sunshine!" he commanded brightly to hide the heartache snaking its way through him. "Don't want to lose you out the door on a turn."

Adams Avenue was its usual overtrafficked weekday morning mess. But while the Brooklyn Bridge was congested, at least it was in motion. Once across the river and driving on the East Side, Ray knew shortcuts uptown. They'd arrived at Canal and Hudson Streets without stopping for a single red light.

"I should go in with you," Ray thought aloud.

"What for?"

"To hear what the opthamologist says. Says exactly. You never tell me anything specific."

Jesse didn't deny it.

Five minutes later, as they neared the corner of Seventh and Twentieth, Ray decided, "I'll park and come in. I can drive you to the office."

"You'll never find parking here." Jesse was realistic. "And there are scads of cabs going downtown. Go home, Ray! Go to work. Earn money. Lots of money. Buy me diamonds. I'm 40—Holly Golightly says I can wear diamonds." Jesse leaned over and bussed Ray's cheek. "Lousy job shaving," he commented without a hint of malice. Then he was out of the car, jauntily swinging his attaché as he neared the huge gray stone building housing the doctor's office. He stopped for a glance backward, saw Ray illegally double-parked, grinned, gave a jerking thumb gesture signifying "Get outta here!" and slipped indoors.

Ray clutched the steering wheel tightly. What if Jesse never walked out that door again? Someday that would happen. Then what? What are you going to do then, Ray? In his peripheral vision, a car glided by, its driver giving him the finger and shouting "Whaddaya own the whole damn street?"

two

As he entered D'Agostino's, Ray had to trace a detour. At the second of the two glass doors leading into the supermarket, a five-foot wooden stepladder had been splayed open. Someone was astride its scaffold, reaching up to the automated device connecting the doors to a ceiling-mounted, geared mechanism. Ray couldn't see the fellow's face, only his thick, matte-black curly hair. But the repairman's body—clad in a heavy rugby shirt, knee-length, wide-wale corduroy shorts, off-white woolen socks, and clunky, heavily stained ankle-length work boots—was tight and muscular. His buttocks and thighs (exactly at eye level) and his calves (slightly lower) were so well modeled, so evenly tanned that they implied perfection throughout. Ray had learned over years of man-watching exactly what might correctly be inferred from a fragment: a hand and wrist held outside a car window; a shoulder blade and neck muscle glimpsed in a department store dressing room just as a V-neck was pulled on.

Possessed of who-knew-what unsuspected brass, Ray whistled sexily and crooned à la Streisand, "Hel-lo, gor-geous!" adding as he passed, "Don't fall!"

The guy looked down, bulky yellow plastic-lensed goggles framing and partly obscuring his cute, squarish, masculine face. "I won't," he said, sounding amused.

Surprised by his own daring, Ray snatched up a shopping basket and sped into the protective anonymity of the produce aisle. There he managed to find his grocery list and attempted to concentrate.

Brooklyn Heights was littered with fetching workmen of all ages and races, especially during the day. Ray would race out of his home office in the morning carrying a trash basket he'd failed to put out the night before, only to be greeted by the glowering face of a sanitation worker, a young Botticelli who menaced, "Next time have it out! Or I won't take it!" Or he'd be wedging into a parking spot and some Verrochio archangel with rolled-up sleeves and a Marlboro dangling off his lower lip would lean out the window of a pickup Ray had beaten out and yell obscenities, suggesting Ray learn how to drive—sonofabitch! The studly Puerto Rican adolescents who delivered pizza and Chinese at lunchtime wore skin-tight shirts and jeans, and flirted brazenly. The African-American son of the newsstand owner on Joralemon Street wore the least amount of clothing legal as he helped out during the summer: iridescent basketball tees and one memorable, shimmering, lilac-hued Speedo, lubricious against his bittersweet chocolate skin. The beauty and abundance of the men had been a standing joke between Ray and Jesse since they'd moved there, along with the understanding that these fellows were heterosexual and thus unobtainable. Besides which, even if you did fulfill the fantasy and have sex with one, what could you possibly talk about afterward? The latest Sondheim musical? The newest dance-club drug? So Ray concentrated on his food shopping and forgot the young repairman.

The stepladder was still there, but vacant, when Ray paid for his groceries ten minutes later. He sighed. But right outside the supermarket, he was surprised to see the workman, loitering against the back doors of his paint-splattered van, parked not ten feet away in the adjacent alley. He was clearly waiting for Ray, because as soon as he espied him, he turned, opened the doors, and climbed in.

Nervous yet undeniably intrigued, Ray stopped at the van's back door, shifting his grocery bags in case he needed an excuse for his halt. The mechanic was faced away, rifling through storage shelves built into the inner sides of the truck, doing so in a way that more than hinted that he was showing off his body.

When he glanced at Ray, Ray responded with a smile and what his mom called a great big Midwestern "Hello."

"Hello, yourself," the workman said. Slight outer-boroughs accent. "You know," he added, "you go around saying things like you said to me in there, you could get into trouble."

Ray shrugged. "I never do that. I just couldn't help myself."

A pause to assess the implied compliment.

"Not that I'm personally offended. But some guys..." the repairman trailed off. He swiveled around, holding powerful-looking snub-nose pliers in one hand.

Ray couldn't help feeling the man was flirting, giving Ray front and back views. Uncertain yet emboldened, he said, "So, what time do you get off work?" Oldest pickup line in the book.

"Coupla hours. I got one more stop in Caroll Gardens. Why?"

It's now or never, Ray thought. "I live nearby. Thought you might want to stop by for a beer."

The workman lifted the massive goggles off his face and used them to brush the thick shock of hair. The eyes disclosed were glorious: the palest green, lashes like an old film starlet's, set in high cheekbones. He leaned on one booted foot, which provocatively canted his lower torso forward. "I can get a beer anywhere."

With the revelation of those eyes, Ray's heart had thudded in his chest, a double whammy, given the erection he already had. Say it, he thought, panic-stricken lest he never see those eyes again. "How about I throw in a blow job?" Ray hoped he sounded cool and measured.

No change on the young face—he looked to be about 22, 23. And now Ray noticed that besides his solid physique and electrifying eyes, he also possessed a good complexion—evenly tanned, natural crimson to signify health, no marks or blemishes. "Well," the workman temporized, "I'm not sure when I'll be done here. Or the other place. Gotta be home by..."

Ray dropped the grocery bags and took out his wallet. In it, his card for Klavier Stuecke Records. "My address and phone number." Handing over the card, he noted the square-tipped, stubby fingers covered with cross-cuts—some old, a few fresh—that took hold of the card. "I live two blocks down, around the corner." Ray was casual as before. "Park in the garageway. No one'll ticket you." He wondered if he was coming on too aggressive, if he seemed too needy.

The repairman glanced at the card. "Like I said, I'm not sure when I'll be done." His voice hadn't fluctuated since they'd begun speaking, so Ray wasn't able to assess what might be at play behind the inexpressive face. But then Ray had also kept his voice to a masculine monotone. The workman didn't return the card, perhaps a good sign. Instead he slid it into one of the pockets in his shorts—a better sign—and turned to look for another tool.

Ray couldn't help feeling a bit dismissed. "Hope you find the time," he said brightly. "Bye!"

Half a block later, stopped at the traffic light at Montague Street, Ray thought, well, I was close, but somehow I screwed it up. His nerve in talking to the guy, never mind trying to pick him up, amazed him. He'd never done anything like that in his life. Certainly not with anyone whose sexuality he wasn't sure of. Hardly even with men he was certain were gay. In fact, Jesse used to tease that if he hadn't repeatedly pursued Ray over a period of months, they'd never have ended up together.

Nerve. Chutzpah, J.K. would call it: J.K. Callaway, Ray's best friend. J.K. had been in New York City more than two decades and used Yiddish words as though he were a member of Temple Beth-El and not an occasional attendee at St. Mary's Roman Catholic Church. Ray decided to call him the minute he got home. J.K. had more chutzpah than Bette Midler. He'd be shocked.

As for the young workman, he was sexy, and those eyes, my God, those eyes! He had definitely flirted with Ray, but almost casually, as though he flirted all the time and it meant nothing. Maybe that was true. Someone that cute! He must get hit on ten times a day. All of which suggested that it was unlikely Ray would hear from him. Probably for the best, Ray concluded. Struck as he was, excited as he'd been, he still felt queasy with the idea of touching anyone but Jesse, no matter how much his quite ill and thus celibate lover insisted it would merely be hygienically sound for someone as sex-starved as Ray to do so. Anyway, Ray had plenty to keep him busy that afternoon.

Otto was laying in wait and tested edging past Ray's legs at the office door. Ray's hands were busy, and the little Persian slid inside with a triumphant meow, speeding out of reach under the desk. Ray would pry him out later. He trooped upstairs to put the groceries away, popped a beer, took the rest of the six-pack down to the office's half fridge. He tapped the speed dial that would bring him J.K.'s voice.

Who did not pick up the phone. Who was instead, disgustingly, talking to someone else. Ray hit play on the answering machine and listened to a message from a college-bookstore customer he'd been playing phone tag with. He phoned that number and got the record department buyer. He'd barely hung up that call—with a substantial order to invoice and pack—when another customer phoned, needing more stock of the Horowitz CD.

He checked the small reserve area and found sufficient copies of all the required items. That meant he didn't need to go to the storage area his little company rented several blocks away in a local warehouse. He counted the CDs into stacks on the big old work table, all the while sparring with Otto, who'd taken a defensive position atop a mass of flattened-out cardboard boxes and who seemed determined to make up for his exile by a vigorous defense of the spot. The phone rang: the second customer, adding another title. Then, since he was on the phone, Ray speed dialed Jesse's work number and spoke to his lover's secretary, Tasha, who reported that Jesse was at lunch with some colleagues, but that he'd arrived at 11:30 that morning in a good mood. Ray didn't know what that meant. Jesse was always in a good mood, no matter how he felt, no matter how good or terrible the news involved.

He filled and sealed two boxes, then toyed with Otto until the cat extended its claws and hissed. They reconciled, and Ray went to the front office computer to input information and generate invoices, bills of lading, and mailing labels. He taped up the orders and set the boxes by the office door for UPS. He sipped at his beer and hit J.K.'s number again.

This time he answered. "This had better be crucial. I'm stepping out the door this very moment."

"It is crucial," Ray assured him.

"Meaning the topic is," J.K. clarified, "A, sex. B, money. C, me."

"Sex."

"No! You *did not* have sex!" J.K. protested into the receiver.

"I *almost* had sex."

"Bor-ring! *Almost* doesn't count."

"With a very cute repairman. At D'Agostino's," Ray added. "He was fixing the automatic doors when I walked in. He was waiting for me outside and we talked and I offered to do him and gave him my phone number."

There was an intake of breath from the other end of the phone. Then: "Raymond Henriques, I know now why I keep you as my friend. You have *completely* made my afternoon. You have restored my faith in the sexual appetite of the American working man, not to mention the inexorable action of human bodily fluids. I am sitting down again," J.K. declared. "I am taking off my jacket. I expect to hear every detail. Gloss over any item at your peril."

A half hour of details, it turned out. A great many more than Ray thought were needed. J.K.'s own romantic and sexual life must be pretty sparse for this level of obsession with a single, merely potential occurrence in Ray's life. But what were friends for? J.K. had come to Ray's aid on more than one occasion, and as for the situation with Jesse's health, J.K. was possibly the most knowledgeable man in New York, had the best instincts in the world, and could be counted on without question. So Ray humored him, even if it meant having to invent details and repeat, "It was a flirtation. Nothing will come of it."

"Nothing will come of it because your hard-up, horny working mensch perceived you were…*unserious*!" J.K. replied, his most severe put-down. "Some far less attractive, far less worthy, far less ambivalent queen shall shortly reap the rewards of your petit dalliance, believe you me."

Ray did believe J.K. So much so that when he heard a tap on the office door to the street, Ray remained on the phone listening to J.K. go on about his "moral cowardice" while he got up to see who it was, and when he looked out and saw first the paint-splattered van parked across the concrete driveway, then the curly dark head of the repairman, Ray almost didn't believe it.

"Someone's at the door," he said to J.K. in a hushed voice.

"It's not him, is it? Mr. Sexy Repairman?"

Seeing the fellow moving back toward the van's door, Ray unlocked the door. "UPS," he lied. "Gotta go."

"Call back the second he's gone!" J.K. demanded. "We're not done discussing this encounter or its ramifications."

"Right. Sure," Ray agreed. Then, door finally open, he called, "I was on the phone." Seeing the dark head turn and those amazing eyes, visible through gray sunglass lenses, he added, "You made it! Great!"

"The other job was canceled. I had free time," the repairman said. "Am I parked OK? I'm blocking the sidewalk."

"Anything bigger than a bike will block it. I've got a parking decal you can put in the window that says you're here on business."

Ray left the door open and located the decal, brought to the workman peering down Joralemon Street at a police car.

"I can't get another ticket. My boss'll go ballistic."

"Hang this from the mirror in your window. If you get a ticket, I'll pay."

Back inside, the phone rang. Ray hoped it wasn't J.K. It wasn't. It was, however, the second customer he'd spoken to earlier, asking if he could modify his order yet again. Ray said sure and entered the revision directly onto the computer screen, still scrolled to "billing." He'd have to exchange the outer label, and reopen and repack the box. Hell!

When he turned around, the office door was closed and the repairman was inside, staring out the window at the street. Ray still couldn't believe he was there.

Ray joined him at the window, just in time to see the police car stop and a heavyset female cop get out, check the van, then get back into the patrol car and move on. "What'd I tell you?" Ray said.

The repairman filled the office with his presence; his smell, a complex fragrance Ray couldn't quite figure out. A mixture, he theorized, of machine oil, aftershave, maybe natural musk. Ray wanted to touch the younger man, only inches away, so badly that he was actually trembling.

"I just can't get another ticket," the workman apologized, facing Ray. "Three this year already. It comes out of my pay."

"I understand. No problem."

The visitor looked around at the office with its metal framed Music Festivals of Europe posters on the walls, the cabinets of CD albums. "This is what? A German record company? 'Blue Danube Waltz'? Oom-pah-pah bands?"

Ray laughed. "No, keyboard music. Piano, some organ and guitar. Mostly classical stuff—*klavierstuecke* means keyboard pieces. How about that beer?" Ray turned to the half fridge and the mechanic was there, palms out.

He presented his soiled, square hands, with their stubby fingers and mangled fingernails, skin all cut up. A few of the incisions looked fresh. "I'm all greasy. Better wash up."

"I'll show you the john."

Ray led him out of the office, past the storage area, where Otto stretched and ostentatiously yawned as they passed by, into the master suite. Ray blushed as they entered the large room. He pointed out the lavatory. As the repairman entered, Ray said, "You want mercurochrome or bandages on those cuts? They look pretty raw."

"Sure. Alcohol, peroxide, whatever." He ran the tap.

Ray had to graze him to reach the medicine cabinet.

The repairman held his hands over the sink. Ray poured alcohol over them, dabbed them dry with a facecloth, carefully wrapped Band-Aids across the two newest-looking gashes. From this proximity, the repairman was the same height as Ray: eyes level. Less prepossessing now. Even younger. More vulnerable. Ray felt less apprehensive, less unsure. He still didn't know what would happen, but it didn't trouble him. He was simply pleased by the man's presence—so close, so easygoing, so unassuming.

"Now how about that beer?"

Ray thought the fellow looked longingly at the bed as they passed out of the bedroom and back into the office. Or was Ray deceiving himself? The beers were waiting on the desk, and as there was only one chair, they leaned against cabinets, a few feet apart as they snapped open and chugged down the brews.

"So, you what? Work and live here too?"

Ray explained the setup.

"How did you get into this line? It's pretty unusual, right?"

Ray explained that he'd been an A&R man at EMI/Capitol Records. He mentioned popular artists the guy might have heard of. "Gigi Gertz!" The workman was duly impressed. "You don't mind not working with pop stars anymore?"

"I had no choice, if I wanted to stay in the city. How's that brew? Need another?" During the discussion they'd become more equal in Ray's mind. The power had even shifted in his favor.

"Don't want to drink and drive. Maybe I should be taking off. Gotta get back to the Island. It'll be an hour with the traffic and all."

Ray knew he would have to act immediately, or what J.K. had predicted—him doing all the work and someone else reaping the rewards—would come to pass. He was no longer unsettled by the man's good looks, nor by the thought that what he intended was disloyal to Jesse. His focus had shifted to how to get the young man undressed easily, gracefully, not too aggressively. Ray extended a hand and brushed the front of the guy's shorts, then said in a calm and measured voice, "I'm not being a very good host, am I? I did promise more than beer."

"Well, ye-e-eah," the younger man answered. Now he was the one who was nervous, adding, "Look, it's OK if..."

Perversely enough, his uncertainty convinced Ray not to stop what he had started. Ray caressed the repairman's bulge through the corduroy. It wasn't large, but it was hard, and that seemed to validate anything that might happen. "I think we've got a winner here. Let's go into the bedroom," Ray said in what he hoped was a reassuring yet sultry voice. "It's more comfortable."

Refusing to relinquish his corduroy prize, he towed the young man along the corridor by degrees, gripping his belt to draw him along.

Once across the bedroom doorsill, Ray released the shorts and used both hands to lift the rugby shirt. When the repairman made a gesture of hesitation, Ray reassured him. "Don't be nervous. I'm not going to do anything you don't want me to do. OK?"

The raised shirt disclosed the athletic chest and flat abdomen Ray had imagined. The repairman's torso was by no means huge, thickly muscled, or perfectly "cut," but it was without an inch of fat and hairless but for an inky penumbra circling each nipple and a tuft rising above and below his navel, fading into tanned skin.

"It's not that," the workman said. "It's just that I don't...you know, do this kind of thing."

Ray wasn't listening. He let instinct take over, taking hold of the man's torso and nibbling one nipple, then kneading it between his fingertips as he moved his lips and teeth to the other. Back and forth, once, twice, thrice. When he perceived the repairman would not try to free himself, Ray let go and slowly kissed down the tummy, engrossed in delineating with the tip of his tongue the nearly invisible line of hair evanescing into the reinforced waistband of the promised land of underwear. Ray paused in his descent only to dally at—circumscribe with the tip of his tongue, teasingly explore—the vortex of belly button. He employed those few seconds of distraction to effortlessly unbuckle the belt, unbutton the pantsfront. The corduroy shorts drifted down, settling gently around densely stockinged ankles. Ray knelt, never for a second ceasing to caress the young man's briefs and, with hands and mouth, never pausing in his stroking of the cotton-enclosed bottom.

Ray was like a child receiving a long-awaited present, so temptingly close, he so eager for it, yet willing to restrain himself from tearing off the wrapping to savor the prospect a few seconds longer. He was conscious of how unconditionally lust had been set free in him as well as by how thoroughly he intended to experience this fellow, and this fellow's sex, when he made out a low moan: basso, guttural. Only with the greatest effort was Ray able to momentarily force his face away from the snowy field of Jockey cotton to glance up and discover from where those sounds emanated, what they were meant to express.

The young workman's head was thrown back. When his face swung into view again, just beyond his flat pectorals with their erect nipples, the voluptuous green eyes appeared smudged, three-quarters shut, his lips a blur. Ray sat back on his knees to relish the sensual victory, then slowly nudged the repairman backward, step succeeding step, all the while taunting him by running his teeth back and forth across the Jockey-covered swelling—until the younger man turned muzzy and stumbling.

At that instant Ray drew down the underpants, freeing a perfectly shaped penis, which sprung out, shuddering. He also released that specific and individual bouquet he had detected before, intensified tenfold. Essence of Man, they'd called it in the movie *Barbarella*. Ray nudged the guy one more time a bit harder so he couldn't help but lose his balance. He floundered, then dropped backward, landing athwart the edge of the bed's mattress.

All but deranged by the sight and smell, Ray moved in, attacking the longed-for lower torso with face and hands, teeth and lips and tongue in a barrage of kissing and sucking. Ray consolidated all effort, the entirety of his existence, toward a single end: producing in the sexy workman a thrashing, teeth-clenching, mattress-thumping, unsmotherable, earth-shattering, gut-borne roar of orgasm.

When he began to come, the repairman rose off the bed as though intending to levitate, gasping and groaning, before softly subsiding, panting, deflating back onto the bed. Ray at last allowed the fellow's hands to detach his face from the still-vibrating body. Sated, relenting, Ray hunched on his heels, surveying the scene, then joined the repairman on the chenille.

The guy attempted to rise, fell back exhausted. "God. I needed that!"

Me too, Ray thought. He had come without touching himself.

Holding the well-muscled arm, he looked at the left hand, the one he had not bandaged. A gold ring on the scarred third finger. "Married," he mumbled.

"Yeah," a little laugh, "but that don't mean I get treated like this at home. And lately," he added more darkly, "I don't get much at all." Then, lest he seem disloyal, he went on, "It's all since the last kid was born. You know, she's had woman illness, that kind of thing."

"You have kids?"

"Two boys and a girl. Eight, six, and two. Want to see their pictures?"

"When did you start? When you were 12?"

"You think I'm a kid?" half sitting up. "I'll be 31."

"I'd never have guessed it."

"You're what," green eyes scrutinizing, "35?"

"Close," Ray said.

"But never married, right?"

"Never married," Ray admitted.

"Which is why you sent me to the ceiling a few minutes ago."

Ray was flattered. Jesse had never complimented him like that. "You liked it?"

"I think I already expressed my appreciation," the repairman laughed, rolled closer to Ray. "Everyone says for good head, you gotta go gay."

"And now you know which gay to go to," Ray said, feeling esteemed, giddily so. Which was why he was emboldened to add, "Maybe when you're in the area…?" He touched a hot shoulder, "You around a lot fixing automatic doors?"

"I haven't been. This other guy, older guy, who works there too, he asked for Brooklyn and Manhattan jobs. But he's ticked off a few customers. I could ask for the route…drop by. I couldn't say when, exactly. That OK?"

"I'm here all day. You've got my card. Give a call."

Their faces were inches away from each other. Those eyes!

"You like it, right? Being gay? Doing stuff to guys?"

Ray wasn't sure exactly what he was being asked. "I like doing stuff to you." Then he added. "Why?"

The workman turned away, looked up at the ceiling. "She was my high school sweetheart. We went to the prom in May, graduated in June, got married in September. Everyone thought she was knocked up. But she wasn't. We've known each other since we were, like, in second grade. I hung with her brothers. I like her folks and all. We do things together with her family all the time. The beach. Deep-sea fishing. Barbecues. The whole nine yards."

It came out affectionately, yet rueful. Ray didn't know how to answer. "Sounds comfortable."

"It's comfortable." Again the workman's tone was mixed. "Unlike my friggin' job." He sat up, stretched. "Which can be a bitch. Now I gotta fight traffic all the way back to Massapequa. When instead I could sleep all afternoon. You ever do that, you know, working so close to bed?"

"Not often," Ray admitted. "The phone rings. Orders to be filled."

"The john's that way?" Pointing. Then the repairman was up, winking at Ray as he pulled on his Jockeys, his shorts, and buckled up. All Ray could think was: Look at that body! Look at that face!

He could have stayed in bed and waited and watched the guy come out again, but it might have embarrassed him. So Ray got up and was straightening his clothing when the repairman entered, checking his watch, all business.

"I'm gonna be right in rush hour traffic."

Ray led him back through the hall to the office and street door. As he stepped out, Ray said, "By the way, you know my name. From the card and all. You are…?"

"Oh, right. Mike. Mike Tedesco." His handshake was butch, one of the Band-Aids flapped off.

"Mike from Massapequa," Ray mused. "See ya around."

"Sure." Hearty. Then, in a different tone, "You know, maybe sometime, you can show me some other stuff. Other gay stuff," he added conspiratorially. "You know what I mean?"

Ray didn't have a clue. "Sure," he said as though he did.

Mike hopped into the van, and it dashed into a break in the Joralemon

Street traffic, moving so fast that he was gone before Ray remembered the parking decal was still in the truck. Maybe Mike would see it and come back. If not today, then another time.

Ray closed and locked the office, then drifted through the lower floor, stroking the cat, meandering into the bedroom—so unexpectedly redolent with Mike's fragrance. Jesus, it's strong, Ray thought. I've got to spray in here before Jesse comes home.

He decided he should change the bedcover, too, just in case. Chuck the cat out the door, open the windows, and totally sanitize the place. But just glancing at the bed turned Ray on so much that all he could do was lie back in the midst of that fragrance—Essence of Mike Tedesco—and replay it in his mind. He become aroused again, and ended up masturbating.

three

The phone clamoring. Someone steadily clubbing the door. The doorbell beckoning. Ray massaged an eye open to salmon-colored afternoon light percolating through shutters into the bedroom. The clock read 4:15. He'd napped what? A half hour? More? He tumbled out of bed. In the hall, Otto waylaid him, brushing against him, sidling between legs, all but tripping him.

"No cat food here. If you're hungry, go home," Ray told the cat.

Sable and Chris were at the office door: just as they were supposed to be. Sable shaded her eyes with a hand, peering in. Chris bounced around in time to the music on his earphones, turning to hammer an especially rhythmic drumbeat on the window with a ringed knuckle. Ray waved to get their attention. The phone machine had picked up and begun recording an endless message from J.K. Callaway, berating Ray for his lack of consideration, his failure to accept responsibility, his kindergartner's sense of time; Ray couldn't be certain what else exactly; nothing new, nor unanticipated.

"OK, puss, out you go." Ray nudged Otto into the driveway.

"ToeToe!" Sable called out her baby name for the cat. She dropped her school bags and, instead of coming in, went after the cat, who'd stopped in the driveway to turn and deliver a dirty look. "Sable, stay out of the street," Ray warned. Chris bopped into the office, drumming every surface he could find as he entered, oblivious to anything else.

"So I raped her!" Ray sang into one of the boy's ears, lifting one earphone a half inch. "Then I stabbed her! Then I killed her! Da da da!"

The boy beamed, took off the earphones. "It's not *that* song."

"Par-*don*! My mistake! Any chance you can keep your sister from being run over while I pick up my phone messages?"

"Yeah. OK." Then, staring at Ray, "You were sleeping."

"That right?"

"Your hair's sticking up in back. Your clothes are wrinkled. Your pants are unbuckled. Either that or..." The young face went slack.

"Care to speculate further, Sherlock?"

"I'll get the Slug." Chris dropped his pack and sauntered out.

Ray punched the phone machine to replay. Sable entered as J.K.'s message rewound. She was, naturally enough, holding Otto, picturesquely drooped across her arms as though to prove to Ray that yes, he belonged here.

"Uncle Ray, can't I just—"

"We have *no* cat food. And you know he makes Uncle Jesse sick."

"OK," the little girl said. "Can I play with him outside?"

"Only till I get my calls. And when you come in, wash your hands thoroughly."

"Face too," Chris added. "The cat slobbered all over her." Chris dropped into a hunch against a cabinet, intent upon rewinding the cassette in his Walkman, when J.K.'s message began aloud. After a few seconds, Chris asked, "What's *his* problem?"

Ray laughed. "A typical adult problem of having no life and wanting to live vicariously though other people."

"Good thing *you're* not like that."

"Consider yourself lucky that neither I nor your mother is like that."

"She can barely find time to live *her* life," Chris astutely commented.

"What's with this latest character?" Ray probed. "Alcohol? Drugs? Abuse?"

"He's just a jerk." Then, "The Slug says it's a sex-magic thing." And when

Ray looked skeptical, "Those aren't her exact words. But close. They all but put a gate on the bedroom door."

"That can't last," Ray said.

Chris snickered and it came out high, almost a whinny. Surprised, embarrassed by the sound he'd made, he became sober and fitted the headphones back on.

J.K. was still talking, though now his ranting voice was lower. Ray hit replay and sifted the message for data. None apparent: all fume.

Ray played the other messages that had logged in while he'd napped: a voice he didn't immediately recognize. "Mike here. Guess you know why I'm calling. I've got your parking thing. Didn't see it till I'd gotten to Ditmars Avenue. Don't worry. I'll bring it back. Not sure when. But soon. I definitely want more of that honey."

"What honey?" Sable asked, finally indoors, the cat abandoned. "Can I have honey? On toast, please. And peanut butter too. I'm hungry."

Unsurprisingly, Mike hadn't left a phone number where he could be reached. What was the name of the company he worked for? Wasn't it painted on the side of the truck? Ray couldn't recall. Even if he had known, he wasn't about to phone him. Mike was married; he wouldn't be back, despite his conspiratorial bull about wanting to do more "gay stuff." Kiss the parking sticker good-bye.

A half hour later, upstairs, Ray began to prepare dinner. Sable, snacks eaten, homework spread on the crumb-covered table, hummed as she colored in a natural history map of Long Island for social studies. Her brother had his earphones back on, and groaned over geometry proofs. Ray didn't get how he concentrated with the music blasting so loud in his ears all the time. But every once in a while, the boy would look up, startled, as though he'd expected them to vanish while his focus lay elsewhere. Or he would look up and read Ray's lips as he and Sable chatted, and Ray spiced and dredged the round roast, diced the carrots, peeled new potatoes.

Ray thought about how different his sister's children were. Chris so resembled his father that Kathy might have been nothing but a receptacle for a cloned reproduction. At least physically, since Ray had only met Chris's father three times and had never spent as much as an hour alone with him. Still, as Chris grew, he favored his sire to an astonishing degree, which had to occasionally freak out his mother, who'd divorced the man a decade earlier.

Long-limbed, big-boned, gangly, already Ray's height, strawberry-blond, Chris had one advantage over his begetter: He lived close enough to a large urban center to already have a highly developed sense of fashion, even some style. His hair was cut modishly, his clothing scrupulously chosen by color and cut to emphasize his fair WASP looks. Hardly a mallrat, the two times he and Ray found themselves in a men's store, the boy had spent an hour trying on garments, not minding Ray's running commentary, better suited to a homosexual twice the boy's age: "That shirt has too much gray. It dulls your eyes. How about one with more green in it?" Or "Not cashmere. You need a bulkier sweater. To hide how slim you are." Which the boy accepted, followed. And once, when a hovering, simpering salesman asked if he was dressing for a girlfriend, Chris sneered, "I dress for myself." Then, revolving in place like a model, he asked, "How do I look?" The clerk sang, "Fabulous! The Zoli Agency is waiting!" A line Ray repeated whenever the boy was being too obviously vain.

Sable's father had been half Puerto Rican, half African-American, so she was a less-standard model than her brother. True, they shared big, velvety, chocolate-brown eyes, the same eyes as their mother's, the same eyes as Ray's, inherited from their father and allegedly from prior generations of Portuguese Sephardics who'd emigrated to Holland in the 16th century. But where Chris was tall and rangy, even at nine Sable was voluptuous, compact and shapely, all satin, from her nimbus of soft, frizzy red hair to her downy cheeks.

Her father, Ivan Dominguez—defunct via a salvo of .38 slugs in a trash-filled lot off Atlantic Avenue—had been a sexy, flirtatious guy, bright, ironic, physically desirable, charming. And so it was difficult for Ray to think of Ivan as nothing more than a local drug dealer, until his life ended prematurely in the mode so emblematic of the vocation. By then, Ivan was deemed an "error," long gone from all of their daily lives. But Sable favored neither her father nor her mother: She was a synthesis of their best features, genetically and in her disposition: fun-loving, quicksilver, tactful, and affectionate. Even her older brother, who'd protect her to the death but who after all was a teen and called her "Slug," could be found gaping at her marvelous belief in herself and others, in her unceasing trust that the world would treat her well, and do so for a very long time.

Ray found himself thinking how his sister Kathy would cream over Mike Tedesco if she ever laid eyes on him. It was odd how attractive Ray had always found his sister's choices in men, now matter how badly they turned out, and how much Kathy was attracted by his men—the few she'd seen. As recently as last Christmas they'd sat in this very room munching butter cookies, with Jesse and the kids still in pajamas on the living room carpet playing with presents in front of the over-ornamented blue spruce as the stereo played a new CD of

German carols, and Kathy had said "You know, Rags, even sick, he's exception-
ally cute, your Jesse. I played the field, and look at the mess I made. You held
to your guns. The minute you saw him, you knew he was the one. You ended
up getting the best guy."

"I didn't know we were competing," Ray had replied, and it sounded disingenuous even to him. So he added, "He's not sick. Just HIV positive." At which
Kathy had drawn back a few inches. "Don't do this to yourself, Rags."

"Do what?"

"I know you've stood by me through a lot of crap. But unless you squarely
face facts, I won't be around when your crystal palace comes crashing down."

He knew that his face had set hard. But then Sable was suddenly bouncing
between them, demanding attention, and the moment had passed.

Ray heard a car door slam shut. He checked out the window, and yes, it
was Jesse, exiting a taxi and staring at Otto, still lurking in the driveway.

"Go meet your Uncle Jess," Ray said. "Carry his attaché case,"

Sable jumped up, yelled out the window that Jesse should wait, she was
coming, and rushed out of the apartment. The pot roast was almost braised. In
a minute Ray would throw the vegetables and herb bouquet into the pot, add
chicken stock (no wine, not with the HIV), and let it cook. As usual, Jesse's timing couldn't be better.

"I should help too," Chris said, surprising Ray. Then he understood.
Chris had been gazing out the window. He had turned a somewhat shocked
face to Ray, no doubt because of how slowly Jesse was ascending, even with
Sable toting the attaché.

"OK. But don't let him see why."

"Don't worry," Chris understood the implications, "I won't."

A minute later Ray heard their customary teasing salutations.

Before dinner, once the table was cleared and the kids were settled in front
of the TV in the other room, Jesse withdrew a manila folder from the attaché
like some prestidigitator and scattered its multicolored contents across bread
plates and napkins. He'd always loved surprises; he especially loved being the
bearer of surprising news. "Think you can you spare me 12 days of your busy
schedule beginning next Friday?" he began mischievously.

"What? Why?" Ray all but fell over a dining room table chair trying to get
to the brochures. Only after Jesse had pulled him into the adjacent chair and
pushed the flyers and catalogues in front of him did Ray comprehend. He
looked from Jesse to the vivid photos: cerulean seascapes, bone-white yachts
anchored in unruffled baylets, catamarans scampering across spume-flecked

waves, waterskiers gyrating in midair, scuba divers slithering through multihued reefs. "What is all this?" He finally asked.

"All this, young master Raymond, is Magic Time!" Jesse said with a flourish. "It is also Providenciales, most developed of the Turks and Caicos Islands. British West Indies. The CEO of our company built a house there, and as it's empty, he's offered to let us use it. One hour from Miami by jet. A cleaning woman, a car, and a speedboat accompany the house."

"But…how?" Ray was thrilled, Jesse was tickled to see.

"After a meeting a few days ago, he said he heard I was feeling low and wanted me to rest up," Jesse said. He reached into the inner pocket of his suit jacket and withdrew a sheaf of airline tickets. "These and the tourist board stuff were on my desk when I got back from lunch." He watched Ray's eyes widen. "Whaddaya t'ink, kiddo?"

Ray's warm Iberian eyes answered "Yes!" before he could say a word.

Ray reached for Jesse's hand. "This is so great!"

Kathy naturally chose that moment to phone and ask if they could keep the children with them overnight. She'd really appreciate it, she told Jesse.

Jesse said sure, and after he hung up, Ray raised his eyebrows several times à la Groucho Marx and said darkly, "Sex-magic. According to Sable."

When Jesse mentioned the night's change of plans over dinner, the kids seemed unsurprised. Sable, in fact, reminded him that both had changes of clothing in the spare bedroom drawer from their three-day Christmas visit. Chris seemed disinterested, and when Jesse interrogated him while collecting the dinner dishes, he shrugged and said, "The way Mom and I are getting along lately, I'd move in here with you guys in a minute."

"What do you think?" Jesse asked Ray, after telling him what Chris had said. "Should we have him move in?" He knew Ray would never bring it up himself.

"Let's wait until after the Caribbean trip," Ray said sensibly,

"You mean in case it becomes a long-term situation?"

Ray groaned in response. "If I wanted kids, I would've had them."

"C'mon!" Jesse insisted, tickling Ray. "It'll be fun. Then, in a louder voice, to the kids, "Who'll help their exhausted old uncle tumble downstairs? Chris?"

It wasn't until 15 minutes later that Ray at last went down to check how Jesse was. He was huddled under quilts, a little querulous. "You left the windows open."

"I was airing it out. I blew some guy in here today."

"Finally!" Jesse declared. He sat up, inquisitive, no longer sorry for himself.

He wrapped himself more thoroughly in the quilt and listened to Ray, whom he had to prompt for details. Even though Jesse was sure it had been a hot, sexually satisfying encounter, he appreciated like hell how much Ray downplayed each detail.

"Well, I'm glad. You needed it. I hope he's coming by again," Jesse said.

"He won't."

"But you realize him wanting to come back was the unconscious message behind keeping the parking decal. This way he *has* to return," Jesse insisted. "Believe me, Ray!"

"If you say so, Sigmund." Ray pushed Jesse down onto the bed. "Now go to sleep." He lay atop the quilt, face close to Jesse. "You are falling asleep...."

"And clever, seductive, libidinous you," Jesse went on, "will keep him coming back for more. Teasing him with gratification. Eventually you'll expose him to all kinds of perversions, training him, as you trained me, to be your personal sex slave."

"Yeah, sure, right!" Ray giggled. "All thought out, except...he's married."

"So what?" Jesse countered. "You're married."

Ray was about to protest that he wasn't, or that it wasn't the same, with the same significance or responsibilities, but Jesse stopped him with a hand over his mouth. "Keep him coming back, Ray. You need it. *We* need it."

While Ray murmured protestations, Jesse yawned elaborately. Relieved now. Ray would have a two-week vacation in the sun. And someone waiting for him when he got back. Jesse needn't too much worry about his marvelous man.

In a startlingly short time Jesse was sound asleep. Ray got off the bed, closed the door, and went upstairs to pry Sable away from the TV and tug her sleepily into the guest-room bed. He made himself a weak vodka tonic and watched the 10 o'clock news with Chris. He annoyed Chris into showering and brushing his teeth. Ray looked over a new Franz Liszt biography he'd gotten in the mail.

He called Chris over and told him that he and Jesse had to go away a few weeks because of Jesse's health. He watched the young face, gauging it for trouble. But no, Chris seemed to understand. So Ray went on, saying that if, when they returned, Chris still wanted to try out living with them, it was fine with them. Better if Chris and his mother could work out something. But otherwise...OK?

Chris said sure and told Ray he was the best, and Jesse too, and, still smelling of soap, he kissed Ray's cheek and padded off to bed. Ray went back to the account of young Liszt's schooling.

A half hour later he suddenly stopped reading. Outside, Joralemon Street was abruptly silent, not a car going by, not a word spoken, as though he were inside a cabin deep in the country and not in the middle of a city.

This is my life, Ray thought: Jesse asleep downstairs, the kids asleep two rooms over, Kathy and Dan possibly resting between bouts of lovemaking. Me tired yet satisfied. So well-loved. Why was it, Ray wondered, that he also felt a shiver of foreboding, as though an unseen abyss were opening beneath his feet?

four

The paper upon which the letter had been transcribed was multi-ply, creamed ivory, a plush bed for the slate-gray embossed logo to rest upon as well as an impeccable foil for the slightly overinked blue-black type. Ray held it up to the near-noon, late-November sunlight, and the weave wasn't so much observable as smokily suggested, the way intense pigments on an overcast day are implied but not actually visible from the converse of a stained-glass window. The dense single-lined text of the letter was nearly as abstruse. It was in French, naturally enough, as was the correspondent, Mlle. Frederique Le Cerf. Freddie the Deer—or Doe, to be exact—wrote from a company in the Second *Arrondisement* of Paris. And while the greater part was everyday French, intelligible to someone with Ray's college credentials, at paragraph three it veered treacherously into Gallic business terminology—

words he'd never laid eyes on, simulating English but surely dissimilar.

This ought not to have been a surprise: It *was* after all a business letter, regarding the leasing of the North American rights to Albert Ferber's recording of Faure's *Theme and Variations* along with several barcaroles and nocturnes. Ray felt certain Mlle. Le Cerf was saying that the rights were available and could be leased for a specific fee, biographical data and photos of the late pianist to be included. And since CDs tended to be longer in duration than LPs or cassettes, the company, Disques TransMontaines, would throw in, at a slight extra cost, an earlier taping—not on the LP—that Ferber had done of the *Ballade in F# Major*, almost 15 minutes more of music. Excellent! If only Ray could be sure that was indeed what the letter said.

He'd written to them in English, which someone there apparently comprehended, despite their reply in their own tongue. Before accepting their terms, he needed to be absolutely certain he knew what it was he was agreeing to.

Who could help? J.K. Callaway could. He read *Le Figaro Litterraire* over morning coffee, Huysmans and Yourcenar in the original. Except Ray didn't want to call him. J.K. was being something of a bitch these days. These weeks, in fact. Almost since the day Ray had had sex with the repairman. As though J.K. accurately intuited that Ray was keeping something from him.

They'd known each other for years, he and J.K., since a meeting one breezy, sunny August afternoon in a social security office on Rector Street in Lower Manhattan not long after Ray had arrived from Illinois. When he'd successfully interviewed for a job, Ray remembered he'd lost his card years before and had no record of its number. To be employed he'd need a new one. J.K. was Ray's first real acquaintance in New York, his first grown-up friend.

Unlike Ray, J.K. had never worked, never had a social security number. "I never dreamt I'd need one," he'd explained guilelessly, and then burst out laughing. A large, kaleidoscopic, euphonious laugh indicative of generosity of spirit and love of life; a laugh Ray later discovered was all that, but also more—a practiced, premeditated element of J.K.'s scrupulously assembled New York City persona.

They'd been alone, in opposite chairs, in the small, surprisingly tastefully decorated lounge of the federal office, J.K. clad in a charcoal three-piece suit of a type he still favored. A suit that made him resemble a securities broker more than an English lit professor. Ray wore chinos and a tweed sport jacket. Even before J.K. had opened his mouth to ask, "Are you *really* reading that book? No one reads Turgenev anymore! Or *do* they?" Ray had known J.K. was gay.

He wasn't exactly sure why. J.K. didn't look different than any other New Yorker. He was attractive, with thick, straight, mahogany hair—let long to fall in front—shrewd black eyes flecked with bits of pale blue and gray, and square-jawed, broad, Irish-American features. J.K.'s physique was more substantial than Ray's own just-over medium-height and weight, yet he didn't look tall or hulking. He was blooming, healthy, not overmuscled. His gestures and intonation were neither studiedly macho nor effeminate.

Even so, Ray knew, and J.K. knew he knew, and after they'd finished their business at social security, he'd waited for Ray and they sauntered to a local Chock Full o' Nuts, where they rapidly discovered they were the same age, came from similar backgrounds (J.K. from rural Pennsylvania), shared the same taste in music, books, and films, and lived only a few blocks apart in the East Village. And where they also rapidly deduced they'd probably become immediate pals, but that the sexual attraction between them hovered between one and zero. J.K. then revealed another aspect of his character: directness. Munching his second order of raisin toast, he'd asked, "Boys or girls?" Disconcerted, but seeing no reason to equivocate, Ray had replied, "Boys. Or rather, one boy. I even know what he looks like. But I've yet to meet him. You?"

J.K. had shrugged. "Boys too. But my granduncle Francis Xavier, a confirmed bachelor who knows everything, assured me I would never have a great love, only flirtations. He quoted Oscar Wilde at me, whom he reveres not as a pervert but as an Irish loyalist: 'A man who loves himself is assured of a lifelong affair.' " At which J.K. had let out his trademark guffaw.

It was then J.K. clarified what his initials stood for. John Kevin, or Joseph Kenneth, something tiresome like that. "No one but immediate family calls me anything but J.K.," he'd maintained. So Ray fell in line and forgot the real name.

A year later to the date that they had first met, J.K. treated Ray to dinner at a West Village bistro, and Ray, who had that very week met Jesse Vaughan Moody, told J.K., "I'm sure of it. This is the one." To which a soberly rapt J.K. had asked, "The Tom Sawyer to your Huck Finn?" Persuaded it was, he'd announced, "Tell me everything. Everything! And you can rely on me utterly until the end of time."

In the beginning he did tell him everything; he was so madly in love, he couldn't restrain himself. And while that telling had greatly diminished over the years, abrupt moments did recur when J.K. would waylay Ray, reminding him of the request he'd never dreamt he'd have to fulfill forever.

Alas, dear Jesse couldn't be of any help with the letter. When they were in the Caribbean a month before, they'd taken an afternoon junket via single-engine Cessna over an otherworldly, multihued, aquamarine bay to Cap Haitien, the picture-book harbor city on the northernmost peninsula of the island of Haiti. Once there, Jesse had marveled at Ray's spoken French; although, in truth, most townspeople they had business with—at the café, the art gallery, some boutiques—spoke excellent, liltingly accented English.

It had been a magical side trip. Their entire holiday had been dappled with unanticipated enchantments: the facility with which they learned to snorkel, the hours Ray (Jesse tired easily) passed in diaphanous waters, buoyant atop a realm of neon-green ribbonfish, tiny silversides, and two-toned octopi gliding over bone-white expanses of limestone sea floor irregularly defined by seductively beckoning seaweed. The beaches had been almost eye-hurting bright, uninhabited, temperate. The islanders they'd met were reticent, gratifyingly nonmaterial, dignified, and, after a week, somewhat cordial. The weather had been miraculously clement. And the rain—he'd never forget how the rain fell only upon specific inland districts. From the north-facing lanai of the house they observed it just hanging there, like an illustration of rain, motionless for hours at a time over a single location. When they drove to dine in town, rain still flowed, a definable drape across the two-lane highway. And when they drove home again hours later, its boundary remained at the exact same spot they'd first espied it.

So Jesse was no help.

On the other hand, Ray was to lunch in a half hour with a more recently met friend, Liesl Sieghart, at a Chinese place on Montague Street. Ray was sure she knew French, although she'd denied it. Who knew why? Perhaps because she was German-born.

It was increasingly clear Ray would either have to remain in the dark about the letter's potential shadings or phone J.K. and plead with him to parse its text for secret meanings.

So Ray dialed J.K.'s office at Hunter College, still wondering what, exactly, he'd done to raise J.K.'s hackles and prepared to acknowledge his fault, wherever it lay, and offer an act of contrition.

The machine picked up, and Ray was about to leave a message when a woman's voice came on. "Yes, can I help you?"

"I'm trying to reach J.K. This is his friend, Ray."

"He's not here," she said, sounding peculiar.

"And you are?" he tried.

"Dr. Knipper," she said, and now he remembered the woman.

"If you hang up, I'll call again and leave a voice-mail."

"Well. You're Ray?" she asked, distracted.

"Ray Henriques. I think you and I have met. Can I leave a message for J.K.?"

"Wait!" she said. "OK, you're on the list. Actually, J.K.'s at home. He's been out of the office five days now. I'm only allowed to tell certain people. He gave me a list." Then she added darkly, "You know J.K. You have his home number?"

"Yeah, but we haven't spoken in almost a week. My fault, entirely. It's not that new flu going around?"

"A bit more serious," Dr. Knipper said. "You should speak to J.K. yourself."

"If you're trying to scare me, you're succeeding."

"Oh, Ray," the voice fractured. She withdrew from the phone and returned with a bit more control. "It's the pneumonia. You know, whatever it's called. He was taken by ambulance last Friday. They only just released him from the hospital yesterday. He didn't want anyone to know. But he can't be there alone."

Ray battled stupor. He wasn't sure what she meant by saying he knew what the pneumonia was called. So he asked the question she might be able to answer. "Is he alone now? If so, I'll go right over and—"

"Maxine's been there all morning. His assistant from the office? And a grad student, Brad Stone, slept over last night and will again tonight."

"I'm not supposed to know?" Ray asked. Something icy clutched his spine. "Is that what J.K. said?" Before she could answer, "Pneumocystis? Is that what he has?"

"Yes. Yes to both questions. He said you already had someone to take care of and he didn't want to overburden you."

"How long...for how long has he been, you know, seroconverted?"

"I don't know. He told me it came as a shock, that he didn't know until the doctor at the hospital took tests` last Friday. He said...there are some treatments now. And he'll be back at work soon."

"Yes, sure. He's right. My partner's at work now," Ray said as brightly as possible. "I'll try J.K. at home. Thanks. You were right to tell me. Really," he added to reassure her. "Don't let him yell at you."

"I only wish he were well enough to yell at me."

After she'd hung up, Ray sat holding the receiver. Why should he be so surprised, he asked himself. The *truly* surprising thing was that Ray hadn't tested positive. They had to all be infected, no? He and J.K. and Jesse and every damn kid who'd arrived in Manhattan from Peru, Illinois, and Wheatland, Pennsylvania, and Asheboro, North Carolina in 1979 and 1980, 22, 23 years old, just out of college, ambitious for careers, looking for the love of their life. It had been another three, four years before anyone really said what was happening, recognized the abhorrence that silently tightened its grip on Jesse and so many thousands of others. And now J.K. too. Brave, bold, confident J.K. This was going to be difficult. J.K. always lived his life as though it were open-ended, not over at 80 or even 100. And now...

Maxine answered the phone and said J.K. was asleep. She'd tell him Ray called when he woke up. If he really had to come, she suggested 5 or 6. J.K. was most alert then. She'd be leaving and Brad would be arriving to spell her.

Ray checked and realized he had five minutes to get to Gold Lotus and meet Liesl. He took the letter just in case, swearing at his image in the bathroom mirror as he brushed his unruly mop. Haircut tomorrow, he decided. He wondered whether to tell Liesl about J.K. He'd see.

He made it to the restaurant on time, but Liesl was, not surprisingly, 15 minutes late. She more than compensated by appearing remarkably sexy in an outfit Ray had never seen: totally unsuitable for the afternoon, natch, but pure Liesl—black vinyl wraparound skirt, matching boots, and lacy jet camisole, all barely penned in by her knee-length ponyskin coat. This, with her petite, coquettish good looks, fair complexion, and feather-cut platinum hair—tips frosted pale orange—gained the attention of the entire by now quite full restaurant, mostly male office workers on lunch hour. Liesl ordered them martinis and after tasting hers with a pointed tongue, announced, "If you say no to this proposal, darling Ray-mond, I'll have my Mafia ex-lover encase you in concrete and dump you over the promenade. You know who I mean, the one with the *gran Napoletano salcizze.* He owes me a favor."

Her glamour and effervescence lifted Ray's spirits instantly, sweeping thoughts of J.K. from his mind. "Say no to what?" he asked. Today even her drowned light blue eyes, her one poor feature, didn't bother him. "What proposal?"

"Simply this, Ray-mond! My ex-lover Vin-*cent* from Montreal—you know, the one with the penis so long he can sodomize himself? I told you all about him—he's making this movie. Actually, he's shot it and is editing in Astoria—that's Long Island, yes? Not far away from here? He needs a musical score. Something serious and elegant. Classic. Up-to-date. I told him you'd be perfect, because you know classical music inside out. Don't say no."

"I've never scored a movie," Ray said, then quickly added, "I didn't say no."

"From what Vin-*cent* said, it's just recording. You know how to do that."

"I suspect it's somewhat more complicated than that," Ray said. "But I'll talk to him and see what he's thinking about. Vincent what?"

"Vin-*cent* Mau-*rette.* From Montreal." She leaned over the table to kiss him, almost knocking over their martinis. She went on to explain the movie.

Ray gathered that it was an independent production financed by the Canadian Film Board, about love and philosophy and ecology, to be exhibited in cinemas as well as on public television. Ray let Liesl take over the conversation, which soon veered off Vincent and how intellectual yet sensitive he was, to her current ex-lover, Masahiro Kita, a sculptor (penis short, if monstrously thick) completing a gigantic bronze representation of the space age, intended for some corporate plaza in Singapore, and from him to her future ex-lover, Fedya Zulkov, the skinny, redheaded devil of a Byelorussian cellist (medium-size penis, but with an immense head) who had taken Berlin by storm only last week—she was so happy, she could die.

Liesl never seemed to have a current lover, only various species of ex-lover. Each was a genius, dazzling if emotionally volatile, which was why she couldn't live with them longer than three months at a time and often slipped away for good at 4 A.M. as they slumbered, benumbed by drugs, stupefied by copulatory excess. She had twice appeared at Ray's door at some uncivilized hour and slept over, once even sliding into bed alongside Ray's nephew Chris, another overnight guest, dead to the world. "He smells so young," Liesl had said. "I'm sure he won't mind." The next morning as Ray and Jesse ate breakfast, the astonished boy crept from the guest room, and no amount of talk could ever adequately explain the vision he'd awakened to: a nearly nude, incredibly sexy woman. He'd asked about her for months. Ray and Jesse joked whenever they came upon a colorful individual at a cocktail party who reminded them of one of Liesl's ex-lovers—they'd only met a few. They'd say, "Donald. Afro-American math prodigy. Ten-inch fireman's hose. Terrible memory; possibly early Alzheimers." Or "Herbert. Virtuoso in commodity futures. Can predict through the next century with 98% accuracy. Minuscule equipment; scrotum the size of the Bronx. Orgasms by the gallon."

Liesl ordered her usual four-course meal, baffling the waiter, who naturally assumed, because she was so small, she'd never eat half of it. As she chatted on, she slowly, methodically ate every bite on the various plates, Ray looking on with his customary amusement and mystification at precisely where she put it all.

It did, of course, take time: an hour and a half, at the end of which the majority of colunchers were gone. That was when Ray chose to pull out the letter from Mlle. Le Cerf. As expected, Liesl brushed it aside. "Ray-mond. For shame! French? Why not Hottentot?"

Before he could answer, a massive man sporting sheaves of plaited, shoulder-length butterscotch hair and wearing a neutral-toned, pebbled overcoat, pulled a chair to the table. Liesl leapt up, squealing, "Vin-*cent! Du gruesse knabe!*"

spilling crumbs, hugging and kissing the newcomer, looking like a small mobile shadow against a skyscraper.

Vincent Maurette appeared no older than Ray's nephew, despite his impressive stature and two-day growth of reddish down upon his gaunt, equine face. He appeared shy, reticent, adoring Liesl, all but ignoring Ray after they'd been introduced. Like Ray, he let her natter on, let her fire away a zillion questions he modestly answered. He drank only water—a pitcher in minutes, then another—and waited until Liesl had gone to the ladies' room before gazing intently at Ray with small eyes the same cobalt hue of comic-book heroes, inappropriately set in almond-shaped sockets, making him appear both languid and shrewd. In his silky, inaptly high tenor, he asked, "So, *cher*, what did Liesl tell you?"

"That you need someone to score a film. I've never—"

Maurette's huge, soft hand fell atop Ray's, stopping him from going on. "Listen now, *cher*, the film: one hour and 19 minutes after it's fully edited," he all but whispered, fixing Ray with his suboceanic blue eyes. "Of which 39 minutes require music. Nineteenth century. Perhaps Viennese or German. The first theme for piano. Lonely, classic, when we first hear it. But emotion-drenched when repeated at the end. It comes twice. Either whole or in part. Maybe three, three and a half minutes. Second theme. Orchestral or concerto. Romantic but not sweet or cloying. Grand, broad, and sweeping. A memorable melody. Not precisely a waltz. But if so, somehow off-kilter. Perhaps seven minutes total. It'll be presented in three segments before it's heard completely. I have a pianist who can sight-read and record the piece for laying down later. Any ideas, *cher*?"

As he'd spoken—his voice never rising in decibels, forcing Ray to listen more closely—his big hand had lain atop Ray's, letting his imperturbably probing eyes do their work. Even so, Ray realized Maurette had all the while been caressing his fingers, applying a constant motion of pressure to stroke and warm him.

Despite this, Ray had not been distracted. Maurette's voice, with its oddly velvet sheen and hint of French-Canadian allied to a Midwest twang, had somehow penetrated Ray's mind, instantly evoking response.

"Do you know the Sibelius Third Symphony?" Ray asked. "There's an andante, a sort of interrupted waltz that goes a little nuts, then comes back to itself, that I think might work. It's in three parts and can be broken apart and put together again. For the piano theme, I'm thinking of the Chopin Prelude in G. Played by Frederic Lamond or Jorge Bolet. Oh, and it's been orchestrated by Jean Francaix, and I have recording of that too."

"Can you make me a cassette, *cher*?" Maurette prompted.

"Sure. This afternoon." This was so easy, Ray thought it couldn't be happening.

"Call me in the morning and we'll arrange for the studio messenger to pick up the cassette. I'll have him carry a letter of intent. That's a precontract agreement."

"Then what?" Ray asked.

"Then, *cher*, you come to the studio and watch the rough cut with me. Together we lay out the music time-wise. You record what you need, all the pieces, then you lay it down in the editing room alongside the film on a separate track. I'll show you, You've used magnetic tape, *cher*?"

"Thirty-five and 75 millimeter."

"Then it's easy, *cher*. If we need the live piano version of the Sibelius waltz, my man comes into the studio and you record him. Then we'll lay it down alongside the film. Simple? Yes?" The beckoning voice would not be denied.

"It sounds simple, but I'm sure it's much more complicated than that."

The big hand calmed him. "It is simple…for professionals. You'll see. The money's not much, only a few thousand, since it's a small-budget film. But maybe later on, *cher*…." The eyes narrowed, as though looking through a gunsight. "Yes?"

"If you like the selections," Ray clarified. "But if not—"

"We'll worry if it happens. Now tell me what Liesl says about me." The voice became even more intimate, ingratiating. "Personally. No bull, eh, *cher*?"

"Nothing bad."

The hand went on stroking and the gunsight eyes still held him, until Ray blurted out, "She says you're very well-endowed," quickly, mischievously. Then appending, "And that you're heterosexual."

A smile on the fleshy, sharply outlined, as though carved, upper lip. "She didn't tell you my nickname, *cher*? No? 'Backdoor Maurette'? No?" A satin laugh, and when Ray must have looked startled, the smile widened. "And given such a…proclivity, how would I be totally hetero, tell me that, eh, *cher*? Unless I'm a fool! But never," he added quickly, "with anyone I work with." Ray began to relax, until Maurette said, "That is to say, at the time I happen to be working with them."

"I have a lover," Ray panicked, feeling a fool saying it. "Twelve years."

"I'd be willing to overlook that," Maurette murmured, continuing to smile, then suddenly dropping his other huge hand to get a better hold as Ray surreptitiously attempted to withdraw his own. "Liesl said I'd like you… And I do, *cher*. But first comes the soundtrack! Eh, *mon cher* Raymond?"

Ray at last managed to retract his hand, slowly, by stages, and when he was free, he pulled out the letter, folded over to show only the bottom third—with the words he found so troublesome—and handed it to Maurette.

The filmmaker perused it with his usual calm. "I see this on film contracts all the time. This clause," pointing to it, "means no further negotiations. It's a set agreement. This other phrase says that any changes to individual parts of the agreement that may occur in the future will not in any way alter the general import of the contract."

Nothing crucial, true; but on the other hand Ray would have never guessed what those idioms stood for.

Liesl flounced to the table and drew on her ponyskin coat. "Haven't you two left to go make love yet? That was all I could think of for two nights. My love thumb is sore from fantasizing it."

Maurette laughed and called her names in German that Ray didn't quite get and grabbed her closely. Liesl squealed, giggled, and together the two of them kissed and hugged and laughed, all but stumbling out of the restaurant into a conveniently parked taxi on Montague Street. While Liesl searched for an address in her purse, Maurette extended one weighty hand to shake Ray's and to hold onto him while he again fixed him with his eyes and melodramatically intoned, "Tomorrow the tape. Next day the studio. Then who knows? Maybe Hollywood! Eh, *cher*?"

five

At first glance, as he approached the townhouse on foot, Ray wasn't certain what to make of the long, buff-colored van sitting in his driveway. The walk home had been unexpectedly crowded and noisy, filled with preteens on some sort of field trip, and he'd allowed himself to become annoyed and distracted by their shoving and squawking, so he was ready to believe the van belonged to some delivery man who'd despaired of finding a parking spot in this residential area and had finally left the vehicle out of frustration, indifferent—or resigned—to getting a ticket. As Ray drew nearer, the lettering on the truck's side, BRANAGH ENGINEERING & REPAIR, MASSAPEQUA, LONG ISLAND, grew clearer: a heavy sans serif, with a clawhammer pictured as the upright in the capital B, a wrench drawn in the E, and a Phillips-head screwdriver supporting the R. Across the rear sliding door someone had used another lettering to spell out

"Angela-Sue" in quotes, as though…what? Naming the truck? Dedicating it to her? Inside the truck there was little to see. A dusty set of snap-on sunglasses nestled amid $2 or so worth of small change on the passenger side of the dashboard, partially covered by a Yankees commemorative baseball cap. Then Ray noticed it—his parking decal—hanging from the rearview mirror, twisted among an ancient set of amber-colored rosary beads, a blue Smurf toy that had seen palmier days, an old rabbit's foot, and a funerary remembrance card featuring a hippie-looking Jesus in an engineer's jumpsuit zipped open to the navel, out of which he seemed to have produced, like magic, the burning heart he held serenely before him. While the van Mike Tedesco had driven the first time Ray met him had also been a Branagh truck, it had been heavily splattered with paint, composed of a yard-sale jumble of differently painted fenders, the lettering inside a painted-on benday, as though applied all in one piece. This must be an official company truck. But if it was Mike's—and the loose change on display seemed to suggest it was: What city-dweller would be foolish enough to tempt a break-in with that kind of display?—where was he?

Inside the office, a handful of messages blinked on Ray's answering machine. The first was from Liesl, almost indifferently warning him she'd be late for lunch. No kidding. Another, longer, slower message was from J.K., of all people, sounding raspy-voiced: Bacall after a long night. "They said you want to come by. I look like shit, OK? Otherwise you're welcome. Bring something gorgeously romantic to listen to. I'm having politically incorrect fantasies about one of my sitters."

Brad, the grad student, Ray guessed. Maybe Ray should leave now? Close up for the afternoon, subway into Manhattan and…

Ray hit the replay button, thinking he'd be able to better gauge from rehearing the message whether J.K. would merely put up with his visit or whether he really, really wanted Ray to come and was, as usual, being psuedo-blasé. But a knock on the door interrupted him. Peering in through a window was Mike: the black hair grown almost into a nimbus around his face. The gray-lensed sunglasses, almost transparent in the pewter-colored afternoon— they must be light-sensitive—revealed a tormenting hint of those sea-green eyes. He wore yet another version of the rugby shirt, this one long-sleeved with wider stripes in faded shades of emerald, ivory, and crimson. Over that he sported a fluffy khaki down vest. But replacing his corduroy shorts were a pair of overwashed forest-green twill work slacks that fit him even more snugly. The same stained boots as before. He held a brown paper bag that appeared to contain slices of pizza.

"Hey!" Mike greeted Ray. No touching. Nothing like that as he stepped into the office and again temptingly raised the paper sack, front edge plucked open, exposed to release its spicy aroma. "Hungry?" Mike asked, his eyebrows dancing. Any plan Ray might have had about taking off for J.K.'s place vanished. He came back, Ray thought. He came back for more. He even brought food!

Ray was about to say something stupid like he'd take his pepperoni without pizza, but thought better of it.

"Just ate lunch. C'mon in."

Mike made himself comfortable on the edge of Ray's desk and carefully peeled back a crumpled end of the paper bag.

"You mind?"

"No. Sit in the desk chair if you want. Something to drink?"

The gray sunglasses came off, were plunged into the space between the top button of the rugby shirt and the tender concavity beneath his Adam's apple. "Got any brewskis?" A little glance to check if he was going beyond bounds.

He wolfed down a slice of pizza and was working on the second by the time Ray came back with two opened beers and joined him on the desk-edge.

Mike chugged down half the beer, then sighed. "I work too hard. I stopped by before. Brought back your parking thing." He motioned outside to the van, took another slug of beer, then attacked the second slice of pizza. His teeth were white, sharp, perfectly even. "I'm starving."

"Hold onto the decal," Ray said, wondering if he was going to far, too fast. "For, you know, when you're in the neighborhood again?" he added, as though Mike would have so much else to do in the area *but* see Ray. How often could automatic doors go kablooey anyway? "I've got another decal." He didn't. Not yet.

"And if you're out, I can park and nap."

So Mike *was* planning to return.

Mike kept eating, sipping the beer, gliding slowly into gratification. He glanced at his hands—as nicked and cut up as before. "I'm a slob. I shoulda washed!" His little grin: that checking look again. Ray was reminded of a documentary he'd seen of primates in groups, how younger males kept doing that repetitive checking, with an almost apologetic little grin, just before they cornered and climbed onto a female. The voiceover explained that their repeated checking gesture was to render them younger, less of a threat, perhaps evoking the protective, nurturing side of the female about to be mounted.

"I won't tell anyone," Ray confided. "But you can wash whenever you want. You know where it is," he gestured at the corridor.

"Think I'll need mercurochrome? Bandages?" Mike asked, inspecting his wounded fingers again. "Will you help?" His little-boy routine was by no means unappealing. Ray had a sudden image of Mike bare, on his back, legs up as Ray screwed him.

Mike almost spoiled the little-boy act with an unexpected, resonant belch. He looked astonished, then shook his head. "Can't take me anywhere!"

"I know one place I can take you," Ray said. He liked playing with this guy. And when Mike responded with a half eager look, Ray enjoyed teasing him by saying, "The bathroom! To heal your wounds."

They were nearly face to face in the lavatory, at the sink, undergoing what was increasingly appearing to be their own little arcane pre-sex ritual involving blood and fingers, rubbing alcohol and Band-Aids, when the phone rang. A minute later Ray thought he heard a familiar voice leaving a message. "I should get that."

He grabbed the receiver just as J.K. was about to hang up.

"You spend as much time in the loo as a 14-year-old boy!" J.K said when Ray told him why he hadn't picked up the phone. "I'm hoping *not* for the same reason!" He must be feeling better; his voice was less raspy. J.K. explained that he had a short—but as expected from him—exacting list of "sundries" he'd appreciate if Ray might bring by. He couldn't very well ask the mellifluously named Brad Stone to buy him emery boards and Vaseline, now, could he? The lad might think he was up to something deviant. That is, if Ray was still planning to come.

Ray said he was coming. He wrote down J.K.'s list on the unopened envelope of a telephone bill and at last managed to get his loquacious friend off the phone without arousing suspicion that he was being rushed or, in his own words, eschewed—J.K. abominated being *eschewed.*

Mike wasn't in the bathroom. He was in the bedroom. On top of the bed covers, without any clothing on, lying back, looking at the ceiling, perhaps looking at nothing at all, idly fondling his comely, medium-size, rigid penis in his bandaged hand. Ray gazed at him, a bit voyeuristically, feeling vibrations purring inside himself spread out into the room, via the hardwood floors and by way of the Tabriz Persian carpet, until Mike, in bed, must have also sensed the reverb, and dropped his gaze to look at Ray.

"Hey!" In this odd light his green eyes were luminescent.

"Hey, kiddo!" Ray unbuckled and dropped his denims, touching himself through his designer briefs as much to exhibit himself as to communicate his excitement. He used one shoe-tip to draw off the other. Reversed the action with a socked toe. Kicked away the shoes and trousers. Slowly unbuttoned his pale blue oxford, deciding at the last minute to keep on the chest-hugging guinea tee, all the while measuring how well he was holding Mike's attention. When he was satisfied that Mike's interest was high—the man's situation itself was a clue to begin with, no?—Ray descended onto the bed, directly atop Mike, who quickly turned away—signifying he wouldn't kiss (a shame but no real surprise), otherwise letting Ray do whatever he wanted.

Ray was more assured, less fearful Mike would try to stop him, suddenly change his mind, abruptly get up and leave. More confident, Ray now had the security of lavishing more time and invention at foreplay. After all, this naked man in Ray's bed was a knockout with a gracefully masculine body: Homage must be paid. Mike was so tangibly close, so openly Ray's own, such a superb specimen. Not since his first night with the 22-year-old Jesse Vaughan Moody had he experienced this.

After talking with other gay men, Ray often tried to recall if, like some of them, it had been his father's physicality that had first attracted him to men. But in truth, he didn't have a specific—or even general—memory of his father's body (as others often so vividly had) and he found it difficult to credit those (mental health) professionals who insisted that an infant-era attempted and rejected father-son "romance" was the inevitable turning point in every gay man's life.

The more Ray strove to recollect, the more he realized his fidgety, intelligent, open-hearted, at times carping, and frequently self-deprecating father never wore anything more revealing than a pair of Bermuda shorts and kneesocks, topped by an elbow-sleeved sports shirt. Ray definitely *did not* recall seeing his father nude, or him lifting him to the toilet rim to pee, as J.K. remembered his own father; nor showering at an open-air beach cabana, as Jesse recalled his. Ray couldn't even recall seeing his father wearing a bathing suit, and doubted he had ever worn one.

No one in Ray's family—not his father, not his mother, not his aunts or his uncles or cousins—had been physically prepossessing. Intellects, yes, and great lovers of books, as Jesse so clearly was. Neither the Henriques nor Egger family was at all physical. Maybe because like many Midwesterners of their generation, it had been drummed into them that the body was animal, swinish, bestial, lower class. That might help explain why, as adolescents, Ray and his sister had so easily discarded the emotional and intellectual to veer into the rocky shoals of the corporeal.

Actually, it started before then, because if there had been no one in their family, and not that many opportunities in their tiresome suburb, around young

Ray to inspire him to grow up an androphile, there had been instead one single, miraculous fortuity: a neighbor of maybe 25 or so, Nick Stepner, a newly-wed who had moved in a few doors down and across the street from the Henriqueses.

In fair weather, from the first hint of spring through the middle of November, Nick would spend hour upon hour washing, polishing, detailing, and otherwise pampering the newly bought apple-green Mustang convertible parked in his driveway. To avoid getting splashed or dirtied, Nick wore as little as possible. Any prolonged sunshine, no matter the season, was motive enough for him to take off his shirt. It was especially remarkable how throughout those seemingly endless, humid, sweltering central Illinois mid Augusts, Nick labored at the fortunate auto clad in nothing but tiny, hip-hugging, ice-blue cotton shorts. Yes, Nick Stepner had been the first man Ray had ever stopped to look at, and remained to gaze at, gawk at, wonder over.

A year older than Ray and equally observant, Kathy also noticed how Nick's thick shock of strawberry-blond hair patterned itself into a point low upon his nape before diffusing into a fuzz across his shoulders that shone in afternoon sunlight like golden powder. They had looked—each of them, brother and sister, alone and together—at how the blond, fine hair reappeared at the dimpled lower back, where Nick's spine dove into the loose-fitting, belt-less waist of his shorts, indicating that his near-shelf of a rear end was finely dusted with particles of it. While in front, the pale shoulder hair only glittered when it happened to be backlit, then seemed to vanish from the wide, bare geometry of clavicles and pectorals, as though exiled by such rigorous virility. It returned, guilefully, at first barely visible, a fine golden haze surrounding each baby-pink nipple, eventually gathering in an inverted delta at Nick's breastbone, and from there plunging in an attenuated orange-gold effulgence headlong down his body and into his shorts, only to be resurrected once again as gold dust defining his upper thighs, knees, and calves. The red and straw-colored fur and Nick's slender, perfect physique, along with his sweet-natured, forthcoming personality, had kept Ray from zipping past on his three-speed Raleigh. Instead he'd stopped to admire, and as Nick had turned out to be friendly, he'd talk to Ray, explaining what he was doing, how and why, assuming all the time that it was the apple of *his* eye, the shiny green car, that was the object of Ray's apparent lust, and not himself.

They'd never spoken of it, Kathy and Ray, only noticed each other noticing, hanging around when the Mustang received attention. After Nick moved away—Ray was a young teen by then—he'd begun to look around and observe other men, mostly his peers in phys ed class, in the gym or outside on the scruffily grassed high school track and field or in the vast, resounding, odorous municipal swimming pool. Ray came to stand in awe at the male human body, beginning with his own, not insubstantial, example, moving on to silently venerate various schoolmates.

He'd been amazed not only by the body as a whole but even more by the extreme thoughtfulness of its detailing: astounded for example, by the abrupt yet fluid manner by which the front upper thighs connected to the groin, sometimes so jarring an abutment that long, contoured veins rose on either side, the way vast continental shelves subducting one another drive up coastal promontories, mesas, and arroyos. He'd marveled at the depth and extreme softness yet also the strength and surface tension at each side-hollow lying between, almost within, the protection of a sinewy shoulder and a meaty bicep. He'd been endlessly intrigued by the delicacy of the tiny central basin between the symmetrically sculptural neck bones, as well as by the inflexibility of the sternum, flanked as it was by the low mounds of softer breasts. He'd been stunned by how buttocks arose as a superlative to and yet also a harmonization with the broad backs of the legs, and how barely visible connective sinews joined their abrupt dimensionality to the bisected, spine-knobbed, otherwise antithetical flat plane of the back.

If physical man was a miracle that Ray could and did openly adore, and if Jesse in his unassuming perfection had been a divulgence, then Mike from Massapequa was a prodigy. Every aspect was more defined, more pronounced, more subtly colored, more sublimely molded even than the lover whom Ray had grown accustomed to adore. Seeing this, feeling it, Ray could show no greater respect but to make love to every aspect of Mike, from the only possibly ugly inch—the red-skinned ridged heel behind his foot—to possibly the most lovely—the mellow-tan baby-ass nape—before actually taking his penis in his mouth, so that by the time that occurred, Mike was simultaneously aroused beyond his previous experience yet also tranquilized, as though he'd been macerated in fine oil: his skin atingle, breathing sporadic, his manhandled body stimulated yet ready for more of anything Ray might offer.

It was then that something unexpected occurred. Mike had been recumbent, observing Ray. Gradually he raised himself, abdomen muscle by clear-cut abdomen muscle, and began to touch Ray.

Preoccupied, distracted as he was, Ray wasn't sure whether Mike was clumsily trying to get rid of the close-fitting A-shirt Ray was still wearing, or even if he was completely conscious of what he was up to; his touching seemed so uninstructed, so fumbling. Ray helped a bit, raising his body, lifting an edge of the shirt himself, so Mike would see how to do it. He did, unskillfully caressing the hot skin of Ray's chest and back, but he also reached farther down. In response, Ray hoisted himself a few inches so Mike could get his hands on the front of Ray's underwear, which appeared to be his intention. He touched Ray there, briefly, amateurishly—if excitingly—not so much caressing Ray or fondling him or holding him very long, as certifying him, or perhaps assuring himself of Ray's masculinity before he sank back once again onto the bed, where he went on to occasionally, inexpertly stroke Ray's shoulders.

Less than a minute later Ray thought he heard Mike murmur words he at first thought might be directions or wishes, then supposed to be fantasy elements ripped out of context, words he at first couldn't discern, until he did at last clearly hear, "Yeah…that's it!…Big man!…Do that…big man…big man!" And while Ray couldn't tell if the reference was to his well-developed shoulders or to his genitals—larger than Mike's; Mike had so recently handled both—he was pleased by it, and even more pleased that Mike was still mumbling those words when he began to arch his back and thrash his legs as he let himself orgasm inside Ray.

After a while the stillness as they lay alongside each other—no longer even breathing hard—was broken by a gurgling from within Mike's abdomen.

"Sounds like the pizza wasn't enough?" Ray suggested.

"It's *never* enough. Since I was 12 I've eaten like a horse. And I'm still hungry. My father-in-law says I have the metabolism of a hummingbird. Ever see one of them? How they hover in the air 'cause they beat their wings so fast?"

"I could make you a sandwich," Ray offered.

"No, thanks. I'll be eating as soon as I get home. If I don't clean my plate and have seconds, my wife thinks there's something wrong with me."

Silence again, stillness. Ray wondered whether he should mention Mike's touching him. Would it encourage or embarrass Mike?

"I'll bet the van threw you off." Mike had a joke in his voice.

"A little. But I don't know too many guys with any kind of van."

"I sorta got promoted. 'Member I told you this older guy was tickin' off people? He pissed off one guy real bad, and Branagh—that's my boss—gave me the primo route. That's Queens, Manhattan, and Brooklyn. The other guy got my route. Long Island. Closer to home. But this route is a little less work for a little more money. We earn based on what he can charge. He charges more in the city."

Mike's stomach began rumbling again, and he sat up, muttering. As he did, he inadvertently brushed Ray's upper thigh. He started to whisk away his hand, but Ray's own hand darted out and held it against his upper thigh. He slowly guided Mike's hand the short, crucial distance to his groin, to his still not yet softened erection inside his underwear. Mike's eyes were a little startled, his handsome face forming questions.

"You did it before," Ray explained serenely. "I figured you were curious, and might want to do a little more but weren't sure how I'd like it."

Mike shrugged. Not about to let on to anything. He did let Ray continue to maneuver his hand into stroking and caressing him. When Ray lifted his own hand away, Mike continued to caress him, and together they watched Mike's hand, still somewhat awkward and fumbling, as it addressed Ray's hard-on through his briefs.

"Big," Mike said with something in his voice that Ray couldn't quite reach a conclusion about: not awe, nor fear, something he'd never come across before.

"I'm guessing," Ray began, "that despite what a great-looking guy you are, you don't have a hell of a lot of opportunity to do stuff…like this. Why not take advantage of it when you can? Even if you are a little unsure."

Mike lifted his wondrous green eyes to search Ray's face. "It's not that I'm unsure. I know what I'd *like* to do…I've seen guy stuff in pornos and all, you know…and…I'd like to do *everything*. It's just…" He shifted his hand from off Ray's crotch to his lower torso, his bare stomach. "It's not that I don't like you or…I guess I still gotta convince myself, you know."

Before Ray could ask what he meant, Mike completely lifted his hand, which had risen up to Ray's chest. "Now I gotta take off!"

Ray felt something more needed to be spoken, clear as it now was to him that this was hardly going to be a verbal relationship. He stopped Mike as he was climbing off the bed, a hand grasping Mike's hand. "Listen! Take your time, OK? Move at your own pace. I'll go with you. I'm cool with that. Understand?"

Mike's eyes seemed to open fully, almost blindingly green, before they returned back to their muffled brilliance. "Yeah, sure. OK. Thanks." He sounded at the same time satisfied and noncommittal.

This time Ray did remain lolling atop the bed covers until Mike had come out of the bathroom again and got dressed. Ray pulled on only a pair of denims to see him to the door. They parted, as before, without touching, without any farewell more definite or meaningful than "See you later" and "Yeah, later."

Ray went back to bed to undress again and masturbate in the atmosphere of tossed bedclothes and the lingering odor of Mike Tedesco. Only now, it wasn't just a moment-by-moment replay of what had already happened but a projection into the future. Given what had transpired today, there was suddenly now a real possibility that whatever Ray had fantasized might happen. If not soon, then at some coming time. This was getting distinctly interesting.

Jesse

November 1992

six

The first few times, Ray had helped him with the infusolator. But when he'd gotten home today, Jesse had immediately noticed the note telling him that Ray was at J.K.'s due to a "minor" emergency. Whatever that meant. Given J.K.'s dependency upon Ray for the smallest things, that might signify J.K. had broken a fingernail or that he'd been beaten nearly to death by a hustler. The note asked would Jesse be able to do the infusolator by himself? Or maybe not, maybe he'd wait until Ray got home? That ought to be shortly before dinnertime.

Jesse decided he would do it himself. He'd learned how at the hospital, observing the step-by-step demonstrations before and after they'd installed it in his chest, and while awkward, it wasn't difficult. Hook up the medicine and other squishy plastic bags to the intravenous rack. Open each bag with a quick twist of the wrist. Test the point to see if anything comes out. Let the tube hang to his chest. Get comfortable with a book or TV remote. Snap open the stopper on the infusolator. Use the peroxide and cotton balls to cleanse the area, particularly the skin around the plastic opening a few inches above his heart. Insert the needlelike tip from the hanging tube into the infusolator. Watch it trickle into him, drop by drop, hour after hour. Think "positive, life-enhancing" thoughts. Replace it with each of the two other tube tips, cleansing chest and plastic before and after. Remove when empty. Snap infusolator closed. Rewash.

He'd better get used to doing it himself, no? What if the doctor told him he'd have to do it more than once a day? And at the office too? No, that wouldn't be a good idea, letting people at Casper, Vine see how ill he was, despite how great they'd been about it so far.

Ray had arranged the medical supplies in the lower section of the dining room sideboard. The medical stand with its arms for hanging the plastic bags—the DHPG itself, as well as the electrolyte-and-sugar solution—he'd placed in the living room corner between the curtained window and a bookcase. A contemporary looking, snakelike reading lamp had been coiled around one arm of the IV rack to drop to the big, Danish, redwood and caramel-leather reading chair Ray had bought a few months after they moved in together. The idea was to downplay the medical aspect: Make it a hip sitting area. It sort of worked.

He'd always thought of the Danish number as Ray's chair and usually settled on the sofa or perched in the Bloomie's barrel seat. But when they'd gotten home from that pre-op hospital meeting with doctors, registered nurses, and a social worker, Ray said, "This is the best spot, Jess. I know you don't like this chair, but it can be comfortable." Which was funny because Jesse adored the chair, and every opportunity he had that Ray wasn't there, he'd luxuriate in its firm, sensuous contours, stretching across it, using the arms as supports, a head rest, taking pleasure from leather sticking to his skin—like a jealous boyfriend—in summer or when he sweated from fever.

Even before the surgery, they'd worked out not only how Jesse would receive the three-hour infusions, but also what might happen later if he became differently incapacitated. It was an easy decision to convert the upstairs bedroom into a prospective sickroom, and even though it was a flight of stairs up, it was near the kitchen and living room, steps from a full bath. But what if the kids slept overnight, Jesse asked. Where would they go? Ray would empty out Klavier Stuecke's storage room next to his office, or reorganize it to leave room to open out the folding bed for the night.

Jesse hadn't been able to convey his real anxiety: It would be the first time he and Ray slept in a different room—not counting a few business trips each had taken—in 12 years. Jesse was uneasy, fearful, though he understood that it had to happen eventually: Like most healthy people, even in sleep Ray emitted bacteria, and the more unable Jesse became at fighting off bacterial assault, the more isolated he would have to be. Ray slept so deeply that he didn't know how awake Jesse often was, despite fatigue. He'd jolt awake at 4 A.M. in the big bed—Ray ten feet away—light the tiny reading lamp, or put on the headphones and listen to jazz or classical music and gaze at his lover. Read, sketchily. Listen to music, dreamily. Think.

Mostly he thought about the past: his and Ray's. And he wondered about the future: Ray's, since he had no future. As for their future together, that seemed little more than a ongoing separation. That's what the sickroom upstairs signified, another, further, physical distancing from Ray.

It had begun at his diagnosis, with their no longer being able to have unprotected sex. Ray had not come close to complaining, of course, but Jesse felt the millimeters of plastic between them whenever Ray fucked him or sucked him off had been a momentous step, first in a series of barriers the disease would construct between them. The pace increased a year ago when shingles appeared on Jesse's waist—the initial excruciatingly painful indicator of the virus's active presence—and lest Ray in any way exacerbate the torture by accidentally brushing against him during sleep, Ray had slept on the folding cot, although it was placed next to their bed.

The shingles had disappeared at last, replaced by a variety of minor, less tormenting ailments, some dermatological, others neuropathic. Ray once more slept on the folding bed. Then Jesse's T-cell count dropped more than a hundred points. Ray and the cot journeyed across the big bedroom. Six months ago a bronchial infection appeared that Jesse's physician was certain originated from a daylong cold Ray had, an infection he'd quickly thrown off, which lingered for weeks in Jesse. This sleep setup became permanent. Due to the virus's progress, the two no longer had sex with each other, no longer slept in the same bed, no longer kissed or nuzzled or touched, except mornings and nights when Ray disinfected him.

Meaning that HIV had accomplished what no one else had been able to: not society, which barely tolerated them together; not Jesse's background, which insisted it was morally and ethically wrong; not even his mother, who despised his homosexuality and everything and everyone connected to it with a Fundamentalist Christian zealot's passion, with the hatred of a woman betrayed and robbed. Knowing what HIV had done to them hurt Jesse more than knowing he no longer had a future.

That was an odd sidelight, how with this single procedure Jesse had realized he was going to die, and how instantly he'd accepted the fact. Naturally, he'd gone through all the steps from denial to acceptance before, in the days after the diagnosis, but now, well, now it was indisputable. Medical intervention had been critical, therefore it couldn't be more authentic, could it? In a way that delivered him from what he'd only now recognized had been apprehension. Before, everything had existed in a possible future, the way that, as a child, the illustrations in his Jules Verne novels had existed. Now, while it might not be as dramatic as pneumonia—or shingles or a bronchial infection—it meant he had a few months, a year if he dawdled.

He had no intention of dawdling. Not for his sake and not for Ray's. He'd never enjoyed being ill. He still remembered his childhood illnesses: recurring bouts of tonsillitis, his throat so swollen he couldn't even swallow water, at times could barely breathe; and the dull ache after his tonsils had been removed that all the ice cream in the world couldn't assuage. Or the itching, burning, scaling, hideous allergies he'd weathered when he was eight, nine, ten years old. Allergies that had returned lately.

The manifestation that brought everything into focus, to a single point, was so much less of a proclamation than any of those minor illnesses would have been, the only indication of something really wrong being a totally sensationless cloud in his left eye. But while not painful, it announced the insidious virus unchecked, growing every day more powerful, depleting him slowly, as though his life were a savings account and he were withdrawing daily without ever depositing. Becoming lackadaisical had grown easy, to not bother to fight, to accept walking more slowly and thinking less sharply, to allow himself to sleep later every day: a kind of movie-star dream of death, an oh-so-languid surrender to diminished capacity.

Jesse believed he'd pretty much fulfilled the nearly perfect arc of his intended life, and it would be, at the very least, unaesthetic to loiter on and allow the lovely curve to be marred by an unsightly trailing-off.

He knew the high point of the arc: when he'd been made copy chief, following three successful print ad campaigns with industry awards and a substantial pay raise, a new corner office, a vice presidency on its way. That same month he and Ray, already living together several years, decided to have a commitment ceremony. They invited both families, although only Ray's had come, Jesse's line represented by a second cousin, Alexa, who happened to live in the city. But

Mona and Harve Henriques had driven out from Illinois, along with Ray's two aunts, Jana and Rose. Dressed as bridesmaids were Alexa and Kathy (there with her newest husband and the three-and-a-half-year-old Chris, who'd been their cherubic, somewhat confused, blond ringbearer), while Kai Morito from Jesse's workplace had been usher, with J.K. as best man. All in formal wear—morning suits, ascots, cummerbunds—with flowers and live music and a stout, gray-haired clergywoman from the North Fork. Four couples and three singles from Casper, Vine drove out too, including a partner. Another dozen came from EMI/Capitol. Running the entire three-ring circus was J.K., who'd contrived their wedding to rival something in *Modern Bride*, taking place at a loaned, ten-bedroom "equestrian estate" in rural Long Island on an early-May Saturday.

Ray and Jesse awakened the next morning with Chris between them. He had crawled out of the apparently noisier and more active bedroom of his mother. As the toddler slumbered, they discussed kids, concluding yes—either their own or their families' children would definitely be part of their lives.

Later that summer they'd rented a monster house on the beach at Fire Island Pines, with J.K. and the newly met Liesl as housemates. It had been wonderful, magical, the best summer ever. By fall, Ray was promoted and they could afford winter vacations; London at Christmas, Cancun in February. Life had been good.

And had continued good, losing glitter here and there, slowly, inexorably as the epidemic grew and began striking people around them, the circle drawing tighter and tighter, finally striking them. Yet, if he were sworn in front of a courtroom, Jesse would have to tell the truth: The past 12 years had delivered so much more than he'd ever expected, had so totally fulfilled his hopes and dreams that nothing—no illness, no separation, no loss—could take from him the belief that although he'd been undeserving, he'd been wonderfully gifted.

Growing up as basically an only child in a rigorously staid, ultra-Christian, tradition-drenched Southern family in a state capital no bigger than most Northern mill towns, Jesse had been certain that what he'd come to think of as his "daydreaming" would always remain exactly that. An only child, because it was only once he turned 13 that a second pregnancy happened, surprising no one as much as Adele Vaughan Moody, née Carstairs, who fumed, who barely spoke to her husband the last four months she carried. By then Jesse had come to figure out those elements needed for defending himself, and for waging guerrilla war against his mother, who seemed to want only one thing—to ingest him whole. Or was it to become him? To live his life for him? It seemed to vary.

Childhood illness turned out to be an unanticipated weapon in their ongoing skirmishes. Mostly because Adele—while she could become as self-sacrificing and loyal as any woman on earth—feared certain infectious illnesses, especially those that might disfigure her lovely facial features. How many times had she retold the pitiful saga of her cousin, May Dunwoodie, a prepossessing young lady slated to marry a Lee of Virginia, who'd lost all in a toss of the medical dice when she'd contracted scarlatina and been left "disfeatured; socially no better than a Nigrah washerwoman."

Jesse's inexplicable facial rashes, his abruptly swollen lips, his blooming acne—reactions to foods or flowers—threw the fear of facial damage into his mother so intensely that she (blissfully!) kept away, not merely while he was actually affected but often long after, leaving him in the care of Mrs. Greene, their plump, sweet-tempered cook and housekeeper, who'd never previously hinted at interest or ability in befriending him, or in defending him from the Scylla of his mother's emotional clutch and the Charybdis of her uncontrollable temper.

During the second year of dermal afflictions, Adele withdrew almost altogether from Jesse, no longer requiring him on local forays or shopping trips downtown where formerly he'd been her escort, package-bearer, pet, and victim. She now went alone, or with a woman friend; she even learned to drive.

Jesse remained at home, idle at first, at loose ends, but then eventually much occupied: In good weather, he'd scavenge the lush thickets and disordered groves of the sizable acreage surrounding the Moody house, down to deeply crevassed Foxglove Creek, across the wide meadows to the hickory wood, wherein still lay the perilous ruins of a long-abandoned, cedar-slatted, Confederate ammunition depot. He wandered as far as the Napier's tobacco farm on the one end (always busy, filled with machinery and people) to the granite quarries on the other, playing solitary as a polecat (since Adele had long declared no boy in town good enough to be befriended) for hours at a time, pretending to be both Chingachcook and Natty Bumpo, Lieutenant Lightfoot Harry and Colonel Burnsides, Jim Hawkins and Long John Silver, Huck and Jim, Robinson Crusoe and Friday, Ned Tannen and Captain Nemo: his storybook heroes, their beloved coadventurers, loving companions, and sworn enemies all in one, sometimes mixed together.

In this fashion he grew tanned and agile, energetic and enduring, audacious and daring. In Adele's words, when she bothered to notice him, "nothing better than one of those grease-haired, half breed Cherokees stumbling by the feedstore."

Evenings, stormy days, and freezing weather, the boy remained solitary indoors, often for hours at a time, at Mrs. Greene's table, watching her bake and roast and steam, listening to her chitchat and anecdotes and eventually, when he'd come to trust her, relating his dreams for the future.

Unlike Adele Vaughan Moody, née Carstairs, Mrs. Greene (Lylah, he discovered was her first, musical, name) did not dash his wishes, saying, "What foolishness! You'll certainly not go off North to live and kill your poor mother with a heart attack. You'll stay here and work in the law offices of your poppa's partners." Or "You don't know what you're saying, boy! You shall not reside with your best male friend forever. You shall marry a girl of good lineage and raise a family and carry on the Moody name. Who fills your head with such cowboy drivel?"

No, Mrs. Greene would instead talk of someone she knew (she never said whom) who had gone to a big Northern city and uncovered not cheats and ogres, but kind and gallant folk, and how that person had thrived; she even once spoke of her cousin Antoine, whom she'd described as artistic and elegant, and how he'd traveled up to Philadelphia and found himself not a woman—he'd disdained such since he was a child—but a young gentleman of similar tastes, and how they'd moved in together and were the toast of their social set. Suggesting that if Jesse wanted to do the same, there was precedent, even if it were—she had to apologize—colored.

The part of the dream he'd never been able to tell her during those intimate chats—forever permeated in his memory by the fragrance of vanilla and almond extracts, freshly baked biscuits and pies, overripe banana mixed with honeysuckle and jasmine during the spring months, spruce and Georgia pine during the fall—was his dream-companion. Sympathetic as he came to know Mrs. Greene to be, he'd never been able to bring himself to confide in her what this companion would be like, because it was so opposite of what he thought she dreamt. His friend wouldn't be elegant, wouldn't dress in fresh-starched shirts with triangles of scented handkerchiefs, wouldn't visit for tea and sip at aperitifs.

His companion would be strong, masterful, manly, unpretty, scarred or crag-faced, someone who'd unthinkingly remove his shirt in public as backwoods workmen did laboring at the old Indian quarries, and like them, he'd be sinewy and rock-bodied, unashamed and natural-acting—as ready to shake your hand in friendship as strike you for some offense or scorn you for being a fool.

No question in Jesse's mind but that Daddy Moody didn't fit the mold. Once he almost had. Jesse remembered how when he was four, they taken a summer vacation to the beaches of Georgia and how after playing in surf and sand every day, his daddy would take him by the hand into a roofless bathhouse where, among other boys and men, he'd remove his and Jesse's sand-choked bathing suits and rinse them in the shower while they stood nude and washed themselves with soap and water, the curious boy looking at everyone else. And how his daddy lifted him onto the built-in wood benches between lockers of the changing room and dried him with a towel, while his own huge, slabby body glittered with water droplets among the fine, curling mats of chocolate-colored hair. Day after day for two weeks they shared the ritual, and it had given the little boy ample opportunity to observe not only his father's body, but also that of other men and boys. Even then his daddy's belly had been round, his elbows, knees, and back tending toward fat. The child had asked if he'd look like him when he grew up, and Daddy Moody had said, "No, son, you favor the Carstairs, not the Moodys. You're refined and fine-boned. You'll grow up slender. Lissome, like your mother."

As predicted, fine-boned and lissome, refined and slender he became by the time he was 13, partly due to heredity, partly due to the illnesses that had kept him indoors playing alone in the toy room, sitting in the kitchen; partly from his imagination-filled athletics out of doors; while his daddy swelled from slab to flab, from thick-bodied to larded with pounds of extra flesh. Then it was, wishing more than ever to share his outdoor adventures with some beloved youth his age, that Jesse began to recall those other men and boys he'd seen at the beach that lovely summer, men wiry and muscled, skin so taut that shower water sprang off as though burned. The teenage Jesse began to witness his own fluids flow hot as he slept, as he washed in the tub, and with those unexplained spasms of his growing body, a concomitant longing, almost an agony, grew in him to be alongside one of those men, to touch him and be touched back, to clasp him around the shoulders, clench him by the waist, grasp and stroke, knead and punch those powerful limbs.

"Preternaturally gifted as a young a scholar" was how the high school dean described Jesse when recommending him to colleges, despite his mother's constant criticism of him as "dreamy, lazy, and know-nothing." Possibly because of all the reading he had done on his own, thrown back upon his own resources as he'd so long been, examining in detail the 20-volume *Encyclopedia Americana*, the two-volume *Columbia Dictionary*, the giant *Oxford Atlas*, H.G.Wells's *Story of History*, and Bury's *History of Greece*—in fact most of the books in his father's office, some previously unread, their pages uncut. So Jesse had been admitted to a small, prestigious, barely Southern, East Coast university, where in the first few weeks he'd discovered, to his astonishment, that everything so far in his life had not made him the complete loser and fool he'd for years considered himself (that his mother insisted he was), but instead a handsome, poised, self-possessed youth: someone desirable.

Not only desirable to girls—who, like Mrs. Greene's cousin, Jesse had never quite gotten the point of. The first well-built young man who'd dropped to his knees and sucked Jesse's cock in the shower room merely confirmed what his slightly older, more sophisticated dormmate, Pryor Fleck, laughingly said: "You damned innocent child! Don't you know that with your rotogravure face and your illustrated-book body, with your thick chestnut hair and your great golden eyes, you are as the god Apollo to this dorm, possibly to the whole damn school! Get all you want, boy. But don't spread too much if you want to keep your reputation."

Jesse had thus peered around more closely, and if at first the slumbering old red-brick and black-walnut-shaded campus had appeared to offer a plenitude of young men exactly his type, he'd soon enough come to realize that pretty much all of them possessed one serious failing or another, from stupidity and cupidity to vulgarity and effeminacy. Accosted on one of his near-daily runs and persuaded into joining the track and field team, Jesse instantly lighted upon its captain, upperclassman jock Beau Wheeling, who seemed the least defective of lads, and even though Beau was "going steady" with a junior named Nancy Janeck, Jesse had in Pry Fleck's words, "publicly and privately set his cap" for Beau, and after a few weeks of siege—both subtle and overt—had maneuvered the craggily handsome strawberry-blond into his bed, whereupon Beau demonstrated a remarkable amatory aptitude, for one so ostensibly heterosexual, in what Pry always referred to as "the Hellenic arts."

Beau remained in Jesse's bed until he graduated, by which point Jesse had almost mastered several noncurriculum assignments, including critical lessons in the male ego as well as barely squeaking through a course in what was needed to keep a male-male relationship going. His sophomore year, Jesse's "chosen" was even more open to public scrutiny: Yancey Eubanks, the popular, devil-may-care quarterback of the Swamp Foxes, was known to be in love with grain alcohol, himself, football, money, and Jesse—in that order. By the end of the year, Jesse had reversed the order, and in so doing also managed to haul the maladroit Foxes to near the top of their league as well as attract an NFL offer for Yancey to play professionally. Of course, Jesse thereupon consolidated his fame as a heartbreaker by very publicly dumping Yancey in the middle of the final home game, driving off at halftime in the sapphire-blue and white Maserati roadster of a Savannah millionaire playboy, "Val" (Valentine) De Spain.

De Spain lasted a summer, and his social connections and largesse for once even managed to partially shut the ever critical mouth of Adele Moody, née Carstairs. At last, however, the precise nature of her son's various "friendships" was made clear to her, and the horrified Adele, by this time no longer totally encumbered with the full-time occupation of ruining the life of her young daughter, turned her attention back to perform an identical service for her son. She applied untold pressures upon Jesse. A rather embarrassed Daddy Moody— who scarcely comprehended what the term *invert* meant, never mind what it might entail—was forced to threaten the boy that he'd have to "shape up" or leave college and be thrown upon his own resources. Jesse's allowance was cut, and what he didn't receive was sent to the perfidious Pry Fleck, bribed by Adele into spying and reporting. Even more humiliating, Jesse was coerced to present himself at the offices of a Freudian psychiatrist who claimed to be able to cure what Jesse thought of as his natural sexuality.

Made uncertain by all this of what he'd believed to be his preordained trajectory in life and more than a little chastened by what even Jesse had to admit were three unsuccessful love affairs in a row, he subsided into a decline in his junior year. He took a dorm room of his own, threatened Pry Fleck's life, scorned his former pals in the lesbigay campus club, dropped off the team, ceased attending athletic events, and shunned the gyms and locker rooms where his lithe body was in high demand. Instead he took to skulking about campus, lurking in off-quad coffeehouses and beaneries, moping about the library, sulking upon the lawns, dressed in outsized and seldom laundered all-black garb. He let his hair and beard grow long and uncombed. He took up cigarette and pot smoking. He spoke to no one. Refused to answer questions in or out of class. Walked out in the middle of exams. Didn't hand in term papers.

Meanwhile, Adele insisted on dragging him away from the college and "temptation" every opportunity she saw—each holiday and long weekend—and while he was home, she pushed Jesse into heterosexual liaisons. She almost no longer cared whom he associated with, so long as it was a female. The tenth time his mother introduced him to a "nice girl" and pressured him to drive her home, Jesse did so, parked and necked with the willing young lady, and ended up persuading her to perform oral sex on him. Legal prosecution was barely averted. Jesse seemed very near a total breakdown. He advanced into his senior year by a cat's whisker.

That interim summer he remained at home but took up residence in a room over the garage, furnished by the previous owners for a chauffeur, and in which he'd played often as a child. His by now thoroughly alarmed father avoided him, and even the rapacious Adele momentarily ceased her demands. Jesse had hoped to spend time, as he had done years before, with Mrs. Greene. But the cook had grown old, was now half deaf, and seemed unclear about exactly whom Jesse was. His sister, now seven, tried to befriend him. After a bit, and mostly because Jesse knew they shared physical and verbal abuse at the same hands, they ended up bonding a little.

He managed to clean himself up enough to complete his final courses and graduate from college. He cut his hair and shaved his beard, and dressed sufficiently well to occasionally hustle the bar of the best hotel in his college town: The only sex he now pursued was geared toward fattening his savings account, for he sensed he'd soon be on his own. Jesse had scored an impressively profitable john not an hour before what would be his final meeting with the quack psychologist. Ostentatiously counting twenties in front of the shrink, Jesse not only explained where it came from but exactly how—and how often—he had labored to earn it. Consequently, he was physically ejected—guffawing—from the office.

On the street, still laughing, Jesse had run into a classmate who'd long had a crush on him. She was unusually somber and told Jesse she was about to be interviewed by an advertising agency that had sent its headhunter to the school. Partly to accompany her—she was so nervous, and after all had always been kind to him—and partly as a giggle, Jesse also interviewed. Because of his many literature and social studies classes, the personnel man assumed he'd wish to be a copywriter. They had a great time, he and the interviewer, Jesse on the spot creating ridiculous ad slogans and absurd campaigns for imaginary items of clothing and personal care. They periodically went off in gales of laughter. It had been a great hoot. No wonder Jesse was astounded two weeks later when he received a letter from the ad agency with an offer to join the copy department.

He'd told his father of the offer (assuming he'd tell then Adele) and without bothering to attend his own commencement ceremony, had moved to New York a week later. The job was perfect: He became part of a team on new accounts; a half dozen other young people and two experienced ones. He found a studio apartment near Gramercy Park and desultorily furnished it. He began spending weekend nights at the city's many gay bars and dance clubs, the bathhouses and sex clubs. It was his first years of college all over again: Jesse discovered that without having done anything specifically about it, he was now more physically desirable than ever, able to land virtually every handsome, muscular guy he chose. He whored around for two years, never meeting anyone he wanted to see more than a few times, but at least if he was a slut, he slutted around more privately than he'd done as a college lowerclassman, if still with that single aim in mind: to find his dream companion.

Just as Jesse was beginning to think he'd once more failed, some friends had taken him to a party at a nearby apartment of a man named J.K. Callaway. They thought Jesse and J.K. would get along great. And while they looked good together and indeed, had good sex twice, it turned out not to be J.K. but a pal of his, one Ray Henriques, reencountered on a beach towel on the "tar beach" of J.K.'s apartment building, who actually was the first man to ask if Jesse was seeing anyone, if Jesse was serious about looking to settle down, if he wanted to be married to another man.

They'd seen each other around for some months before that serendipitous rooftop tanning session, at various clubs and bars, and of course they had officially met once before, at J.K.'s party. Jesse had been drawn to Ray's slightly off features—his odd mixture of thick, dark blond hair with too deeply set, soft-brown, almost Latin eyes, his prominent, ambiguously ethnic nose, his massive-shouldered, small-hipped body with its constantly active oversize hands, square elbows and knees: an awkward blending of physical anomalies that not only held together, but, suffused by Ray's enormous energy and alertness, strongly attracted. But if Jesse had been attracted, he'd also been offended when Ray, passing by, had said "'Scuse me, Huck." Sensitive that he still had a noticeable accent, Jesse had taken it as hostile remark.

At their rooftop encounter months later—relaxed in the warm sun, mollified with marijuana and tall, icy lemonades—the two of them alone together for a long while as J.K. dropped downstairs to his flat to take a phone call, Ray corrected the misunderstanding, explaining he had intended anything but offense: Huckleberry Finn was his absolute favorite; in fact, he used to jerk off to the illustration of the Clemens character when he was growing up. Did Jesse, by chance, have a photo of himself he didn't mind getting semen-smeared?

That evening they left J.K.'s together and ended up in bed, and while Jesse was by now used to men lavishing affection upon him, he'd seldom met anyone like Ray, who demanded so much of the same in return.

"You're awfully pretty, kiddo," Ray muttered into Jesse's ear, after sex, unwilling to let him move an inch away. "But you're awfully spoiled too."

"Here I was thinking you were far too aggressive and vain for me to have anything to do with," Jesse had replied. "Much too demanding."

Ray chuckled. "I guess this affair is totally doomed from the beginning!"

"Totally fucking doomed," Jesse agreed with a laugh.

Now, as he drowsed, Jesse recalled waking up in the hospital a week ago, the infusolator surgically installed a few hours earlier, feeling his entire chest area around the new thing quite sore, as if someone had punched him there, which was how the doctor had predicted it would hurt. Ray had been watching him sleep, waiting for him to wake up, and when he had, Ray had almost jumped out of the chair at him, asking, "How do you feel, kiddo? Terrible, huh?"

While the DHPG finished dripping into him and the other stuff began, the phone rang, and Jesse let the machine pick up, knowing it was his mother making her nightly call of demands, claims and complaints, alarms, anxieties, and manipulations. She'd begun phoning him two and a half years ago, the day Jesse's father died, filled with new apprehensions and the very same old lies, with long-used pleas, exhausted attempts at evoking guilt, and fresh maneuvers at disturbing his life. He'd been forced to deal with her after all—he'd had to return home for the funeral, and while there, he was impressed by how small and frail and helpless Adele appeared. Of course, that didn't last long. Soon enough she was up to her old tricks again. Even so, Jesse felt he was now at a considerable advantage over her. His life was so good, he could afford to be gracious and giving, especially to one so unhappy and lacking. Besides which, he was 800 miles away, reachable only by phone. So he listened to every third word she said, and if that included something absolutely demanding reponse, he usually offered one. But once the phone was hung up, he more or less forgot about her. Meanwhile, Adele seemed momentarily placated, if by no means satisfied—she would *never* be satisfied—and so they'd resumed some kind of relationship, in which their roles, if not reversed, were at least altered from how they'd always been, to the point that he believed he could no longer be worked upon by the force of her wiles and passions. For the moment, that is, because implacability was her middle name and she would never cease trying until she'd gotten what she wished. Which was why, more and more as he felt himself weakening and letting go, he sometimes didn't pick up the phone when he knew it was her, didn't take her messages, didn't listen.

When he awoke an hour later the tubes were all empty and Ray was reaching up to the IV rack, removing them, bending down to disinfect Jesse's chest with the cotton balls and peroxide. He looked terribly gaunt and pale, really upset. As Jesse watched, a tear rolled down one of Ray's cheeks. Jesse touched it. Ray saw he was awake, and tried to talk, tried to tell him about visiting J.K. He could barely get the words out, he was so disconcerted.

So Jesse said for them both: "J.K.'s got it too!" Jesse had already known that before today, of course; he had intuited it the last time they'd all been together a few weeks ago. Something about J.K.'s skin tone, his suddenly depleted face when seen at an angle. The by now unmistakable signature of the disease. Of course, he hadn't said anything at the time. Why bother? It would come in its own time. Now it had come.

Ray nodded.

"Poor Ray. Nothing but bad news. You deserve better."

"No, no!" Ever kind, ever ready to cheer Jesse up, Ray went on to say, "Not all bad. I met a friend of Liesl's at lunch. He wants me to find music to score a movie he directed. A small movie. A small, independent film."

"That does sound like good news."

They talked about that for a few minutes. Jesse found himself distracted, cogitating about being a boy again, suddenly free, long hair swept by wind, limbs elastic with vigor, leaping across small chasms and flying over the blue grass pursuing purple-black "darning needles." Now look at me, he wanted to say, a lump in a chair hours at a time, passive, receiving what may or may not save my life. Why start? It would only upset Ray more.

He'd settled onto an ottoman at Jesse's knees. "And another thing happened today," Ray said. "I saw that straight guy again. Do you remember me telling you about him? The married guy? The workman?"

"Mr. Yummy Repairman? Was it nice?" Jesse hoped it was.

"Well, pretty much the same as before. I sucked him off again. But this time he touched me," Ray said, a quiver in his voice. "My dick. My shoulders. Not for long or anything, but it was kind of exciting. Maybe he really is interested in trying out stuff."

"You deserve someone to adore you," Jesse said.

"I've got you. This is enough. I don't need more."

seven

Resolute, machinery-nicked fingers reached down and delicately yet firmly pulled Ray's face from where he was lapping at a shallow, palm-size pool of skin amid the crest of a thigh and the undulation of flesh stippled with black hair, all of it not so much flesh-colored in the mid afternoon bedroom's light, but instead, oddly, shades of cerulean, as though the body he attended so diligently wasn't strictly human, but instead protean, godlike. At times Olympian ivory, others a Cimmerian duskiness, and today, surprisingly, overwhelmingly, ultramarine.

Ray was about to lodge some complex yet sure-to-gratify amorous protest when Mike took advantage of the slight separation to turn himself over in the large, tousled bed, exposing surprising new fields of his body to the possibility of tactile and buccal penetration. So gratifying a sight it was—three distinct solid geometries accompanied by transoceanic hues of spine, skin, and but-tock—that Ray wasn't at first certain he was hearing correctly when the young mechanic reached behind himself with one strong, scarred hand, roughly lifted aside a pale azure–tinted ass cheek, and murmured that Ray should "push that big thing in." Before Ray could dither, Mike's second hand joined the first in roughly reexposing the aperture, and Mike reiterated, making the invitation unequivocal.

Not since the first time he'd inserted the head of his penis inside a man's rectum two decades before had Ray undergone such a welter of thoughts and emotions. Really? Me? Are you sure? Don't you have this upside down? Aren't you the straight one, I the...? And like this? Now? Without a condom? Unprotected? What about disease? Have you considered the consequences? Do you even know the consequences? Have you thought this out? And what about...? What about *everything*?

Mike had to repeat himself a third time. This time it came out imperious, even querulous—well, are you or aren't you, and if not, why not?—so there could be no doubt what he meant, despite Ray's many questions. So for Ray now there could be no stopping—how do you tell a beautiful man with that incredibly muscled, soft-skinned rear end who's demanding to be fucked that you won't fuck him?—no, nothing to do but go ahead with it. Ray noticed that despite his qualms, his questions, he'd not lost a smidgen of stiffness himself; he was more rigid than ever, pulsing like an erratically beating heart against the linens gathered around his lower limbs at the foot of the bed.

He settled for whispering—"Tell me if I'm hurting you"—into Mike's exquisite right ear as he spit on his cock head and slowly tucked himself inside. Before him, as though in moving fresco, deltoids and lats flexed, bunched, and relaxed in ever changing formations as Mike's anatomically textbook spine rip-pled like a banner waved in acquiescence. Ray's shamed, eager face brushed against and was immersed within the warm, dry mass of Mike's black hair, that from this close disclosed miniscule streaks of other tints, whether natural or from the lighting he couldn't tell—hot orange, sapphire, magenta—while from below he felt himself slowly forcing open a closely stitched purse of fine, warm silk. Ray felt the physique beneath him tense abruptly, shudder twice, like a big dog shaking off a sudden downpour, and he tensed himself against being shak-en off altogether. Instead Mike slowly exhaled, then sighed, signaling an immense letting go. With it, an unexpected pulling inward, clutch, loosening, clutch again. Mike's head fell forward, deeper into the pillows, his long arms—whirled about with dark hair—suddenly stretched wide in either direction; his buttocks rose, clasping, grasping, towing Ray in more intimately, until he was gliding into the longed-for boudoir. At the same time, an odor was released into the air between their bodies, unquestionably anal, yet flowery, sickly sweet, like dead orchids.

Ray brushed Mike's right shoulder with his lower lip, coming away with the taste of salt and something else, something like aluminum. He accompanied the kiss with a manual counterpart, slowly caressing first one hot-skinned, hard-nippled breast, then the other with his left hand, as his right hand continued to hold himself slightly off the mattress. He felt unable to stop himself from beginning to push in and out, still not quite believing it was happening, still alert for any minute alteration in position, muscular torsion, or internal tension that would signal an error had occurred and must be quickly rectified. The signal never arrived. Instead, after maybe five long minutes of lying inert, Mike seemed to abruptly come to his senses. He raised his head, then that amazing back; he reached around with both strong, scarred hands and grasped Ray's buttocks as though for confirmation, then slid his rough-skinned paws along Ray's thighs and stomach as if verifying their texture, heft, and density. Once again his head fell forward to the pillows, now spread apart so his face lay between them, a quarter inch from the bottom sheet. Once again his body convulsed so intensely that Ray thought he was about to be thrust off. Again he was clutched even more securely, and after pausing a bit to get a good hold on the ground gained, Ray finally figured what the hell, Mike must know what he wants, and allowed his body to take over, transforming him into a heedless, impassive, unceasing, machined piston. He fell forward completely onto Mike's body, lifting it only so he might twirl an erect nipple, rhythmically brush the sternum, caress the burning, furred belly, clench the travertine hard-on, all thoughts of potential harm not so much vanished or forgotten as put aside, made irrelevant, held apart for some other time, while he attended to what—to his amazement—had become their conjunct pleasure.

It had been more than a year since he'd screwed anyone, and he reveled in the renewed exhibition of his skill, techniques honed for years with guys before his lover, then perfected with Jesse. Not to mention his penned energy and the potency he believed he both represented and fulfilled. Every once in a while the torso beneath him suddenly shuddered or spasmed uncontrollably, but Ray no longer dreamt of stopping, only of readjusting to its vagaries, varying his speed, lunge, his angle of entrance, and once, when he lifted Mike's head and turned it to him to try to gauge whether it indicated pain or pleasure, the face was so evidently out of it, the younger man so entranced by the narrative his insides were relating, Ray had to smile through the sweat streaming off his forehead, and lean closer to taunt, "Hurting? Want me to stop?" knowing damned well he was viewing, enjoying, the opposite.

Mike panted, sounded almost panicked as he gulped out "No!" in response. He thrust out both hands and again wrapped them them behind himself to get a greater purchase on Ray's body. "No," he gasped, whispered. "Don't stop. Keep going!" so fervently, his eyes so shadowed and sea-green, Ray felt certain Mike could probably himself orgasm this way, so he continued to mindlessly jackhammer until both were sweating freely, the bed vibrating violently, and he was becoming a single, growing, compelling impulse from within, witches' fingers itching his groin a quarter inch under the skin, bubbling lava welling toward freedom, and he suddenly had the thought, *I couldn't possibly come inside him*, attempted to pull away, to draw himself out of Mike, only to find himself gripped inside even more tightly. Ray fought it a few fruitless seconds, then relented. Distracted by too much else happening, he plunged deeper, lunged with greater force, until the familiar, quotidian yet ever new, self-igniting wonder nucleated from a pin-spot abyss within his lower body, was suspended, throbbing radiation, threatened to grow algebraically, to become a hydrogen blast, to shatter flesh, bones, boundaries, skin, himself, Mike, the room, earth beneath, sky above, everything.

"You didn't come, did you?" Ray managed to gasp out. A quick view of Mike's overturned body showed the smallish, still-rigid dick, all but glowering amidst the thicket of dark, sweat-matted hair. Still panting, not yet fully recovered himself, Ray reached to take hold of it, rolled himself over Mike's body in comma, and began to suck. He came remarkably quickly, a few minutes later; came so hard, it was all Ray could do to keep him atop the bed. After that, he'd barely turned around to furtively slobber into a tissue as Mike leapt off the bed, pitching through the bathroom doorway.

Ray lay on his back, intensely satisfied, thoroughly gratified, unable to figure out how he would speak to Mike about the condom issue. If they were going to do this again—hadn't Mike once said he wanted to?—wouldn't they need some ground rules? Or would Mike feel, having given in like this, that it would be insulting to assume he did it with anyone else? He could easily take umbrage, not come back, and Ray knew that was almost the last thing he wanted, especially after today. Ray would have to say something. Downplay it. It wouldn't be easy, would require tons of tact. Still, for both their sakes, he had to.

He must have been daydreaming, because Mike was already out of the john, dressing himself, saying, "Jeez. It's late. Don't want to get caught in traffic."

Ray located and managed to slip on a pair of shorts, yet Mike was dressed and already in the hallway, past the office, about to go. Ray stopped him at the door.

"Hold on! Hold on a second."

"Gotta go. I'm a working man."

"I know. I know. But, listen, what we did back there?"

"Great, man! Jeez! You know I wasn't sure I could…Then you…And I just…and…It really felt…I don't know…But OK!"

"We should have used a condom," Ray said. "I should have put on a condom. There are diseases out there, everywhere, and…It's my fault. Sorry."

"Hey, no problem, man. You're OK, right? Not sick." Not a question.

"No, I'm not sick. But I *might* be sick—"

"You been tested and all, right?" That's how confident Mike was. And how blasé, as he asked for confirmation of what he already felt he damned well knew. "Been tested and found out you don't have it, right?"

"I *have* been tested, and I'm *not* positive. But I *could* be."

"But you're *not*." One for Mike. Ipso facto: "So we're cool."

"Right. But…like…" Ray stumbled, trying to make his point without overdoing it. "But just…like…just think about it? OK? That's all I'm saying."

"I'll think about it, all right," Mike's tone of voice giggled, leered. "Hell, I can think about being blown all day!" He all but whooped in joy. "Hey, and maybe next time I'll take my turn. You know! On top. What say?"

And he was out the door, getting into the van, the engine running, the truck pointed into 4 o'clock traffic. Just like that. Leaving Ray at the partly opened downstairs door, wearing nothing but a rumpled old pair of linen shorts that didn't button, didn't even zip up all the way, as four teenage girls half sauntered, half danced by, animated by their release from class, dressed alike in the tripartite layered uniform of the local Catholic school. Seeing Ray standing there, they kept looking back, yet at the same time kept trying to keep each other from looking back, sniggering, saying things about him as they poked each other, one almost dropping her school books, as the little group lurched forward, passed a projecting stoop out of sight three houses down the block.

"You shouldn't *assume* it, that's all," Ray uttered at the empty sidewalk, only now finding the words he ought to have said to Mike. "You shouldn't *assume* I'm not sick!" he repeated, too late for it to do any good. "That's what I should have told him."

He closed the street door, and almost mechanically checked the answering machine; he'd thought he'd heard it turn on twice to answer while they'd been in the bedroom. But no, there was only one message on the machine, and when he played it back it wasn't a customer with an order, or J.K. with a some elaborate new symptom or complaint. It was Chris, sounding hollow-toned, surrounded by stunned air, as though he were hunched over at the bottom of a well, meaning he was probably in the gymnasium hallway at school. Chris saying he'd be home an hour later then usual due to softball practice, which was usually Wednesday but had been put off till today because Coach Choumans had been sick yesterday, remember how he'd come home an hour early then? And start dinner without him, if they had to.

"Yeah, right. And who'll eat it?" Ray said aloud. "You'll probably ingest more than half of whatever I cook, hungry as I'll be after all that exercise, especially with your sister living with her mother and now that your gay Uncle Jesse eats like a hummingbird."

He dredged up a T-shirt from a mess of clothes he would never have dared leave thrown around before and slipped on black plastic sandals he'd bought by the dozen on 14th Street—from mainland China, all man-made, "no natural materials," the bottom sole's decal proclaimed smugly. Upstairs, he was instantly drawn to the fridge by sudden hunger. He stood at the opposite counter, and ate—chunk by knife-cut chunk—a half-pound slab of dill-flavored Havarti, washing it down with a bottle of Heineken. Comfort food. A typically Northern European snack for the little Dutch boy he still could be. Polished that off, washed out the bottle before doing the same to his mouth, gargling water off the metal tap, slightly hitting his teeth on the brass, determined not to smell when he went to check the guest bedroom.

Jesse was still sleeping within, despite the late afternoon hour, despite how much sleeping he'd done already today, and despite a full night of sleep, admittedly interrupted (Jesse up at midnight when Ray had first dropped off, up again later, Ray had heard him, barely awakening, at 3:32 A.M.); despite how much he'd slept in the past week, coming home early, Tuesday by taxi from work, and more or less collapsing into bed. Despite three days so far this week, two last week and the week before. Inescapable conclusions should be apparent, then, that it was incremental. Rapidly incremental and that next week, perhaps, it would be four days. Maybe in a month it would be all five workdays, Jesse sleeping longer and longer, dreamlessly lying there, letting existence elapse, all energy slowly seeping out, becoming every day more pallid, more starkly fair, increasingly slender and sweet-tempered, eating less and less, needing to be washed less and less, slipping inexorably into his destiny as the sleeping prince of Brooklyn Heights.

"Hey, kiddo!" he murmured, kissing the nearly colorless skin, as the limbs oh so slowly reconfigured themselves and Jesse's eyelids uncemented long enough to disclose his eyes, chestnut-hued in this low light, the eyeballs dry and bright, if sensitive and fluttery, as Jesse rolled a slim arm to wanly grasp the end of Ray's big nose.

"Hey there, sexy!" Jesse whispered, his own ultrasensitive nostrils vibrating like a pony's. "You smell like you do whenever you just came. Been jerking off?"

"Thinking of you," Ray half lifted Jesse's lightweight upper torso and slid himself under it, making of himself another pillow against the bed's padded backboard. "You gonna get up in a little while for dinner? Chris gets in late today. I'll make chicken broth. Not too strong. You'll eat some, won't you?"

"Anything for you, big nose." His own nose was busily sniffing, his face registering and not uncritically liking what it detected. Mike's body sweat. Mike's ass smell, Ray found himself thinking, smeared all over his body, oozing into the T-shirt and shorts. He ought to have showered before coming up here.

"That straight guy came by," Ray explained, extra blasé. "Mike? From Massapequa? That's probably what you're picking up, you ol' Carolina bloodhound."

"Oh," a slackening, now that it was explained. A stifled yawn. "I'll have broth. When?"

" 'Bout an hour." Ray would shower in the meantime. "Or…right now if you want."

"No," Jesse said. "I want to see Chris. I missed him yesterday. Right?"

"Right, you missed him, but he stopped in and kissed you."

"What should I do, Ray?" The question from out of nowhere.

"Do about what?"

"You know…about work and all?"

"Nothing. Wait. Wait till they bring it up."

"They're heavily hinting already." A slightly bemused fact that Jesse didn't seem the least bit sad or angry about.

"What do *you* want to do?"

"God, hon, I don't care. I just want to sleep. That's what I want to do, and that's not so good, is it?"

"Could be worse. It's sure easy for me. Compared to what it might be."

"And here I thought I'd wear you out. Guess I'm a failure." Jesse yawned again, his body going even more limp against Ray, who slid himself out. "Where you going?"

"To clean up. Because I stink. Also to make chicken broth."

"Make sure I get up tomorrow morning," Jesse said, snuggling into the down comforter, ready to sleep again. "Wake me up in the morning. If I manage to get to the office, I'll arrange everything to let them give me leave from work."

A crucial step, one Ray had been thinking about for days now, kvetching to Liesl, to J.K., anyone who'd listen, as he kept trying to figure out how to bring it up. And here Jesse was bringing it up himself, so casual about it. Just like him not to be any trouble. Not even while dying.

"Good idea. But don't you think it's a big step?"

"I guess," Jesse was almost asleep. "Not such a big...step...any...more... now...that..." And he was already headed back into slumber.

A hand reached out for Ray, stopping him. "He...fuck...you...?" Jesse slurred the question. So he *had* smelled everything. "Mike from...Massa...pee...?"

"I fucked him," Ray replied. "It was a surprise."

"Why? Straight...guys...aren't so...dense," Jesse said half amused, more than half asleep, "know what...to do...with a..." Jesse was lightly snoring, totally out. Ray stared at him a few seconds more, unable to pull himself away.

He knew very well what was going on, although he could not prevent it. His adorato was dying: He was already well on his way in his dying. Each extra hour of sleep Jesse added on was momentous, another milestone in his dying, in their separation; so cunning because all that sleep should be healing him, and instead it was the opposite. It was an ongoing process, his sleeping, his dying, Ray's knowing it, already in progress, which was why it permeated every moment of his existence, yes even as Ray climaxed inside Mike's smooth and warm as hot silk ass, and as he watched those girls passing, inexpertly flirting on the sidewalk and as he stood in the kitchen, one sandaled foot curved atop the other, and attempted to drown out Joralemon Street traffic and chewed, cheese crumbing down his chin; as he billed invoices in his office, merely mechanical, until paused in awe, waylaid, listening to Gieseking's impeccable pedaling in Debussy's *Footsteps in the Snow.* Even then he was grieving, Margaret are you grieving? Over Goldengrove unleaving? Leaves like the things of man. You with your fresh thoughts care for...Grieving and who could he tell? Who would understand it for the actuality it was and not mere fear, or paranoia, or even anticipation of a separation that had already begun to embroider the unstretchable minutes of the quotidian...? No one. No one but Jesse, really. Jesse, who was the last one he could tell. Jesse, who was become an ever growing fist of darkness, mere inches from his own left auricle. God, how could this be happening...Stop! Do something! Stop! Take a shower. Call, J.K. Make broth. Do something, anything, you idiot! Stop right now!

Right now, Jesse thought, partly thought, thought in that subconscious way of thinking that was getting to be so familiar the more he dozed off, this is where it all becomes interesting: This is where past and some unknown future try to fit together, little Jimmie Rae Wurtz from back home sharing licks on an ice cream cone with Liesl, 22 years apart; Ray's sister Kathy, aged 34, driving past with a car full of boys he hadn't recalled seeing since he'd been a high school sophomore. Driving a two-tone '58 DeSoto Fireflite coupe, gull-wing fins swooping in chartreuse, anodized gold trim outlining a side-body inset of pure flame; ensconced in Naugahyde, everyone singing *The Love Boat* theme song, the hood ornament not the stylized gunsight and bullet he'd recollected but a slick Casey Donovan—porn star as tiny, metallic, thrust-forward, bare-assed Hermes, winged feet, flying helmet, caduceus and all—until Kathy started honking the horn to get attention, honking insistently, through which he could make out the insistent whispered strains of an enormous chorus singing "Do the Hustle," although why he didn't know and…awake now…the honking was outside, a truck or van down on the street, through two rooms, Ray just now closing the thick front door to click shut over the double-paned storm door, left open before to welcome, maybe even look for, Chris, coming home late, closed now to block the noise, much softer now.

Jesse turned in bed, pretended to be asleep when Ray checked in to see if it had awakened him, checked Jesse's forehead again—automatically it seemed these days—for fever; not *if*—there always was—but for how high it might be. Then he was gone, the bedroom door a half inch ajar, and Jesse turned into the soft pillow he held to his chest, a down, all-giving lover, his only allowed companion in bed anymore, so still now he could give attention to other matters, to follow his own erratic heartbeat, for instance, or the tiny thunder of blood pulsing his exposed temple, a slight uncomfortableness, not that unpleasant, somewhere in his scrotum.

Jesse had heard them fucking before, heard them in his sleep-not-sleep, dream-not-dream, and he had thought it was something else happening, someone knocking on the door had somehow been imaged by way of explication, someone trying to get in, but he knew, awake or asleep, what it really had been, and he'd noted it in passing on to a deeper dream level, without comment, or rancor, oh, there's Ray fucking downstairs, good for Ray, not stopping to think whom he was with—for a second he'd dreamed it was Zeb Hogwood, that silly redhead boy on the softball team only 11 years old, when Jesse last saw him, in the wisped smoke of raked leaf fires off denuded November elms, standing in the street before his house, ankle high in them, less than an hour before he'd been struck by an out-of-control bread truck. *Good for Ray,* Jesse had thought. *I always meant to fuck that Hogwood boy on account of his his long skinny legs and big shelf of a butt.* Then Hogwood had turned into Chris, Kathy's boy, standing there, rake in hand, and Jesse had to giggle in his sleep at how naughty the thought had become, Chris and Ray, although of course the two boys were one, almost, similar as they were physically, and it was only a dream anyway, so why worry?

Only now he was awake, and he lay there almost floating, eyes closed, and listened carefully to every sound Ray made, no matter how small or difficult at first to figure out. Wasn't that *thut-thut-thut* him cutting celery on the green plastic board? Yes, and the *clup, clup, clup,* him chopping carrots next. A murmured cymbal smash of soup kettle to lid, softer smash against the sink, *gluggle gluggle* must be tapwater shrilling as the pot filled. Another smash as it brushed against the metal of the range, *plop plop plop, pluup, plop,* as the veggies were tossed in, bigger *pluaaawp* of chicken parts. Details of him in the kitchen: little grunts erupting from Ray's throat without him realizing as he chose herbs, sprinkling them, reminding himself almost aloud what to do next, what went where when. The intensity with which he'd hunt down a sprig of parsley and chop chop chop almost maniacally, eyes aglitter, knives in two hands like some psycho, before catching himself with a smile, a blasé "*sera suffit!*" The way he'd frown and look down at a spill on his T-shirt—he never wore aprons—and his half-lifted-in-a-laugh lips with which he looked up again, catching Jesse's eye. Mad chemist, delicate hand-sculpting artist, a little triumphant "Ta-da!" then honestly modest as it was served, tasted, admired. "No, no," his protestations. "It's the recipe. I swear it. A kindergartner could do it!" Then, later, when they were alone, "That ragout, kiddo, was it any good? Or just…"

If this was all, all life offered, Jesse found himself thinking before he subsided back into the mysteriously inviting Tantalus of lush pillow and sheets that yet never brought rest, I'd take it—have taken it, haven't I—but I'll take it, even take it from here, a room apart, without a sight of him, just his sounds, from a tousled bed, from this fugue of sleep, this dreaming life, forever.

eight

"Naturally enough, before it happened, I thought, well, it wouldn't be all that bad if I were forced to loll about all the time. I mean I *do* have about a thousand unread books in one room or another in this place. I figured, well, I'd just take the time and catch up on all that reading I've wanted to do. Those volumes and volumes of Trollope and Thackeray, not to mention the collected works of Henry Fielding, Daniel Defoe, and Tobias Smollett, whom you've never even heard of, although you are allegedly one of my more educated friends."

"I've heard of Smollett," Ray disputed mildly. He was in a highback chair near the double-hung windows that let a bit of cooler air into the large, overheated bedroom. Next to him was a lamp table littered with periodicals. Ray was clipping the lower left-hand corner of J.K'.s magazine covers, which he would later on place atop the commode downstairs in the building lobby.

Mostly *New Yorkers* and *Atlantic Monthlys*, but also a few *Vanity Fairs* and—just so J.K.could feel he might keep up what he believed to be his reputation in the building for being radical and naughty—an issue of *Playgirl* containing, among its pages of photos of sportive Santa Barbara City College studmuffins, a series of extraordinary shots of a smallish, fattish, brown-skinned fellow from a little known South Pacific atoll who'd been born with a double penis: split in the middle, growing two equal-size shafts complete with urethra and glans. "All the women want to see me without my shorts," the modest fellow observed. "When they see me, they want me to pleasure them," J.K. had read out with glee, adding, "They prefer me to many younger, stronger fellows," before tossing the magazine to Ray with a braying "*Next!*"

"Didn't Smollett write *The Expedition of Humphry Clinker?*" Ray asked.

"Which *you've* never read," J.K. declared from the big bed where he was splayed out, huge satin pillows dragged in from the sofa. As much, Ray thought, to bring out the rainbow tones of the watered-silk pajamas J.K. had on—what he referred to as his Aurora Borealis—as to be leaned against. "...Or read six pages of."

"Ten pages," Ray agreed.

"Whereas I've read the three best-known novels, *Clinker, Roderick Random,* and *Peregrine Pickle,* and have on tap two others among his 30 collected volumes. Including *The Misadventures of a Flea.*"

"You're making that title up," Ray said without emotion, dropping another magazine onto the growing pile around his cowboy boots.

"Am not. See for yourself. Top shelf, library, left of the reading chair. The set is dove gray trimmed with cinnamon. However, all that is quite immaterial as it seems I will read none of them. Nor my Fielding. Nor my Defoe. Nor even my lovely calfskin-bound set of Aphra Behn. But shall instead incessantly watch daytime television."

"Your mind will turn into tapioca and treacle," Ray warned.

"It may have already," J.K. tartly replied, alluding to AIDS dementia.

"True," Ray agreed. Why whitewash it with hard-as-nails J.K.? "Any more?"

"No. Until *La Peste* made its appearance, I was up to snuff."

"Any other mindless tasks you'd like done?"

"How's your sock darning? Never mind. That's it for now. So...to get back to what I was saying. It's hardly daytime serials or talk shows I'm watching. Instead—and here, sweetie, is where it's so intriguing—instead, there's this program that shows every afternoon from 3 to 5 a...1930s musical!"

J.K.'s pajama top was unbuttoned, his carefully hairless chest bearing the slightest hint of black fuzz making a comeback. Not as naturally masculine as Mike's abdomen. Still…

"He's discovered Busby Berkeley! Only about a decade after everyone else!"

"Worse! I've discovered Fred and Ginger *two* decades after everyone else. I've now seen all the films they made together at least twice. Forget the bios like *The Story of Vernon and Irene Castle* and the much later, color *The Barkleys of Broadway*. Forget even *Roberta* and *Flying Down to Rio*, except for that "Night and Day" dance number I could watch forever."

"Choreographed by Busby Berkeley," Ray put in, trying not to be too obvious as he continued to size up his oldest gay friend. It was the oddest thing, but that recent bout of pneumocystis had really done wonders. J.K. had lost about ten pounds, which had before given him that pumped up "puff"; now mercifully gone. As a result he was more attractive than he'd looked in years. Ray might tell him that, to cheer him up. But J.K.would scoff, reply that Ray's physical tastes were bizarre: finding skin-bones-and-sinew Latino fighters on cable TV to be the height of beauty. Not to mention his eerie, ongoing obsession with poor Jesse. Then J.K. would moan over how far he'd strayed from the weight and muscle development of his (by no means unshared) criterion, Aeneas Anderson, the current porn darling and star of *Tie Me Up, Then Go Down.*

"Sure. Sure. I know all about Berkeley," J.K. allowed. "But it's the three films in the middle. *Shall We Dance, The Gay Divorcee,* and *Top Hat,* all choreographed by Astaire himself, with, I believe, Hermes Pan, which, I've decided, after multiple viewings, are the masterpieces. Among the handful of great films of the decade. *Rules of the Game, The Blue Angel, Dinner at Eight, King Kong, The Women, Metropolis, Wuthering Heights, A Night at the Opera, Gone With the Wind, 42nd Street*—and those three! The thing is," J.K. seemed honestly perplexed, "I can't for the life of me figure out which one of the three is *the one,* the *ne plus ultra.*"

J.K. pouted picturesquely against the pillows as though in deepest thought, totally unaware that a two-inch diamond shape of scrotum was showing through the improperly buttoned fly of his pajamas. Ray didn't remember seeing his old pal this exhibitionistic in years and wondered how unconscious it was, or if J.K. was horny all the time, the way Jesse had been during his first symptoms. Luckily so, for Ray, the way things had turned out, because not long after, sex between them had ceased. Ray knew J.K. would be shocked if told he was showing off, declare he'd never dream of having sex with someone he knew as well as Ray. So rigid. And Ray had to admit he was a little surprised by his own excitement looking at J.K. today. Still, he also had to admit, there was something unquestionably sexy about an attractive guy on his sickbed—vulnerable, available—even if he was a "sistuh."

"*Shall We Dance* has all that Gershwin music, of course," J.K. went on blithely, oblivious to the fact that he was being inspected like government Grade A meat. "And it has Fred tap dancing in the engine room to keep up with the machinery of the ocean liner. While *Top Hat* has the 'Pick Yourself Up' number and all that Russian business: *Hor chi'chornia*! And Astaire's takeoff on Martha Graham. *And* he never danced better."

"Ginger danced backwards. In heels!" Ray butted in, wondering what J.K. and Mike from Massapequa would be like together in that big bed. Actually, not together so much as laid out, side by side, awaiting Ray. Arms behind their heads, dicks at attention. As Ray swooped over them, pausing to lick a navel here, nip at a nipple there. All that black hair and white skin!

"Then, yesterday, they aired *The Gay Divorcee* again," J.K. brooded, "and I find I'm leaning toward *that* as the absolute summit of their art. Think of it! The story is fun yet not that complicated. In featured roles are," J.K. ticked them off, "the astonishingly dizzy Edward Everett Horton, the extremely droll Eric Blore, the incomparable Alice Brady, the perky, still, I believe, teenage Betty Grable, and that fellow who plays the Italian."

"Signor Tonetti at your ser-veese!" Ray mimicked the actor. In a way, that role reminded Ray of both J.K. (the preening, the casual vanity) and Mike.

"Thank you, sweetie! Who is the best, bar none, fake Italian in movies. Then there's the music. The very silly, very cute, 'Let's Knock Knees' number. Remember? At the summer resort? Everyone supposedly outdoors wearing those Adrian resort-wear numbers? Then, later on in the film, that 15 minute-long, four-part, 'Continental' number, designed to the tits in black and white, where dozens of dancers line up in complementary light and dark outfits, *en suite*? Simply unparalleled!"

"Not to mention the art deco interiors everywhere," Ray recalled. It had been years since he'd seen J.K. even close to naked, never mind in bed. Not since that time at the Pines, the fourth night of a ghastly heat inversion over the metro area, when Jesse, J.K., and that boy—what was his name? The big Texan. Rowdy? Howdy?—tranquilized by a '75 St. Emilion and sensimilla grass, spread out on those huge air mattresses following a midnight ocean swim, and Ray had come outside and seen them there, lined up and ready, and gone from one to the other, beginning with the Texan, ending with Jesse, kissing and lightly licking each, forehead to toes, before they'd paired off for side-by-side sex. J.K. had never once afterward alluded to that night, from which Ray had to assume he was not totally averse to what had occurred...What was Ray thinking? J.K. wouldn't permit anything like that! Keep it in your pants, stupid! You fuck a straight man and suddenly you want to have sex all day long with anyone even vaguely breathing?

"Those interiors in the hotel were," J.K. went on, "naturally, influenced by Syrie Maugham. But the details! The sconces! The etched glass! The doorknobs! Did you know, by the way, that they had to change the title from the stage play, which had been called *The Gay Divorce*? The Hays Office film censors felt that no divorce could be gay; whereas, I guess, a divorcee could easily be. You're not paying a whit of attention."

Ray, who wasn't paying a whit of attention, denied it.

"Liar! You're sitting there with a major woody. Since when, exactly, has the impression of Syrie Maugham's tone-on-tone upholstery brought on erections?"

"I was thinking how hot you looked and how easy it would be to—"

"In the words of Alice Brady, you're beginning to fascinate me, and I resent that in any man." Even so, J.K. grabbed a pillow and put it in front of his body. "It's that repairman, isn't it? The one with the truck! You've seen him again!"

"I screwed his brains out yesterday."

"How did you persuade him?"

"He persuaded me."

"Wanda the Witch was right. Yesterday's trade *is* tomorrow's competition. I trust," J.K. added aloofly, "that you after you mindlessly screw the poor thing, you're also laboring to raise his gay consciousness?"

"I've never given it a thought. He comes and goes too quickly for political indoctrination."

"But it's your responsibility!"

"You sure Aeneas Anderson gives queer theory seminars after every screen fuck?"

"He might," J.K. said.

"He might also fly unaided. I somehow doubt it."

"Well, I don't believe I care for this Mike from Massachusetts."

"Massapequa," Ray said, content with the idea that J.K. didn't care for Mike.

"From wherever. Taking him up doesn't sound healthy. Jesse must agree."

"Jesse couldn't be happier about it."

"Don't tell me you recount the lurid details to him?" J.K. was aghast.

"He hangs on every lurid detail! He's thrilled by the very idea of Mike."

"And to think," J.K. spoke to the room, "I've nursed this viper in my bosom."

"Actually," Ray rose ominously, "you've not let me near your bosom in years."

"Down, boy!" J.K. commanded. His eyes held an instant of uncertainty about whether Ray was joking that Ray found indecently delightful.

"OK," Ray replied, locating where he'd thrown his sweater and leather jacket, then putting them on, "but if *you* won't put out, I'll find a sick friend who *will*." Before zipping the jacket, he pulled out his Scotch tam and drew it down over his temples, then made a lunge at J.K., who almost fell off the bed trying to get away.

"You are sick! Sick!" J.K. declared from the other side of the bed. "That straight boy has you obsessed with sex."

"I'm leaving now," Ray leaned forward, presenting one cheek. "A kiss?"

"Out! Out, I say! Wait! Don't forget the magazines!"

"Dream of me," Ray signed off swoonily, from the doorway.

Before leaving the flat, he checked the library for the Sterne book. He was surprised not to find it. Instead, among the other 15 volumes, was a volume titled *The History and Adventures of an Atom*. He wondered whether he should bring the error to J.K.'s attention. Perhaps not. J.K. was feeling good these days. Why bring him down?

The rickety glass and half-timbered elevator was empty. Ditto the long, well kept, dark-tiled, butter-colored corridor. But as he scattered the magazines upon the commode in the oversize, circa 1925 space, Ray could make out through the locked lobby door some guy checking his front hall mailbox. With that dopey snowflake-patterned wool cap and to-the-knees loden coat and rubber galoshes against the shitty November weather, he had to be straight. Straight and probably married. Which had to mean something different to Ray, who these days fucked a straight, married man. He made certain that several pages of nude male photos were faced up on display among the magazines. As he held the lobby door open for the guy—not bad close-up: mid 20s; clear complexion; brightly flecked pale gray eyes; long, narrow, amusing, possibly Gallic nose; curly reddish hair escaping from under the cap's confines.

"Free magazines," Ray said in a hearty voice. "Check them out!"

Out on the street, Ray found himself smiling, then unable to stop laughing. He stopped at a nearby brownstone porch to arrange his pants cuffs outside his boots, knowing it was an excuse to look back and see if the guy had stepped out of the building again. No. Too bad.

Ray found today that he was looking at men much more closely: on the subway platform, within the half-filled subway car, once it arrived, on the second platform in Astoria, where he got out, along those long Long Island streets leading to the studio—dampened by a brief, frigid downpour he'd missed while traveling underground. No, he wasn't looking *more closely*, he was looking at them *differently*, as though each man carried some until-now unsuspected potentiality, and might turn around as he was leaving the subway, hand Ray a phone number, and casually say, "My wife works days, 9 to 5. Give me a call." Not since he'd come to Manhattan years ago had Ray looked at every male in his age range as though he were sexually available. Not necessarily desirable, but available—which wasn't the same; but in another sense was.

For years, like every other gay man in an urban setting, he'd trained himself to follow the unwritten code of who to stare at, who to flirt with in public—and who not. At the same time he had tutored himself in the complex prognostications that ruled the body language of men who would flirt back. Mostly gay men, but not always just gay men, especially given the occasional straight who was very obviously with a woman, and who at the same time flirted with him outrageously. Ray had also educated himself to read those usually obvious clues beyond wedding rings that meant a man was not only not interested in other men, but opposed to any possibility: the obtuse, leaden-eyed response to an appreciative glance, sometimes followed by fidgeting or slumping as though the seat had become suddenly uncomfortable (at times he'd get up, change seats, even change subway cars); the annoyed contempt of a raised upper lip; the undisguised frown, usually preceded by surprise, as though the man were saying, *What? You've got to be kidding!*; and the digusted lift of a shoulder, just before a newspaper came up and blanked out the guy's face; the calculated, abruptly turned back; the openly sneering stare-you-down glare; the holier-than-thou "I see you but I'm not going to even acknowledge you exist beyond a field of generalized molecules." All were indications that Ray's notice had been noticed and definitely not relished, not taken for what it was—curious appreciation—but instead disdained. So, while it had been limiting, and occasionally embarrassing if the other guy turned out to be uncool or a nutcase, for the most part it had been a comprehensible, even dependable, world system of signs and symbols, all held neatly in place. Not really that dissimilar from the world of high school and college locker rooms with its learned yet unspoken semiotics of exactly where you could look and where not; precisely how long you could stare and after what moment it became unsound.

He'd gone along with it, accepted it for years, even seen in its shorthand some utility, but now, since that last afternoon tryst with Mike, Ray began to wonder if all those tacit understandings he'd taken for granted for years might instead be ciphers, a tissue of nonverbal language with no reliability at all, hiding, covering over, when not actually *misconveying* crucial information. He could no longer assume that even those most standardized gestures or that unchanging masculine vernacular now signified anything beyond, say, an immediate sensation of awkwardness or self-consciousness. If he thought about it in that way, it wasn't all that dissimilar to AIDS, was it? The disease that was so frightening partly because it hit you so low, all but obliterating the long-held, commonly held, assumption that unless you went in a freak accident, that as a white American male you'd probably live until 79 or 80 before dying of a heart attack, a stroke, cancer. And, like AIDS, once Ray grasped the enormous fallacy that lay at the heart of the quickly summed-up male-male approach system, it quickly added up to a gradual unmooring, a steady but certain disconnection.

He shot up the curved, polished black-and-white granite steps and through the late '40s glass-brick and anodized-steel doorway, where slender, overdressed, and undercosmetized Tonya Toyota (slight acne, facial pitting) greeted him by biting even harder on the perpetual pencil in her mouth, motioning with her hairdo: "He's already in! Number 6!" Her Brooklyn-Queens accent emerged when she added, "Cawfee or someting?"

"Maybe later, Tone. Thanks."

Ray treaded the three-story-high central corridor past a score of office doors, peeling off the heaviest layer of outerwear as he went. Almost a century before, the three-block long structure had been a film studio for silent two-reelers and had lain abandoned, underused until a few years ago when the owner's clever grandchildren inherited it, checked it over, and decided to replaster, repaint, fix the plumbing, and redesign a bit before renting it out inexpensively to craftspeople working in the city's tiny, tenacious, independent film community. The Hollywoodized film noir lobby had been added years ago during a previous, failed attempt to bring it up to date, but the 20-square-foot cubicle offices were newly assembled and quickly rented out. The building's back half, however, remained almost original, its former, true, immense size left as it was, complete with hung-off-the-patterned-tin sky-lighted-ceiling movable light fixtures, and double metal tracks for scrims and backgrounds. A handful of other configurations, at first baffling, had also been left on the immense, unpainted, concrete floor, Ray supposed in case it was ever again fully utilized: giant metal bases he'd been assured held revolving stages; man-size clamps to secure 60-foot gantries; even a tenth-of-a-mile-long narrow gauge rail for tracking shots. Hung off the far end were semienclosed chambers of differing sizes: photo developing rooms, a minuscule theater, sound and sight editing spaces. Inside the smallest, Maurette was at work, editing film.

"Ah, *cher!*" his childlike face and youthful voice always surprised Ray. "Just as Liesl tells me, you are like a psychic. You come exactly when I need you. Come sit!" He made room on the wooden garden bench that had been brought indoors and placed at the editing machines to more comfortably accommodate his bulk. "I'm up to frame 1300." He moved aside for Ray to get in front of the kinescope machine and watch the four-inch screen and listen to the tinny soundtrack.

After a half dozen frames of lead-in and chalk-marked ID frames, the scene he'd been editing began and Ray recognized it immediately. They'd worked on it a few days ago. The soundtrack was aligned perfectly. Dialogue was crisp and clear, and the quiet, increasingly insistent piano piece Ray had brought in to build tension had the subtle crescendo Maurette had been looking for.

"Good! Eh, *cher?* I told you you'd be perfect for this project."

"That's one piece," Ray admitted.

"One? We've done four so far and they're all good. Excellent. I've never had it so good for a soundtrack. But listen, and you will probably hate me for this, but remember what I told you on the phone day before yesterday? That I thought this other scene with the two women at the windows also needed music? I've decided it absolutely has to have it! Music. Not dialogue or background sounds, as before. You know which one I mean, eh, *cher?*" Before Ray could say anything, Maurette enthused, "Believe me, it will work if you find precisely the right piece to fit, and I know you will. Something haunting but spare. Something thrilling. An oboe solo? Or a high coronet?"

Ray reached into his coat and pulled out his Walkman. He placed the headphones over the big man's thick head of butterscotch hair, arranged them over his ears, and turned it on to play what he'd prepared that morning—after he'd finished his paperwork for his record company, after he'd washed the kitchen floor, after he'd phoned Jesse—who'd gone back to work that morning despite telling Ray he was going to resign and had remained ever since, almost two weeks—just before he'd visited J.K.

The music was something Ray had heard for the first time a week ago at the Chinese laundry on Clark Street where he brought Jesse's oxford and tattersall work shirts and where, until that day, he'd heard nothing but '60s and '70s oldies—from Buffalo Springfield and Melanie to the Bee Gees and Elton John—coming out of the little pink plastic boom box set high upon a shelf, where Mr. Chun kept rubberband-wrapped stacks of laundry ticket booklets and a healthy, if leggy, fuschia geranium. All Ray knew about the laundry owner was that he was second generation and had finished community college and started up his own furniture business—which hadn't done particularly well, so when his dad became ill, the son had stepped into the old man's shoes, ran the shop, and eventually inherited it. All the more shocking then, because this piece of music hadn't been from the radio but instead a cassette, and Ray had been so struck by the wild, forlorn beauty of the music, he'd asked Chun about it. "It's some old-time melody from my dad's home province. Shen-shi," the laundry owner said, determined not to give up much. But Ray remained at the counter, the brown paper-wrapped bundles of shirts he'd already picked up under his arms, for the music's five-minute length. Then he'd asked if he could look at the cassette. That proved to be all but useless: just hand-scrawled ideographs. Half suspicious, half amused, Chun had looked up from the big iron mangle where he was pressing an ivory-hued sheet and asked, "You really like that Chink stuff?" Ray said he very much liked it. "That number is called something like 'Song for Courtier's Ghost.' Some title, huh?" Chun had added, spraying starch from a plastic plant waterer across the surface until the pima cotton shone, before bringing the curved, steaming top to smash down in clouds of steam. "It's from a Chinese opera my grandpa used to listen to. You ever hear one of those? Screechy, high voices. Lots of drums and cymbals and shit! He told me this opera hadn't been staged in a long time," Chun added, automatically lifting the mangle's lid and readjusting the cloth before letting it fall again with a whoosh of compression. Ray replied that it was beautiful. "What instrument is playing the music?" It sounded so weird, almost otherplanetary, like no other instrument he'd heard. "Chinese violin!" Chun said, between regular mangle smashes. And when Ray looked perplexed, he added, "It's kind of hard to explain." Yesterday, a week later, as Ray had passed by the laundry windows on a food-shopping trip, Chun had called him over with a clawlike gesture of his fingers. Inside the shop he'd shown Ray a photo of the violin from some old magazine. In the snapshot, an elderly man dressed in what Ray considered Mandarin regalia sat in a chair, the instrument held between his legs as though it were a cello. Yet it was only violin size, save for its triple-extended sound board, and the man played it with two implements, a catgut bow below—where the strings crossed the f hole for the lower register—and a series of five leather plectra upon the other hand's fingers that plucked, strummed, and picked out harmony for a second melody almost two feet higher. "There you go! The Chinese violin," Chun said, then surprised Ray by handing him a cassette of "The Courtier's Ghost Song," saying, "Enjoy, man!" brushing off any payment. Ray played it several times last night and again this morning, when he'd rerecorded it.

He now watched closely as Maurette listened to the music, the other man's big left arm raised in the air, following the irregular rhythm, his eyes closed, his lips slightly apart. Clearly he liked it as much as Ray had, and before the tape ended he began butting Ray with a fist, then hugging Ray, all but smothering him within his cashmere-sweatered bulk. "This is it! This is perfect for the scene. Very weird. Wonderful."

Then began the work of retiming the track and laying it alongside the film. Now he had to wait for Maurette to do his part. That would take far longer, both because of the precision needed and also because of how painstaking Maurette was about everything. This would be the fifth time Ray sat alongside the bigger man in the small, enclosed space, and like those previous times, he almost immediately noticed—couldn't help notice, felt himself almost overcome by—Maurette's body odor. Not that Maurette wasn't hygienic: He was; Liesl, now dating him regularly, told Ray how much time he spent in the shower, in a bathtub. No, it wasn't that. And the body odor wasn't in any way foul. In fact—and this was sort of the problem for Ray—it was an oversweet smell. As though the Canadian filmmaker were an overripe c asaba melon. Honeyed. Sugary. Almost sticky sweet. The first time they'd been boxed in together like this, the smell had been persistent and uncomfortable. Ray had at first been reminded of something he'd read years ago about H.G. Wells, a small, by then elderly novelist, who'd wed a woman a quarter his age. Asked whether she had married Wells for his brilliant mind, his astounding imagination, or for his witty, incisive manner, she'd answered: "No. It's because he smells like honey."

Someone else in Ray's life had smelled like honey, like Maurette. After that first afternoon within the editing area, Ray was disturbed trying to recall whom it could be. Nearly a week went by before he remembered: In college, vague about what field to specialize in, he'd majored in the arts and minored in social sciences. That meant taking several "normal" and "abnormal" psychology courses if he were to do any federal or state government-paid teaching.

One such course involved a minimum of two hours per week spent in "hands-on experience." Ray's choices for fieldwork had been: 1) a local middle school, where he'd observe and later help a school guidance counselor; 2) a nearby after-school program at a beat-up community center for "disadvantaged" kids in the only area of his hometown he supposed might, in a stretch, be considered a ghetto; and 3) his eventual choice, assistant to the sports program at a county mental institution. He chose the last because he and his sister Kathy had lived not far from it and summers they'd bicycle past the walls of the big old place to get to their favorite lakefront park for swimming. It marked the halfway point in the 40-minute bike ride, so they chose it as a spot to stop, rest, and sip chilled copper-flavored tap water from his father's Korean War-era Army thermos. The drab, weather-stained, much chipped at, story-and-a-half-high walls around the lofty Victorian-era buildings had been the perfect height and at the best angle to lean oneself and one's bike against. Especially at one corner, where two huge, inexpertly pruned peach trees provided vast pools of indigo shade on even the steamiest August afternoon. In addition, they'd given free fruit. Some admittedly chalky, or worse, wormy; others firm fleshed, ripe, messily delectable.

The site had originally served as a utopian academy, instituted, funded and superintended by one of the more recherché of an array of mid 19th-century dissenting sects that seemed to arise overnight within the fertile, anthracite-black soiled Central Illinois floodplain. As with many other such brotherhoods, obligatory community self-sufficiency was postulated—explaining the amplitude of tilled fields, the copious outbuildings for domesticated animals, the many irregularly rounded hills of still-bounteous orchards. All of which had composed—since before Ray's birth—a model farm, jewel in the crown of a flourishing downstate agribusiness. From its elevation high upon a pink granite outcrop with sweeping views of the plantations, the college had for decades sent enlightened graduates into an unsuspecting, usually uncaring world. Once the sect was dissolved (due to rigid celibacy and pecuniary fatigue) the school and dorm buildings were sold, first to the state to be transformed into an orphanage, then, decades later, when that endeavor foundered for lack of abandoned offspring, it was overhauled and renovated to be a "home" for the neurologically unreliable and those dangerous to themselves or others hailing from Illinois's central 19 counties. It was redesignated the DeLane Home, a casual corruption of a late 17th-century French-born explorer and settler, allegedly half Thomas Jefferson and half George Washington Carver—one Alphonse-Phillipe-Olivier-Marie Arnauld, Chevalier de Leigne. With a Pavlovian loathing for the unalike tied to an instinctive affinity for colorful turns of phrase, Ray and Kathy's child-hood pals had called the place "Dee Lane for Dee Insane."

At DeLane—the peach trees just brown branches with scarcely visible hints of green bud, that mid March Saturday morning of Ray's college junior year—he'd received his job description, and he'd instantly sneered at it as beneath contempt: He was to organize a dozen adolescent and young male inmates into a softball game. He soon discovered how Herculean, how unreal-izable a task he'd been given. After a winter spent locked up inside, the inmates were unquestionably pleased to be able to get outside to enjoy the weather. A few even recognized Ray's strategy—i.e., to play a sport. Several repeatedly, vociferously claimed to grasp what needed to be done with the sporting equip-ment that Ray spent a half hour handing out and helping them put on—every time. Several even managed not to drop, lose, or otherwise forsake the equip-ment as they became beguiled by the wonders of nature, swindled by clamor-ing voices inside their heads, or led astray by other, not as easily explicable, seductions. Just as Ray had succeeded in finally coordinating the pitcher, bat-ter, and catcher to operate more or less together, he would look up and espy the shortstop squatting on the ground experimenting upon a ladybug, a right fielder standing on his head against a wall, the first baseman upset, having just urinated all over himself, and the outfielders scattered in the far distance, intent upon their individual errands. Getting any batter to swing—never mind hit—a ball pitched from a mere few feet away turned out to be an idealistic dream, a momentous accomplishment. Ray had to run with each "walked" ball and to catch most of the so-called thrown or batted balls. The first game at DeLane he managed to get played lasted four and a half hours and consisted of two innings—well, one and eight-ninths, to be precise. Driving away that evening, he considered the option of checking himself in at the main desk, or failing that, slamming at 80 miles an hour into the trunk of one of those stal-wart peach trees.

He hadn't, of course. He'd returned to DeLane, Saturday after Saturday as March ended and April suffused the play area with a new distraction—peach blossoms covering everything, everyone—and he'd returned throughout May and June. He'd tried to stop, had accosted his psych professor in the corridor after that first failure and explained how impossible it was. The simian little man with unclipped eyebrows had agitated his head and gleefully agreed, "Yes. Yes. Quite impossible. Keep me posted." So Ray had returned to DeLane, and he'd kept the professor posted—his final, self-condemning term paper further detailing his many failures at the home earned him an A, with the handwritten comment—"Excellent powers of observation!"—but had never even acknowledged, never mind addressed, the issue of why even bother to try to get them to play that Ray had raised. And then, for some reason Ray could never figure out—had it become a habit? was it because the guys were expecting him?—after college classes had ended for the summer, he had still returned to DeLane. Throughout July—with yet another distraction, those achingly ripe peaches, some of which simply thudded right into your outstretched-to-catch-a-ball glove—and August and September, right through October, when at last it became too cold to go out, and indoors they'd held a victory party for the DeLane Lames—their own name for the team by then, though he suspected sly, paranoid Willy Parsons had come up with it.

Not that Ray had ever conned himself into thinking he'd ever form one or two softball teams out of the youths—nor end up playing a full nine-inning game. No, negative, tempestuous James Carcopolous would never stand for anything as defining and final as a full game. Nor would ever contrary Larry Tomkins bat in the general direction of home plate more than twice per game. Dennis Whately would, naturally, not cease to vanish from the playing field by at least every mid-game, to be found napping in a bed of nasturtiums or raking leaves with a brochure, or counting bricks in a wall. But skinny, one-eyed Jeffrey Washington would cheer anyway, no matter who was at bat or what they did. And the utterly unstrung Robert de Luca would agree from the sidelines, looking seemingly anywhere but at the game, while shouting, "That was a good one! A good one!"—even at strikeouts and unmistakable foul balls. The ever apprehensive Joytisha Chandra invariably halted the game at some point to arrive at the plate, mumbling "Very important! Very important!" then whispered in Ray's ear that he'd masturbated nine times the previous day, before returning, mumbling again, to his shortstop spot mid-field. So, it would never be a real game. But they would have fun: each of them assuring Ray in their own specific way, at one time or another, that he was doing them a service, helping them, or at least letting time pass differently for them.

"As good as the *The Avengers!*" Willy Parsons, their prized hebephrenic schizoid whiz kid had assured Ray, who accepted the compliment for the big deal it was meant to be. It had been Willy, 6'4", weighing something like 350 pounds and still gaining, who'd smelled like honey. Willy, who was the least apparently disturbed of the group, who'd figured out how useful Ray could be and had maneuvered him into driving Willy (sometimes Joytisha and Robert and Jeff too) off grounds, although with doctors' approval, in his little sedan over to the White Castle, off an interstate ramp five miles away, for hamburgers. They'd gather in a booth farthest from the main door, and Willy would hold a sort of court, while they all overate and overdrank and overtalked and had a pretty good time, while not pissing off the customary patrons too badly. Willy had explained DeLane's men's wing politics to Ray in all its aspects, along with complete (and, it turned out, quite accurate) assessments of the male nurses, administrators, and in particular, individual psychiatrists' weaknesses and strengths. It was Willy who had finagled Ray into taking him back home to Chilocathe for a visit by train. They'd slept over in the same bedroom, and the next day stood in the middle of his family and their neighbors' apparently boundless, newly sown farmland, the ebony earth extending as far as one could see, ponderous, breathing, saturating the air with potential. As Ray had tried to assess what he was feeling exactly and put it into words—that immense sky, those massed battalions of clouds, the immeasurable geometry of tract after tract of land—Willy had come along and said, "Smells like horseshit, doesn't it? Miles and miles and miles of horseshit!" On the train ride back to DeLane he'd stunned Ray, saying, "Well, you're just lucky I decided against running away and staying home on this trip, thus ruining your life." When asked why he hadn't run away, Willy had devastatingly summed up what even Ray hadn't failed to notice of his parents' barely controlled mental fragility. Willy had concluded, "So you see, if I came home, first *he'd* crack, then shortly afterward *she'd* crack. That's why I have to stay away." Willy with his long, flaccid, indifferently shaved face, lusterless, ill-kept lank hair, black eyes nearly popping out of their sockets, nose and mouth so petitely sculpted as to be baby size; with his smarmily exact vocabulary and just-too-low-to-be-properly-heard voice as though he were always just about to let you in on something really good. On the last day Ray was at DeLane, Willy intimated, "I blew De Luca this morning so he'd give you a home run," giggling at the shock on Ray's face. Willy snickered again when the usually thoroughly distracted De Luca smashed the ball way past center, in a perfect arc not even Ray could have caught, and provided the team with its first official home run. Again it was Willy, who after all the boys had, in their inimitable ways, said good-bye at the end of that second summer when Ray announced he was leaving Illinois, moving to New York, who had hugged Ray last, and for a long time. Just as Ray began to think it might be for sentimental reasons, Willy whispered, "Your pocket!" Inside, Ray later found an address and phone number in Manhattan next to the words "Best Inexpensive Female Escort Service." Willy Parsons.

And now it was Maurette who was finished for the moment and who said, "Tomorrow, eh, *cher*? We'll do some more," before picking Ray up out of the bench and swinging him around and around the small canvas walled chamber, in his pleasure—smelling from close up just like cloverleaf honey.

nine

The bedroom walls were, for some reason he couldn't quite figure out, a sullen greenish gray, the identical tint of the apples one dissects to make pie. Outside, whenever enough of a opening showed through the fluttering, pulled-down window shade, Ray could make out the same leaden skies as earlier today, when it had timidly drizzled, just before Mike had arrived. The air was a bit more specific now; it seemed to approximate solidity, it was so thick, precipitation almost palpable. It also seemed to conceal sound, allowing some subdued, omnipresent undertone to keep humming. He wouldn't be surprised if thunder began to rumble from afar, or if the walls abruptly whitened with the biting, exploring fingers of lightning.

He was bumped out of his musing by the unmistakable flush of the toilet. Both sink taps surged, then were quickly shut: Mike washing up. Ray supposed he should get out of bed. He didn't. Too lazy. Too bushed. Another workout. Like the last time. Only today he hadn't waited for a second invitation but fitted himself in as soon as requested. Stayed in longer too. Less surprised, more composed, he'd taken his time: taken longer to orgasm, taken a longer, slower time to then turn Mike over and suck him off. Perversely, the more eager for climax Mike became thanks to his efforts, the more Ray dawdled and toyed with him, putting it off, indefinitely if possible, until Mike reached down to caress Ray's face and whisperingly implore him. He'd relented, almost instantly brought him off.

He assumed now that Mike would flee the bathroom, throw on underwear, pull up his work pants, and hurl himself headlong toward the front door still buttoning his shirt. Afterward, Ray would come back to nap. The air was so dense it insisted on sleep.

He was surprised when Mike exited, face freshly washed, black hair sleek and wet, and instead of drawing on his Jockeys and socks, dropped back onto the bed. "Gonna rain in a minute, really come down," Mike announced, rolling his arms behind his head, cradling the mop of black hair that, in the room's underwater illumination, glinted violet and indigo wherever it retained moisture.

As Mike's remark didn't appear to invite comment, Ray said nothing. Nor did he turn over and transparently stare at Mike as he would have done if it were Jesse next to him. He knew by now that instead of permitting himself to be admired, Mike would become restless, uneasy. Why wasn't he leaving? The threatening weather? Did he want to wait it out before driving off? Or did he want, instead, to talk? Open up? He hadn't. *They* hadn't talked so far. At least not the way gay men always talked in bed, after sex. Even men who'd never met before. *Especially* men who'd never met before. Maybe that was about to happen: that abrupt exposure that had converted each of Ray's earlier sexual forays into little school rooms, learning sessions, with flashes of perception into people's lives, insights into strangers' decisions and motivations. Surely that was one meaning of the phrase *education sentimentale?*

That was also one of the unexpected surprises—one of the real premiums—of being gay: how directly you could enter another's life. Ray would never forget the first time it happened, nor its varied impressions upon him. It had been maybe his fourth or fifth sexual encounter, only the second time he'd taken anyone back to his junior year off-campus flat. He'd lived in a small, nearly featureless room—only big enough for a single bed, desk, and chair—with a bath across the corridor, one of six rent-outs: four upstairs and two, including his, on the ground floor. The more public rooms—kitchen, breakfast nook, and small "den" (with TV) of what had once been a single-family brick house—separated him from the other, larger, first-floor bedroom, occupied by the outgoing Jamake ("Geoff to my friends") Shields, a popular exchange student from Sierra Leone. Ray's room was virtually at the back door, farthest from the stairs up, allowing him to easily hide a guest without the others knowing. This fact, Gilbert and Louis—the look-alike, think-alike engineering school dweebs who dormed in pristine rooms side by side on the second floor—repeatedly mentioned, attempting to bait Ray whenever he had the mischance to be in the den or breakfast nook with them; affecting that they knew some loathsome secret they couldn't possibly about his private life. Due to them and to Ray's circumspection, it wasn't until the first day of the Christmas vacation, once he'd ascertained no one would be in the house, that he'd brought another student to his room. It was two months later that he got up enough nerve to permit another's presence.

What almost made him decide not to the second time was that he'd met the man not at school but downtown, where he'd gone to catch *And the Ship Sails On*, the latest Fellini movie, a bizarre offering set in the opera world that he'd enjoyed but wasn't sure he understood. Checking the bus stop timetable outside the theater afterward, he discovered he had more than a half hour to kill. The polar February weather prompted him into a coffee shop, to a table from where he'd easily be able to see the bus approach. It was only after Ray had defrosted his chilled fingers around a mug of hot cider that the man entered, bought coffee, carried it to the table across from Ray's, kept staring at him, and when Ray acknowledged him, joined him.

Herb was about 45 years old. Herb was craggily handsome, with ice-blue eyes of a voltage only a few watts less electrifying than Paul Newman's and a shock of hair so jet black it reflected blue and green in the overhead fluorescence. Herb appeared to be in great physical shape, attested to by a knitted pullover that gripped his shoulders, biceps, and forearms, and slacks that hugged his thighs, buttocks, and calves in a cashmere embrace. The entire outfit, including the car coat that reversed to a black-fur lining and the authoritative-looking wristwatch that later proved to be an Omega Submariner, looked even to Ray's untutored eyes carefully selected and expensive. Herb owned that futuristic-looking, British racing green Jaguar XK-E coupe—complete with rear spoiler—parked across the street. And even more meaningful than any of that, Herb desired Ray with an unmasked craving that was almost amusing. Indeed, Herb shamelessly sported a Brooks Brothers trouser-bound hard-on of some heft and kept trying to get as close to Ray on the shared banquette as humanly possible without them actually sharing a common cellular structure. Herb calmly proposed a menu of libidinous activities, many of which Ray had never heard of, that he, that they, might engage in once they were out of this place and "somewhere quiet." With all this talk, it was just a few minutes before Herb began to stroke Ray's thigh not far from his own Rogers-Peet herringbone-covered hard-on.

Later, in Ray's bed, so narrow they'd barely been able to remain upon it during their athletics, as their suddenly inactive bodies misted into the near-frigid air and the sheets began to cool enough so they no longer adhered to burning skin, Herb began to talk. He confessed that he was married, which surprised Ray twice: first by its factuality, second by how it glamorized Herb even more. He was president of a nationally known corporation with local headquarters, and lived in what Ray had heard was the most exclusive street of the most costly neighborhood for a good hundred miles square.

They were lying face to face, gingerly touching each other: Ray admiring Herb's sinewy neck muscles and solid chest, the two distinct, uneven lines carved into his brow, the barely visible crow's-feet tracery ornamenting his eyes; Herb unable to get enough of the newness of Ray's skin, the natural flatness of his stomach, the tautness of his arm muscles. "Funny thing is," Herb had run an elegantly manicured fingernail along Ray's sternum, "I've got a boy your age. What are you, 20? He's at college too."

"And probably," Ray joked, "he's just freshly fucked and sucked to oblivion by someone's father."

"I wish!" Herb replied. "But I strongly doubt it, given how dull he is." The more he talked, the more Herb revealed unexpected, at times extraordinary, facts about himself and his family. He'd met his wife while trying to seduce her older brother. That brother had thrown his sister at Herb, explaining how it would provide the two young men with many more chances to be together without raising suspicion—this being pre-Stonewall times. Barely a month after the wedding rice had settled, his brother-in-law accepted a permanent position at a university in newly occupied Hokkaido, Japan. Herb had seen him maybe five times in the decades since; and they'd only had sex twice, briefly, in drab hotel suites. Several times Herb had come across men— they seemed to get younger and younger, Herb remarked—who reminded him of his brother-in-law as a youth. Having learned his lesson, he'd instantly bedded them. Over the years, two youths had come to work for him and were now his second and third in command, one purportedly straight, the other gay—both still occasional bedmates, especially while away on business trips. At times they introduced Herb to other available, willing young men, often in intriguing combinations. Thus, he'd not missed much during the decade just then ending, the so called freewheeling '70s. All of which more or less explained why Herb remained married. The other justification had to do with his wife, whom he characterized as intelligent, attractive, affluent in her own right, well-connected, and quite social. They'd brought forth two children in the first three years of their union, after which they'd moved to a sizable dwelling with only vaguely neighboring bedrooms. She'd never since objected to Herb's unspoken policy of sexual dereliction—save for annual wedding anniversary nights when, if he were sufficiently sober, he performed his husbandly duty. Herb presumed she contented herself with flirtations with pool guys, passionate afternoons with delivery boys, and romances with men—and possibly women—of their circle. She'd as much as told him from the start that she'd wanted Herb for his looks, for his style, but mostly for his sound genetic makeup. As for the payoff of the desired DNA, aside from his all-American good looks, their first boy was so utterly everyday as to defy Mendelian science. "Maybe," Herb mused, "instead of being such a wonderful father, I should have sexually abused him? Beaten him? Sent him to black boots in a factory at age ten? At least then he'd have *something*! What did I know? I was young and foolish!" Their second boy, with his equally clean-cut, corn-fed, clothing-shop advertising looks, followed so closely in his sibling's footsteps—little league baseball, football, Eagle Scouts, equestrian camp, swim team—that Herb had just about lost hope. Then, during his second year of high school, the boy felicitously swerved from the straight and narrow to be declared a "problem teen," complete with obnoxious behavior, miserable grades, unexplained truancy, unsavory associates, a small disreputable tattoo, even a suspicion of drug abuse. Alas, Herb moaned, before he could enjoy the boy, he had met a girl his mother approved of, had fallen in love, and quickly married—and was now living at home and majoring in business management!—humdrum as his brother. When pressed, Herb guessed he ought to be grateful they weren't serial killers—or Wall Street attorneys! Still he lamented, while kissing, as he counted every hair on Ray's abdomen, that he'd turned out to be such a disastrous male role model; left alone to carry the flag of queerdom and nonconformism.

The longer Herb talked, the more Ray came to understand that he was telling Ray all this not because they were going to see each other frequently from now on, or even see each other regularly, but because they *weren't* going to see each other again.

After Herb, others had offered what his pal J.K. called "Sexbed Confessions." The most surprising were: 1) the pretty, muscular, tough, strawberry-blond bantamweight—he wouldn't take no for an answer and all but raped Ray—who it turned out, was renowned as Rustie LaRue, the foremost drag performer in Chicago; 2) the sensuous, laid-back Greek-American stud who, as he was being serviced, had grabbed Ray's hand and shoved it extremely deep inside his rectum, who'd later been revealed as a highly decorated motorcycle policeman; and 3) the cutish, thin, undeniably nerdy guy (plastic-rimmed glasses, incoherent haircut, ill-fitting clothing) who, during sex, emitted a loud, fairly inventive barrage of verbal trash and who afterward casually owned up to being the oversalaried star of a comedy series that even Ray, who seldom watched TV, had heard of—on hiatus, he said, visiting his grandparents in the nearby town.

Each man he slept with had a singular history. It might focus upon his upbringing, say, or upon his background. One otherwise unexceptional fellow turned out to have been born in Shanghai, China, into a missionary family and as a toddler had to be hidden two days among a load of bok choy and white radishes in a farmer's cart as the disguised family and their terrified retainers fled, while, gaining ever closer behind them, strafing Zero planes and tank gunners of the Japanese army overran the city. Another, a pink-and-chartreuse-haired punker with needle tracks on both arms giggled as he revealed being the beloved, pampered, only nephew of a reigning—openly antigay—cardinal of the Catholic church. Another's father was a famous pop artist known for his drinking and womanizing. Yet another, as an infant, had been the miraculous sole survivor of a commercial airline crash, in which he'd lost his parents and siblings. Then came the stories each man told of his first sexual encounters. The identical twins who'd made out with each other and now double-bedded men. The fellow who'd grown up sleeping in a bed with two cousins, male and female, who...

"As you probably guessed," Mike suddenly said, "I'm in no hurry today." His words carried the hint of some emotion threading through them. Was it resentment?

"No hurry." Ray was always even-tempered with Mike. "I'm not going anywhere."

He did wish Mike would come closer, where Ray could touch him, maybe even hold him. But like face-to-face kissing—so far, taboo—that also seemed to not be in the cards, probably because it was "too gay" for the young repairman.

"I figure," Mike went on, "it makes no sense to put myself out for a boss who doesn't really care."

This, Ray could tell, was an invitation to ask what was wrong.

Ray tried to couch it in Mike's own lingo: "Boss breaking your chops?"

"Nah. He's not bad," Mike said. But just as Ray thought, whoa, wait a minute, our signals got crossed, Mike quickly added, "I guess it's my own fault, thinking he'd want me to have the better route just because I'm a better worker. Compared to someone who's falling down on the job, who he's known most of his life."

Ray tried to recall what Mike had said about this earlier. It had been weeks before, when they'd first met, and had something to do with the disposing of routes for Mike and the other guy who repaired electronic entryways. The Brooklyn-Manhattan, or "city" route, was the preferable one. Mike worked that route when he and Ray first met, which was how they'd met in the first place. Because usually Mike had the "island"—i.e., Queens and Nassau county— route. Mike had been pulled in to take over the city route because of complaints about the regular repairman. Wasn't that what he'd said? And since then, Mike had been trying to get the city route permanently—more jobs, larger commissions per job. It sounded as though he'd finally made a bid for the route, only to be rebuffed.

"Happens all the time," Ray shrugged it off. "They old friends or what?"

Mike sighed. "Well they're both old…I guess, yeah…I shouldn't have been surprised when he let him keep the route. The boss probably figures he can always send me to troubleshoot. Some places won't even let this guy get out of the truck."

"He's that bad?"

"But you know…it was something I earned. Something I deserved," Mike added, and the hurt in his voice was evident. "Something I wanted really bad."

Ray was supposed to say something. He was older and a professional, so he could take the path of the wise elder: That's life, kid. Grow up, let it go. But he was also nearly naked after having just fucked and blown Mike, and so, for the moment, an equal; so he could also do a you-been-screwed-man thing. He tried to find another way. Maybe the Socratic method?

"He just said no? Your boss? You can't have the city route, period?"

"Nothing that definite. He said the other guy would hold onto it for now. I'd still get some days on the route, and of course, I'd go whenever a customer hates his guts."

"And you get those commissions?" Ray probed.

"Yeah. So it's better than before, I guess, when I didn't have anything in the city. Still, that guy doesn't appreciate being here. He just puts away brews in some bar and watches the game whenever he's here. Told me himself. He could do that anywhere!"

The Socratic method seemed to be working, so he'd stick to it. "Whereas you...appreciate it more," Ray tried.

"You gotta admit, I'm doing new things," Mike half snorted. But before Ray could respond, he went on, "You know, I drive around, and I walk around. I see things. I go places and shit when I'm here. I don't waste my time on a barstool."

So Mike felt he was being cheated out of more than a position. While vague, he clearly had reasons for being on his own in Brooklyn and Manhattan. Interesting.

"Want to know what I think?" Ray asked. "One, you've been screwed. The old boy network, as usual, is working against you. Two, you're probably using your time here better than he is. And you should continue to do so whenever you have the chance. Three, this setup doesn't sound like it's forever. You might be able to work your way in slowly. And four, it might all change for the better if he continues to screw up and more customers complain."

Mike didn't say anything for a while. Ray could almost see him mentally sorting out what he'd said. "Maybe," Mike slowly, at last, admitted, "maybe what you say is possible. But!" He suddenly punched his fists into the air. "But what gets me, is—it was something I wanted. And I never get what I want. Fucking never."

The window shade all at once began juttering against the ledge. The illumination dimmed, became grayer and greener than ever. Ray listened for advancing thunder or lightning. He realized that Mike, having reached into himself for the source of his pain, was now speaking about it in particulars, opening up to Ray, talking about the past, about his thwarted desires, then returning to where he now worked, going into the personalities of himself, the other repairman, and their boss, speaking of how fast he'd learned right on the job, how much better he'd done there than he or anyone else had expected. As Mike quietly, insistently spoke of his triumphs, and as Ray began to comprehend how little they actually were in the world's terms and yet how much Mike needed them, Ray felt his heart suddenly turn toward Mike, turn and open to him. He was unsure how to express it exactly, in ways acceptable to Mike. But he felt it, and wanted Mike to know he felt it.

Before he could figure out how to do so, rain abruptly struck the bedroom window, only inches away, interrupting Mike's recitation, sounding like handfuls of pebbles tossed in an agreed-upon signal. A second later it was repeated even more forcefully. Mike stopped talking and sat up. Ray did so too, and a second later he joined Mike, who had turned to face the window. The wind-tortured canvas shade, dancing out of control, out of their grasp, snapped with a crack and rapidly rolled itself all the way up, as though by phantom fingers. Ray barely had the time and sense to pull the window sash down before the inundation arrived. The noise on the glass grew so deafening, Mike could not have been heard had he continued talking, unless he'd shouted. The two knelt on the mattress, silent, side by side, faces nearly touching, elbows on the window sill. The room was cast in darkness, highlighted by unheard lightning—like the interior of a deeply submerged berth. They were children, freshly landed, awestruck, on some uncharted subterranean floor fathoms below.

Ray wondered if he should begin making love to Mike again. But a glimpse confirmed that, although surprised, Mike remained sullen. Sex would fail to distract him.

Ray turned and flattened himself back on the bed. For what felt like a long time, rain came down in torrential, disfigured sheets, quickly modulating from resounding to earsplitting. Mike remained at the window, forehead against the ever moving screen of rain on glass, as though trying to peer through to the other side—or daring it to get him.

"I once wanted something bad. Something I never got," Ray said, and immediately wondered why he'd uttered the words—indeed *if* he'd said them aloud—and if so, if he'd said them so quietly Mike hadn't heard him.

Mike heard: "Not something stupid like a route on a job, I'll bet."

"It was pretty stupid. A ring. I wanted an onyx ring."

Mike turned, slid down, not next to Ray, but higher, on a plumped pillow.

"Just an ordinary ring," Ray said. "You must have seen one."

"One of those flat black stones set in gold?" Mike asked.

"This one was in a silver setting. They're not uncommon. All kinds of guys have them...But somehow I got it into my head to want one and...well, I could never get one. At the time, what with my allowance and all, that kind of a ring cost too much, even to save up for. I told my sister to tell my parents I wanted it, but she never did. Or she did and they didn't listen, because year after year my birthday came and went and I never got the ring. I must have been, oh, 13. Of course, when I was about to graduate from high school, my dad asked if I wanted the school ring. So maybe Kathy had said something and they had been

...listening, after all. But it wasn't onyx, so I said no. Later, when I finished college, I didn't even tell them a college ring was available."

"You could afford one now, right?" Mike said. "Why not get one?"

"I don't know...Because it's too late...Because it had to be given to me, not something I bought for myself...Or because some things in life should remain wanted...I don't know. But for a long time, when I was a kid, it just drove me nuts wanting that ring. And not getting it. It just...I don't know, festered in me. Then one day it made no difference."

"Something else came along and took its place, right?"

Jesse took its place, Ray thought. Jesse, who was worth ten billion onyx rings. "Something else took its place."

They lay side by side, silent, close to dozing, for a few minutes, until Ray realized the rain had stopped. The walls began to silver over, brightening slowly. Mike looked up, then hauled himself out of bed. He began to dress, not with his usual speed but thoughtfully. Around them everywhere, Ray heard dripping water.

At the front door Ray said, "I meant to tell you, in case you happen to be around here and are thinking of stopping by, I'll be away for two weeks."

"Vacation?"

"The Caribbean. Me and my partner. Maybe another couple we know. A guy I help record for sometimes and his woman friend."

"Sounds pretty sophisticated," Mike said, and for the first time since it had begun to rain, that sparkle was back in his eyes.

"We're just hanging out," Ray downplayed it. "We all need rest."

Mike stopped him from opening the front door. "What you told me before? About that ring and all? You weren't just making that up, right?"

"Why would I do that?"

Mike shrugged. "You know, so I wouldn't feel so bad."

He was so close, Ray embraced him, feeling a second of surprise, a hint of resistance, before Mike awkwardly relented, allowed himself to be hugged. Ray almost unconsciously inhaled the familiar mixture: Mike's particular attar, the dry hair, the fusty down vest. Ray let go first and opened the door to a piercing breath of post-rain ozone along with the stereophonic dripping of rain from overhead trees.

The sidewalk was drenched; where it met the ground, inch-high fountains bubbled. Mike's multicolored van was glossily damp, the chrome looked just polished, window glass still rippling tears of rainwater, roof and fenders bedecked with storm-torn leaves. At the beveled edge of the cobblestone street, an oil slick exuding out of a patch of repair-work pitch, previously invisible, was stirred by mirrors of new ditchwater into displaying an irregular slice of prism.

"I did that so you won't feel so bad," Ray declared, meaning the embrace. "What I said about the onyx ring was true."

ten

The daily jet from Miami was just alighting as they drove up to the hurricane fence enclosing the tarmac-surfaced disembarkation area. The two-lane approach road to the two immense Quonset huts that served as the airport's departure and arrival lounges (as well as housing British West Indies Customs and Immigration) was all but impassable. A motley of passenger cars—mostly Ford Cortinas and Opel Olympias with a smattering of Chevys—of varied vintage and in condition ranging from glittering new to fenderless, evidently belonging to those picking up or dropping off friends and relatives, were parked amidst the more uniform, somewhat dented, almost totally American (Chevy Impalas and Ford Galaxies) fleet of ten- to 20-year-old official taxis—all repainted authorized shades of pale blue. And those were towered over by newer, better-kept, ten- and 12-passenger vans, embellished with identifying logos for anyone to easily read their resort of origin upon the island. The closest parking lot being a half mile of a hottish walk away, every vehicle was illegally double parked along the tiny bit of plantless brown verge intended to remain bare and serve as the airport road's emergency shoulder.

No matter, they'd been assured by the cabdriver when they'd arrived a week ago, since all of the island's tiny band of policemen were at this moment within the two overarching structures. Either they were directing the surge of human traffic coming and going or, more likely, they had changed into different uniforms, since to survive on such low wages they were forced to become customs inspectors or immigration officials during the frantic three hours, six days a week, when commercial flights were in service.

Arriving late, Ray crept the jeep—a *sportif* yellow Wrangler, it had come along with the house they were staying in—through the languid, polyglot traffic. He spotted an ATV pull out of what may have been a spot. The dark-skinned driver of the battered tangerine-and-cream Falcon van directly ahead hesitated fatally, doubtless wondering if he could fit (he could, just), and thus allowing Ray the seconds required to shoot ahead and sneak in, managing to park with what in Brooklyn Heights would be a largesse of four inches front and back. The van driver saw his error too late and regretted it. Leaning out the driver's side window, he bellowed that it was his spot: He had seen it first. Ray and Jesse jogged past his flavorful shouting, adroitly fitted themselves around the bumpers and fender mirrors of the porridge of barely moving vehicles, and made it to an oddly unoccupied few square feet of fencing from where they might witness the disembarkation.

They'd arrived just in time to see the stopped 1011 unfurl its stairway onto the ground and to witness the side hatches pop open. Liesl was the third person out—leave it to her to finagle first-class seats out of a coach ticket. Emerging from the dim interior into the midday tropical glare, even with jet-black sunglasses on she was forced to flinch, although it didn't stop her from scanning the area for them. Last night, sitting around the pool after dinner, Jesse and Ray had speculated on how she would be dressed, coming from near-freezing New York. Both agreed, whatever else she'd wear, she'd have on the Alpine white leather jacket, with its belts and buckles, buttons and zippers: her official bad-girl look. And sure enough, here Liesl was, her hair glinting metallic white, it was so very blond; she wore a tiny white bias-cut cotton shift that exhibited her petite figure, low-heeled tan sandal-like pumps, a spotted beige-on-ivory scarf wrapped loosely about her neck, and yes, there was her oversize white leather jacket barely around her shoulders as she swiveled and twisted, pouting at the top of the stairs, looking for all the world like somebody's idea of a fashion model—calmly ignoring the competing invasive flickers of paparazzi and equatorial temperatures.

As Ray had also predicted last night, Maurette was not behind Liesl. Nor would he show up once all the passengers had exited. But she'd spotted them, perhaps even heard them calling her name over the tumult. Instantly she dropped her matching '50s white leather octagonal carry-on, shucked the jacket off her shoulders, pushed out her tits, and gave them a big kissy-mouth, complete with a single full-body shimmy, pretending she was some movie starlet. Ray and Jesse shouted hurrahs in appreciation, and weren't really surprised that they were joined in their applause. Even a few flashbulbs sparkled before a young, lean, tea-colored, official-looking native approached her with a big smile and graciously offered to carry her bag inside to customs, grinning and sneaking peeks as he accompanied her all the way in.

When they had arrived in this exact spot, gotten off the plane and drifted into the gigantic hangar a week before, Ray hadn't been able to shake the feeling that he'd somehow wandered onto the set of a film being made of a Graham Greene novel—it was so altogether picturesque. Not only in its larger aspects, say the great sweep of the arrivals lounge, its dappled light dripping from scores of high-set windows, light that never quite reached the chilled concrete floors. Nor was it merely the outlandish baggage-retrieval area, enclosed by sable velvet ropes like some old grande dame of a movie house. Nor the burnished, massive, teak consoles behind which solemn islanders in sedate uniforms—some swagged with faded ribbands, all smelling of British colonial days—stood, greeting you with a shy smile, as they asked for your visa and air tickets, mellifluously intoning their memorized litany of items forbidden. Nor was it even the passengers on those long, surprisingly fast-moving and quiet lines; the natives on one side a bit more excitable since they were returning home, as they espied friends or relatives in the room behind the wickerwork screens; the American and European expats and tourists, more chicly clad, distinctly summery, some—especially the younger men—casually gripping snorkels, rubber flippers, the newest scuba gear, a canvas wrapped around poles, and a sine curve of plastic that, opened up, would become a sailboard.

Well, yes, it was all that. But it was also the details of arrival. How the official would warmly clasp your hand as he welcomed you, adding with the greatest sincerity, "This is believed by many to be where Christopher Columbus first landed where he reached the Americas. Some historians have pinpointed the spot to Thompson Cove." Or as he assured, "You may use your U.S. dollars.

But remember, if you drive, even though the steering wheel is on the left of the auto, you must drive on the left side of the road." Or another detail: the multi-colored, rather beautiful visa entry seal, depicting a fanciful version of the alleged Columbus landing, so much more complexly larger than the allotted space on the passport's page, it bled onto other stamps. Or, immediately after the visa ritual, once you'd gotten your bags in hand or onto the cheaply rented metal cart, your unhurried departure from the terminal absolutely unharassed by anyone soliciting for transportation or lodging.

Tinged by such an arrival, why shouldn't everything afterward enchant them? The easygoing taxidriver who, when Jesse read off his ad agency boss's winter house location, had commented, "Very fine address, sirs. Continuous offshore breezes in that locality." He'd helped with the bags, was pleased that Jesse sat in the wide, previously paper-strewn front seat next to him, asked if it this was their first visit, and when they said yes, observed sensibly upon the scene all along the island's main north-south artery to Five Cays. "That be the food market," he'd remarked of a low, utterly undistinguished-looking structure next to a minimall. "Air condition," he'd added. "Everyone shop there. High and low." A fact qualified a few miles later by, "Past Stubb's Creek crossroads, under those mango trees, a fresh market arises Thursday mornings until noon. Produce from island farms. If you never drink Santo Domingo coffee, you might take a trial run. Excellent roast. Sell everything there but fish." And another mile along, when another double-laned road bisected theirs, "Highway leads to South Dock. Every afternoon but Sunday be best fresh fish market. Right now the grouper is running large and sweet. You ever taste? The Rolls-Royce of fish. Baked in tinfoil is best." Then, as they turned onto a road that soon gave way to gravel, "This be Bay Estates Road. Exclusive new development, mostly for American expats. Only the old commissioner's residence remain from olden times. It now modernized as Mariner Hotel Yacht club."

A quarter mile in, the gravel had given way to a rain-rutted dirt road, where they'd been approached by an open-bodied, khaki-colored Korean War vintage jeep, driven by an extremely tanned, slender, good-looking blond fellow not quite 40, wearing matching khaki undershirt and shorts, although not the expected uniform boots but instead pediatric sandals. Both vehicles stopped so the drivers faced each other. The cabbie repeated the address where he was taking Ray and Jesse. "Admirable place," the jeep driver remarked, then went on in pure Oxbridge inflection, "Simon Woodcock. I'm what's said to pass for the law *and* for the administrative staff here in Bay Estates. That shack," pointing to a small cottage behind, "is my office, if you ever have need, as well as being where

I live. Why not come by for a drink, once you're settled?" His warm brown eyes were set in sun-browned skin that crinkled around the edges of his mouth, nose, and eyes as he laughed good-bye. He lurched the jeep forward, but just as suddenly staggered it back to the taxi before they'd even moved. "If you're here next week and you could stand a scrap of adventure, a few of us will be diving around an engulfed fortification several cays northeast of here."

As they drove on, the infrequent, rather runty, single-story cottages on the right had soon given way to a body of water the cabdriver called Chalk Sound, a vast smooth inlet of a dozen shades of calming turquoise waters ornamented with scudding carmine and ivory ketches, catamarans, and even a good-size trimaran. On their left continued the Caicos Banks sector of the Caribbean Sea, fronted every eighth of a mile or so, by yet another large, somewhat distinctively designed, two- or three-story wood-and-glass-veranda-girted edifice perched high enough upon its own stone dais to avoid most hurricane stormwaters from off the close by, multicolored bay.

The house they were to stay in was the tenth in the row, surrounded by gardens of ground-hugging succulents, dotted about with a few low-growing bristly palms and wind-stunted, bushy, shade-giving papayas. Inside the deep, cool, completely encircling porch, a half dozen rooms and baths surrounded the square living room with its 30-foot-high skylighted cupola. Within 24 hours there they'd discovered how the house itself regulated temperature. Air was cooled in the shady veranda and surrounding rooms via louvered windows; naturally heated, it rose into the triangular-shaped ceiling pitch of each chamber and within the central room's more elevated concavity. After sunset, once external temperatures fell, one closed the doors and windows and gradually the trapped hot air descended, warming the place.

By then they'd also discovered the flashy speedboat tied to the pier at the end of the terrace. They'd explored the wide bayfront terrace, with its to-the-water's-edge swimming pool from which one might hover, floating, isolated from, yet feeling oneself a part of, the amazingly colorful bay. They'd found the CB radio on the kitchen counter and figured out how to use it; had discovered awaiting them in a kitchen far more conveniently modern than their own, the frozen "arrival meal" and in a wine rack an accompanying, not flinty, Australian Chardonnay. They'd napped—Jesse longer, natch, but not by much—and lazed out of doors, reading, playing checkers, mostly just lying there watching the baywaters undress slowly in scores of shades between celadon and milk-jade green until the sun had begun to repaint it with oranges and reds seconds before it plummeted from view.

For the next week, everything had been delightful. Even having to visit Simon Woodcock (Ray loved saying his name) to obtain commercial water to fill the cistern that constituted the entire cooling basement beneath the house wasn't that troublesome. Ray had envisioned finding Simon alone, the administrator being so contrite, he'd offer to share his own shower—with a casual, mutual wank thrown in. But while he was at home and courteous, Woodcock wasn't alone. Several older, more out-of-shape, shorts-and-singlet-clad, beer-guzzling fellows were arranged around a card table. And Simon was far more interested in the bridge game he'd been rousted from—and whether Jesse and Ray also played—than any erotic fun Ray might propose. He definitely lost points, and Simon had lost interest, when told they did not play bridge. And despite that setback, once again they had enough water in which to bathe.

By then, too, they'd been twice to the supermarket and to the weekly outdoor market (what *were* some of those objects for sale purporting to be fruits and vegetables?). They had discovered fresh daily croissants and baguettes at the French bakery in the minimall; and had visited the oddly unbustling South Dock—all but closed for the day. Following a tip from a net-mending sailor, they had headed farther east, to Cooper Jack Bight marina, a bit more lively, where they'd managed to purchase a large, flat, not-cheap grouper out of a trawler's deck hold. Once home, they'd baked it in foil, as recommended, on the outside barbecue—bony but delicious. The next day they'd taken the motorboat on a sightseeing tour of the west and south sides of the island. Once they'd passed around South Bluff they'd found scrumptious, white-sanded, totally vacant beaches to sprawl upon, all the way to the Malcolm's Road sector. Later on and for days afterward Ray had snorkeled to his heart's content off the house's little pier within the shallow, chalky, limestone floored "Banks" waters. While downtown getting daily newspapers, he'd found out that a movie was to be shown at the Blue Hills Lodge that night. But with so much free television—openly pilfered by a 30-foot-wide satellite dish (the "Microwave Tower" was its sobriquet) erected by the local chamber of commerce—covering North America west to Chicago, South America down to Sao Paolo, who needed a movie theater? Unless one wanted company. They didn't.

Best of all, in the past week Jesse had flourished. Within a day his high, thin, almost squeaky morning and nighttime coughing had vanished. His face relaxed first, then his body. He was resting outside, in the shade of the porch or out in the sun. He stayed in the pool longer each day. With the sun, rest, and sea air, he was eating more. His sleeping, already curtailed in those weeks he'd returned to work—if emphasized on weekends—became nearly normal. Ray still drove out on daily errands without his company, but increasingly Jesse rode shotgun. And he was allowing himself to be talked into joining the Woodcock diving expedition—once they arrived at the fort he would decide whether to dive. His slender but by no means gaunt body looked svelte in the little Speedo briefs Ray had brought and made him wear. With only a bit of sun on him, Jesse's chestnut hair had begun to shimmer as the warm dry air helped it wave and then curl. His fair skin quickly took a golden tone that looked almost edible against his predominantly white summer shorts and T-shirts. Jesse soon looked as alluring as when they'd first met, years before. And whenever they went out on the island, people, especially women, gazed at Jesse, just as they had done when he and Ray first met.

For Ray it felt like a last-minute reprieve from the governor's mansion, an unexpected remission just as one was being anesthetized for life-saving surgery. All of Jesse's pills were working as intended, and no medical machinery—a few hours away in Miami in an emergency—was needed. Jesse still had to sleep alone in an adjoining bedroom. He still had to be hand-washed twice daily. He could still use light-fingered massages with warmed oils for his aggrieved skin. But even with all that, Ray found that he himself could, for the first time in two years, unwind a bit. So he looked upon the island house as a blessed place, heaven sent. And now Liesl was here with them, the three of them reconciled, almost as though they were reliving that Fire Island summer again (J.K. alone not here), although to be honest, he was glad Maurette—and his work—had not come with her.

They lingered behind the wickerwork screens set apart for friends and relatives, trying to catch glimpses of Liesl, Jesse refusing one of the dozen or so seats, Ray trying not to too obviously stare at the others also waiting, the few natives—a younger woman with a baby sleeping sloped across her front in some kind of cloth rigging, a slender, handsome grandfather in a straw fedora leaning upon a silver-headed cane, someone's heavyset husband or middle-aged brother unable to tear himself away from the *Miami Herald* racing pages. The remainder in the lounge were what J.K.—fascinated as he was repulsed—would call Eurotrash; mostly men, a few women, all around 30 years old, even that prematurely gray fellow with the Hollywood hair, none clad in anything but shorts and surf sandals, loose-fitting A-shirts, an occasional baseball cap. Except of course for the glamorous nymph concealed behind a huge, floppy, brimmed hat and oversize sunglasses, her lower torso swathed in some botanically patterned sarong, above which she had clasped a brocaded ivory vest of northern Indian provenance.

One wicker gate flew open and two people entered, a tall, sunburned, jet-haired man, not at all bad-looking—even with the prominent aquiline nose and carefully overpolished effect—clad in loose-fitting khakis, brilliant brown, yellow, red, white, green Hawaiian shirt open most of the way in front, complimented by gleaming, nearly crimson huaraches. He was toting the white leather octagonal bag in addition to his own off-the-shoulder one, and Liesl, alongside him, neglectfully dangled her leather jacket. In an instant the enigmatic waiting dryad shoved herself through the crowd and at them. The new arrival had just set down Liesl's bag and turned to take her hand in parting. A second later, he was hefting the floppy-brimmed woman who had all but leapt into his arms, wrapping her legs around his waist in greeting. Meanwhile Liesl stepped back, sneering, to survey the scene.

"I'll never understand what women see in some guys!" Ray said, half turning to Jesse, who, it turned out, wasn't there to listen. After a second, Ray picked him out at the back wall, stooped over the water fountain. He shouldn't be drinking the local tap water, what with amoebas and paramecia and...

"There you are! And here I am! Just as promised!"

Liesl had him in a combination half nelson and ear-gripping head hug.

He hugged her back, enough to get her hands off his face, then awkwardly kissed her. He pulled away, commenting, "God! You're so white," all he could think to say. "Like a photo negative. The sun here is really hot! You'll need quarts of sunscreen."

"Don't you remember, stupid, sweet, darling, dopey, forgetful Ray? I tan perfectly easily, with only a spray of the stuff once an afternoon."

He guided her just enough to be able to see beyond her to where the other couple still clumsily smooched, although by now all four of their feet were on the ground.

"Who are those people? He looks like a stage baron in a French farce."

"Clever you! Loic was an actor back in France! Now, of course, he doesn't need to work at all. Because of her," Liesl's voice dropped to a near whisper. "The grasping little cunt! And from what I discovered beneath an American Airlines blanket, there's quite a bit of him to grasp." She covered her mouth uselessly, since she laughed at her bawdy witticism right through her fingers. "Is Jesse back at the house?"

"No, he came with me. He's here. He's fine. Much better." And when Liesl looked surprised and dubious, he added, "You'll see. He's like a changed person. This trip was exactly the thing for him." Seeing the look on her face unaltered, he went on, "Really, Liesl. I almost hope..."

She wasn't listening to Ray, or looking at him, or even walking beside him any longer, but had halted and was staring ahead. He saw her shocked demeanor fail to turn into joyful surprise, saw her consciously rearrange her face with a constructed smile, felt her withdraw from his encircling arm, heard her whisper harshly, "Stop doing this to yourself, Ray-mond! For all our sakes. Before it's too late!"

She dashed ahead, he saw, past the elegant, still-awaiting grandfather to Jesse, coming up right behind him with a wan smile. As Liesl clasped Jesse around the shoulders, Ray now saw how frail those shoulders were. As she lightly caressed his lips, he made out how delicate that face had become. And as Jesse wrapped his arms about Liesl, Ray perceived for the first time how feeble those forearms had become, the bright bracelet of bone beneath the bare skin, a 17th-century Divine had written. As Liesl and Jesse enfolded, Ray acknowledged the pallor beneath Jesse's fraudulent suntan, the extreme erosion beneath the perfectly unbroken greensward, the walking death sentence he had somehow convinced himself didn't exist, that Liesl had comprehended in a twinkling.

Stop doing this to yourself, her words repeated in his mind, and Ray turned from their encounter desolated, hollowed. He found his feet moving him out of the lounge, past the high-set open doors, his arms still carrying Liesl's bag and jacket, their dazzling, bleached surfaces glittering in the abrupt, unquenchable blare of the outside sun, just the way scores of flashbulbs go off on every side, illuminating the corpse carried out of the murder house.

eleven

The hot little itching fingers had returned. This time not in his stomach but lower, somewhere in his nether intestinal tract. He wasn't sure where; all he knew was that it had nothing to do with the food, nor the bottled water, nor the sip and a half of beer he'd tasted last night.

This morning, it had begun in his stomach and had lasted a while. He didn't know why. He'd merely drunk rice milk, gentler than velvet on the stomach, slowly chewed half a croissant: comfort food, despite which he'd ended up in his lav—luckily they each had their own—four times already since he'd awakened today. First, half hunched over the bowl as the grinding cramps had excavated him, replaced by the hot itching fingers, tiny ferrets in his guts, followed by the intense burning, during which something—it might have been dross drizzling off freshly smelted steel—seared its way out of him to stain and stink up the water bowl. Relief arrived and was brief. After a few minutes another series of convulsions started, this time in corkscrew motions, as though a giant hand had gotten in and was gripping his entrails, twisting them, getting ready for one final yank. Next, the hot itching fingers returned, immediately followed by the sopping furnace slag. In between the spasms he'd held himself, arms almost painfully contorted around his midsection, as though if he held it like that, it wouldn't burst apart, able to do little but breathe slowly and shallowly, his eyesight shattering images as though reality were a late Braque, his hearing stunned by high-pitched ringing.

As it all slowly subsided, he was able to see, hear, begin to relax, huddled over his kneecaps, counting the pale green tiles—the color of at least one stripe of the bay waters outside—sunk into the surrounding greater number of beige ones. And to observe the stately, otherworldly scurrying of yet another translucent scorpion that apparently lived under the sink, hurrying a few inches from cover to cover, carefully avoiding contact with the not much bigger, stupider looking, pale ecru house lizards that endlessly patrolled the ceiling and walls, busily hunting, first by smell then by sight. So continually were their heads revolving more than 300 degrees to stare after possible prey while they hung upside down, that in only a few days he and Ray had come to call them "Linda Blairs."

Directly, the pain left—the cramps, the hot little itching fingers, the flaming steam too—and he was able to stand, to clean himself up, to stagger to bed to rest a while.

Luckily Liesl was here and so Ray was distracted, not checking in on him every ten minutes. They'd barely noticed him leave the veranda, hadn't bothered to stop talking. As he reemerged, both had gestured him over to their puffed-pillow chaise lounges, and he'd brought a lightweight chair and sat between them, reaching out to touch them lightly, simultaneously. After a few minutes, he felt better. And remained feeling better while they went indoors to change for the boating jaunt. Fortunately Liesl wasn't all that vain, or saved being vain for the U.S., because she had changed into another bathing suit, loose-fitting shift, sunhat and sandals and was back out even before Ray. She was looking lovely as he and she waited beside the jeep, in the almost directly overhead shade of two trees and the front overhang, her telling him he didn't have to go diving today, probably shouldn't, she'd support him in the decision against Ray if he started in on Jesse. "I know," he had answered her. "But I feel pretty good. I may go in."

He *had* felt pretty good throughout the ride along the Leeward Highway beyond the hotels and resort clubs to the public yacht marina at the Leeward Going-In docks. Felt good when the six of them—Simon Woodcock and his bridge and drinking buddies David Cordier and Kai Thommsen—jumped onto the 30-foot vessel that would take them away. He'd remained OK throughout the half hour cruise, slowly edging past first Mangrove Cay then Little Cay, before they could open up the throttle and speed out to sea. He'd avoided the multiple cans of beer that were opened, the cigarettes and joints that were passed around, focusing instead on the gorgeous day, emerald waves, unstirring tapestry of utterly cloudless blue sky any direction he gazed at along the immense horizon, the sun not too hot, the breezes and sea spray just enough, all of it utterly pleasant, so conducive to rest and relaxation, that he'd done just that, spread out on his back with generous gobs of sunscreen all over him, laid out upon a section of planking above the hold where they stocked their under-water gear, Liesl's straw hat over most of his face, as he rocked with the slight seas and was lulled almost into a nap.

They stopped at a low, almost treeless, unnamed cay filled with iguanas, some as large as Alsatians, all seemingly friendly, or at least unhostile. Ray, Kai, and David had dove overboard, swum to shore, and wandered unmolested among the active, partly curious reptiles, and had returned ten minutes later, ready for more brewskis, a little agog with the experience. Not long after, they approached another islet, also uninhabited, this one with pristine rather than gray-brown beaches, and as they'd slowed and rounded a little promontory, they'd been able to make out, clearly evident on the far end of the man-high yel-lowy spikes of some succulents, the unmistakable gray and black bricks of an old building. Actually, all they could make out along the sheer cliff was a single wall of varying height, some 20 feet long, yet obviously broken from its origi-nal, somewhat greater size, with two circular and one octangular windows. It must have been the back wall of the fortification, and he could well believe David's explanation that the little harbor directly in front had hosted the entire little fort but had dropped below sea level, around the same time of the collapse and total destruction of Port Royal, Jamaica, 300 hundred miles southwest, in a nearly direct line, and possibly along the exact same geocline—possibly even from the same event: some gigantic underwater earthquake that had sent that bustling 17th-century city hurtling into its marine mausoleum.

Equal in antiquity, this fort had been far smaller, probably only an outpost set up by the British to secure the waters between the Bahamas, the Caicos, Inagua, and the outlying islands against the Dutch and French who had claimed larger, richer islands and ports. From 29 feet above, looking over the side of the boat through nearly transparent waters, one could make out its wavering out-line below, walls of dark rock amid drifts of sand, and what looked to be bro-ken curves of towers and donjons.

He'd just that moment decided to content himself with sitting next to Liesl and Kai at the wheel while the others dove into the dilapidation when the hot itching fingers returned, and he'd all but stamped his foot in aggravation. After five minutes it hadn't gone away. But neither had it turned into the crushing cramps, nor had he felt any burning diarrhea. So, when Simon turned to him and said, "A tank for you?" to Liesl's obvious consternation and Ray's equally evident pleasure, he'd said "Sure," thinking what the hell, if it won't go away, at least I can distract myself a little from it.

Ray insisted that he put on the skin-tight rubber shirt none of the others wore, to ensure that his infusolator—not used these two weeks—remained dry and uninfected. Despite that, he was very well distracted the minute he fell backward into the clear, buoyant water and descended headfirst, letting the tank's weight draw him down as they'd been instructed at the diving pool at Erebus Spa three times last week when he and Ray had taken lessons for such an occasion. There, after the initial scuba tank experiences, they had dove into ocean, the rougher, dirtier waters at the northern edge of the island. But here, as he plummeted headfirst, easily making out the bubble trails of the three who'd gone before him, the waters were otherwise marvelously pellucid. When he saw the bottom slowly approach, he slowly jackknifed, watching the others do the same, 20 feet apart, and as he settled to the bottom he noticed that except for the definite distant accumulation of shattered man-made walls, like most of the Caribbean, it was a nearly bare and flat marine topography, except for the occasional interlaced curtains of seaweed stretching upward, and the broad ottomans of fuschia and orange-red coral bedded amid wider pillows of already dead coral, housed now in dusty-looking ivory-colored shells. The sand-ed floor was easy to walk on, sparsely occupied by sea anemones, sea cucumbers, lurking crabs, poorly hidden octopi. His view was steady and clear, disturbed only by sudden torrents of synchronized schools of yellowfin and abruptly pirouetting showers of silversides, everything entwined by neon green filaments of sea ribbon flashily diving to avert the ovoid apertures of puffed-up white-and-carmine-striped farmer fish, all of them easy to distinguish, all of them seemingly unfamiliar with humans wearing breathing apparatus, all foolishly unafraid. Distracted by the beauty, the wildness, the unsuspected loveliness of it all, he no longer felt any discomfort within himself, but instead a sort of calm, an inclination to become one with his surroundings.

That had to be Ray, his dark blue swim trunks floating about his waist, waving him over to join David and Simon, who'd gone around a corner of the ruin and found something of interest—he could see Simon's arm waving Ray forward. As he lifted off and glided toward the walls and the others, his peripheral vision tugged his gaze down where he spotted what seemed to be a metal cauldron, possibly once used for cooking within a giant inglenook, now fallen and barnacled over. He swerved to catch at the exposed handle and tug it up, but whatever had filled the cauldron in the intervening centuries—sand, water, animals—now held it down tight. Instead, his own course through the water was affected, his path distorted; he had to work his finned feet extra just to remain aloft.

As a result of this deviation, if he were no closer to them, he had at least gotten himself at an angle and within view of the three others and could now make them out gathered closely at one particular, unremarkable wall of the former fort. Simon and David were using pulled-off pieces of seaweed wrapped around their hands to rub at the stonework as though cleansing it, doubtless of algae, perhaps also of coral growth, in order to read some inscription. Given Simon's body language, this was something new and thrilling. Excited to see the discovery himself, he swam toward them as fast as he could.

Approaching the first two edges of fortress wall, of what must have been a battlement now somewhat tilted, he felt as though he were in a chamber, and, instinctively troubled, he looked up, where he only saw water rising to the surface, lighted at one juncture by a saturated brightness of sunlight. He was about to look down again when he saw it, more of a feeling—somber and foreboding—than a true sighting, as though the shadow but not the object itself had suddenly interposed itself between the water above, with its coruscated surface, and himself, 30 feet down. So strange a sensation it made upon his mind that he stopped where he was and looked again.

From here, directly in the center of what had to have once been some tower room rising several stories—despite the large clumps of damage—first the stonework walls, then the darkened waters defined a vertical tunnel. There! There it was again, the blackest of shadows coasting above him, still too fast and far off to be exactly determined. And there! There it was again, larger, lower down, as though spiraling below along the invisible gyre at the bottom of which he stood, curious, rapt.

Twice it spiraled down closer before he realized it was not the shadow of something appalling, but the appalling object itself, a large, bluish-black barracuda. He felt the hair tingle on the nape of his neck, saw the hair rise on his forearms. In a few more turns it would be caught in the delimited helix of the walls. He must move slowly out of what might easily become a snare. He step-swum slowly, backwards, away from the others just ahead, yet he hoped toward freedom, or at least toward more space, continuing to look up at the shadow, now vanished, not yet ready to sigh in relief, and there! There it was again! Continuing to gyrate down into the ruined tower room, gliding in through a ruin of window, sweeping half around, sliding back out through another, lower chink in the wall. Ever looking up, he slowly edged backward, checking, as he attempted to get out of its path.

Abruptly his view was disturbed by two separate schools of fish—one looking like giant tetras but with single undulating neon-yellow stripes, the other of what might be silver-blue anchovy. Where had the shadow of doom gone? As long as he could see it, he might be anxious but not panic. But now...and there it was, back in the tower room, entering as he'd entered before, swirling about, gliding back out the same way, the big fish slipping directly past him, not two yards away. It appeared to be about eight feet long, far blacker then he'd thought, the blue highlights deriving from the remora that hitchhiked off its massive cartilaged back: huge, smoothly flowing, per-fectly suited, oddly alluring.

The little wiggle it made as it slipped past him was the signal he'd been taught to watch for. That specific motion, they were told in diving class, meant it had picked him up on one or more of its various kinds of sonar and would return to investigate more closely, barracudas being reserved yet reasonably inquisitive. He knew what to do, not stay perfectly still as instinct dictated, but jump as it hurtled past, punching it if possible as it went by as hard as he could, aiming for the eyes side of its head.

He rotated slowly, spotted it at a distance, turned a bit, and caught a glimpse of the other three divers, stopped at the wall, looking his way. Ray had evidently witnessed the black shape sliding near him, had gestured to the oth-ers, and they had all deviated toward him and begun to gesticulate. He looked away, caught the jet shadow in the dim depths behind him, out of the others' view, now just above head level, revolving to once again approach.

OK, he thought, this is where my stomach gives out and I simply shit up the entire ocean. But he had to giggle at the thought, because his stomach had-n't been so calm all day. He hadn't felt so alive all day. So oddly in charge.

It came toward him, black and bullet-shaped, and it turned aside at the last minute, precisely as had been predicted, to allow its skin-sunk sensitive anten-nae and flesh-filled radar to envision him standing there. He reached out fast, as instructed, not to punch—why hurt such an amazing creature?—but to slide his hand along its side, the bumpy, hard cartilage feeling matte and leathery. From the frilled gills on through the divided tail, as he caressed it, the mysterious organism seemed to shiver all over—before it swam away.

Now he could more clearly make out Ray, his body language signaling that he was panic stricken, trying to come toward him, but wisely being firmly held back by the others, standing at the other side of what they rightly recognized as a built-in mantrap. He looked away and rotated again, watching the long dark shadow perform a low, flat, looping figure eight, then head back toward him again. This time, as it approached he moved directly into its path, and although scent and/or curiosity drew it, before he could caress it, it flinched away. Refusing to be touched, it glided into the tower room, as though perhaps aimed toward the others, but then swerved suddenly and fled out through the ruin of window, as it had done earlier.

Five more times the barracuda approached, each at the apex of its exploratory figure eight, each from a slightly differing angle, including once from so directly above that he might reach up and touch the open mouth, the hooked teeth. And each time it approached him, as it neared him, it flinched more apparently away from his reach, from his touch, from his grasp, it seemed, and each time its figure eight became even more distorted, distended, wobbly too, so that once, after passing him, it missed by only an inch a wall of the fort, veered sharply to avoid butting its head into it, scraped its side against the wall's algae and barnacles. Five times, during which, slowly, then surely, he came to realize it would never harm him, never come any nearer to him, certainly never attack or even try to nip at him.

Following the close call with the fort wall, the barracuda shimmied away, much more uneasy, angled itself upward, and took off. It came into his view only once more, 20 feet above his head, in a slovenly sine curve, before absconding from the scene altogether. When he could no longer see it, he felt not release but dejection. Perhaps even rejection. More strangely, something rose from his throat into his mouth. Acid reflux, it must be, yet wasn't this exactly what ancient writers called the unparalleled bitterness of gall?

When he was certain the shadow had departed for good, he turned to check the others, and found himself almost within Ray's encircling arms. The others were close around him too, Simon gesturing that they should ascend. He allowed them to take him up with them. At the surface he felt the sun burning even through the slickness of water and oils on his skin. He permitted himself to be helped up the ladder into the back of the boat, all the while feeling as though some catastrophe had occurred, not that one had been averted.

Not the others. The minute they had their breathing tubes out of their mouths and their face masks off, they were whooping, grouping themselves around him, helping him remove the tanks off his back, unbuckling the halter that held them in place, removing the arm guidelines, all of them talking at once, asking him questions, complimenting him, expressing awe.

"What? What? What happened?" Liesl, detached him from them, taking him all to herself. "Tell me, Jes-se!" She looked at his face, as though aware of what he was feeling, and took what he felt seriously. He couldn't answer her, had to look away.

"I've never seen anything like it! I still can't believe it!" Simon insisted, the loudest, the most unrelenting of them, as he popped open one, then another beer can, and distributed them about. "I've been diving 20 years and never saw the like of it. Have you, Dave?"

"Never," he declared through a face full of beer suds. "Didn't think it possible!"

"What happened?" Liesl demanded,

"What happened?" Simon echoed her. "What happened is that your little pal here tamed a giant barracuda with his bare hands!"

"One bare hand!" Ray corrected, almost choking it out through the beer. Like the others, he was elated. So frightened before. Now elated by the passing of danger. But what did they know? Any of them?

"What? How did he tame him?" Liesl asked, uncertain whether she was being ridiculed.

"Damn thing swam right down at him out of nowhere," Simon said. "Black as night and big as a house. And instead of freezing, like most first divers would do, or punching out at it as Dave or I or any experienced diver might do, all the while we were pissing into our bath trunks, Hard-as-Nails here reached out and *petted* the damn thing!"

"Caressed it," Dave corrected.

"And it swam away?" Liesl asked.

"Hell no! It came back! Again and again! And cool as a cucumber, he reached out for it. Completely enchanted and utterly befuddled the damn thing. You should have seen it. It went ga-ga. Swung about lopsided and all. Didn't know where it was."

"Nearly broke its head against a wall," Ray said

"Got a good scrape along one side on that wall, it was so bewitched."

"Is this true?" Liesl asked, herself a little charmed.

He shrugged, tried to get away. She insisted he answer.

"I suppose!"

"But why? Why would it do something like that?"

"It was under a magic spell!" Dave opined.

"Enraptured!" Simon added.

"Jes-se?" she asked. "Is that so?"

His stomach was hard and calm now, so he sipped at the beer, wondering whether he would pay for it later tonight. "No," he answered placidly.

"Then why?" Typical Liesl: She couldn't let well enough alone. She had to know.

"Because it was horrified of me," he said coldly, looking at the others' uncomprehending faces. He sought out Ray's eyes, locked on them. "Horrified!" he repeated. "And because...because I guess barracudas smell dead meat. And even though they're fascinated by it, they won't come near it."

"What?" Simon scoffed. "What dead meat?"

"They eat dead meat all the time!" Dave disparaged. "You chum dead flesh to bait them out into the open, onto the surface."

"You don't know what you're talking about!" Simon dismissed him. "Kai!" He jumped up and went to the other, beer can popping open, "You should have seen this thing! It was a beauty! Must be a size record for the area!"

And so the group broke up and the incident was laid to rest.

Much later that night, back at the house after dinner, after he and Liesl had washed and dried the dishes and she had gone to bed, he pulled on a sweater and went outside to look for Ray. He found him down on the rim of the terrace, at the convergence of the vast, jet-black, moonless, star-specked sky and the bay water, sporadically salted with phosphorescence. He was seated across a chaise, looking out to sea.

Ray reached for him, made him sit in front of him, and held him around the shoulders. It was a warming, protective gesture, purest Ray, and he tried to respond in turn, to show Ray how much he really loved him without saying a word.

After a while, Ray whispered, "I'll never forget what happened today, Buster Brown. Never!" Then, after a very long pause, "Weren't you even a little scared?

He pondered before asking, "Of what? That I would die?"

Soon they went back in and to bed, separately, as usual these days.

When he got up a half hour later to get water from his bathroom, he heard what he thought was murmuring behind Ray's bedroom door. He'd been unable to sleep for fatigue, and first thought it might be Leisl and Ray, also unable to sleep, quietly talking.

Edging open the other bedroom door, he was startled to see he'd made a mistake. The lights were out. All he could see in the dim, horizontally slatted, bedroom light was Ray's naked form, as long and dark upon the lighter colored mattress as that barracuda had been in the water. Like the beast, Ray's body appeared to be in motion: an irregular sudden slight vibration of his arms and legs, as though he were swimming. Or perhaps Ray was dreaming, and in his dream he was involved in far more strenuous activity, battling the great creature, even; all of it tamped down, streamlined by sleep. And now Ray was grunting, not quite calling out, not fully saying words, but meaning to. Then he was vibrating again.

He'd witnessed this behavior before. When they'd slept together regularly and Ray had nightmares.

He thought of waking Ray, of doing something, saying something to console him. But that was absurd, wasn't it? Soon enough, no consolation would be possible for Ray. Would it?

He edged back out of the bedroom and quietly shut the door.

twelve

Chris was alone in the bookshelf-lined conference room that doubled as a faculty library. He sat at the huge, dark slate conference table, his hands in front of him as though for inspection, as though they belonged to someone else and were being looked at for the first time—extremities: connected, useful, peculiar despite all that.

Ray could only guess what the boy might be thinking. He must have known Ray had been called by the principal. He had to know he'd done something wrong. He possibly didn't believe it was wrong. His face didn't have anything about it of shame or guilt. More that increasingly frequent gaze Ray had at first taken for blank until he realized it actually asked, *You don't believe that I actually care, do you?* That and a general puffiness and sleepiness about his features that confirmed the efficacy of testosterone throughout his body, thickening his eyelids, ripening his lower lip, plumping out his cheeks.

Secondary sex characteristics, like nipples instantly inflated by a breeze against a shirt's cotton-and-linen weave, or earlobes heavy and flushed long after some snippet of sexual reference had been heard and absorbed. All inherent in being 13 years old and male. Ray could recall it happening to himself and his friends at that age. Once while they were out bicycle riding and had stopped along a path in a mile-long meadow to throw themselves down onto the grass to sip warm soda pop and rest, Denny Slawson, his sister Kathy's so-called steady boyfriend and classmate, had turned to Ray, his face swollen with hormones like Chris's was now, a pouting so utterly desirable that Ray had forced his own drinking straw into Denny's soda can, not so much because he was thirsty, but to get nearer to him. Their two cheeks had brushed each other, caressed each other as they competed to empty the can. That, naturally enough, had led to them pushing each other over, pummeling each other, wrestling each other. Hidden from view by acres of four-foot grass, they'd suddenly, slowly, deeply lip kissed, then French-kissed for maybe 20 minutes. They'd separated only when their mouths, their nostrils, their faces were almost raw, inflamed by such a previously untried yet enthusiastic collision. They'd then broken apart, climbed onto their bikes and rode on. They'd never repeated the experiment, never done anything else of the sort together. After Kathy and Denny began seeing other people, Denny and Ray had grown apart. Years later, after Denny married, Ray returned home from college one summer and came across him in a diner off the local interstate. They'd converged from different sections to pay at the cash register and immediately began to play catch-up, swapping life histories. As they stepped out of the diner, Denny said, "Good thing I met Trudy. Because you almost ruined my love life." "Why me?" Ray asked. "Well, you set such high standards in kissing, I couldn't marry anyone until I found a girl who kissed like you did." Denny had blushed a little saying it, but he had not undercut it with some stupid homophobic remark, so once Denny got into the driver's seat, Ray had leaned over the open window and said, "I kiss even better now," adding with a wink, "Get more practice." Denny began to roll up the car window. "Don't even start with me, Ray. Let me stay a happy man!" Both men had laughed.

Chris's fingers were tapping the striated nonpattern of the tabletop. Before he got too distracted, Ray thought he'd better get into the conference room.

"Oh, hi!" Chris seemed surprised. Then, Ray guessed in a show of a jot of contrition, he added, "You weren't like, too busy or anything to come?"

"Well, I'm here, so I guess I wasn't too busy."

Ray sat at the conference table opposite Chris, who pulled his hands closer to his body and glared intently at the table.

"Sorry," Chris said. Then, "You talked to Klebold?" and quickly added, "I don't know why *he's* involved. Nothing happened in school. Anywhere *near* school. And we were off the school bus."

"Would you rather the school called me? Or the police?"

"It was nothing," Chris defended himself. "Things happen all the time."

"How about letting me decide? What exactly happened?"

"Nothing."

"Chris? Am I ever unfair or unjust to you?"

That eventually evoked a reluctant negative.

"Then tell me…And trust me."

A full minute of Chris looking at his hands again. While he decided if he believed what he'd just agreed to: i.e., that Ray was fair and just and could be trusted. A decision was made: "We'd just gotten off the school bus, and I was walking the little monster home," the words exploded out of him, as though he'd been waiting for exactly this. "Paul Kooj and Barry Yakuzi were behind us, acting like jerks. Bothering her, grabbing at her hood and stuff. And she turned around to yell at them to leave her alone. That's when Barry said Sable had nigger hair. He said she was a nigger bitch. I told him to take it back and when he didn't…well, you know the rest…."

"The rest?"

"I popped him."

This was somewhat different from what the principal had told Ray.

"Japanese are racists. They hate black people," Chris added.

"What you just said is racist! Some Japanese people are racist. Some aren't. Right?"

"I guess," Chris admitted, pouting. Then, "I'm not sorry. And I'm not apologizing."

Ray sighed. "This is the complete truth and nothing but? You'd swear it in court?"

Chris put his hand on his heart.

"Did your sister say anything to Barry before you hit him?"

Chris smiled and said in a quiet voice, "She told him, 'I like my nigger hair.' And then she said, 'And everyone knows Jap boys have tiny wee-wees.' "

Ray had to laugh. "It sounds to me like she didn't need your protection."

"Those kids are JDs. They'll grow up to be junkies. Especially Paul."

Ray was silent a minute. "What you did, Chris, is called displaced anger. Who besides your mother and her boyfriend are you angry with?"

"No one." Said too quickly.

"Know what I think?" Ray asked. "I think you did an Otto. Remember how whenever Uncle Jesse and I used to go away for a week or two to the Island, even though you and Sable would come over and play with Otto, and even though he was well-fed and taken care of, he always managed to make doody somewhere outside of his litter box? Remember that?"

Chris was being circumspect. "I don't know…Maybe."

"Well, I think that's what you did yesterday."

"You mean I was wrong?"

"It's not so much that you were wrong. I don't know. Maybe you were right and Barry is a racist thug. The thing is, you acted out of proportion to how much you were provoked. Your little sister acted appropriately. Maybe it has to do with you being a teenager and acting out. Or it may be 100% the Otto effect. Or half and half. I'd like you to think about that while I go tell Klebold he's a gullible jerk for listening to those kids."

Chris looked up with a mischievous smile that said he approved of Ray.

"I'm not kidding, Chris!" Ray warned. "I want you to think this over!"

The principal was busy with another parent, so Ray sat at his secretary's desk and began to write a note, explaining what Chris had told him. The other parent came out of the office, not obviously either Paul or Barry's mother, so it must have been anther matter.

Ray went into the big office, sat down in the chair still warm from the woman before him, across from the principal's large, neat desk and repeated what Chris had told him, concluding, "He's never lied to me before. I have no reason to believe he's lying now."

Klebold had not expected this development. A second of alarm was all he showed in his large matte brown eyes. Then they hooded over again. He phoned his secretary and had her write up a pass for Chris to return to class. When he hung up, he said, "This information changes the situation. Why didn't he tell me?"

"He told me." Ray said the obvious. Then, to soften it, "Chris doesn't have a history of opening up to people unless he knows them."

"I see. OK. Now what?"

"I'll discipline him for his impulsiveness and for striking the Yakuzi boy," Ray said firmly. "But I'll be damned if I punish him for standing up for his sister against bigots. Taking care of prejudice should be this school's job."

Klebold glanced at the manila folder of papers on his desk, and as he did, his mostly bald pate, already somewhat shiny, reflected the overhead ringed lightbulb, making it seem he was sporting a neon halo, only slightly askew.

"Do you plan to take this any further?" the principal asked.

Meaning, would Ray bring an action against the kids?

"Not," Ray bargained, "if you tell their parents what really happened."

"Paul Kooj's parents physically abuse him. He comes to school with lesions, black eyes. I don't want to have to be—"

"Me either," Ray interrupted. "Forget about Paul. Concentrate on the Yakuzi boy. He's the one who said those hateful things."

Klebold sighed, looked up, leaned back, and the illuminated nimbus slipped backward until it was out of sight. "You'll deal with your son?"

"My nephew. Yes. I just saw him. He's thinking various things over."

"You understand that prejudice is…well, it's like a recurring cancer," Klebold began. "You think you've eradicated it, and then another nasty black spot pops up."

"Few know as well as I do," Ray said. "Or Chris either."

He waited for Klebold to comment, to ask what Ray meant. He didn't.

In the conference room, Chris now had the hall pass in his hands to fiddle with. He looked up when Ray came in. "I've been thinking about what you said…I guess you're right. I didn't have to hit him. I probably did overreact. But I don't think it was like the way Otto acted when you went away…" He was carefully reading Ray's face for a reaction. "I don't know. I've got to think about that more…But now what do I when I see those jokers again?" Chris asked, sensibly enough.

"Nothing. You do nothing. You say nothing. Stay as far away as possible. You and Sable. You get on another bus. Walk a block out of your way if you have to."

"But what if—"

"They're afraid of you now. And after what I said in there, they'll realize they've been caught in a lie. They're defeated for the moment. The last thing you should do is to let them know that you know it too—or gloat about it. If you do, this incident could turn into guerrilla warfare. Do you understand why?"

"Not really…Well, maybe a little."

"Believe me," Ray said. "It might. Let it go now."

The period bell rang.

"It's 1 o'clock. What's your next class?"

"Double-period social studies. Mr. Bennett. He's OK."

"Then go. And try to have a good rest of the day." Chris almost sprang up out his chair. "Hey! Don't I get a kiss?"

Chris looked around to see if anyone was looking through the two glass windows between offices and the conference room. No one. So he came over and pecked Ray's cheek.

Ray let him leave. He continued sitting in the book-lined room while listening to the shuffle of hundreds of sneakers not ten feet away in the hallway as the student body changed classes, some, like Chris, for the last time of the day. Long sections of Ray's own teen years had been passed in a combination middle school–high school, but one amazingly different from this extremely urban facility that might have been an office building or small factory, given its brick walls, regulation steel-sashed windows, grime-dulled alabaster pediments and facings, with no outdoor spaces but an open-to-the-air fourth-floor gymnasium, impenetrably girdled atop and on all sides by fortified iron fencing. Sable's grade school, just down the block, was firmly attached to this one by a two-story "modern" (i.e., 1950s) glass-and-steel cantilever structure with faculty parking below. While Ray could understand why the buildings had to be so massive and well-defended, they nevertheless represented school as prison, an idea opposed to his experience. Ray's own adolescent school years had been spent on the broad, half-moon-shaped flood plain encompassed by the confluence of the Wabash and Ohio Rivers. Of the 15 buildings that made up the two schools he attended for seven years—barely connected by low, well-lighted, semi-open corridors—only three were taller than a single story: the double-height cafeteria, gym, and auditorium. It was a campus, laid out on 15 acres, surrounded by another 25 acres of municipal park land. Raised in the early 1960s to accommodate the eruption of his postwar generation, the educational institutions had seemed anything but institutional: They'd been easygoing in layout and style, admitting the outdoors via sliding doors that opened to paved terraces; classroom "pods" ringed by internal courtyards, sitting areas, lawns. The structural elements were of strong but lightweight materials painted in bright colors. The schools had been centrally heated and cooled, with the latest in PA systems, interbuilding telephones, equipment of all kinds. They'd been looked forward to, not dreaded, allowing students to be comfy, not imprisoned. For most, it felt like an extension of their own suburban split-level homes. For less affluent students, like Denny Slawson, bussed in from single-crop farm areas, school was a paradise of modern conveniences they didn't possess at home: televisions, air conditioners, kitchens with large ranges and electric dishwashers, laundry rooms. Of course, Ray realized that was a different, more artless time to grow up in. Even so, the rigors of what Chris and even Sable had to contend with on a daily basis coming and going from school seemed excessive—and unnecessary. More than once he'd tried to persuade Kathy to return home to live with their parents, or at least nearby, so the children could grow up there, attend those schools, and maybe make it to age 21 without being mugged or shot at. Kathy argued that she was a CPA, specializing in theatrical-venue accounting—seasonal budgeting, arts-grant preparations, tax returns, and box office receipts. In the metro area she had all the business she needed, even turned some away. In south central Illinois, she'd go broke in a month. But Ray argued back, couldn't she *not* specialize in the theater or ballet? Sure, but why should she? After all, the only reason she got into accounting was because she'd discovered there was a need for it in theater. In this way, she was still able to be a respected, needed, at times crucial element of the artistic worlds she adored, that she'd hankered after since she was ten, that she'd never be able to break into through her acting or dancing talents. She saw dozens of performances and rehearsals for free. She hung around with artists and performers. She didn't want to give that up.

When the noise outside had died down and the period bell rang again, following the *slapslapslap* of a single pair of feet in the hall, Ray also got up to leave. In the outer chamber, Klebold's secretary looked up from the cabinet where she was filing. Removing some papers from her teeth, she said, "He favors you a great deal." Before Ray could fathom what she meant: "Your boy? He looks just like you." There was concern on her intelligent, dark face. "He's never been here before," she added, pointedly.

"Let's hope this is the last time," Ray answered.

Her words unaccountably brightened him as he walked down the staircase to the front door, out of school. The afternoon had turned from cloudy and threatening to pale gray, almost white, as though the predicted snow was gathering, hovering, just out of reach behind the white curtain it had raised. The silver blue Regal, squat in the parking lot among shinier, newer, more intensely painted vehicles, looked drab and old; it definitely needed washing. Even so, Ray had to admit he was in much better spirits than before. No one had questioned either his authority or his parenting skills. The boy was being amenable. Ray could only be relieved. All he had needed in his life now was more trouble. While not gone, for the moment this firestorm seemed under control.

Traffic was no more annoying than usual, and no one was blocking his driveway, so he could put the car in the garage. Tomorrow was Saturday. He'd give Chris the car keys, make him take the car out, wash it, and put it back in.

Chris would doubtless see this as something positive (on the way to Ray's promise of teaching him how to drive) rather than punishment, it was yet another
item in a planned increase in the boy's general responsibility. In the coming
months Ray would need his help more than ever.

Jesse was at work, had been since the Caribbean trip. To Ray's relief. Maybe
that trip was exactly what he'd needed to get a second chance going. Yeah, sure.
And I've got a bridge to sell you in Brooklyn.

Downstairs were two messages on the phone machine. One for business.
The more recent one a hang-up. Ray took off his suit and tie, dress shoes and
shirt. He was hunting for his denims when the buzzer sounded, instantly
resounding.

"Hey! You home?"

Mike from Massapequa.

"I'll buzz you in. Wait till I get some clothes on."

"Why bother?" Mike asked and was buzzed in.

Today Mike was wearing his heavy-twill, dull-green work trousers, his
usual stout, paint-stained work boots, and puffy, quilted tan vest over a forest-
green work shirt unbuttoned halfway to the white of his undershirt, which rose
almost to the tender hollow of his throat, allowing barely any black chest hair
to escape. A dark green felt baseball cap sat awry on his head, the attached fuzzy
earmuff flaps strapped up across the crown, held by a built-in buckle. Mike's
face looked a little smudged with pink-red, as did the tip of his nose, the apples
in his cheeks, the point of his chin—from the frosty weather. Or was that liquor
on his breath? His turquoise eyes seemed especially sparkling.

They met in the office area, the single blast of cold air gone with the slam
of the door. "Fuckin' look at you," Mike said, clearly happy that Ray had not
put on more clothing. "Just what I want." Mike was at him, his hands all over
Ray's chest, hoisting his T-shirt, roughly feeling him up. "I came by before. And
phoned. Whaddaya, playing hard to get?" he nuzzled Ray's neck, one rough
hand around Ray's waist in ownership, the other rubbing against the front of
Ray's briefs.

"I was out. Just got in."

"Terrif timing!" The undershirt was now over Ray's head, so Mike could
rub one nipple. "'Cause I want you…now. That OK with you?"

Slight liquor on his breath. Ray wondered whether Mike wasn't a little
drunk, horny, and now he was going to pull him into the bedroom, throw him
down and make good on his three-times-now promised offer to screw him.

"Sure. OK."

"Onaconna you're my guy. I can do what I want with my guy, can't I?"

"Sure, Mike. Whatever you want." Less worried than bemused. While Mike was a little awkward, he clearly didn't mean any harm.

"Good!" Another nuzzling under Ray's chin, a few light bites at his Adam's apple, as though confirming for himself that it was a man he had in hand. This time, however, the gesture knocked Mike's cap off so it landed on the nearby desk. Abruptly he withdrew, grabbed Ray by the arm, pulled him through the corridor, half stumbling, into the bedroom, where he tossed Ray toward the bed. Before Ray could register what was going on, Mike had ripped off his vest and dropped to his knees in front of the bed, where he flung that mass of black-haired head directly into Ray's groin, pulling back a second to mumble "Not hurtin' ya, am I?" before he began rapaciously nibbling at the front of Ray's briefs.

"No."

Mike had found the quickly hardened configuration he'd been looking for and now avidly bit and licked at it through the white cotton, using his hands, his mouth, dropping to gnaw at the lower bulge of scrotum, slavering, munching his way up all the way to the cotton enclosed tip. When he'd reached the triple waistband, he nipped at it with his teeth, murmuring plaintively, until Ray, surprised but also unwilling to stop the live-action porno occurring right in his lap, simply pulled down the waistband, freeing the thing for Mike's instant, gourmand gratification. His hands now unencumbered, Mike used them to remove his shirt and undershirt, to unbuckle his work pants and pull them down, to strip himself out of the confinement of his jockeys, and, nudely comfortable, to resettle on the carpet at the foot of the bed, with Ray in his mouth, where he continued to labor and murmur to both their satisfaction.

Mike's efforts, Ray found himself assessing, were somewhat better than those of a first timer, perhaps more like an underpracticed avid amateur. Ray was a little larger and thicker than normal, so it was natural Mike would gag a few times, but it didn't in any way stop him. Instead he let Ray reangle the two of them so he would no longer stifle. He didn't ask Ray to look away from what he was doing, as many tyros would: Possibly he understood that half the excitement of the act—especially the first time—lay in its visual component. And when he kept taking it out of his mouth, to lick along the shaft and nuzzle the testicles, Ray stopped him, wanting Mike to retain the suction he'd built up; Mike didn't complain. He seemed to grasp why and he didn't do that again.

That he'd been drinking earlier and that liquor had released Mike's inhibitions was now apparent. It was also evident that he'd wanted to do this before, perhaps from the first time he'd come here. It was similar to allowing himself to be anally penetrated: Mike seemed to need only the most minor of adjustments to get into it and to do it fairly well. This suggested, as it really almost had to, that he'd performed these acts before. Probably, given exactly how practiced he was and how technically rusty he was, not all that recently. Yet definitely before. And more than once. Possibly over a period of time.

Ray had been lying back. He sat up and tried to haul Mike up by his midsection. "Turn around. Move your legs up here. I'll do you too. We'll sixty-nine."

That required adjustment. Their heights weren't that different; but being side by side wasn't a good fit, so their proportions must have been off. On the other hand, after a little experimentation, it turned out that Mike on top of Ray, in Ray's mouth, with Mike's head over Ray, was great, a perfect fit. Mike must have done this before too, as he adapted to it instantly, his own titillation undeterred to even stop for a second going at Ray.

Given their excitement, this probably would be brief and effective. It was. First Ray came, and seconds later Mike did too.

Mike didn't stick around as he had the last time. He was in the bathroom almost as soon as he got out of bed, spitting out and washing up. Then he was out again, all traces of outdoors or alcohol-induced color on his face gone as he hurriedly redressed. Ray got up languidly and drew on a pair of flannel surfer shorts to see him out the door. "Let's do that again," Ray said without emphasis. "Cool!" was Mike's equally blasé reply.

Ray augmented the shorts with an old sweatshirt and pair of woolen socks, gathering his piles of discarded underwear off the bedroom carpet and dumping it into the laundry hamper, then ran upstairs to see how Jesse was. Still asleep, unsurprisingly. Ray was disappointed he couldn't immediately report what had just happened. What about when Jesse was gone? Would he still want to tell him things? *Don't head in that direction, Ray,* he warned himself. *Don't even start...*

Standing at the kitchen counter nibbling pickled herring fork-fished from a jar, he was close enough to catch the phone on its first ring.

"Those two central hairs on my left eyebrow are standing up," J.K. declared, without bothering to identify himself. "And you know what that means?"

Ray checked into the other room to see that Jesse hadn't awakened.

"I've got to take this downstairs. Call you back?"

He hung up, took the jar of herring with him, and redialed J.K., who repeated his enigmatic opening.

"I could say it means you're pregnant," Ray responded. "But it doubtless means you're somehow telepathically aware that I was just sucked off by a straight man."

Rare silence greeted that. Then a breathy: "Not Mack from Mississippi?"

Ray had long ceased to correct J.K. "The very same."

More silence while J.K. absorbed the enormity of that fact. Irritated, he asked, "Given that news, how could you possibly be eating? *What* are you eating?"

"Fish!"

"Don't get smart with me."

"Pickled herring, I swear it. Mike was a little liquored up. I was in my underwear. From the second he got in he was all over me like a cheap suit. Blow Job City. After a while I deigned to reciprocate." He smacked his lips on the fish.

"Am I supposed to ask if he was any good?"

"He's done it before. More than once. Not recently, though."

"Meaning...?" J.K. started off. "Your Mick from Mineola was what? A stick boy in Marrakesh from the age of six?"

"Un-likely!" they said simultaneously

"Had an older brother?" J.K. tried, "No, two older brothers? Who demanded daily oral satisfaction?"

"If," Ray pointed out, "Mike even has older brothers and if they have half of Mike's looks, they would have easily gotten all they needed outside the family home."

"Yet he knew how to blow and likes getting shafted?" J.K. posed. "Wait a minute! It's coming. It's coming, It's—"

Together they said, "Reform school!"

"Cute younger kid," J.K. glibly explained. "Easy mark for the older boys and the guards. Probably was servicing the whole dorm, front and back. From age 11 to 13, when he was finally released."

"It's possible," Ray admitted, as he'd considered it too. "But somehow he doesn't strike me as the reform-school type. He's too...earnest."

"Meaning what? Too stupid?" J.K. asked.

"Not stupid. But not brilliant. A modicum of street sense. Bit of an ego. But distinctly *not* the overwhelming, typical mother-idolized Guido. So...no reform school!"

"Is...a...puzzlement!" J.K. agreed, faux Thai accent in place. "Meanwhile, you, my lad, are a, so-to-speak, lucky stiff...Which is probably one origin of that term."

They spoke about Jesse. They spoke abut Chris at school. They spoke about Liesl and Maurette dating. They spoke about what J.K.'s hunky student Brad Stone was up to: i.e., nothing with J.K. They spoke about J.K. slowly giving up his classes, then moving into his own planned retirement. When he said he didn't want that to arrive too early, Ray reminded him of all those '30s films he wanted to rewatch, ad infinitum.

"Actually, I'm reading again." He clarified, "Contemporary liter-a-chure!"

"Anything good?"

"Nothing musical," J.K. quickly said, a barb at Ray who mostly read music books. J.K.then named two or three titles he referred to as *gayishche* novels that were "not entirely awful"—the highest praise he'd give anything written in the last 60 years—which he would loan Ray. "Oh, and I perused one exasperatingly twee tome-ette that's gotten the most astonishing blurbs, surely all earned by the author personally, upon his extremely nelly knees. Although from the cover pics, one wonders how desperate the literati must be in the Midlands for even that to be likely."

J.K. nattered on: He mentioned the author to a visiting Oxonian in the departmental office at school, who after hearing the name, had pulled a very long, very sour face and huffed, "Mistreats his canaries, I'm told. Doesn't earn a quid off his books. Still, the bastard might at least line their cages." By that point Ray was hardly paying attention, because after all, who cared about third-rate Yorkshire poofters?

"Maybe," J.K. suddenly offered, interrupting himself about the damned, doomed scribbler, "before he got married, your Mark from Montana had a homosociable affair with a close pal? Such affair being long enough for him to absorb a few techniques such as enjoying anal p. and giving fair head. Yet not long enough to perfect them. And, in fact, as he got married so young and immediately began making babies, I'd even wager your Mitch from Missouri was, as they put it, scared straight by the little queer affairette."

"Bingo!" Ray said.

"You mean I'm right?" J.K. exulted.

"Who knows? But that's my own latest theory. Gotta go, Chris is here. Can't let him see me sitting here eating…with a boner."

"You say the sweetest things to me. But won't you ever ask your Miles from Michigan the source of his expertise?" J.K. wondered.

"Miles from where in Michigan?" Ray asked. Then, "No, I seriously doubt it."

"But don't you *want* to know?"

"Not as much as you do. Anyway, why would I do anything to spoil what is fast becoming my hottest mutual sex since Jesse?"

"Betty Friedan is right," J.K. waxed indignant. "All men *are* pigs!" Then he added plaintively, "Maybe Max from Miami's a bristle or two less of a pig than you, and will volunteer an explanation?"

"Sure he will, J.K. Along with the cure for AIDS."

thirteen

"Well, then, thank you all for the presentation," Max Vine said, standing up. "Becky, you and Thaddeus better clarify those numbers before we show this to the client's group next Tuesday. Otherwise I see no problems here. Good job, Jesse. As usual. That's it, right? Nothing else on the agenda?"

He brushed right by Jesse, who immediately began to get up too, stopped by Max's large, florid hand on his shoulder, holding him back in his chair. The others, however, stood, all gathering around Jesse and congratulating him for the campaign, approximately six months in the works from its inception last spring and now more or less ready to go. Then Max was out of the meeting room, the others following. Becky alone remained where she was in the doorway, half turned toward the others in the corridor, until they were all gone, when she turned to him and half closed the door. "The numbers are fine. They're never going to be more exact."

"When *you're* the agency president and you're shown a preview presentation," he began, "you too will manage to find something wrong with it. Even some tiny detail you're sure must be right."

"Yeah, sure!" she scoffed. "When I'm agency president!"

"Could happen." Jesse got up trying not to look as fatigued as he felt. "Realistically, you've got a better shot than I do." She moved to let him pass. "In fact, I'm probably your main obstacle to the job. Once I'm out of here, the sky's the limit." Her handsome face, set in her hard "we'll get the bastards" mode all day and throughout the meeting, now seemed to melt, and she looked like a little girl, looked the way she must have on her first day of school, down on Mott Street, wearing double pigtails and holding a lunch box tightly to her chest, warily inspecting the other children as her mother wiped her face with a tongue-wetted handkerchief and warned in her pidgin Cantonese and English to behave and reminded her how to raise her hand to go to the bathroom.

"Jeez, Jess! Don't say that!"

"Jeez, Beck! Don't be such a schmuck. I didn't drag you kicking and screaming all the way up to this point just to have you wimp out on me. You're my hand-picked successor, and everyone in this company knows it, from Max Vine on down to the ladies who clean the offices and read everyone's foolishly unshredded memos. Just do me proud, OK?" He opened the door and started out the door. "Oh, and for chrissake, if Thad De Pasquale is as heterosexual as he claims, get into his pants, and tell me what's in there."

"Can't be all that much!" she riposted, back in form again.

"Well, he acts like it's plenty, and I'd like to know for sure."

"So that's it?" she asked. "You just split? Without a gold-watch ceremony or going-away party or anything?"

"Have to keep up the fiction that I'm going to get better and return some day," he laughed. "You know, keep the commoners happy in their ignorance. That way they won't be too upset to think they've been working alongside a plague carrier all this time."

"My time here hasn't been wasted after all," Becky commented, taking his arm as he slowly moved along the corridor. "Looks like a smidgen of my realism has finally penetrated you."

"Enlightened cynicism, Beck, old girl. Call it for what it is. And believe me, I perfected the concept long before you came along, way back in college."

As they walked on, she leaned into him closer, in intimacy. Before she got sentimental, he lightly shoved her off. "Go concoct better numbers for Max!"

He appreciated her momentary slack-jawed shock. Then her laugh. She waved the presentation papers and strode off down the corridor to her office, hips swaying, all femme and sassy. She restored his faith in egotism. Hell, she might even see the famous De Pasquale pepperoni close up some day.

His own secretary had no calls or papers for him. Tasha was already appointed to a new position for another executive starting on Monday and was enjoying her time off, reading a fashion magazine at her desk.

Inside the office, he quietly locked the door, then unlocked it. She wouldn't bother to push in, unless he said she might. His desk was clear, the presentation having been the very last work he'd do for Casper, Vine. To continue the myth that he was taking a medical leave of absence, he'd have to remain in the office a while longer today, as the others went off to lunch and returned a few hours later. He'd white-lied to Becky. Max had, naturally, a while back proposed a going-away lunch. Something tasteful, for just a handful of them. But he knew he'd be unable to put down anything more than a cup of tea and maybe a few spoonfuls of soft dessert. Rather than let them see how bad it was, he'd vetoed the idea. He knew it was all vanity. Soon enough, everyone would know how badly off he was. Yet something in him persuaded him this was the right way to do it. He'd been a star at the agency from the beginning, first as *enfant terrible*, fresh out of college, later as an aggressive team player when the new CEO had aimed for and achieved his takeover of the other partners, continuing through his carefully selected, yet once chosen, 100% patronage of the new agency stars, right up to Thaddeus and more recently Becky Lo. Within a month of joining the agency's creative division, every newcomer figured out *the* place to be was within The East Corner Gang, as Jesse's group was called because of their location, more or less surrounding his office (far from the other execs) and more recently—due to Becky's presence and increased role—more exotically known as The East Palace Court. For every tryout who failed to make the E.P.C. or who dropped out, three more were trying to get in. They worked on the flashiest accounts. They did the most brilliant work. They received the biggest salaries, garnered the most princely bonuses. They had the most fun. And so he would leave here, after a long and excellent run, as he'd come in, having been useful, loyal, and effective. Wasn't that exactly and at all times what Daddy Moody had wanted him to be? He imagined Daddy Moody's spirit would be gladdened by him.

He kicked off his Church loafers and lay down on the little sofa. He couldn't stretch out on it, had to lie on his side and bring up his knees, hold his hands up to his chest. Even then it wasn't very comfortable. As he got into position everything ached, every limb, each particle of his flesh. But this would have to do. A couple of times he'd fallen asleep on the carpet in front of the desk and scared the hell out of Tasha, whose knocking hadn't awakened him and who had for an instant of horror thought him dead. This would suffice for a few hours until he could leave.

Sleep didn't come right away, and he found himself thinking the usual thoughts. Except now there was a new twist. This morning he'd awakened with spots in the extreme left end of his left eye, spots he knew were the stigmata of cytomegalovirus damage upon the surface of his iris. Despite the DHPG infu-solator. Despite all the other meds and precautions. It reckoned faithfully with the increased daily stomach problems, the constant at times blinding headaches, striking out of nowhere, the fatigue that was constant, at times overwhelming. It all added up. The medicines were failing. His immune system was in full retreat. The virus was taking over everywhere.

It had come to him a week ago, at home, perched on the bedroom chair, as he tried once again to visualize the interior of his body as the doctors and New Ageists insisted he do. This time, he'd actually succeeded for a second, and what he'd seen had amazed him: The bold white amoebalike soldiers massed in phalanxes against the virus—represented by black-edged puffy red rhom-boids—had held their ground. Upright and orderly, strong and resistant, they'd held the fort: a single acute spot, perhaps a crucial lymph node, before, all at once, being overwhelmed by reinforcements of the black-edged red things, hordes and hordes of them arriving from everywhere at once, blocking out, obliterating, the good guys.

Oddly, when he'd stopped visualizing, had come to, he hadn't been angry or saddened. Not even all that uneasy. He'd simply witnessed what he had expected for a long time, and objectively speaking, it made sense, seemed "cor-rect." He'd long accepted his demise as a precondition; now he'd simply have to implement it. That was when he'd decided to resign from the agency, to execute all the other legal and medical instruments required. Only one thing remained, and that was calling Adele Vaughan Moody, née Carstairs, and telling her.

He knew that once he told his mother, she would march upon the North like General Lee, instituting a reign of terror, or at least a hurricane of difficul-ties for him, for Ray, for everyone. Yet it had to be done. Couldn't *not* be done. If Jesse was hospitalized and died without her knowledge, Adele was capable of causing far more problems for Ray and everyone else. What, exactly, he couldn't say. Legal hassles, criminal charges…something unimaginable, since Adele was unimaginably self-seeking, unimaginably capable of anything to soothe her ego.

Another reason for getting her up here before he died had tugged at the boundary of his consciousness for several weeks, and it was only today, sitting here at this desk a few minutes before going to the presentation, that he'd been exhausted enough to let down his safeguards and permit the idea to enter fully. The truth was yet another vanity, but what the hell, he had no illusions that he was better than anyone else. He was subject to daydreams and vanities like other people. He could admit why he wanted Adele here. It would give him one of the few chances in life he'd have of being superior to her. She would arrive in a self-generated maelstrom of panic and near-despair. She'd unflinchingly receive the doomed prognosis with antebellum aplomb. Thereupon, she would settle in for the death watch. And it was then, once she'd become accustomed to the idea he was going to die and she couldn't do a damned thing about it, that he would finally and really for the first time in their lives have her at his mercy. He would be lovely to her. Charming. If she brought up the past, he'd dismiss it. If she alluded to her mistreatment of him, he'd forgive her. Perhaps excuse her. He knew her well enough to recognize the contours of each and every corner she would come at him from, and he'd be prepared for her at every one. He would cut her off at every pass, replaster and repaper every approach she'd utilize. Witnessing others sicken and die, he'd arrived at a good idea of how bad it could get for those near the dying. That, and his native wits, honed to perfection by years of politicking at Casper, Vine, would be all he'd need. Ambushed by his graciousness, Adele would at first falter and attempt various rejoinders. She might achieve a few minor ones, but in the end, like everyone else who fought the disease, she would have to admit defeat. In the end, she would have no choice but to recognize that he had more than adequately fulfilled Daddy Moody's, possibly even her own, high criteria. He'd met all those demands in his own manner: successful career, nearly as long a marriage as hers, even helping to raise a family. She would have no option but to reach the realization that he had won the lifetime struggle between them. Which, in Adele's universe of black and white, yes and no, on or off, could mean only that she had lost, utterly and irrevocably, lost her self, lost her purpose in life, lost any edge over him she'd dreamed of possessing. "I'll show you!" she used to bellow, hurling him to the floor, viciously, heedlessly kicking him while he was down. And now, now he'd show her. She'd be the pathetically huddled heap, her only son tortured to death by a disease so dreaded among her country club bridge players, so loathed for its association with swine and Negroes and perversion, she'd never be able to breathe a word to anyone, never mind seek pity for her loss, but must suffer quietly alone or risk utter social ostracism—the very last thing she could bear. It was a complex, rather refined revenge he would exact on Adele: like the Black Queen in *Barbarella* feeding orchids to her prisoners so she might resent them even more; a retribution all the more elegant in that, of all the universe, only he and she—and God, if God were discommoded enough to still frequent this universe—would truly appreciate it.

No time like the present, he told himself, and having nonrestingly rested long enough, he hauled himself off the sofa and edged over to the desk, enfolding himself in the big overdesigned high-tech desk chair. His memory for phone numbers had vanished long before the headaches began; he'd seldom called Adele anyway in the past year. He looked it up in his phone book, and when he did, the number didn't look all that familiar. An 803 area code. Was that right? Utah's area code was 801. And central California was 805. How could his mother's home phone, on the southeast coast, be 803? The three phone numbers did look right. Nor the subsequent four. Had she changed numbers since he'd lived there? It had been more than two decades. He let it ring twice, then hung up, thinking no, this can't be right.

He dialed Tasha, who was still there, and asked her to look up the number in her Rolodex. Sure enough, 803 etc. He dialed again. This time it rang so long—five, six, seven times—that he had to requestion whether it was the right number. Didn't Adele have an answering machine? Hadn't he bought her one a few years back, in an unexpected (and unrepeated) excess of filial piety, as a holiday gift? Which had garnered the expected reply of ingratitude, "Could you have found a less attractive shade? Wasn't there a more hideous one for sale?" Naturally, it perfectly matched her kitchen.

"Yes? This is the Moody Residence!"

It was Adele's voice. Slurred, yes, and unaccountably fluffy, as though awakened from an alcoholic stupor. Or was that merely wishing?

"I didn't wake you, did I? Where's Mrs…" He couldn't remember the live-in woman's name. "…the housekeeper? Why didn't she answer?"

"Jesse?" the unexpected, unaccustomed tone of delight in her voice, made him wonder even more. "Boy? Is that really you?"

"Yes, it's me." What was all this? Greene. Lylah Greene. That was the housekeeper's name. "Why didn't Mrs. Greene answer the phone?"

"Oh, her!" The flat voice he knew so well had returned. "She pretends she's deaf so she doesn't have to answer the phone or do half of what I tell her." Then, in the new, joyful voice, "I heard on the tellyvision that it's snowing up theah."

"Is it?" he asked, and looked out the window. "No. Not yet."

"Lord! Then it's a good thing you called. The tellyvision morning weatherman said a gigantic storm is headed your way. Gigantic," Adele repeated, evidently liking the sound of the word. "Dangerous too. Already dropped ten inches on Chicago and the Midwest. It'll soon be theah. Maybe you ought to leave your office earlier."

"I already am leaving the office earlier. That's one of the reasons I'm calling. I'm taking a medical leave of absence."

Silence from her end. Then in the wary, disapproving tone he'd come to know so well and which he hadn't yet heard during this specific phone call, Adele asked, "You've been let go theah, haven't you?"

"Let go? You mean fired? I'm a vice president and creative director, remember? I can't be fired. But I am taking a leave of absence. As of today. Paid. With benefits. A medical leave of absence. Do you understand?"

Silence on the other end. In a less certain voice, "Lawyer Arbuthnot, you know, Clara-Jean's husband? He took one of those medical leaves of absence, to go have himself a triple coronary bypass. He's been home four months already. There's no saying when he'll return to the law."

"Probably never. Mr. Arbuthnot's 75 if he's a day. And I probably won't return to work either."

"But you're half his age, boy."

She was always lowering his age, no doubt so she could think of herself as younger. "I'll be 41 in May."

"The years do fly by," Adele said, exactly as he knew she would, covering her own vanity and untruth. "You don't mean to tell me you're fit to retire already?"

"Listen, so you'll understand what I'm going to tell you. I know you read the newspapers and watch television news shows and—"

She interrupted him with an elaborate list of exactly which journals she read and which news programs she was devoted to. It was about as he'd anticipated, save for the quirky addition of *The Christian Science Monitor.* When she'd finished itemizing, she sounded as though he was expected to be proud of her.

"Fine. If you're that knowledgeable, then you know what AIDS is. Well, sit down if you aren't already. Because I've got AIDS. And I'm so sick with it, the medicines aren't working anymore. I'm taking a leave of absence because I'm too sick to work. Too sick to do anything. I'm going home to stay until I die there. Do you understand?"

"It's that Jew boy gave you the AIDS!" Exactly as he knew she would.

He'd long ago made the mistake of thinking Adele would be as fascinated by Ray's funny, mixed-up, somehow or other typically American background as he'd been. "No, Ray didn't give it to me. He's not infected. He's not sick with AIDS. Ray's been taking care of me while I've been sick."

"You mean to tell me Jew boys give the AIDS, but they don't get it?"

She was just as bad as he'd thought she would be.

"Jews get AIDS like everyone else. But Ray doesn't have it."

"Well, I'm just a simple Christian woman, but I'll be hanged if I can understand anything you're saying. If that Jew boy and you is...*bedmates*," she spat out the word, which he guessed was better than "sinners together," which she used to call them, "for so long, then how come you got it and he don't?"

"Because I *strayed* on him. Ten years ago. We almost broke up. I don't know what I was thinking at the time. I left Ray and I had other bedmates. One of them must have infected me."

Which of the many questions would she ask first?

"Were they Christians?"

As usual, it came from out of left field.

"The guys I dated? I guess some were. I didn't ask. That's not the point."

"The point being, none of the Christians were good enough for you to sin with?" She asserted. Bravo, Jesse congratulated himself. It had to come out sooner or later; he was batting three out of three so far. "So you have to go back to the Jew boy to sin with?"

"After a few months I realized I truly loved Ray. No one else. So I went back to Ray. He took me back. We've been together since."

That last speech, he knew, would be like successive hammer blows to her heart.

"How are you so sure that Jew boy didn't go off and sin and get the AIDS and give it to you?"

"Because, Mother, he said he didn't he see anyone during the time I was away."

"And you—you fool—you believe him?"

"I believe him, because he was heartbroken that I'd left and overjoyed that I returned. I believe him because he tests negative for the disease."

"You always had to go and do whatever you wanted, didn't you?" Adele derided. Unable to blame Ray, she'd easily swiveled to blame Jesse. "I shouldn't be surprised that you went off, even on your Jew boy, when you did whatever you damn well pleased around this house all the years you were growing up. Stubborn, I always told your daddy. More independent-minded than was ever on my side of the family."

"You may be right and you may be wrong. Whichever, the upshot is I not only test for AIDS, I also have symptoms of the disease. I have terrible headaches. I can't eat. When I do, I can't keep food down. I'm too exhausted to work. I'm going blind. Ray has cared for me. He works at home and he'll care for me till the end. He's an angel, despite what you think. I was a complete moron to leave him for even a minute. And that's all I have to say to you. Period. Ray's been after me to phone you with the news, so as to lessen the shock to you. I've kept putting it off. The only reason I'm bothering to call now is that when the news of my demise arrives, it won't inconvenience you too much." He hoped a little irony would drip in her direction. "I wouldn't expect you to do a thing. Not mourn, not pay any further attention to me. So, good-bye and give my regards to Lylah."

"Who in hell is Lylah?" Adele asked. Then, "Oh! That old idiot house-keeper. You always doted on her more than was good for either of you." She took a breath, he suspected, to get ready to let loose. "You awaken me from a fitful afternoon nap to insult and grieve me, and I don't know what you expect. You were always a cold and calculating child while you were under my roof, independent to a fault and careless of others' consideration, manipulating your daddy against me time and time again, and you seem determined to do me ill from thousands of miles away, at the end of your sinful life!"

That outrage gotten off her chest, Adele fumblingly disconnected the phone, the awkwardness corresponding to how furious she was. Jesse heard the buzzing of the receiver with a deep, if rather frigid, satisfaction.

"That's done!" and he felt lighter. Better. So he wouldn't have the more complicated satisfactions he'd daydreamed of. What of it? This would be better all around.

His French-made Relide table clock, an art deco bagatelle, now read almost 2 o'clock. He took it and placed it on his desk, along with another dozen or so personal office items that Max said would be shipped to him.

Outside his office, Tasha had gone to lunch. He left a note reminding her to send the items. They'd already said good-bye. He drew on his scarf, fitted himself within his heavy ankle-length Chesterfield against the late January chill. Leaving it unbuttoned, he patted gloves and beret in his side pockets, hefted the Hermes attaché case, and stepped out.

Almost no one in the corridors. Wanting to avoid Max or any other exec coming in, he slipped out the side door to the elevator lobby. Empty. Perfect. An elevator opened, was vacant, and he stepped in. Alone, he dropped 24 floors into the long street-to-street marbled foyer, where he almost immediately bumped into Thaddeus.

The larger, younger man, coming in from lunch, looked embarrassed as he mock jovially warned, "Thought you'd escape my clutches, didn't you?"

Thad wore a expensive—probably Gucci—black leather car coat over his casual Friday light gray turtleneck and herringbone slacks. His face was flushed from being outdoors, his thick shock of dark brown curls glistened with diamondlike sparkles of damp, tiny snowflakes just now melting. He looked virile and strong and wonderfully handsome, and Jesse thought back to how he'd fallen for him the minute Thad had walked into his office as a trainee five years ago. They'd carried on a completely platonic relationship shamelessly in public and private since, under the guise of up-and-comer and older mentor.

"Walk me out." Jesse took the younger man's arm and turned him around, headed toward Lexington Avenue. "Help find me a taxi."

Jesse donned his cap but left the gloves pocketed. They passed a gaggle of younger account execs coming into the building who Thad knew and nodded at, and were soon out into the icy chill. Thaddeus blocked him, raising an arm to hail a cab. A bad time for them: post-lunch, a light snow; they would wait a few minutes.

Thad took time off his cab-searching to sulk. "I can't believe I'm not going to see you again."

"I'm not moving to Tibet."

Relief on the young face. "Can I visit you?"

"You can do anything you wish with me, as you very well know," Jesse flirted. "Come visit. Make Ray jealous. So he doesn't take me for granted."

"Come on. He's nuts about you." Thad's head was newly dotted with snowflakes, quick knitting an impromptu lace mantilla that was nearly a nimbus. "We all are!"

"We who?" Jesse flirtatiously demanded, as several empty taxis drove by.

"Everyone! You know how I feel, of course!"

How? Jesse wanted to ask. *How exactly do you feel?*

"The instant I'm gone"—Jesse meant to provoke—"you'll forget me. You'll have your own claque of adored ones. You probably already do."

Unable to resist, he lifted his ungloved hand to Thad's snow-haloed hair. A stubby yellow Checker screeched to a halt in front of them.

Thaddeus intercepted Jesse's hand reaching for the cab door, and held it.

"Give me your blessing," he said, his voice choking up. "Please."

Before Jesse could respond, Thaddeus moved the hand to his lips and kissed it, palm open. Jesse knew then that he'd never see Thaddeus again. He also knew he must fulfill this archaic, not totally understood, observance. He moved his still-held hand to Thad's sweater front, dove cashmere exposed within jet leather. With the tip of his index finger he impressed an inches-high letter X. "First, here. Always here," he said, uncertain what he meant.

Thad released his hand and reached around to bear hug him. In seconds he'd opened the cab's back door, lightly pushed Jesse in, and slammed the door. As the vehicle pulled away, Jesse saw him standing there—tall, strong, tight-jawed mute, tragically unhappy, yet somehow satisfied, instantly rehaloed by snowflakes.

"Good-looking fellow," the turban-clad cabbie said, with a nod back. "Your boy?"

"My boy, Thaddeus," Jesse conceded. He was inexplicably moved. Like the moment with Becky in the hallway, it seemed so...he didn't know...biblical? Antediluvian?

A moment later at a stoplight, he offered the cabbie his address, explaining how it was just a few blocks over the Brooklyn Bridge, saying that by rote so his fare wouldn't be refused, before he settled against the wide, dark brown, Naughahyde seat.

The light snow all around the slow-going taxi thickened second by second, rapidly accumulating on the Checker's cooler metal elements, the chrome window detailing, the blunted hood ornament. The windshield wipers started up with their regular swoosh and thump, swoosh and thump, swoosh and thump. Headlights on autos around them went on, flashing pale gray day into sundown. The turbaned head in the front seat bobbed forward almost to the windshield, as though the driver needed to see more clearly to concentrate—as well he might, hailing from a totally different climate.

By the time they'd arrived downtown, snow was amassing unchallenged on the hoods, roofs, and trunks of parked cars, frosting denuded ginkgo trees, outlining every decorative component of every office building, outlining post boxes, frosting telephone booths, lending traffic poles more height. The bridge, as they neared, then crossed it, had already passed from the beetlelike, wet-black-steel stage into a freshly delineated spun sugar atop bittersweet chocolate. The streets of the Heights were already sunk in white, everything a minimum of two inches of fluffed ice, as though by simply crossing a river they had ventured more incisively into the season. The gentle silence of the downfall muffled most traffic sounds: calls, car horns, and fender benders alike. Now Joralemon Street approached; car choked, it would be inched through for many minutes.

He was put in mind of another time, another day. Summer it had been, perversely, and yes, as he let the memory arrive, he recognized it as the last hour of a two-week stay at Fire Island Pines in late May, years before. Some house J.K. had corented that somehow he and Ray had all been able to stay at for almost no cost. Casper, Vine had been relocating its headquarters and was a mess; Ray was newly unemployed, Jesse taking vacation days long owed. And it turned out to be a scrumptious two weeks. Hot and transparent by day. Cool and star-crazed by night. Just one swift storm had arrived, one night after dinner, tactfully gone by morning. They'd encountered new and old friends, they'd reacquainted themselves, they'd lived at the beach, around the pool, traveling in what even they recognized as a formidably attractive bathing-suited trio through the meat rack and tea dance, the grocery store and discotheque, by lateral taxi to other communities for amusement and to other houses for afternoon drinks, and, after the club had closed, pool parties. He and Ray had made love often and divertingly, indoors and out. J.K. had found a slender cutie named Cecil, a young Alabamba-bred lad with honeyed speech and taffy-colored hair and perfect buns requiring an indefatigable top. And so they'd all been at peace.

But at last the second Sunday had arrived. They'd all four left the house, headed for the harbor where, since it was the end of a holiday weekend and almost sunset, they'd had to wait amidst a hundred others headed back to the city, shoulder bags slung across their tanned torsos, dropped about their sun-darkened legs. The line to the ferry had already grown so long by the time they'd joined that it had strung out beyond the little harbor, along the sidewalk in front of the Pavilion's rear deck and the liquor shop, and soon they'd all moved off the hot concrete path to cool their sandaled and sneakered feet on the dirt road, the single road of the place, utilized by the sole police car and single fire engine. Obliquely angled sunlight spangled each weathered wooden plank of the club's enveloping structure, catching here and there at a metal edge or light fixture, splattering wherever it made contact with pane glass, illuminating as though from within a score of roof-hung pennants, immutably shivering in a marine breeze. The crowd was quiet, not weary of waiting, since like them, Jesse believed, everyone had enjoyed themselves so much, yet even so, eager to move on: men imminent with mass transition.

The ferry arrived, then another, neither of which they could actually see from so far back as they could infer from the sound of docking horns and crew calls, the few disembarking ferrygoers, the half broken statements of others, farther along, of what was going on. The line had just begun moving, step by baby step forward, when all at once they were surrounded by a whiteness in the air. Inch-long doubled wings. Tiny, white, moist sluglike bodies. Blithe and irresolute, simultaneously absorbing and reflecting the last intense minutes of sun like hundreds of fluorescent bulbs. Hundreds of them. Thousands. Scores of thousands.

"Mayflies!" someone whooped, as the soft fluttering insects erupted from below their waiting feet, exploding in twos and threes from out of the earth, from below boot heels and rubber soles, to emerge cool and white into the air, filling every cubic inch between them and the trees and the wooden walls and one another with hundreds of thousands of their numbers. "Mayflies!" others responded; the word passed along, complimenting a growing flutter so softly insistent they had spun about in place to experience it. Boldly outstretched fingers were immediately bejeweled with living, quavering pearls, beards and heads were resurfaced in multiple barrettes of pale insects,

T-shirts reembroidered, shorts freshly brocaded, sandal straps encrusted with alighting and retreating whiteness. Like showgirls from someone's daydream of an all-white Erté fashion show, they slowly edged toward the boats, decorated, encircled, almost silent in wonder. Around them the entire harbor paled and whitened as millions of mayflies continued to eject from the ground and fling themselves into the air for a half day of existence: not eating, not sleeping, not thinking, merely living to mate and mating to once again live.

Individual insects had, for the most part, detached themselves and physically retreated upon reaching the water's edge, and the muted mob of travelers had entered the vessels in near silence, found seats below or rose to the top deck, whispering and murmuring. He and Ray, Cecil and J.K. felt the boat abruptly untether, gradually pivot in the tiny harbor to face forward, for takeoff. For 15 minutes or more, glancing across the boat's churning, V-shaped wake in the bay waters, they had continued to witness the harbor area, unrestrainedly filled with pallid unending confetti, which, as they'd glided away, had resolved into a tall cloud, peculiarly airborne, upwardly driven, an ebullience of pure silver-snow.

"This the address?" the turbaned driver interrupted Jesse's reverie.

He looked out the window, paid, got out, shut the door, lurched from the tree to the metal banister. The stairs were snowed over, already several inches thick. He could only move slowly, very slowly, the frozen railing searing his ungloved hands. He stopped, almost fell, turned and sat down, trying to get at and put on the gloves.

"You need help?" he heard and looked up to see the cabdriver in front of him. The cabbie wore no coat, only a thick brown sweater with a radiantly henna-dyed cotton scarf wrapped several times around his neck. "You live up there? Top of the steps?" and before Jesse could say don't bother, he heard "Come now! Upsa-daisy!"

He was lifted easily, half pulled, half levitated up the steps one after another. Before they reached the top, the doors opened and there was Ray. He came out and down, and two sets of arms now lifted him, completely, high up over the snow, over the step, indoors, into an armchair, hat off, coat opened, still panting, eyesight drifting, home.

"It's a wonderful thing, this snow!" the cabbie said, standing in his dripping sweater and red-orange scarf. He gestured outside, turned around to take it all in, arms opened wide at the glass door to encompass it all. "Never before have I seen so much snow. The whole city is covered!" he exulted. "Now I go home to my children to play with them in all this snow. We will have such fun!"

Before he could thank the driver or offer coffee or money, the turbaned head was gone. Ray was lifting Jesse again, carefully prying the attaché from his warming fingers, taking off his coat and scarf. He hugged Ray as close and hard as he could.

"I chose a good day, didn't I?" he asked. He was filled with joy.

"Kiddo! Any day you choose is a good day."

fourteen

The minute Ray got inside the office, he could hear Sable's voice. She was upstairs giggling, not as though she were being physically tickled, no, but perhaps as though she were being mentally tickled. He was familiar with those chimes of giggles that rose like carbonated water out of her throat, escaping from her not all at once, but as through a carefully prepared time release. Her laughter gurgled and warbled and ended up pealing like many small, imperfectly polished bells, a childish yet in ways grown-up laugh, reflecting both her recent infantine past along with a foretaste of the sexually mature future she would inhabit in not too many years.

On the desk he dropped the ream of printer paper and the two rolls of wrapping tape he'd gone out to purchase, hung his ski cap, and looped his scarf on the door hook. He skinned off the rime-crusted gloves, shook them almost uselessly into the trash can before stuffing them into the pockets of the heavy wool coat he spread to dry across the accommodating back of his office arm-chair. Even with the outer door closed against the weather, it was cool inside. So cool, his clothes remained unthawed. It hadn't been extremely cold yet—nothing like his first winter in Manhattan with its weekly blizzards, staunchly iced sidewalks, six-by-ten-foot banks of unmelted, grime-encased snow all along Chelsea and Murray Hill avenues until late April, long after it was supposed to be spring. In the middle of it all he'd flown home for what his father termed his Aunt Jana's "hippy-dippy" version of a Seder, and had been astonished to arrive amid full blooming daffodils and tulips, trees and lawns emerald green everywhere he drove in south central Illinois. But today wasn't yet Passover, it was still January; it was allowed to be this resolutely cold.

Rubbing his hands, he checked the thermostat: 65. He pushed it up to 70, drew off his sweatshirt, leaving only the waffle-weave Henley; it would be warmer upstairs in the sickroom. Leaning against the wooden banister column, he alternately kicked and shook his boots off his feet, as another peal of laughter percolated through Sable's nine-and-a-half-year-old body from above and proceeded to ripple—sweet, cooling bubbles—just at the surface. In almost instant counterpoint, he made out a lower voice that he'd before only felt as a vibration but not heard, speaking too low for Ray to make out any words, a basso rather than mid baritone voice, so it must be J.K. up there with her rather than Jesse, although he felt certain that the voices issued from the guest bedroom. Sable's laughter ballooned suddenly, rose to a ring, and was stopped by the lower voice. In canon, first her soprano tittering, then his basso muttering ensued, the two voices twining around each other, constructing a little fuguetta which ended in a triad consisting of what was undeniably J.K.'s loud guffaw, Jesse's muted chuckle, and Sable's unceasing carillon of laughter. He pictured her as she rolled back and forth in mirth across the bedcovers. Ray at last managed to kick the dangling boots off his feet entirely. Leaving them in a heap at the bottom of the stairs, he loudly trudged upstairs in his stockinged feet, as though he were an ogre forewarning them of his coming.

He found them almost exactly as he'd expected to. Jesse was sitting up in bed, propped up with a half dozen pillows. Dressed in his flannel pj's, just as Ray had left him not 45 minutes ago, but more wide awake than he'd looked all week and with his hair newly, neatly brushed, doubtless thanks to Sable, who loved to mother him. J.K. was sprawled more or less in the big bedside wing chair, angled 90 degrees to face both Jesse and the more peripatetic Sable. J.K.'s long legs were lifted onto the bed, forming an ivory wool and sky-blue denim accent upon the darker navy-puce-brown-purple-lilac paisley coverlet. Sable was still in her school clothes, predominantly of the red-orange shades she favored, but she'd had taken off her boots and had just returned within the narrow valley of coverlet formed by Jesse's scissor-open legs. Evidently Chris had dropped her here and fled, presumably to play ice hockey once again on the impromptu rink of two-inch-high ice laid atop the surface of St. Anthony's black asphalt schoolyard, a few blocks away, the end result of two months of unremitting precipitation and the inefficient use of rock salt.

The only unexpected member of the domestic scene turned out to be the most active one, and, Ray soon saw, the main occasion of the laughter: Otto, atop the comforter, next to Sable, who tried holding the tawny little cat as he kept leaping up to take on the impossible yet all-too-tempting task of batting and grasping at an extemporaneous cloth ball consisting of a few wool socks rolled together, handled by puppetmaster J.K. Callaway. After an initial twinge of alarm, Ray concluded that it probably no longer made any difference to Jesse's state of health that the cat was in the house, never mind so close to him.

Ray kissed Sable, patted Otto, bussed J.K., and at last, farthest away, held and kissed Jesse, who held him around the neck a second longer to whisper, "Let him stay. He makes her happy." Which Ray answered with a second kiss, higher on Jesse's forehead.

It was only when he'd also sat down that he realized that the coverlet was also littered with playing cards; apparently a game interrupted before he'd arrived.

"J.K. said Otto can live with him." Sable suddenly leapt onto Ray's knees. "And I can visit him whenever I want. Isn't that great?"

"Great!" Ray looked for an adult agreement to this plan. "But maybe your Uncle Jesse would like Otto to visit him a little longer."

"Doesn't Otto make him sick?"

"Not anymore." Jesse stroked her hair. "If he does, Otto will go to J.K. Deal?"

"Deal," she agreed. She and Jesse performed some gestures with their hands that Ray guessed was a secret handshake Sable had learned and tried to teach him.

"What were you playing?" Ray asked.

"Go Fish!" they all yelled gleefully at him. The cat was so startled it jumped into Ray's lap, where he held it, finger-combing its back of knotted fur.

"Wanna play?" Sable asked, gathering the cards, which looked unusually large in her little hands. "J.K. cheats," she stage whispered.

"I do not cheat!" He was indignant. "At least," he clarified, "not at Go Fish!"

Otto seized the opportunity of J.K.'s umbrage to bat the sock ball out of his grasp and chase it off the bed, where Sable joined him, followed seconds later by J.K., who took advantage of being out of sight to once again tickle both girl and cat.

The phone rang, cutting through the din. Jesse picked it up, answered, and in a second handed it to Ray.

"*Cher*, it's me, Maurette. Listen, can you turn on your radio right now?" He gave the station call numbers.

"I'll take it downstairs. Hang up in a few minutes," Ray instructed Jesse.

Down in the office, the heat had not yet substantially gone on. He tuned the receiver to the music station, and a string quartet came through. Classical Viennese. He listened to it on the phone to make the music was the same on Maurette's end. Yes. A slow movement. Arioso. Violin playing solo while the other three strings accompanied. Almost a nocturne. "Sounds like Haydn."

"Not Mozart?" Maurette asked.

Ray knew the last ten Mozart quartets and a few of the earlier ones. He doubted it was Mozart. Nor the six recorded Dittersdorf, nor the four Pleyel string quartets.

"Haydn," he repeated. "Not one of the later, more famous pieces. Not an early one either. Middle period. Opus 54 or Opus 55. Even Opus 42. Beautiful."

"I'll say, and that's exactly what the radio announcer said after he'd played it," Maurette said, "He stopped the CD and played the movement again. So I phoned you."

Then the movement was over, and the performers sailed into a far more chromatic, less aleatory, more orchestral fast section.

"I'd bet money it's one of the three in Opus 54," Ray told Maurette. "I think I have the recording somewhere."

Cradling the phone receiver, he sat at his computer and brought up the program that listed all his music on tape, LPs, and CDs. Haydn's Opus 54 was on a '60s-era Julliard String Quartet LP and also on a tape he'd made to keep from overplaying and thus ruining the precious vinyl. He located the LP quickly within his storeroom shelves because of its vivid scarlet cover. It would be far easier to access the middle movement than on the reel to reel tape. The album's back cover had timings, showing the second quartet with a slow movement marked "Menuetto" lasting a little more than three minutes; less than half the length of the first quartet of the series's adagio or of the third quartet's largo. What he'd heard was short, therefore he felt this might be the piece Maurette had phoned about. He laid the LP on the platter of the burnished-steel Bang and Olufsen automatic turntable, switched the receiver input from radio to phono, and cued the tone arm to drop the needle onto the middle of the disc.

The Menuetto began with a two-measure-long, anthemlike subject, all four instruments playing in unison. The little theme repeated, only this time the first violin broke away from the other strings, a tritone higher, and busily ornamented the motif. The melody repeated again in a closely related, slightly different key, and this time the soloist varied it with trills, transforming the minuet from a miniature concerto into a soprano aria from some wordless chamber opera. The instruments returned to the theme yet again, slower, deeper, the solo violin lustrous with passion, ever more probing in its embellishment. It echoed bleakly, exposed against the three other, nearly muted strings: sounding abandoned as Ariadne, newly awakened, alone, loverless, undeluded, upon Naxos; bereft as Orpheus knowing he'd once more lost Eurydice, this time through his own doing; heartbroken as Dido watching Aeneas's ships sail into history. The theme iterated yet again, ascending higher and unbearably higher, almost more than one could take, before—as though realizing it could not possibly go on—it abruptly fell. It dithered, distracted, appogiatura. The other strings had all fallen away. The violin solo ceased several bars later, in a far key, nearly atonal, barely audible.

He had to ask, "Is that it?"

"Isn't it perfect for the end of the film?" Maurette said—it wasn't a real question. "The last few minutes, as the camera follows him out of the building and onto the street, black with rain? We take out the Sibelius waltz transposed for piano solo and insert this. What do you say?"

"When do you need it?"

"Now."

"Now?"

"Remember I told you Liesl was pulling strings with several of her old boyfriends to get the film to the Berlin Festival?"

"Heinz-Konrad and Jens?"

"She sent it to them. They got it to one of the selection committees, who said yes. Out of competition, of course, but on display! In the version we had at New Year's. It's almost a full edit, but with my Moviola mixes and only half the music." Maurette couldn't hide his excitement. "They want the finished film! Tomorrow! An international courier is already booked on Lufthansa flight 1006 for 8:30 A.M. He's carrying two other films. Heinz-Konrad said he'd carry mine too. I must hand this to him at the airport by 8. We must do it now, Ray. You must come now."

Ray pondered all the variables. Leaving Jesse here with Sable and J.K. and Chris, later, wasn't too bad. But Ray could end up being away an entire night. Away from Jesse. How many more nights together did they have?

"I'll make it up to you, Ray," Maurette began to plead. "My film needs this. I swear. I'll do any—"

"Let me check," Ray interrupted, "before you make any promises you can't keep. I'll see if I can get away." He left the phone and ran upstairs. The scene was a bit more sedate. They were all playing Go Fish, Otto rolling around on the bedspread under the ministrations of J.K.'s free hand. Jesse looked up from his cards: He already knew something was coming. Ray sat next to him and explained.

"That's great news." As always Jesse was pleased for him, encouraging this new career direction. "Go!"

"But I don't know when I'll be home," Ray whined.

"I can put together dinner," J.K. said. "I was going to invite myself anyway," he added sheepishly. "Mizz Sable can help."

"We'll order in," Jesse suggested. "Chinese. I can try some egg drop soup!"

"And I'll get Shrimp Lo Mein!" Sable cheered. "Yay!"

"So, you see, we really don't need you," Jesse added, a tiny smile on his lips.

"You are not indispensable," J.K. added casually.

"Yeah, Uncle Ray," Sable argued, "you're not indisexpensive."

"Well, fine then!" Ray pretended to be wounded. "See if I care. I'll order in my own egg drop soup and my own Shrimp Lo Mein and maybe even some Moo Goo Gai Pan too," he added, for Sable's amusement. She loved hearing Chinese. Even his.

But as he said it, his eyes thanked Jesse.

As Ray had predicted, it took all night. It was more than 16 hours before Maurette finished with the new music and the new details, and he eventually reedited about a quarter of the entire film. Ray had arrived at 5 P.M., cued in the new piece of music until about 9, eaten take-out, helped Maurette a while longer, and fell asleep around midnight on the oversize sofa in the open space adjoining the editing booths, using both of their heavy winter coats over him as a blanket. Now, as he awakened, opalescent daylight drifted through the 50-

foot-high skylight windows and Ray's watch read 6:30. As soon as he sat up, Maurette grabbed his coat and wrapped it around himself against the icy air. He forced a steaming mug of coffee into Ray's hands but continued to huddle around his own cup for warmth. Considering that he hadn't slept all night and had remained working on detailed visuals, Maurette looked amazingly fresh. Ray tried the coffee. As he might have guessed—after all, Maurette was Quebeçois—it was hot and strong.

"We'll clean up and leave right away," Maurette said, even his voice sounding frozen. "We should be at the airport by 7:30 to not miss him."

"If the car starts in this weather," Ray mumbled. And when Maurette looked alarmed, he added, "Don't worry. It usually does."

A new layer of precipitation had accumulated overnight, leaving a thin, rock-hard crust of dirty gray ice on the car, including the windshield and windows. When the plastic ice scrapers proved useless, Ray tossed the dregs of his tepid coffee at the windshield, which melted it. Before that too froze, he labored to scour out a dinner-plate-size section of transparent glass. Maurette's coffee, when tossed at the windshield, only provided a dessert-dish-size viewing screen, but from the Regal's front seat Ray declared it was enough for him to see through. The car heater and defrost vents warmed them, melting the ice enough to connect the viewing ports they'd chipped out.

Side streets were sleeted over and slow going but not far away, Queens Boulevard was already cleared and salted down for the A.M. rush hour. An ice storm arrived just as they were getting onto the cleaner tarmac of the still-uncrowded Van Wyck expressway. Still, they had made excellent time by the time they debouched onto the airport approach road. There, however, only two of three lanes had been cleared, and one of those was more or less impassable, depending upon whether it was filled with windblown snow, fresh sleet, crumbling ice from the third uncleared lane, or all three at once. Even so, they managed to arrive at the gull-wing TWA building, park the car less than a mile from the entrance and get in without more mishap than a bit of Chaplinesque slipping and sliding along the rampway.

Maurette's name was being paged as they arrived at the departure lounge area. As he took the call on the "white phone," Ray checked the telescreen listings of arrivals and departures and noticed that Lufthansa Flight 1006 was delayed an hour. Naturally, given the weather. Five minutes later they managed to connect with the film festival courier and were seated at a crowded, overheated, runway "café" at a series of enormous, mostly iced-over windows, allowing them to presuppose and intuit rather than actually view planes and ground crews coming and going, although what they could see seemed to be happening at a fairly glacial pace. They'd been there, wolfing down breakfast, before the carrier that would later take off as flight 1006 even docked to discharge passengers. The courier pointed out its arrival and, gazing at his watch, said, "It's 8:30 now. They'll be calling the flight at 9:15. It won't lift off until 10. It's a seven-and-a-half-hour flight—seven with tailwinds—but minus six hours for the time difference. So I ought to arrive at Tegel Airport by 2 o'clock and be at the Alte Opernhaus by 3:15 P.M. at the latest. Your film screens when? Six? No problem. Plenty of time!"

The festival courier, Georges Galati, was a long, tall, shambling man aged—Ray guessed—somewhere in his mid 60s. He'd made some reference to having retired early but hadn't said how early, nor why, nor from what line of work. Clearly, however, from his eating habits, his once fine, now worn-looking, slightly *deshabile* clothing, his knowledge of other tongues (he didn't hide his eavesdropping of a French and a German conversation in the café), and his sometimes impenetrable accent, Galati hadn't emigrated to the U.S. but was European born and bred. Equally evident, he still possessed important connections there, especially in Berlin, which allowed him to secure this not very difficult and, Ray supposed, fairly lucrative job hauling films across the ocean. When they'd asked where the other films were, Galati had shrugged, "In cargo somewhere." He went on to tell them that in the past he used to carefully watch to be certain that the films were loaded on planes. But often enough, once he'd moved away from his inspection, bags were sometimes removed from cargo holds, so why should he bother? No need to be anxious, however, as he would be hand-delivering Maurette's film, six big reels divided into a shoulder bag and a hand-held satchel. "Errr-go, if I arrive at Tegel," he said in his most viscous accent, "so does your film."

Galati held his sugar cubes between his teeth Russian style while he sipped his coffee through it. He chain smoked madly, even while eating. His eyes wandered far from their faces, checking out passengers coming and going behind their heads, even while speaking to them sincerely and swearing some truth. Even to Ray, who'd been around a little, Galati seemed oversophisticated, perhaps terminally *ennui*. He seemed to accept as something he could disdain but not do anything about, the fact that Maurette would doubtless not let him—or more accurately, not let the film cans—out of his sight for a second until he'd witnessed them go securely on board the jet.

If Maurette's anxiety amused Galati, he showed it no differently than he displayed any other emotion—which is to say, not very much. His long, puffy, distinctly purplish lower lip might tremble ever so slightly for him to register laughter, but it was only the simultaneous quivering of his densely cartilaged, vein-riddled, all but forested with gray hair nostrils that actually confirmed that he was amused. Galati's extra-long, unclipped gray-brown eyebrows seemed to only operate up and down, and always in unison. His eyes, on the other hand— colored a green so pale it was gray, so pale gray it was the color of dried kinder-garten paste, as though they'd been dyed in his youth but had long since run in the wash—hovered up and down, rolled to the sides, nearly revolved in circles; as a rule, if not always, together, as though some other, far less phlegmatic soul had become trapped within Galati's leonine head, and without his approval was frantically signaling distress. His voice, from mid baritone to deep bass, with an occasional squeak mediating between the two ranges, was probably incompre-hensible whenever he had the slightest head cold, yet was otherwise distinctive, even magisterial.

"A score of filmmakers have I now come to meet because of this"—he all but dismissed his employment—"express avocation!" Galati droned, inhaling his cigarette as though it were the final puff before his execution by firing squad. "Most of them young. Original. Daring. Like yourselves." His head bobbed and his face moved forward a bit to concentrate his intent focus first upon Maurette, then Ray, an effect all but negated by his nearly colorless, flib-bertigibbet eyeballs that pitched in their sockets like paper sailboats in a rain-storm. "And to all of them I have offered one particular story for film." He paused for another drag. "A very good story. And a true one," he allowed, as the smoke seeped from his mouth in several streams at once, giving him the appearance of a careless, incontinent dragon. "And yet," he inhaled as though attempting to swallow all the room's air, "I will tell it to you," he managed to utter, almost strangling on his words, "Tell it one…more…time…" He caught his breath and quickly reiterated. "This, naturally, is true!"

With an introduction like that, it could only be an absurd tale. Yet Ray lis-tened, and after a few minutes, he saw that Maurette, who not seconds ago had begun to nod off with exhaustion, also listened, reawakened, with equal inter-est. Galati further prefaced the tale by saying he could never reveal who had first narrated the incident, only that it had been told to him not long after World War II, and that his narrator had been a participant in the circumstances. He continued to back up his tale by saying he'd also heard it told by others, most-ly old timers, attached to miscellaneous diplomatic corps in various MittelEuropa capitals. Nor would he give the name of the Greek island upon which it had befallen, only that it was a very small one off the Turkish Coast, unimportant really, except in time of war, and then only because it lay directly within a nexus of several much used Aegean-Mediterranean shipping lanes.

The latter was also why the German *Luftwaffe* invaded and then for almost five years held this particular island, Galati told them, instead of the Italian Fascisti infantry who occupied neighboring isles and indeed most of the Aegean during the war. Corrupt, venal, and as casually brutal as the Black Shirts could be, he assured them, they were merely haphazardly violent children compared to the far more premeditated barbarism of the *Wehrmacht*. Which explained why this incident happened on that island and no other.

It was also important to understand that a very old shrine to the Virgin Mary, allegedly housing a miraculous relic, lay in one of the island's three small villages. An archaeologist acquaintance of Galati's had visited, inspecting this site for weeks, concluding that the little chapel was probably one of the first anywhere ever dedicated to the Madonna. It had been erected as a Christian basilica sometime in the fifth century, she thought, atop the site of a Bronze Age temple to Artemis, whose own place of origin was supposedly not far off. Since then, of course, the shrine had endured the depredations of time, the barbarities of war, the enthusiasms of nationalist and religious fervor, not to mention the usual, predictable abuses of architectural fashion. Despite all that, every year during the Feast of the Assumption, the islanders converged in religious celebration upon this smallest hamlet, which was followed by festivities in the *plaka*, including music, dancing, and suitable *tableaux vivants*. As might be assumed, these latter expatiated upon the life of the Virgin, according to Scripture, enacted with local talent, and—crucially—with a young virgin island woman of impeccable repute executing the eponymous role. Again, Galati's scholarly acquaintance had hypothesized that these elements of medieval passion play were merely a perpetuation of far more archaic pieces performed, scenes from the life of the Greek deity in her multiple roles as moon goddess, hunter, and paragon of chastity. But almost immediately after the forces of the Third Reich arrived, the continuance of this ages-old practice was threatened.

The German air force was considered, and considered itself, the elite, the *ne plus ultra* of the Teutonic fighting machine. *Luftwaffe* officers were, as a rule, younger and more cultivated than those in the other armed services. Also better paid and more spoiled. Wherever they encamped, they demanded the finest food, the finest wine, the finest products of civilization; above all they demanded the finest women. While some of the former requirements could be imported, the latter especially were drawn directly from the occupied area. And it would have been no different on this island, save for the fact that if the German air force took all the youngest and most beautiful young women to be their consorts and mistresses, who then would be found to enact the Virgin, come August 15th?

Tradition stipulated that the girl had to be island born and bred. A score of island families had for generations labored in their conjugal beds to maintain an ample supply of candidates. Should the sacred rites be desecrated by any but the most beautiful, island-born virginal girl, seers and prophetesses prognosticated earthquakes, tidal waves, month-long eclipses, drought, famine, untold miseries. What were they to do? Already, the most eligible young women of the island, aged 14 to 18, had been levered by force, threat, or diplomacy out of their parents homes and swept off to live (all well, some like queens) in the air force officers' quarters. And yet another detachment of young Teutonic officers were on their way, due to make landfall in less than a week, with a dozen more mistresses requisitioned. It didn't require a Euclid to determine that the last virgins of all three villages—a mere handful, most of them only 13—would be required to satsify the insatiable lust of those ruffians, and when they had been deflowered, no Virgin-Artemis for years to come would be available to officiate at the Assumption rites. A solution must be found.

Under the guise of holding a funeral supper for an elderly pensioner, a crisis meeting was called. The island's elders, the most important families, and all three priests, their sextons and deacons, gathered under one roof to ponder the dilemma.

Resisting the Germans' demand was futile; and if atrocity tales they'd heard from other less fortunate places were to be believed, probably suicidal. Besides which, the island had never prospered so much as it had since the German air force had set up Aegean headquarters on its shores. Yet when one island spokesman who maintained accommodating terms with the occupiers had jokingly complained to the *Luftwaffe* commandant of the problem, hinting that there might not be enough young girls to go around, he had been waved off with bantering words. The officers would arrive in a few days, he was assured, and they must soon after obtain "household satisfaction." Otherwise he, their leader, couldn't be held responsible for their inability to restrain their natural urge for rapine and plunder. He added that he didn't care how the islanders did it.

Upon hearing this, one merchant of debatable sexual tastes had shouted, "I would sooner wife the monsters myself than allow my poor daughter to do so!" He was almost laughed out of the meeting. But no sooner had he spoken than one of the clerics himself offered to take on the burden. Whereupon the idea, mocked a few minutes before at its introduction, was now reintroduced, yet with a single crucial alteration. It rested upon one of their unspoken leaders, a fishing boat manufacturer of great affluence and influence, to speak aloud what several of them were thinking: "We cannot give them our daughters," he declared, "but we also have sons." Silence greeted this. A net weaver quietly said that his son, like all of the island's youth over the age of 16, had within days of the Germans' arrival fled the island to hide on other shores and help form a resistance army. "That still leaves the boys under 16," the manufacturer replied, implacably. "Every other day, my own boy Mikos assures us that he wishes he were old enough to do his homeland a service as do his elder brothers." Everyone held their breath, for hadn't he just implied he would willingly offer his thirdborn son in sacrifice to the Germans? "As do our patriotic altar boys," the local patriarch spoke up, "also profess their desire to serve their homeland." Soon, one by one, everyone with son, nephew, cousin or servant had made a similar offer.

Before they could take back their words, a vote was held: A dozen boys would be found, the comeliest in the island. They would be dressed like maidens and sent to welcome the new assignment of *Wehrmacht* officers. No one present asked what would happen if the boys refused. They could not refuse; therefore they would not refuse. One of the company, however, the priest of the Assumption shrine himself, did quaveringly wonder in the smallest possible voice what would befall them all should the officers rebuff the boys. They agreed the boys must not only be the most attractive as well as the most obedient. They must also have drummed into their pliable minds that the welfare of the entire populace rested upon their adolescent shoulders.

The decision was made and the boys selected. As their parents had assured one another, the lads trembled at the news, but agreed to the ruse. Soon enough those among the chosen who had no or little carnal experience were exposed to it until they were deemed to be at least exposed if not yet inured to their duty. The night before, as their weeping mothers, aunts, and grateful sisters sewed and wove them the loveliest and finest garments, some of the boys doubted their course, fell on their knees to pray, and displayed a natural hesitation about such an uncertain venture. The next afternoon, however, the boys were clear-eyed and red-lipped, tearless, gracious, soft-spoken and demure, as in their female finery they were introduced to the new arrivals at the well-prepared welcoming banquet. "Oh, ho!" the commandant taunted the island's liaison. "As I thought, you have held back the most beautiful for last. Perhaps," he said, pulling the boat manufacturer's boy onto his ample, green twill lap, "I shall trade in my Mara for this young Miki." Several other high-ranking officers did likewise, and by sunset all of the boys went off arm in arm with German officers.

Their families rushed to the nearest chapel and fell into fervent prayer. They remained praying all night, some until morning. When they dispersed at dawn to go about their usual business, it was with heavy hearts and much trepidation. All day they waited, and little by little it became apparent that there would be no repercussions, that the sacrifice had been accepted, and that island life might continue as it had for months. Soon enough the new island lads were ensconced in officer's quarters. They were seen in public attending string quartet and piano recitals the Germans adored, often dressed, like their sisters, in expensive outfits from Paris, gowns by Balmain and Worth, jewels by Jannequot and Fabergé flown out especially for them. The months went by, then the years, and as the boys reached an age where beards began to grow, they would leave their officer, vanish entirely off the island. But not before first replacing themselves with a younger brother or cousin, who in turn soon was seen listening to Brahms Scherzi and Reger Duo sonatas from behind jeweled fans, with triple strands of matched pearls dripping upon their necks, Chanel's latest fragrance wafting about their bared shoulders, upon which fine lace mantillas were placed by their uniformed German *lieblings*.

Thus the island subsided back into its immemorial seasonal practices; the otherwise occupied invaders hardly ever crossing the paths of those who had been invaded. Among the latter, however, the annual Feast of the Assumption continued to be the most favored and most brilliantly celebrated event, with one fair lass after another ascending the little throne in her sky-blue cape and azure head scarf to impersonate for her brief but glorious six hours the Mother of a Lord who seemed to have looked down with uninterrupted grace upon the fair island and its astute people.

It was only several years later, once word of the retreat of the German forces had been rumored for several weeks, that the *Luftwaffe* commandant and his highest henchmen called the town elders to a meeting. There, as courteously as ever, he thanked the island people for their hospitality, and especially for the loan of their progeny to make their difficult separation from the Fatherland more bearable. They would be leaving now, he told them, returning home to uncertain times. Yet within their minds and hearts they would always retain a great affection for the islanders, and especially for the refinements of this ages-old Greek civilization, surely a people even more cultivated than even their own—indeed possibly the most civilized in the world. Had the officers not noticed the girls were boys? Clearly they had. Some officers had vied for them. Others had not been at all interested. With the expected embarrassments and hesitations, each aging youth who'd been questioned by islanders had made all that clear enough. Baffled, yet relieved, the islanders thanked the Germans for their civility.

Hours after the meeting, the Germans noisily left en masse via the air, naturally leaving all inessentials behind. Among the booty that remained were troves of French champagne, Caspian caviar, fine musical instruments, books, recordings, enough art and craftworks to begin a museum. The loot was divided, carried home by those who had earned it, young women and young men, still clad in their finest haute couture.

A year to the day after the European war had ended, the mayor of the island's largest town called a remembrance gala to be held for the deliverance of the population. Everyone was invited. All the males still alive who had been *Wehrmacht* concubines attended, some by then 21, 22; several now much decorated Greek Army soldiers. No one ever knew if they had agreed upon it in advance or whether it simply seemed the natural thing to do. But each man came dressed in and wore with pride the most expensive tea dress or yacht outfit or evening gown he had been asked to wear by the invaders, his most brilliant emerald necklace or cockatoo tiara, even those men who had come with their wives or fiancées, and even though many had outgrown the finery. For decades afterward the island continued to celebrate their liberation and to honor their saviors. The men eventually grew old and fat, or bony and white-haired, first fathers then grandfathers.

"And to this time, upon that very day, they hold the liberation feast, and the men don what has not in the meantime shredded or fallen into tatters, what they have not given away as a dowry or wedding gift to their own wives and daughters and nieces. They can seen there every year, playing *boccie* or waltzing or simply cackling with laughter over a bottle of *retsina*, sporting a pair of pearl earrings, or an opal brooch, or an aged and yellowed Bruges lace handkerchief pinned to the few hairs left upon their balding heads. And everywhere they go that day in their remnants of apparel," Galati said, "young men stand aside and bow to them, and everyone, young and old alike, applaud."

The courier had no sooner finished his story than his flight was called. He finished his coffee and sauntered off, accompanied by them as far as possible, watched all the way.

An hour later, driving on the Belt Parkway, as they were nearing the

Battery Tunnel approach into Manhattan, Ray said to Maurette, "Do you think he was one of those boys? Galati? And *that's* why he continues to tell the story? And *that's* why he so much wants it made into a film?"

But Maurette was asleep at last, his mouth open, his head against the car window. And with all that would happen, Ray never would remember to ask him again.

fifteen

"Whoa! Wait a minute!" Mike suddenly withdrew from his enthusiastic sexual onslaught. He leaned back, teetering on the edge of the mattress. Before almost falling off backward, he caught himself and managed to stand. His briefs dangled below his knees. His T-shirt was lifted and furled, twisted almost off him, held only at the neck. His face was flushed, his lips mottled and swollen with desire. "Time!" he announced, forming a T with his hands, like the quarterback in an NFL game.

Ray, as undressed as him, flat on his back atop the downstairs bed, looked up in surprise. These days whenever they got together, it was Mike who was the aggressor, dragging him into the bedroom, impelling him into bed, tearing his clothing off, using his hands and teeth to unceasingly nibble and suck at Ray. A bit of a turn-around from their earlier days. But not unwelcome. Ray wasn't complaining.

"Whoa, yourself," Ray said. "You're the one who jumped me."

"Yeah." A little laugh at his own audacity. "I remember."

"So what's wrong?"

"Nothing's wrong." Mike pulled off the undershirt altogether, his torso looking as completely edible as usual whenever it had been uncovered. "Except I think we ought to be a little more careful getting undressed." He dropped his undershirt over his neck and dropped it onto the dresser. Reached down and untangled his briefs, and all but folded them before setting them neatly next to the shirt. He stood naked a second, half leaning forward on one foot, and Ray was reminded of a painting he'd seen years ago in an out-of-the-way museum in a second-tier New England city. It had been a small oil, no taller than two feet and less than half that width, all yellow and gold, ochre and beige, the opulent earth-tone palette deluding him into believing at first that it was Venetian or Flemish, an old master's bagatelle he'd not seen before. The nude, facing forward, had held this very pose, the young man's flood of honeyed curls flecked with pale greens and blues; his pale, golden physique as youthful as Mike's, the flesh almost translucent within its Impressionistic haze of Goya whites and Manet scarlets over Degas grays and tans. The model's tentative attitude, as though he'd just that minute arisen from lovemaking, his implicit motion, his lips thickly parted not as though he were about to speak but as though he were about to lick off them a momentarily recollected flavor, all rendered him so immediate, so alluring, Ray had found himself immobilized before the painting. He'd been astonished when he'd checked the wall plaque to discover it had not been painted centuries ago, but only a hundred years earlier, at the end of the 19th century, painted by—of all people—that elite debutante darling, John Singer Sargent. Could he have been queer? Wouldn't he have had to be gay—or, at least, to have harbored homosexual desire at one time?—to paint that little oil?

"OK! Now I know where everything is," Mike said out loud, rending the illusion that had tied him to a memory. Satisfied, he suddenly surged forward on top of Ray, who was still attempting to get out from under his tangle of clothing and limbs.

"Why do you need to know that?" Ray asked.

"Tell you later," Mike said, blasé. Then, "Come on, guy! Get those pants off! I want what you got in there!" He snarled and bit at Ray until resistance was impossible, and shortly afterward he gave up altogether. Ray's underclothing was manipulated off him, tossed all over the bed, quickly ending up on the carpet.

Twenty minutes later they were stretched out on the bed side by side, untouching, loudly inhaling and exhaling, otherwise no longer moving, their bodies glittering with a silver luminescence of sweat. Ray was again pleased and surprised by the ardency, the unceasing fervor of their physical need for each other, even after, what was it now? Fifteen times? Sixteen? He was all the more amazed because they had fallen into a pattern consistent since that time months ago when Mike had taken him into his mouth. Their sex was virtually identical every time: Mike would undress and blow him a while; he'd blow Mike a while, turn him over, rim him a while, fuck him till he came, turn him over again and blow Mike till he came. Yet there was no mitigation of excitement, no possibility of monotony; each time seemed like the first. Every time he laid eyes on Mike, even if he were outside on the street, simply stepping out of the van, say, or leaning over it, wiping the side windows, Ray was instantly hard for him. And every time Mike got inside the building, he couldn't keep his hands off Ray.

"What was all that about your underwear?" Ray asked.

Mike laughed. He rolled over on his stomach, once more exposing his pert, thickly muscled buttocks, clenching and unclenching them as though he were doing exercises. He laughed again.

"Remember the last time I was here?" His pale green eyes seemed darker today, as though they'd entered a new region, from olive to Russian green, or as though the brightness of the winter day beaming into the room through unshut blinds was a volatile liquid, tinting Mike's irises shades deeper.

Ray said he remembered the last time.

"We were…you know, sort of wild at first? Threw our clothes anywhere?" Mike laughed, unable to keep the joke to himself. "Then I left? As usual, in a hurry?"

"I'm with you so far."

"So three days later, out of the blue, my wife says to me 'Where did you get the fancy underpants?' I ask what she's talking about. She goes to the pile of laundry she's done the day before and picks up this pair of briefs on top of the pile. Holds it up for me. On the waistband I read, 'Calvin Klein.' " Mike laughed again, rolled on the bed, so the two of them were head to head now. "She buys my underwear for me. She washes it and dries it. She irons it. She knows better than I do what brand I wear: Jockey. Fruit of the Loom."

"Oh…shit! What did you say?"

"I knew it was yours," Mike said, unable to stop smirking. "When you get as close to a crotch as I do, even if you're not reading the label, you're bound to notice, right?" He laughs out loud. "So I told her this bullshit story. Told her that I'd gotten soaked on a job and came back wet and my boss told me to change. Said I had no briefs in my locker so he gave me a pair he had wrapped in plastic."

"What did she say to that?"

"Well, she didn't have too hard a time believing they were my boss's underpants, even though you've got to understand, he is sort of a slob, and anything but fashion conscious. She must have thought his wife bought 'em. But she asks 'Should you return them to him now that you've worn them?' And I say, 'What are you, kidding?' So then she wants to know if she should go buy him a pair next time she's out shopping.' I tell her, no, don't bother, I'm sure he's got 20 of 'em. He won't miss one pair.'" Mike looked up at Ray's face. "Jeez, you make me hot! I got to get back to work now and all I can think about is fucking again."

"Let's go." Ray reached for his rear end.

"Forget it." Mike slapped his hand off and sat up on his heels atop the bed.

"So that was it?" Ray said. "Crisis over?"

"So I thought. A few days later we're doing something in the garage, and again, out of the blue she tells me she mentioned the underwear to her mother, right? I'm thinking, holy shit: My wife she really don't know anything about life, but her mother...well, she's home all day doing nothing but watching these daytime TV shows, *Oprah* and *Sally* and whatever. Who knows what she knows? I'm wondering what's coming next." Mike's eyes darkened almost to black with suspense. "You know what my wife says to me? She asks what I think her mother told her?"

Ray played along. "What did her mother tell her?"

Mike laughed, diffusing the suspense ahead of time. "Her mother told my wife that Calvin Klein underwear costs 10 dollars a pair. And if my boss can spend $200 on underwear, she told my wife, he's got money to burn and he ought to give me a raise." Mike rolled the other way laughing harder. "So now they're both after me."

"I usually get them for $7.95," Ray said. "At Bloomingdale's!"

Mike burst out with a fresh peal of laughter. Catching his breath, he finally managed to stammer, "That's all I would have to do! Come home with a bag from Bloomingdale's...." He couldn't stop laughing. "Why not a bag from Tiffany's?" He was on his back again, rolling from side to side on the bed. "They'll make him give me the whole damn company!"

"At any rate," he finally managed to stop laughing long enough to get off the bed and stand up, "I think it's maybe not a good idea to mix up our underwear anymore." So saying, he reached for his briefs folded on the dresser top.

"So you don't think she has any idea about us?" Ray asked. "Your wife?"

"If they were pink silk panties with lace edging I was wearing, she might have a few questions," Mike laughed, with a shrug. Then he thought about what he just said. "I don't mean if I was wearing the pink silk panties." He laughed again, this time enjoying his joke. "Or maybe I did mean that," he said, and laughed so hard at the idea that he almost fell onto the bed again. "Otherwise...otherwise..." he tried again, and finally, "You have no idea how," with another laugh, as he drew his undershirt over his head and smoothed it over his abdomen, "I don't even know what word to use. Suburban? Provincial? Whatever the word is, you have no idea how 'whatever' my wife is. They all are! She, her mother, her sister, her dad. They're great people. Salt of the earth." He began laughing again and caught himself. "I mean if I told them I knew the guy who actually used to record Johnny Mathis and Carly Simon and all, they wouldn't believe a word of it." Next, Mike stepped into and pulled up his heavy forest-green work pants. Buttoning them, he sighed. "I don't know. Sometimes I don't believe any of this." Gazing around the bedroom, he said, "You know, I'll be watching a football game with my dad and brother-in-law at home on a Sunday afternoon, and we're all yelling and eating and hitting on each other with pillows, and I sometimes think, is this real? And sometimes I'm here with you, in this bedroom, doing what we do, and I wonder, is this real? Which one is it? You know what I'm talking about?"

"A little. Are you afraid what they might say if they found out about me?"

"Not really. 'Cause they never will," Mike pronounced confidently, fitting himself into the sleeves of his matching dark green work shirt and pulling it over his back. "Because I'll never tell 'em," he concluded. "No offense." He smiled, a slightly rueful, almost lopsided smile, then went into the bathroom.

Ray said aloud to himself, "Well, stupid. You had to ask, didn't you?"

The room had become chilly, as though Mike were responsible for most of the heat generated, which might have actually been the case. Ray got out of bed and began to get dressed. When Mike came out of the john all buttoned up, his face washed, his hair looking a bit brushed, he came and stood next to the chair next where Ray shifted, pulling on socks.

"Don't you ever miss it? Working with those famous singers?"

"Sometimes," Ray admitted. "I'm doing something interesting now. I'm working in film, finding music, getting it on the soundtrack. This is the first one, but..."

"Tell me something about one of the people you worked with," Mike said, immediately qualifying it, "Someone I might know."

Ray finished dressing by slipping into a pair of docker shoes. He drew Mike down to perch on the mattress and began telling him about a well-known woman vocalist, now a bona fide star, whose name and popular songs Mike had, it turned out, heard on the radio and on beer-garden jukes. Years before, when she was just beginning to break out in the business, she'd come into the studio. Ray was working in another department of the company, but he was intently interested in getting into the artists and repertoire division. An older fellow from that group had taken a liking to Ray and was letting him sit on a few recording sessions. Ray had been in the mixing booth while this guy Tommy mixed the session. That was how he was supposed to learn to do it himself, by watching. That was cool with him. So after he was supposed to go home at 5 o'clock from his white collar marketing job, he'd usually stay another hour or two more with Tommy in the studio, learning what everything on the mixing board and in the mixing room was. Why not? Ray had no one waiting for him at home. He could eat out any time he wanted to. As the weeks went by that spring, he told Mike, Ray remained in the studio after work more and more. Then one night they were in there with this particular young vocalist. She had already recorded a single, one side of which was climbing the charts. She needed to record ten more to make an album—her first. She and his A&R pal didn't get along well. Tommy was phlegmatic, a sort of "let's just do it" guy, while she was high strung and artistic, verging on hysterical. Ray already knew the two didn't work together well. Tommy didn't think much of her voice. He'd told Ray she was a "one-hit wonder," but he'd also admitted that their chemistry was way off. She was too brash for him, Tommy said, too demanding, complained too much, put herself down, swore like a sailor.

On this one night, Ray experienced the two of them in conflict. She was even more tense and nervous than usual and Tommy was even more annoyed than usual, which meant of course that he would die before he showed it. As a result of how unflappable he was, the vocalist kept making mistakes, doing retake after retake, which caused her to be even more tense and nervous, which only made Tommy even colder.

After two hours of shuttlecock between them, Tommy called time, a dinner break, and took off. The vocalist's whole body slumped. She all but fell out of the recording booth and collapsed into the little lounge serving as a general area for the half dozen studios, took out of her oversize purse what looked like a tuna sandwich and a bottle of fruit juice. She was completely disheartened, utterly depressed. When Ray passed back through the lounge from the john, she glanced up, and having seen him in the mixing booth for hours yet not spoken to him, she said, "I'm pretty awful, aren't I?"

Ray didn't believe that. Unlike Tommy, he liked her voice and thought she had much more potential. "Come on. You know you're good," he'd told her.

She insisted she was awful. She didn't think Ray's pal was very friendly; she was sure what he thought of her voice. But what could she do? Tommy had been assigned to her. He was supposed to be the best control mix man at the company. Her agent and all the company bigwigs had chosen him for her because he was known as a "starmaker." She was wasting all this time, and the studio rental was costing how many thousands of dollars of the company's money, and she would have nothing to show for it. She was almost in tears.

Ray had an idea, something that had nagged at him during the hours he'd spent earlier in the mixing booth. Knowing she was temperamental, he was wary of asking and having her blow up at him. But at last he got up his nerve and questioned why she began the chorus after the break following the second verse in the same key, when it ascended too high for her voice by the end of the song?

She told him she did it because it was written that way. He went into the mixing booth and checked the score and brought it out, and together they looked it over. Just as he had thought, and as she was amazed to see, the score read "ad libitum" at the chorus. Meaning it was her choice what key to sing it in. Thoroughly confused, she asked him what key she ought to sing it in.

Ray told her, and he hummed the chorus for her, giving her some idea of how it would work. She joined him, and together they hummed it to the end.

"I can hit all those notes perfectly!" she said. And she tried it again, in full voice, right there, a cappella, in the lounge. It sounded great to both of them. Dropping her sandwich, the vocalist rushed into the booth, placed her headphones back on, and shouted to Ray to play the already recorded instrumental tracks and they'd would tape it this way—"ad libitium."

Still excited that she'd taken his suggestion, Ray fled into the mixing room, hit the button for a fresh tape mix, replayed the laid-down tracks, and listened as she sang the entire song—with the chorus in the lower key. She ended by sailing beautifully up to the C-sharp at the end. After which she laughed, she yelled in triumph, she did a little dance. She asked to do it one more time; she thought she could do it even better. Ray agreed, and they recorded the song again and when they played it back she was right, it was even better. They were replaying it from the tape matrix when Tommy returned from dinner and he heard the song. Before Ray could explain what had happened, Tommy asked, "What'd you do to get her to sound like that? Fuck her?" Ray apologized again, saying he knew it was wrong. But no, Tommy wanted Ray to remain at the mixing table while the vocalist tried out another song. She and Ray ended up discussing that one too, in detail before, during, and after every vocal line they taped. To his surprise, Ray knew enough about music, about the recording process, about the mixing board, and, he discovered, also about the vocalist's range and her abilities and weaknesses, that Tommy left him alone in the booth and went to nap in the little lounge, while together Ray and the vocalist laid down another. They were in the studio until after midnight.

The next morning at work, Ray told Mike, he came in about a half hour late, having gotten home after 1 A.M. and having overslept, only to find a memo on his desk to see his boss. He was nervous. He'd never been late before. He might even have to explain why he'd been late, and he wasn't sure his boss would approve. But it turned out that Ray's boss hadn't even noticed what time he'd come in. However, he had gotten a memo himself, so Ray was sent upstairs to the artist development office. There, a big *macher*, a middle-aged fellow with a frizzed Afro out to here, sporting more gold chains on his chest than the pope had incense, took one look at Ray, and said, "Man, you have gotta lose the necktie if you're going to be in artists and repertoire. Lose the button-down suit too, or you'll give the talent the willies. In fact, you should loosen up your act altogether, man!" When Ray asked what was going on, the big *macher* told him, "You've been transferred here. The broad"—naming the vocalist from the night before—"is telling us she'll only record with you." He went on tell Ray that he was assigned to record her entire new LP, from which the company expected at least one more hit single. Ray would also receive demos from a half dozen other potential artists the company was somewhat interested in. He would have to build his own roster out of them and any other talent he might find in other venues. He didn't think they'd give a newcomer like himself established talents, did he, the big *macher* demanded.

"And that," Ray told Mike, "is how it all started. I did two more albums with her. We got a half dozen Grammy nominations and won one. She recommended me to other artists, and my career was rolling. I did stop wearing suits and ties, but I never put my hair in an Afro or wore gold chains around my neck."

"Jeez," Mike said, stars all but pinwheeling in his unbelievable green eyes. "If you hadn't already just fucked me, after hearing that, I would have let you do me."

"Sure you don't have time to fool around a little more?" Ray asked. But while Mike admitted that he was really tempted, in fact, went for Ray's crotch with both hands, he also said how late it was. He had to go.

As had become his habit, after Mike left, Ray showered. Then, as he did ten times a day, he went upstairs to check on Jesse, who was still bedridden, exhausted.

Not seeing Jesse in bed but noticing the sheets and cover furled off to one side as though he'd gotten out of bed, Ray assumed Jesse had gone to the bathroom, and took advantage of that to get a snack for himself and to check phone messages. Picking at the plastic packet of sliced turkey, he listened for noises from the lavatory but couldn't make out any. He finally decided he was hungry enough to make himself a sandwich, which he ate standing at the counter, swigging down tonic water to help swallow, ending up gargling with the water so that odor-sensitive Jesse would have no reason to be nauseated. Jesse still wasn't in bed. Ray checked the bathroom. Also empty.

Ray called Jesse's name. As he reached the other side of the bed, he panicked. Jesse's body was twisted around, his feet all but bound together by the winding sheet, held in place halfway down one side of the bed, off the floor. The rest of his pajama-clad body was contorted, caught in a snarl of sheets and blankets, one arm stretched out, fingertips just brushing the wallpaper. The other arm and Jesse's head were skewed beneath him, out of sight.

At first he thought Jesse had fallen and hit his head on something. Once Ray had freed his limbs from the meshes of bedding and lifted him onto the bed, Jesse was conscious. He had not hit his head, had not been knocked out. He was conscious, but even through the slightly humid cotton, Ray felt that his skin was blazing hot, uncooled despite his runnels of perspiration. His face and neck were equally searing, and both were a color Ray had never seen on a person, a necrotic gray, the same shade deli meat became after it had spoiled. He was conscious enough, however, that he was trying to say something.

"What is it? Kiddo?" Ray held his ear to Jesse's burning lips. "What?"

He flinched in Ray's grasp, almost as though he'd been electrically shocked. "Hhhhurts…so…much."

The words sliced Ray's heart, reinducing fear, panic. "What hurts? Where?"

"Bbbbback! Chhhhest! Swwwords! Nnnneeedles!"

He flinched again, all but leaping within Ray's arms, convulsing so hard he began sliding out from under Ray's grip. "Hhhhurts so much, Ray!"

He lowered Jesse onto the coverlet, dashed into the bathroom for a thermometer. Even before he'd gotten it wedged between Jesse's lips, he knew what he had to do. Stripping off the pajamas, he felt the incredibly hot skin everywhere on Jesse's body. Cold water bath. He had to call J.K., who'd dealt with the ill before. He must know more about this. But first the bath.

"Hhhhurts, Ray. Hhhhurts!"

Having found his voice, Jesse went on, letting the thermometer fall out of his mouth. The few seconds it had been in his mouth had been enough to get it to register over 104 degrees.

"You're running a high fever, kiddo. We've gotta bring it down." Ray pulled Jesse's now mostly unclothed body up into a standing position. He half carried, half walked him into the bathroom. Shower or bath? Shower or bath? He didn't know for sure, but opted for the shower, and managed to get Jesse inside, and get the cold water turned on over him. Yes, shower, he could keep the door ajar, keep holding Jesse up with the other arm, leaning him into the shower's corner for support. At first Jesse didn't seem to notice the water, the coldness, anything. He was so out of it, half slumped against the tiles, held in place only by Ray's arms. As the water struck Jesse's skin, it began to steam. Was that right? Ray wondered, still holding Jesse in place while he pulled off his own sweatshirt and managed to get his pants off, something of a juggling act.

A few minutes had passed, and the cold water seemed to be working. Jesse was still occasionally flinching, but not so badly, and when Ray clasped him with both arms, his skin was no longer hot and dry but wet and clammy. Jesse had begun speaking again, but it was now gibberish, Ray couldn't make out if he was still complaining of the swords-and-needles pain, but he didn't think so. Ray continued to hold him under the cold spray until Jesse's body began to shudder. No! Couldn't have him chilled.

He manipulated Jesse out of the shower onto the bathroom floor where Jesse immediately began shivering. It started in his legs, ascended to his hips, chest, arms, head, until he was shivering from head to toe. Ray wrapped him around and around in bath towels, but he continued to shudder. Ray half walked, half dragged him out of the bath and into the bedroom, where he gently moved him onto the mattress, athwart the bed, removing the wet towels, replacing them with blankets. Even so, Jesse was shivering so hard now that Ray could hear his teeth chattering, perhaps even his bones knocking against each other. Ray edged himself on top of Jesse, embracing him with his arms and legs, trying to warm him with body heat, murmuring words, trying to warm and comfort him.

After what seemed a long time, Jesse stopped shivering. But a minute later

Jesse was warm, then hot, then sweating. He began flinching again, as though he were trying to jump out of his skin. Ray had to unwrap the blankets, fan him, try to cool him off with ice cubes twisted in a dishtowel on his forehead. When that no longer seemed to work, when Jesse began to moan and convulse again, Ray started the routine all over again, the icy shower, the towels, the chattering and shivering, then back to bed for a warm-up, achieving that for a short while, before the fever started again and Jesse had to be cooled off, then iced up again. Ray did it two times before he realized he was no longer certain what he was doing. He left Jesse in bed, towels and blankets off, ice on his temples, moving just long enough and far enough away, never to lose contact with his body, but to reach the bedroom phone and call J.K.

J.K. heard the panic in Ray's voice, and said, "I'll get a taxi and be right there."

"What the hell is going on, J.K.? What's wrong with him?"

"Sounds like pneumonia. Keep doing what you were doing. I'm leaving now."

"Pneumonia? It's as bad as I thought. Shouldn't I call an ambulance?"

"They'll take hours. Forget it. When I get there and ring, you have him dressed for outside. We'll use the same cab and take him ourselves. Get your medical cards ready."

"Am I doing right here?" Ray asked. "I'm so afraid I'm not doing the right thing," he repeated, but J.K. had already hung up.

He hadn't let go of Jesse for an instant. Now Jesse was tearing at his skin as though it were blankets he was trying to get off his body. Ray put a stop to that, pulled him up, lifted and carried him back into the shower for the ice water treatment.

Semiconscious, Jesse slumped instantly, and Ray had to remain inside the shower with him to hold him up. The two of them were freezing cold when Jesse began shivering again. Ray maneuvered them out, wrapped them both together in towels, calculating he had maybe 20 minutes more before J.K. arrived.

Three more cycles of fever and chills, it turned out. By the time Ray had gotten himself dressed for the street, and Jesse more or less back into his pajamas, with a terry robe around him, and socks on and moosehide slippers on his feet, Jesse was still only semiconscious. He was babbling incoherently, reaching out with his hands at someone or something—who knew. He was seeing right past Ray, clearly hallucinating. They were half on the bed, half on the floor. Ray, who hadn't let go of Jesse for an hour and a half, was kneeling in front of him, dressing him, Jesse spouting gibberish. For an instant, just an instant, in the midst of all the rush and fear and panic and the heat and the cold, Ray suddenly felt himself leave his body and stand apart, as though he weren't there on the bedroom floor but above, looking down into the room, looking down at the scene of the two of them. It lasted only a second, maybe less, but it was so cold and objective that it made Ray pause in his efforts. He felt something strange, what exactly he couldn't say, as though he were looking at it all from someone else's point of view, someone not panicked or fearful but objective, someone simply watching, not feeling. As though some obscenely frozen unseen thing had entered the room and was sharing it with them.

Now Jesse began twisting and turning, hitting out, obviously delusional, thwarting Ray's every attempt to get him fully dressed, to help him, to save him, moaning out loud now, the most terrible noises emerging from his throat, mutterings and groans, animal calls, belches mixed with attempts at throwing up. Ray held him, talked to him, dressed him. "It's going to be all right, Jess. We're getting you to the hospital now. J.K.'s coming. He'll be downstairs with a cab, and we'll get you to the hospital. You've got pneumonia, he thinks, and it's serious, but you're not going to die on me, OK, Buster Brown? Promise me that! I'm with you all the way, kiddo. You hearing your Ray?"

He was all over Jesse, speaking into his mouth, his eyes, his ears, trying at the same time to dress him, to enfold him, to not lose, not lose, not lose him now, not lose him now after so long, not lose him now, and out of his own mouth he heard words he hadn't heard from himself in years, since he was a kid, said slowly, moaned, as though almost torn from his entrails, as he continued to fear and panic and to prepare Jesse for the street, for the cab, for the hospital, for salvation. "Ba...ruch...Ad...o...nai...El...o...him...Ba...ruch...Ad...o... nai... El...o...him." Preparing Jesse for the street, for the cab, for the hospital, for salvation, "Ba...ruch...Ad...o...nai...El...o...him...Ba...ruch." Ray thinking at the same time, *God, if he dies here in my arms, it's all over. All over. Never will I...*

He felt a movement on his face. Through the overwhelming alternating glare of his anger and blackness of his despair, Ray felt a finger move across his cheek, playing a delicate melody on the bridge of his nose, across one eye. Jesse. Jesse responding.

"That you? Buster Brown?" He restrained himself, held it back inside.

The fingers explored a bit more. Jesse's head was thrown back, his eyes now rolling in their sockets. Jesse was no longer flinching or convulsing or shivering; no longer chattering or retching, but shaking subtly, throughout his body, as

Ray held him closer. Yet his fingers spoke on Ray's face, spider feet tapping out a code of survival, so Ray began intoning his litany all over again: "It's going to be all right. We're getting you to the hospital now. J.K.'s coming. He's downstairs, and we'll get you there. You're not going to die, OK, kiddo? You hear me, Buster Brown? You hearing Ray?"

The fingers assured him he was being heard, and through the wonder of even that, enough to cut through his panic and fear, he heard the doorbell, sounding like chimes from on high.

"That's J.K. Gotta get a hat on you, OK, kiddo? It's too cold out," he said, fitting the beret onto Jesse's skull, tearing himself away from him, looking back once, again to make certain he was still there, still alive, before he ran the few feet to the door.

He stuttered and babbled into J.K.'s ascending, worried, but welcome face. J.K. slammed past him into the bedroom. He followed dully. Watched J.K. lift Jesse with difficulty, until he helped. Together they got him to the front door, where J.K. enunciated clearly, as if speaking to a deaf person, "Keys. Wallet. Glasses. Note for Chris."

J.K. held Jesse, instructing, "Good. You've got the keys and glasses. Now the note for Chris. Terrif. Now the wallet. The medical insurance cards inside? Great. Now your coat. Your own hat. Gloves. Scarf. OK. We're ready." Just as the cabbie began blowing his horn down on the street.

J.K. locked up while Ray lifted Jesse in his arms, weighing so little he marveled at how light he was, fitting so perfectly into Ray's arms, his Buster Brown, his kiddo, his Jess, Ray almost smiled at how perfectly he fit. J.K. holding one side of them, steadying them, as they slowly descended the slippery stone steps, going down to the street, Jesse mumbling all the while, perhaps feeling the outside air, and Ray repeating back to him, mantralike, "It's going to be all right. We're getting you to the hospital now. We're going down stairs to the cab now. You're going to get treatment. You're going to be all right. You're not going to die. OK, kiddo? We're getting into the cab now…We're in the backseat of the cab…Are you with me, Jess?…Are you with Ray?"

sixteen

He recognized her the minute she walked into the ICU corridor. He'd never met her, but he knew her immediately, partly due to the manner in which she was dressed—surprisingly fashionable for someone who, after all, was arriving from a small town of little apparent chic on the Southern Atlantic seaboard. Partly due to the colors she'd chosen to wear. Not mourning black, but close enough: a pale, earth-tone silk blouse beneath a charcoal jacket and skirt, umber overcoat, jet cashmere tam and leather gloves. The sole hints of illumination came from a sky-blue wisp of silk scarf loosely knotted around her neck, and a glimmering—as from expiring embers—amber circlet around one bone-white wrist. Even her makeup was low-key.

But mostly he knew Adele Vaughan Moody, née Carstairs, because the face she carried on her inflexible, upright little body so much resembled the face on that ravaged, beloved body still burning as though from fires long banked within; unstoppably burning 12 hours now since Ray had finally been able to check Jesse into the hospital and get him moved up here. It was a body that no longer seemed to observe the simplest customary physical laws of the universe, except perhaps those that decreed that nothing would function as it ought to. It was alone, a small object in a large, high-ceilinged space, connected by a multiplicity of wires, sensors, and cords, a meshwork of communication devices, attached to a half dozen machines with their individually modulated beeping, chiming, aspirating, stridulating sounds; their neon green or titanium white, ever twinkling lines, ever undulating sine curves, ever blinking dashes decorating the room's near-darkness, while, suspended from what looked like an aluminum mizzenmast, miscellaneous globules hovered overhead, plasticene bladders of electrolytes and soluble sugars, opaque pipettes of steroids, inverted syringes of antibiotics that pulsed, dripped, or otherwise induced their contents into the veins of immobilized arms below.

Even inert, Jesse remained the point demarcating the equidistance between Adele, just arrived, erect and quietly quivering at the ICU. information desk, and Ray, at the farthest end of the corridor—papered pale blue with white flocking—not quite legally seated on one of two chairs temporarily placed by janitorial staff during the night. Ray had stationed himself here since yesterday afternoon, all but ignored in a dead-end corner, instead of in the little lounge where he'd been told to wait, half the floor distant. And even from this far away, Adele's face was familiar, though they'd never met. As familiar as her stoic, iron-boned, insufficiently fleshed, erect little build in its overpriced label-wear, like a clothes hanger in a fashion photographer's closet.

He wasn't surprised Adele would be here, although he couldn't figure how, exactly, it was that she'd arrived just before 5 in the morning, what combinations of public and private transportation, air and car, she'd manipulated. Last night, when Chris had met him downstairs in the main waiting area, he'd told Ray of picking up Adele's phone call yesterday, only minutes after he'd gotten home and found Ray's note. Chris repeated Adele's demand to speak to her son and her lack of surprise when she'd been told that Jesse had been taken into emergency care. Chris repeated her interrogation, wanting to know who he was, where Jesse had gone, how long he'd been gone, his condition, the address of the hospital, the name of his doctor, etc.—data the boy was mostly unable to provide. As he forced takeout Chinese on Ray, Chris kept asking how could Adele possibly know when to call, never mind to call at all. He'd arrived home just a few minutes before she called, and he was braced for the note only because he'd been stopped at the porch by snoopy Mrs. Schnell from across the street. It was she who'd told him it was less than ten minutes since Ray and J.K. had carried Jesse off in a taxi, and she was certain to the local emergency room. Chris speculated, "She's some kind of witch! Or else…" His eyebrows rose as his larynx imitated the intoning of a celesta, signifying something weird and spacey. So, yes, Ray had been warned.

Now here she was, fitting the bill exactly as Jesse had for years described it, although naturally arriving after all the dirty work had been done, dressed and acting in her long-decided-upon role of the put-upon widow, mother of an unhappy scion dead set on ruining himself and everyone else.

As he watched her interact with the unit nurse, Ray recognized several of her gestures as those of her son. Jesse's were inflected differently, hers less subtle, less mediated, as though she must be broader to impress herself upon these lesser beings. Unsurprisingly, she was arguing with the ICU station nurse, who was now displaying a file, doubtless Jesse's, with its giant scrawled letters "DNR," signaling that in case of deadly emergency, Jesse was not to be resuscitated, nor any extreme measures taken to save his life. Adele's gloved forefinger continued striking the station's wooden counter in an unvarying rhythm of irritation. Suddenly the nurse pointed to Ray, undoubtedly trying to get rid of Adele by turning the blame on him. Adele turned also, saw him, nodded abruptly, so quickly and with such a tiny movement that Ray couldn't tell whether he'd been noted and greeted or not: She faced the nurse again to continue emphasizing her point.

A minute later Adele was advancing across the corridor at him, her heels striking the tiles—hushed until then—as though they were pistol shots. Her forthright, nearly military approach forced Ray, despite himself, to stand up and prepare to address her. A foot earlier than anyone else might, she stopped and faced him. Her eyes from this close were not Jesse's golden beauties but instead enameled brown, nearly black. Both his and Adele's hands were kept at their sides. She spoke in a fluttery alto voice made known to him by those brief phone conversations over the years after he'd picked up and before he'd called Jesse: "You are Ray-mond. Naturally."

"Yes ma'am," he immediately replied. Nothing extra needed.

"They tell me you accompanied my son to this place yesterday afternoon with a case of pneumocystis pneumonia. I wish to thank you."

Her tone immediately put his teeth on edge. The noblesse oblige of her words went down even worse. "Your thanks aren't necessary," Ray assured her. "It's only what either of us would do for each other. Jesse would camp out here all night long if I were as ill as he is." That settled, he became businesslike. "You'll want to see him. He's in ICU room 5. That door right there."

"In a minute." She moved past him and draped her coat over the other chair. "I have been on the run since yesterday. I need to catch my breath." She didn't sit, however, as he'd assumed she might, but instead placed her headgear atop the coat. "This is a Roman Catholic hospital. I don't understand what my son is…unless another conversion has occurred that I was unapprised of."

Other than Jesse's conversion to queerhood, Ray supposed she meant.

"I was brought up Jewish," Ray rubbed it in before saying, "I'm not observant anymore, and no, neither of us has converted to Catholicism. This is the hospital Jesse's physician is attached to. Luckily it's a good hospital, and close to our home. It only took us minutes to get here yesterday, and they were prepared for us."

He included "ours" and "us" so she couldn't possibly miss his point.

"I'm, of course, astonished," Adele said, sounding in no way astonished, slowly removing her gloves, finger by finger. "I was always led to believe that medical men of your own faith in this region were considered superior."

"Jesse's choice of doctor was his own," Ray countered, ignoring all the probable slurs. "In this, as in all aspects of his life." In effect, telling Adele his relationship with Ray wasn't why Jesse had not taken up with her again after his father's death.

"And this remarkable doctor is…?"

"At 5 A.M.? Still asleep, I suppose," Ray said. "He's due in by 9. He was by again quite late last night."

"You'll be kind enough to keep an eye on my things," she casually commanded as she carefully added her gloves to the pile.

Adele performed a smart, nearly military turn on her heels and entered the ajar doorway of Jesse's room. She remained in the room long enough to surpass her very short limit of visiting time, so that the station nurse had to go in after her. When Adele exited, on the nurse's heels, her superior intrepidity was gone. She didn't quite stagger, but her face was drawn; even her makeup now looked obviously painted on. She hadn't known what to expect and so had received the full force of Jesse's condition all at once. Her slight zigzag toward him revealed her overwhelming shock.

Ray stood and helped her into the chair. He intercepted the nurse, who'd also seen Adele's shock and had started toward them with a plastic cup of water. Ray took it from her and brought it to Adele, whose eyes looked glazed as he handed it to her and ordered her to drink.

"I had no idea…" she was at last able to articulate. "No idea.…"

Ray looked away from her, down at the tile floor.

"Jesse told me he'd phoned you a few weeks ago and said he was…dying."

"I believed he was exaggerating!" she defended herself. "People exaggerate so."

"This is the first major illness he's had," Ray said. "You understand that, don't you?" Still unable to look her in the eyes. "And you understand that if he survives this bout of pneumonia, which is very likely, that he'll be back here, in this hospital, on this very floor possibly, with some other equally deadly illness."

Her face—Jesse's face implacable with age and antipathy—seemed to shake side to side, making Ray ashamed of what he was saying, even as he knew had to say it.

"Believe me when I say I'm not trying to be cruel to you," Ray said. "It's just that…now that you're here, you should know what we've known for months, years now."

"I…know…nothing," Adele sounded operatic. "I understand…none of this."

Ray sighed and looked up at the ceiling.

He felt a hand close over his upon the chair's arm. "Ray-mond. You must tell me what I need to know."

Ray looked down, not at her face, which he could not stand to witness so obviously in distress, but at her hand, closed clawlike upon his own, the nails perfectly manicured, evenly buffed, the shade of coral impeccable, the rings refined, matched jewels rich yet not a carat too garish, as the bony fingers closed over his.

"You must tell me!" she repeated.

He didn't know what kind of box he was opening up now. Why not let her hear it from the doctor?

Ray remembered to tell himself that Jesse was her son, she was seeing her son for the first time since her husband's funeral, for the first time in what was it, five years? Seeing her son firmly in the grasp of slime-fingered death. His own mother's image rose into view, her face undergoing shock, the death of her baby sister in an automobile accident, the stark tragedy on her drawn face as she'd taken the phone call in her kitchen, how she'd hung up the phone and leadenly sat at the breakfast table where 16-year-old Ray had been finishing a bowl of cereal and working on a crossword puzzle, and how when he'd looked up at her, wordlessly questioning the meaning of the call, his mother had for a moment seemed to be someone else too, one of those biblical matriarchs out of his earliest picture books from *schul*, faithful Naomi or ancient Sarah, beloved Rebecca or proud Judith.

And how, when he'd gotten up the nerve to ask her what was wrong, she had simply held out her arms to him, and he'd without a thought rushed into them, taking comfort from one who needed comfort more, feeling her soft, cashmered upper body all about him quivering, her sobbing kept back as she'd uttered, "Now we must be strong. Very strong. God has decided to take your aunt from us." Looking at Adele that way, Ray had no choice but to be kind to her.

So he told her everything. Sparing no detail of what had already happened to Jesse. The blistering headaches. The absolute exhaustion. The wrenching intestinal woes. The nausea. The 20 hours of sleep a day. Nor did he hold back what had happened to others with the disease—making sure she knew that all of it, any of it, might yet afflict her son. Assuring her that it might be two years of hospital visits, more bouts of pneumonia following brain tumors, neuropathological damage following dementia, lethal Kaposi's lesions inside and out. Describing it as he'd seen it, known it, heard about it. Concluding, "Jesse will not get better. He cannot get better. He has no immune system to fight back. All that in there, all those machines and drips, are an external immune system devised by this hospital to get him past this one illness. But he'll be attacked again and again. He can't possibly survive every time. He'll die from one thing or another."

When he'd finished speaking, she held him there a little while longer. When she at last withdrew her hand from his, Ray felt he had done what he had to do. But he also felt mangled, as though he hadn't already known all this for months, years, but was hearing it for the first time himself as he told her. Unable to know what to do now, now that it was all on the table, he stood up and went into Jesse's room.

He looked so small, doll-like, almost a counterfeit, encased in all that technology.

Ray lightly touched the fingers of his right hand. "Hello, kiddo. You awake?" The fingers moved a smidgen against his palm, the eyelids fluttered as though opening but remained shut. "Your mother's here. She came to visit. You know that, right?" The eyelids fluttered again, again remained shut, but two fingers curved in a half inch in signal. He knew she was here. "Go back to sleep." Assent in the fingertips, and no more eyelid fluttering.

It was a tenuous communication they had while the Septra and its alliance of medical infusions did their work, but it was enough for Ray. They'd never needed much in the way of exchanges anyway. A little had always gone a long way, enabling them to be together when they were among others: together and in agreement.

As he stared at Jesse in the bed, the mattress appearing to float as it can-tilevered over the bedstead, Ray was struck by a sudden recollection. It went back to his junior year of high school, in their own living room. He and Kathy had thrown a party for schoolmates, and because their parents would be out that evening, they'd gotten approval to use the living room rather than the chill-ier downstairs finished basement. There had been maybe ten of them—half guys, half girls, 15 to 17 years old, his and Kathy's pals, all good clean fun; a lit-tle dancing to the stereo, his own lightly constructed cocktails, with a single jig-ger of gin or scotch to seven ounces of ginger ale or tonic water. No one had even brought a joint of grass. Everyone pretty much knew each other. Some had dated before. But no one was matched this evening. So everyone was a little wary, on their best behavior, sizing up or reevaluating each other.

He couldn't recall whose suggestion it was; one of the girls, he thought, because he vaguely remembered Suzanne or Donna saying they'd done it before at a pajama party and how amazing it was that it worked. And suddenly all five girls were hunched down on the living room carpet where there was space enough to accommodate Bobby Dineefry's 6'3", long-legged body, and Bobby himself was flat on the carpet, jesting with Kathy and Ursula, who had per-suaded him to try it. While Ray and Miles, Warren and Stephan had stood around and behind the oblong figure Bobby and the girls made—the guys sip-ping their cocktails, scoffing that it couldn't work—the five girls, two on either side, Yolanda at Bobby's feet, had inserted their fingers, just the fingertips, and at the three in Kathy's count had lifted Bobby. Lifted him, using only the pads of their fingers, without any effort at all levitated him off the carpet, raised him first two inches, then six inches, then a foot high, rising themselves, until they had gotten the amazed Bobby—"I feel like I'm floating!"—who had to weigh at least 175 pounds, four feet off the ground.

Warren was next, and he rose as high and might have gone higher if, Ursula complained, he hadn't twitched so much. Stephan, who was the smallest guy, was their best lift of all. The girls floated him over their heads, almost to the ceiling. Miles was next, and he might have also have reached the top if he hadn't popped a noticeable hard-on once he got off the ground, eliciting both comments and laughter from the girls (Kathy: "God, Miles, if I knew you were that easy, I would have dated you years ago."), so they lost their concentration and almost dropped him. Ray and Stephan and Bobby and Warren had to jump in to keep Miles from plummeting and beaning himself. They'd all fallen together, ten of them, in a heap, on the floor, Miles's crotch falling directly under Ray's left hand, so he was able to cop a few good feels of the still rock-hard erection. And Ray had thought that in the laughter and noise, with the many hands upon him, Miles hadn't noticed, hadn't noticed a thing.

No wonder Ray had been surprised months later, when it seemed that Miles not only recalled the incident but also knew what had been meant by it. The school had been called to a fire drill. It was third period, just before lunch, and Ray had been in phys ed, in this case about 60 guys mostly playing basketball or volleyball in the big gymnasium, when the quickly repeated alarms they knew well and that usually elicited appreciation as a welcome intrusion into learning had arrived and this time evoked a great, spontaneous, multithroat "Aw!" by disappointed boys having their fun interrupted. They were forced to line up, dressed as they were, and file into the open-air corridors outside the large gym. Simultaneously, a spring thunderstorm began to gather. Bad planning on the administration's part. In seconds, huge thunderheads developed over the school and everything darkened.

The boys, dressed only in T-shirts and gym shorts, complained of having to leave the building in 50-degree weather and then get soaking wet. Coach Adrian fumed back that they'd be happy enough to get wet if the building were on fire, but he sent his assistant to the principal, who sent him back saying that because of the cold and rain, instead of staying outside, the boys could remain in their downstairs corridor, the one surrounding the locker room.

Ray didn't know whether it was from the beginning of the lineup or only when they got downstairs in the poorly lighted corridors that Miles managed to wedge himself directly behind Ray. He was aware of it only once they were below, in the near darkness, when amidst all the animal roars and birdcalls that the assistant coach was trying to hush, Ray suddenly felt a hand reach around from behind and pull his right hand back, where it was placed directly on a gym-shorts–enclosed erection.

As they were all pushed together, front to back, Ray didn't have to turn much to see it was Miles—Miles who immediately began using Ray's hand to massage himself, all without a word being said. Ray continued, then maneuvered his hand enough so he could reach under Miles's shorts and get right inside the jockstrap to free Miles altogether. He jerked him until he heard Miles beginning to breathe hard. Luckily Miles managed to turn aside so that he splashed against the corridor wall, but Ray held on until he was milked out, at which point Miles removed Ray's fingers one by one, and replaced himself back into his jockstrap. Ray already had his own orgasm—without touching himself—and stared down at the wet spot he'd left on the floor. Less than a minute passed before the period bell rang and the line of boys broke rank and hit the locker room to change.

Miles never said anything about either incident, never approached Ray again for a hand job, and as far as Ray was concerned that was that—just one of many baffling incidents that had shaped his childhood. But not too many years ago, when he was back in Illinois, Ray had encountered Stephan with his wife and their infant in a stroller at the local mall, and while Rosemary had gone into the women's room to change the baby, Ray and Stephan sat outside on a bench and caught up. Among those Stephan mentioned was Miles, who he told Ray was now married for the third time, this time to a 19-year-old bimbo in San Diego. "Big surprise, huh?" Stephan asked; and when Ray asked why it was surprising, Stephan replied, "We always thought Miles was the gay one. Not you. I mean, he was the one who had the jack-off club." When Ray probed for details, he found out that Stephan, Bobby Dineefry, and his younger brother Steve had met a couple of times a week since junior high in Miles's attic bedroom for sometimes hourlong mutual masturbation sessions. It had been Miles's idea, and he was the one who kept it going as long as possible. Even after Bobby and Stephan had begun seriously dating girls and dropped out, Miles had gotten younger boys involved. He didn't seem to care what anyone thought, Stephan said: He'd jerked off two guys at a time, had done them right it in school bathroom, and according to Steve Dineefry, had even begun fellating some of the guys and trying to get them to do him back. "Guess Miles wasn't gay. Just horny as hell," Stephan had concluded. So Ray discovered that for all those years, and except for that single fire alarm incident, he—who'd been looking for, or at least been open to, gay sex—had been ignored, while these straight boys he knew had wild homosexual experiences.

Ray realized he was speaking out loud, telling the story to Jesse, and also realized he'd never told Jesse this story, although he thought surely they'd shared everything about their pasts by now. He was about to turn and leave the room when Jesse's hand rose in the air as far as it could, held down by all the needle intrusions as it was, and Ray took the fingers, which closed in on his palms. Jesse's eyes fluttered open—dun, not gold, in this dimness—and Jesse formed a tiny smile before he subsided onto the bed pillow.

In the corridor Adele looked exactly as pensive as he had left her. Ray went past her, past the nurses' station to the men's room at the opposite far end of the ICU floor. On the way he passed a huddle of people speaking to the nurse receptionist, two young teenage girls, a middle-aged woman, possibly their mother, and two mustachioed, fierce-looking men in their mid 20s. All of them were dark-haired and dark-eyed, bluntly good-looking, thick-bodied, and looked like a family, possibly Hispanic. An hour before Adele arrived, Ray had witnessed a full gurney with medical attachments and a separate breathing apparatus cart wheeled out of the elevator and into ICU room 4. Through all the staff, he'd been able to make out the patient, a wizened white-haired man. One of the teenage girls addressed the nurse, while the others behind her half whispered, half spoke aloud in Spanish to one another.

Once inside the pristine bathroom, Ray stood at the sink and began to wash his face and hands. He looked tired—as he should look, since he'd had virtually no sleep all night—but then again, he didn't look all that bad. He'd pulled all-nighters before. Long ago in college, before term papers were due, before final exams, but after that too, the decade and a half that he—he and Jesse—had partied all around Manhattan and on the Island. Too bad he hadn't asked Chris to bring a razor. Maybe J.K. would bring one later today? He'd have to call both of them…oh, and get back to Maurette, who'd phoned last evening and, according to Chris, had seemed very happy, bubbling over with what he'd called great news. Probably the film had won an award in Berlin. Good for Maurette. But that probably also meant an American distributor had been found for the film. Which probably meant it would play here. Which probably meant Maurette would be able to shoot another film. Which probably meant Ray would be able to score another film, which probably meant…what? That was five probablys. What did it mean exactly? That Ray had a new source of employment? What difference did that make with Jesse barely able to open his eyes, burning in there like a century-old Susquehanna County coal seam fire?

He'd run out of paper towels and just went into the nearest stall to use toilet paper when someone charged into the men's room and ran to the third toilet, slamming the door behind him. Ray heard what sounded like a thud, horrendous retching, followed by vomiting. The toilet was flushed once and then again as the fellow continued to retch. When Ray stepped out, he could see under the stall door sufficiently to make out the man still kneeling at the other toilet. Only now he was sobbing, a low guttural sobbing that rose in pitch and volume and ended in a cry, "*Oh, papi! No muerate! Mi abuelito cariño, me escuche, no dejarnos!*" After he had cried out, he began retching again, seemingly unable to vomit, flushed the toilet anyway, and again sobbed his plea to his grandfather to not leave them. It was clear from even the little Ray could see of his shoes and pants that he was one of the two men out in the corridor, one of the rugged, angry-looking young men. Yet here, where he thought he wasn't seen or heard, he sounded like a forsaken six-year-old. When he began again a third time, it was so painful to listen to that Ray had to lean against the wall.

The door flew open and the other young man shouted, *"Raul! Donde esta?"* Ray had the presence of mind to exit. But a few minutes later, when he'd arrived back at the double seats next to Adele and the family was gathered again at the door of room 4, he thought that Raul threw him a foul glance. He pretended not to see.

By then, anyway, his attention was divided. He'd barely sat when Adele looked up and said in her quavering voice, "You were in the room with my son a far longer time than I was and no one came to shoo you out."

"I went to the men's room too," Ray said.

"I saw you go into the men's room. I meant before that. She!" Adele's bony nose pointed like a rifle at the nurse receptionist. "She told me I could stay five minutes a time every 20 minutes. You were inside that room with my son more than ten minutes."

He couldn't be sure whether she was kidding.

"And what kind of hospital is this, anyway?" She changed gears instantly. "Do you see that? Do you see all those…them, there!"

"Their grandfather was brought in here an hour ago. I think he's dying."

"Why should I care about those kind of people's grandfather?" she asked. "Now at Doctors Hospital back home, they wouldn't be tolerated. Not tolerated."

A male resident stepped out of IC4 and approached the family. He spoke to the mother, but the eldest girl faced him and translated for the others, blocking her mouth with a hand whenever the resident spoke, until finally Ray could tell she was doing so to keep from crying, to hold herself together, as he told her the worst possible news. She nevertheless managed to ask him, and he assented to letting them in one at a time to see the old man at the extremity of his life. As soon as the resident walked away, an explosion of grief erupted from the family. It was a pitiful to behold and to hear.

"Will you listen to them?" Adele snapped. "Like animals! I assure you, Doctors Hospital would not abide this…jamboree." Her foot tapped the floor, and a second later she snapped again. "When that wonder-working doctor arrives, I shall have my son moved to Doctors Hospital! This very day!" Her decision made, she marched to the nurses' station making an exaggerated detour around the family gathered at room 4.

The nurse receptionist was in for an earful of Adele Vaughan Moody, née Carstairs, and she managed to at last pass her off to the resident, who kept shaking his head at everything she said. When she returned to where Ray was seated, she remained standing.

"I have just received the most astounding, the most unnatural information," she declared. "That doctor in training or whomever he is, said to my face that my son is too ill to be moved to Doctors Hospital, despite the obvious deficiencies of this facility."

Ray might have told her that.

"Even more astonishing, he told me I would be unable to transfer him if he were in far better health. And why, do you think, that is? Because, I have just been apprised, that sort of transfer could only be effected by my son, or failing his ability, my son's next of kin. Are you aware whom they have surely mistakenly have written down as my son, Jesse Vaughan Moody's next of kin? Not his mother, Adele Moody, née Carstairs. No! Instead, one who shares none of his names, one who shares not a drop of blood with him."

Ray knew very well who was listed as Jesse's next of kin: Ray.

"That was Jesse's decision," Ray said. "When he was still well enough to make the decision. As was his decision to not be resuscitated or have any extraordinary methods used should he be dying. We've been in this hospital before, meeting with social workers, physicians, and attorneys, working out Jesse's wishes about what's now happening to him."

Unswayed by fact, she stood her ground: "Working it out behind my back."

"No, regardless of your back...I was surprised to see you here. Jesse led me to believe you wouldn't be coming. That you didn't care. You hung up the phone on him. It took several of us many months to persuade him to call you. He wouldn't."

"Then why in the world would you insist?"

"Because I have a mother. And I would want her to know."

That seemed to stop Adele momentarily. Clearly, it had never crossed her mind that he would have a mother.

"Be that as it may, I will take up this absurd matter of next of kin with the physician and my lawyer."

"We have copies of his medical power of attorney at home and right here in that file behind her desk. It was signed and notarized two years ago, appointing me. Not you."

"And why wouldn't you take his medical power of attorney? As you've taken everything that's his? As you've taken his health and life from him?"

Behind them a great wail went up at IC4. The old man had died. Adele turned and stamped her feet. "Why can't you behave? What is wrong with you people?"

Ray was infuriated. Before he said or did something he'd regret, he stood up and went into Jesse's room, hearing her call out, "I am his mother. I am next of kin. Not you. Not some piece of paper."

Out of the corner of his eye he saw the receptionist, another nurse, and the resident all approach Adele. He knew that, despite her protests, they'd escort her away.

Jesse was asleep, luckily, and had heard nothing. Ray stayed with him a long time. When he exited, Adele's streetwear was gone from the two chairs, and so was his. So, for that matter were the two chairs. He found his coat at the nurses' station, where he was told he could no longer remain. Rather than be near Adele in the little lobby where, when he passed, he saw her sitting, fuming, holding her clothing to her chest as though it would be snatched from her at knifepoint by the sobbing teenage Hispanic girls also in the room, he dropped down to the next floor. It was going to be a long morning, a long vigil, and he realized he should have listened to Jesse. But then he told himself she was acting so badly because she was upset at seeing her son so ill. Possibly feeling guilty, blaming herself for hanging up on him, not rushing here weeks ago. Once she'd become accustomed to the hospital and to Ray, she would be human again.

In the basement-floor cafeteria he got coffee and a sweet roll and a *Times*, but the front page remained a blur even after ten minutes of looking at it. He was still incensed at her behavior, at her brutal insensitivity toward those poor people… Half an hour later Raul and his brother also came into the cafeteria. They sat at a far table, but Raul nodded stiffly at Ray as they got up to leave, passing nearby.

"Me siento mucho por su abuelo," Ray said, sorry for the loss of their grandfather.

The two young men stopped and looked at him. *"Y ella?"* Raul asked, *"Su madre?"*

She wasn't his mother, Ray told them, but the mother of his *marido*—his husband.

They shook their heads, understanding him, reached out and each patted his shoulder. *"Es difícil esta vida,"* Raul said. *"Pero el amor, verdadamente ya es mas difícil."*

An hour later he was still staring at the top margin of the newspaper where he'd written what Raul said, translated as: "Life is difficult. But to love truly is even more difficult."

seventeen

Sunlight, glorious and all-seeing, aureoled the nurse's head as he glided in front of the window and leaned forward to shut off the valve connecting the no longer flowing, thick golden liquid from above into Jesse's arm. The chestnut-brown face with its exotic, almost Chinese eyes, flared nostrils, nearly white outlined lips seemed to glow from within, as though the man's love of life had to express itself into surrounding space. The nurse opened the valve to another hanging globule, and silver-white liquid began to flow. He watched it, still embellished by light from behind, tapping it lightly with a flick of a forefinger, and seemed pleased. But then he spoke too softly for Jesse to make out the words, and it was too tiring to keep asking him to repeat himself, so Jesse simply smiled back and mumbled what he hoped would sound like thanks.

J.K. replaced the nurse, the pale pink skin against black hair, black eyebrows and dark eyes contrasting with the nearly monotone melted-chocolate skin, eyes, and hair of the nurse, and the contrast was charming. The pale yellow plastic scoop of chipped ice in one of J.K.'s hands, the pale blue pitcher in his other, were so cute and friendly, and surely they signified that the nurse had asked if Jesse had wanted more ice for his fever-sore-filled mouth. He hadn't, and it wasn't that sore. Still, he opened his mouth, and J.K. bent down, allowing his own handsomely Celtic dark head to be haloed from the sun, and he gently spooned the ice onto his warm tongue where it instantly cooled and melted. So nice. J.K. sitting there, asking if he wanted more. So nice. The halo making such a glow around him, if he could only see himself like this. If only all of them could: the nurse, J.K., Liesl, Ray when he arrived, and the funniest of all, Adele, trying so hard, failing so utterly, yet also haloed, hallowed, divine if only she knew, they knew, what he knew. The humor of it all filled him with laughter deep inside, and he wondered whether laughter wasn't inappropriate, and he tried to stifle it but it came out anyway, as a tiny, high-pitched belch, which was even funnier.

"Of course everyone agrees that *Swingtime* has the single most embarrassing moment of Astaire's entire career," J.K. was continuing a line of conversation he'd begun and of course instantly stopped—as though it were full of state secrets—until the nurse had left again. He held J.K. near him, in that chair there, so he could see the light all around his head as he spoke. "I'm referring of course to the Mister Bojangles's number in which he puts on blackface and dances. Of course, everyone in 1936 wore blackface and thought nothing of it, and after all it was meant as an homage by Astaire to the famous tap dancer. Also, whatever embarrassment accrues is immediately vitiated in the second part of the dance when the chorines move away and Astaire begins to dance with the three shadows on the walls. Do you remember that, Jesse? One large shadow in the middle, two small shadows on either side, as though he were tracked in a triple-glassed mirror somehow. And that is absolute magic. Magic that even the movie's stupid ending with them all laughing can't take away from. It was there," J.K. paused dramatically, "right there, in that dance with the shadows, that it came to me, what I'll call the whole thing. There and of course five minutes later, when the nightclub is empty and Astaire and Rogers have broken up, seemingly irrevocably, and the two of them find themselves first walking through the vacant club, then dancing despite themselves, and in the dance they express everything they've felt, and after that there's no turning back—they're together for good. Are you ready now? Get this title. This is what I'll call my thesis: 'Reflection and Shadow: The Role of Dance as Subconscious Gesture in the films of Astaire and Rogers.' What do you think?"

Through the ice he mumbled he thought it was wonderful. Had J.K. told Ray?

"Well, not yet. You see, old scout, that's going to be something else. Remember how I said I'd take care of him for you? You know, in case...? Well, I'm going to have to take back that promise. I don't think I'm going to be able to. I know I don't look all that bad, but...I seroconverted almost as long ago as you did, and, well, I'm going to have to face facts. If I want to finish the thesis and leave something behind, I'm going to have to take up my sister's offer to move up to Massachusetts. Now that the boys are out of their house, they've got an entire wing I can stay in. Her husband arranged for the Center for the Humanities at U. Mass. to let me be connected with them to work on the thing. So I'll close down my place here sometime in February, I think. April first at the latest. That's when the lease is up...I know you hate me for that."

Of course he didn't hate J.K. He was happy for him.

"Well, then, Ray-Boy will hate me. But I just don't have that long myself. My last two blood works were really bad. We're calling each of what's left of my T-cells by name these days. Herbert. Annabel. Jethro. Caleb. Eleanora. That's it, folks!"

Funny...but Ray would understand. He'd have to. And it wasn't far. Amherst.

"And for once I'll be doing what everyone in my family wants. Instead of doing something to spite them. You understand that, right? How important it is to gather everything together, now that it's coming to a close?"

To gather the essences, yes, Jesse knew. To eliminate the dross—by whatever means at hand—then to gather the essences.

"That's why you can deal with her, isn't it?" J.K. asked, nodding behind himself to where Jesse assumed the waiting room was, explaining, "Lady Bracknell?"

Meaning Adele. Yes, that was why. Why and how.

Then Liesl was floating above J.K., blondly angelic, also haloed. And with her, Ray. Ray whom he could no longer protect, but who would come through it all, if what he'd seen was true...eventually.

They were all talking for a moment, which was funny but confusing, then he concentrated on Liesl, and she shushed the others anyway and was saying something about Berlin. He muttered through the ice for her to explain.

"The long and short of it," she said, as though the discussion had been going on for a while already, "is that Ray has to go to California with Maurette and do it there."

"No, I don't, Liesl!" Ray protested.

Do what, Jesse wanted to know.

"It's not important, Jess. Don't listen to her."

"My darling Maurette's film? *Echoes of Tomorrow?*" Liesl said. "Well, it won a directing award at Berlin. Not the Silver Bear, but some kind of baby bear. Maybe a cub?" She laughed at herself. "Whatever it's called. Anyway the sound and the music were picked out for special merit, and so of course there's going to be an American release of the film. Some distribution company attached to Paramount."

"MGM-Sony," Ray put in.

"Whoever. So they want Ray to fly to Los Angeles to remix the master soundtrack for the film's American release. Is that right, Ray-mond?"

"I'm not going," Ray replied.

Of course Ray was going, Jesse said. He had to go to California. That was one of the things he'd seen while he was feverish. Ray driving down Washington Boulevard in Culver City turning left into the old MGM studio gate. He'd seen it. Ray had to go.

"Is that where they're recording it?" Liesl asked.

"How should I know? I'm not going!"

When did he have to go, Jesse asked.

"I'm not sure," Liesl answered. "A month to six weeks from now."

"I'm not going to California while Jess needs me here. Period."

Liesl began talking about Maurette, and how excited he was, how he'd flown to Berlin and gotten there the day of the ceremony, on a hunch, her hunch of course, and how he'd called from backstage at the OpernHaus after getting the award, with distribution offers from five countries already, and how everyone talked about the music and both Sony and FNAC had approached him about a soundtrack album and…"

A soundtrack? Jesse interrupted her. Is that why Ray would go to Los Angeles? Then he definitely had to go.

"Liesl," Ray warned, "if you don't stop this instant, I swear they'll find your body cut in little pieces all over the Lower East Side."

So she stopped, and the nurse came in and sent them all out except Ray, and J.K. and Liesl said they'd wait outside and come back when Ray was done, and he sat there where J.K. had been, Ray looking so harassed and worried, but excited too about the film, the award, the record, all of it, despite his protests. Jesse could read it on his face.

So he let Ray do his concerned-lover routine, asking every question under the sun, until he was asked out. That was when Jesse told him what he had seen during the 48 hours or so that he was so feverish: the horrible things, the really horrible things, he'd seen, but also the wonderful things, and included in those wonderful things, he'd seen Ray in California, Ray driving a teal convertible into the MGM studio gates which Ray had never seen before, and Jesse knew, he absolutely knew that was what Ray would do, had to do, could not *not* do.

Ray held his ground. "I'm staying where I'm needed."

Ray would go, Jesse assured him. Six weeks from now. Jesse wouldn't need him, and so he'd go with Maurette. Which was right, because that was what had to happen. He'd seen it, he'd envisioned it.

"C'mon, kiddo, you were delirious. Those were hallucinations."

Jesse insisted they were visions. Horrible ones and wonderful ones, all true.

"Fine. Well, then maybe you had a vision about *this?*" Ray reached into his coat pocket and pulled out an envelope. "While I was waiting to at the elevator to come up here, I was served with this." He opened it. "It's a subpoena. To appear at family court. Your mother is trying to take your medical power of attorney from me."

He knew. Hadn't Ray noticed her lawyer with her in the sitting room? They'd been in together yesterday and today.

"I can't exactly say I sit in the waiting room when your mother is in there. The air gets a little close for me. Liesl and J.K. enjoy spying. But I do recall passing and seeing a tall, yellow-faced, orange-haired individual in a suit and tie. I should have guessed they were together."

He told Ray he'd instantly figured out Adele was up to some legal shenanigans the second he'd laid eyes on Hugh Butterworth Jr. She'd had his father in her pocket for decades. And now the son. Adele, of course, had refused to talk about it, but it made no difference. And, of course, she would lose.

"Lose or win, I've got to appear tomorrow morning, 10 A.M. at family court down on Jay Street. So I'll be late coming here, OK?"

He told Ray to bring Liesl with him to court. Even though she didn't practice law much anymore, she was, after all, a member of the New York State Bar.

"I'd forgotten that," Ray admitted.

He told Ray that Adele would lose, and that would only enrage her all the more. He'd seen it all while he was feverish. Ray would have to take extra care once Adele lost, because when she didn't get what she wanted, she became even more dangerous.

Ray set his jaw as though preparing himself for her onslaught, looking so cute when he tried to look determined that Jesse could kiss him. But, of course, there was no way to prepare for all the contingencies with Adele. Determination would help, but it would not be enough, really. What was needed was ruthlessness. Jesse had been ruthless with Adele, which was why he'd triumphed. Of course she'd never forgiven him. Ray could never be ruthless enough. Which was why Liesl had to be there. Liesl could be as ruthless as Adele if it meant protecting Jesse.

Ray listened and set his face even more determinedly, which was adorable, so Jesse tried another tack; he tried to explain to Ray some of what he'd seen and why he was so sure it was a true vision.

"I told you before, I'm not going west while you need me. No discussion."

That was when he got up the nerve to tell Ray he had envisioned something wrong with Sable. Some health problem. Not necessarily fatal, but serious. Before he'd finished, Ray got out of the chair quietly and took two steps back, so now he was haloed.

"What are you talking about?"

Jesse thought that, given Ray's reaction, he already knew what Jesse was talking about. He tried to get Ray to sit down again, but all he got was Ray's hand, held in his own, while Ray remained standing and said what had happened the night before.

In between Ray's hospital visits at 5 o'clock and 10 o'clock the previous night, he'd gone to dinner at Kathy's apartment. Chris joined him, but not Kathy's boyfriend, who was out with friends from work. It had been a great evening, almost old times, only missing Jesse to be complete. Afterward, while Ray and Kathy were doing the dishes, Chris and Sable had been playing on the rug in front of the TV and Chris had been tickling her, when he said he'd felt something weird under her left arm. He got up and reported it to Ray and Kathy, and they'd found it too. A swollen, hard-as-a-rock little lymph node. Kathy immediately began to worry. Sable had been logy and without energy all month. By no means her usual effervescent self. She'd attributed it to Chris being away, to the weather—Sable had also had two colds and the flu already this winter—but now Kathy was concerned. A quick phone call to J.K. proved useless as he was out, so Kathy had called an actress she knew who was married to a surgeon, and he took the phone and asked Kathy to check if any of Sable's other lymph nodes were swollen. She did a fast check, and found one other one. He advised her to take Sable to a pediatrician. They were going in this afternoon, after school. How had Jesse known that? He definitely hadn't told him last night. Jesse was barely conscious last night anyway. Had Kathy called?

Jesse didn't know what to say. He'd seen in his visions what it was, seen right into Sable's body as though she were transparent—one of those plastic anatomical display models used in schools—seen how white the blood became, how thickened the lymph nodes had become: He was almost certain it was leukemia, but he couldn't bring himself to say that to Ray. Especially since he'd sensed something wrong with her for almost a year now, as though being fatally ill himself conveyed along with it some other, hitherto unexplored ability to tell whom else was ill and even how they were ill.

He repeated to Ray that what Sable had was serious but not necessarily fatal. He repeated that Adele would lose in court tomorrow and become even more menacing for Ray. He repeated that Ray would fly to Los Angeles in six weeks to oversee the remix and commercial recording to Maurette's soundtrack. He wanted Ray to look around very carefully during that trip, because he thought Ray would relocate not too far away.

He'd seen a hillside. Big old trees. Very green. Semitropical flowers everywhere.

Ray dropped his hand, as though jolted by electricity, and stared. Jesse grasped for Ray's hand again and managed to grip only the ends of his fingers as he kept talking. He knew Ray didn't want to hear any of this. The last thing he wanted was to have to go, but he had to be prepared for everything now, everything and anything. Did he understand?

"No, I don't understand," Ray's words lied for him. "You're better. The Septra and everything worked. You're not going anywhere but home, as soon as you get better. The doctor said he expects the pneumocystis will be totally wiped out in a few days. Anything else is just anxiety. You're going to be better, you hear, and maybe even so much better that I'll relent and go to L.A. for the damned soundtrack. But that's it! You got that? That's it."

Ray was totally panicked, totally adamant, totally crazed about it, so Jesse satisfied himself with making Ray comfortable again and getting him to give him his entire hand and then sit and calm down, which took maybe another half hour, after which Jesse was so tired he fell asleep, contented that he hadn't chased Ray off for good. Not now. Not this time. And maybe from now on he should just keep his mouth shut about what he'd seen, what he knew, so out of it already himself, half in, half out, that he couldn't really share the frenzy, the hysteria that streamed from every pore of Ray's core, filling the room almost as much as all those tiny curlicues of strings inside what looked like bubbles that Jesse saw whenever he looked, especially in the sunlight, so pervasive they might be the very stuff of existence...so comforting...

$*\ *\ *$

Jesse was sleeping at last, so Ray was able to slowly extrude his hand and check all the tubes and wires connecting him, unwind the light blanket from Jesse's feet where it was always getting caught up, wrapped, twisted, as though Jesse were dancing the Madison for chrissake, instead of simply lying in bed, and once he was certain Jesse wouldn't wake up immediately, he left the room, thankfully a regular single-patient room, no longer an IC unit two floors up, and edged along the wall where it opened to the waiting room, where luckily Liesl was present but not J.K. nor the Monster and her henchman.

He showed her the subpoena, and she agreed with Jesse that she had to join him in family court. She'd have to make a call to cancel lunch just in case, but it wasn't a problem. And she'd call in a favor and find out what judge would be presiding, she said, copying down the number and section of the warrant on a pad. It would be in private chambers, she thought: just the five of them. That done, he had to apologize to her. He'd argued with Jesse about something stupid, tiring him out for Liesl. He was asleep now. But she was OK with that too. She'd go into the room and read her magazine while Jesse slept, be there when he woke up.

The morning's sunlight was so strong when he got out of the hospital that he unzipped his leather jacket again and enjoyed the warm air on his throat and face. He wondered if it would get hot enough this afternoon to melt this dirty, weeks-old ice and snow or if instead it would warm up just enough to melt the top layer, which would refreeze again tonight, as it had done several times already since the winter had set in, rendering some sections of ice banks distinctly layered, cut through top to bottom like geological strata, detailing ages, not days. Maybe today; it was almost balmy.

He kept the driver's side window half down. He was headed toward the Brooklyn Bridge, selecting side-street shortcuts to avoid the usual mess, on his way into Manhattan to check out a few places around Canal Street that still sold 35 millimeter magnetic recording tape on giant reels. He'd noticed his supply was running short in the office. Due to the various ins and outs of the labyrinth formed by one-way streets, he ended up about three blocks from home and was stopped at a traffic signal when he noticed straight ahead, in the midst of parallel parking on the left side of the street, what looked exactly like Mike from Massapequa's van. Same back, same color. What baffled him was that this cross road was residential; in fact, all of this area was residential—he didn't think there was a restaurant or store for several blocks. If that was Mike, why was he stopping? A door on one of the larger apartment buildings?

The light turned green, and he slowly went forward, crossing the side street and pulling up to the van. Which, as he neared it, he now confirmed was indeed Mike's. Mike, however, was not inside, so Ray pulled up past it and looked around. The only good-size apartment building with a glass-doored lobby was number 70 on the right, but it didn't look like one of those electronic doors Mike worked on. Maybe he was wrong? Or was it the other driver, not Mike, using it today?

He'd pulled up a few inches more, past two bare trees, when to his left he spotted Mike. He was down several steps below street level at 75, inside the tiny glass-doored lobby to a standard four-story, 30-foot-wide building. He was dressed as Ray always saw him, forest-green pants and work shirt, big tan down-filled vest, his corduroy hat with the ear muffs buttoned together over the crown, his usual yellow plastic wrap-around sunglasses. Mike faced away from the street, ringing a bell on the side wall panel.

Before Ray could do anything but register the scene, someone in the car behind started honking like mad. Baffled by what he'd seen, afraid Mike would notice him and think he was following, or worse, spying on him, Ray shot forward. But he turned at the next corner and after several minutes was back. The van remained parked. Mike was no longer visible in the lobby—doubtless he'd been let into the building.

Again a driver honked at him. This time he drove straight up Joralemon to Adams, to the bridge and into Manhattan. He tried not to think about what he'd seen. Mike was probably there having sex with someone else. But that was so obvious that Ray was sure it couldn't be true. But then he had to ask himself why Mike shouldn't be having sex with some other guy? He and Mike weren't lovers. They had no agreement to not to see others. And in truth, Mike might have taken the whole AIDS and condom speech as preapproval for him seeing other guys—instead of as the general warning it was intended—as long as he wore a condom with the other guy. Ray had been on top so far, and while Mike sporadically talked about fucking Ray, he hadn't so far and, Ray guessed, probably wouldn't. True, he sucked Mike off, but he wasn't convinced one could get infected that way unless a whole host of factors was involved. Besides which, Mike, while gorgeous and sexy as hell, was married to someone: a woman. While Ray was undoubtedly married to Jesse. And at the moment he had his hands full enough without worrying about this.

He'd justified it all so perfectly that he ceased to think about it by the time he'd parked on Canal Street. An hour later he was back home, packing away the new tapes when Maurette phoned. He'd just gotten back to town and was completely buoyant, a balloon on a string headed into the atmosphere. Ray hoped not to bring him down while trying to convey his problems with Jesse and how they would impact any upcoming travel plans.

"I understand absolutely, *cher*. Absolutely. But let's just say you could travel and go with me to L.A. and rerecord and remix the soundtrack, tell me how you would do it? This is purely speculative, you understand. Completely pie in the sky, *cher*. But still you must have thought about it a little bit?"

Ray admitted he had.

"So what's it going to cost to tell me?"

So that someone else could do it? Ray wanted to know.

"You know I hope not, *cher*. But you would do what—keep the score as it lays out in the film, right? Chronologically. But that's not enough for an album. So what else?"

Ray wasn't happy about being pumped so someone else could do the job, he had to admit, but he wasn't leaving Maurette with much of a choice, so despite himself, he talked about the ideas he had. Of course all the music that he'd used in the film would appear on the soundtrack—in full time. So the Sibelius symphony movement, of which about three minutes appeared on the film's track, would be run its full eight minutes. And he thought the piano transcription of it, which they'd cut from the film, would be reprised later, maybe at track 10. "The Courtier's Ghost Song," with the Chinese violin, which had replaced it, would also appear completely, adding another six minutes. He'd already figured that to 40 minutes. Then he'd thought to add in an intro and epilogue using music not in the film but similar to both the Sibelius transcription and the Chopin they'd used—the Albert Ferber recordings of a Faure's barcarole and nocturne.

"My *maman* played Faure's nocturnes at home!" Maurette said, thrilled. "One in F, I think. I don't recall. I love that music!"

Ray knew he was being more than a little disingenuous. Now that he'd obtained the rights to reissue the Albert Ferber Faure works, having them on the soundtrack would repay Klavier Stuecke's licensing fees. And if the film or the music were hits, everyone would suddenly want the music on a CD by itself and Ray would have that ready. Even so, he added, "Of course this is just speculative."

"Completely and totally speculative, *cher*!" Maurette agreed.

The two of them lying to each other like that: Ray knowing Maurette would move heaven and earth to get him into that studio in Culver City; Maurette knowing that Ray wanted it as badly and would look for some way to join him in California and be part of what was looking artistically potent and possibly quite profitable. An odd sensation: recognizing that they were admitting to exploiting each other for the good of both of them; a feeling Ray had never had before. Strangely adult.

Ended by the buzzing of the doorbell.

And there, if Ray needed more confusion in his life, more of a twisting around in his mind, was Mike, dressed just as he'd seen him not an hour and a half before, a few streets away, pushing into the office, saying "Man! You look so good you'd better take those clothes off before I rip them off. Excuse me, yeah? Gotta use the john!" Shooting past Ray standing stock still in the office, as he headed toward the bathroom.

A half hour later Mike climaxed with even more than his ordinary vocal outburst.

The two remained in bed, Ray and Mike both exhausted.

"He's not here today?" Mike asked. And before Ray could ask who, he added, "The last few times I was by, I sort of sensed you wanted to get rid of me so you could check upstairs."

"Was I that obvious? No, he's in the hospital. He's doing a little better today."

And since Mike had opened the gates, Ray decided to do the same. "I'm actually surprised to see you. A few hours ago I drove past 75 Clark Street, and I thought I saw you going into the building."

"I did. I came here first. But there was no answer."

"I was at the hospital," Ray said. He'd said it, he would ask nothing more.

"Remember," Mike asked, "when I told you I planned to use these work trips to get to know the city more?"

Ray did.

"About a month ago I passed the Brooklyn Museum, and something about the signs across the front, I don't know, attracted me. American Impressionists, it said. Hell, I had only the foggiest idea what that meant. But I liked the painting in front. So I parked and went in. Felt a little funny at first, dressed like this. But no one cared, and I really liked those paintings. Told my wife about it that night. I might have been talking to the wall for all she cared. At any rate, I went back again, and while I was there the second time I met this woman and we got to talking and she took me around the show and told me all about the artists and what they were trying to do. We ended up coming back to her place, 75 Clark Street, you know, and…doing it. She's about 55. Divorced. Used to be a dancer. Still has a terrific body! Amazing body! Better than my wife at half her age, even though her face is older. She works part time. I saw her another time. Another time that you were out. She doesn't blow as good as you, but I like to screw her."

Mike spoke so matter-of-factly about it that Ray was intrigued. Whatever remnant of fear he might have had about Mike contracting disease had vanished.

"So you went there and fucked her. Then you came here so I could fuck you?"

"Yeah!" Mike laughed. He'd probably never put it that bluntly to himself. "Cool, huh?" and before Ray could respond, he added, "If I had told you before you fucked me, would it have been hotter for you?"

"It's always hot with you. So…I know about her. Does she know about me?"

"Not exactly. But when we first met I told her I did it with guys too. I think that turned her on even more. By the way, she gave me some books. One on American art and one on Impressionism. Why don't you give me some music to listen to?" Mike leaned over the edge of the bed and went into his pants pockets and pulled out a crumpled piece of small notebook paper. "Here. I copied down some music I heard on the radio."

Ray read:

Bach Toecata in Dee

Beethoven Pastoral Symfony

Barber's DiMaggio

"I know that last one can't be right," Mike said. "You know, there was traffic, and I heard the guy say it over the radio."

"Could it be Samuel Barber's 'Adagio'? His 'Adagio for Strings'?"

"Yeah, that sounds right. You have that?

"I have them all. You have a cassette deck? CD player?"

"Cassette deck." Mike's face was all lit up. He looked about 12 years old. "So, how's that movie work going?"

"It's going really well. The movie I scored won a prize in Germany. It's going to be shown here this year." Even as he said it, Ray suspected what kind of reaction he'd receive from Mike. Despite that, he charged on. "The director wants me to go to Los Angeles to record a soundtrack."

"No shit! To Hollywood?!" he all but crowed. "You are the man! The! *Man!* And I am," dropping his head onto Ray's abdomen and nuzzling there, "I am the…o-fish-yul cocksucker to *the man!* O-fish-yul fuck boy to *the man!*"

eighteen

Gratifyingly, the judge's antechamber was not especially dirty. Gratifyingly and also surprisingly, as just about every other locale she'd been in since she'd arrived in this horrifying city had been, in her opinion, astoundingly filthy. Beginning with the rented automobile that had taken her to the hotel from the airport—how could they refer to that mobile house of licentiousness, filled with bottle upon bottle of liquor, as a limousine, she'd never in her life understand. Not to mention that hotel lobby and the hotel lavatory—scandalous—which despite her note to the cleaning staff along with a $5 bill had not improved in cleanliness one jot. Not one jot. But luckily she had come prepared with her own washcloths and towel. And soap too. Who would blame her for not touching what they provided? Even the walls of that shower and bathtub were doubtless covered with bacteria. She'd bathe with her own notions, thank you very much, even if it meant having to give herself sink-baths. Meanwhile, she couldn't even begin to discuss the conditions within that hospital. Hospital, her left foot! The place was a hellhole, no better than a concentration camp. The staff were the lowest sort, and even worse than the colored folk—who at least knew to behave when she spoke to them—the place was crawling with Asian Indians, perhaps the single most uppity dark-skinned people God in his Infinite Wisdom had seen fit to place upon this earth. And that, despite the allegedly sanitized condition of humanity following upon the Great Flood. Asian Indians, moreover, affecting to be medical staff, although what good in the world could they hope to do with nearly a billion of their own people back home starving? How could they presume to help anyone at all when they couldn't even control their own appetites and desist from breeding like Norwegian rats?

That young fool, Hugh Butterworth Jr., sitting there, simpering as he rifled through copies of automobile racing magazines he kept hidden in his attaché case as though it were pornography, had actually claimed to her face not to notice how appalling those pseudomedics were, nor how ghastly that quagmire of a hospital had been. But then what else could be expected from a person who'd spent years studying in a university on the plains of New Jersey, of all places, Ivy League college or not? What was wrong with the boy that he couldn't attend a school that had well enough educated for life his father, two uncles, numberless cousins, *and* a grandfather? Doubtless those blighted years passed in New Jersey had habituated him to the rudeness, accustomed him to the dirt, blinded him to the ignorance, made acceptable the lowest levels of service, and perhaps he was not fabricating when he claimed not to be offended by talkback-to-your-face Indians? She didn't know how much longer she could possibly abide it, any of it, but then, perhaps these days of sacrifice and torment were coming to an end, as surely they must, once the legal authority on the other side of that door had ruled in her favor.

This morning, as they had arrived at the vacant antechamber, Hugh Jr. had informed her that he'd at least done a bit of the investigating he'd been hired to do: The judge, he apprised her, was a woman of about her own years. Undoubtedly, she assumed, herself a mother. So, yes, she'd been gratified by that news, late as it had come, for hadn't she been up most of the night praying and worrying? Surely no woman, no mother in her right mind would allow this farce of illegality to continue a second longer. Imagine the humiliation should it ever get back home—and Hugh Jr. had been warned that she would very well know *how* it had gotten back—having your own firstborn's life in the hands of a stranger, a Hebrew? It was beyond comprehension. It must be righted immediately.

Then, on top of that, no sooner had that fool of a boy calmed her with the news that the judge was a woman, than he'd nearly frightened her out of her wits by saying, "And I believe she's white." He *believed* she was white. What else could she be? That was simply inconceivable, even in this Slough of the Devil. For herself, she wanted to see the judge's name—and had been not affrighted that it was Collins, Mary Collins, a good Christian name, although Lord knew that other kind never were shy to appropriate a name, no matter how Christian or honorable, for themselves.

In fact, she'd for the first time since she'd arrived in this Yankee town felt her old self again, when *he* had sauntered into the antechamber, acting as though butter wouldn't melt in his mouth, and even worse, accompanied by that lovely yellow-haired girl who'd been at the hospital every day. Now why in the world couldn't have Jesse taken up with her? She was so lovely and polite. The children would have been adorable. And while she was equivocal since she was, after all, European, and a Hun at that, at least she wasn't One Who'd Killed Christ. But even that joy had been short-lived and had led to heart palpitations requiring two deep sniffs of her special salts when Hugh Jr. had naturally enough asked to know what that Lisa girl was doing in what was supposed to be a private legal session, and *he* had the effrontery to reply that she was present in her capacity as his legal counsel. Well, she could have died on the spot. And that fool Hugh Jr. had actually said, "Well, then that's all right, then." *All right, then*?! Could anyone have been prepared for such betrayal?

And before she'd even gotten her breath back, some large brown person in a uniform had come into the room and called them to order, although they were in no way disorderly, not even *him*, and opened the double doors to the judge's chambers, and they went in and found seats around the table desk where the judge was seated. She welcomed them, removing her glasses, wearing a very feminine, frilled blouse gathered at the neck with ribbons, a sensible enough looking woman who'd lived long enough to know what was what, this Judge Collins, although she had to admit she'd expected someone petite and well, rather a bit more delicately featured, whereas this woman was rather large-boned, her facial features rather broad, in the Mediterranean sense, her abundant hair brown with glints of red, and now she could just kick herself, because after all, if the judge were married, she probably wasn't a Collins herself. Only one way to find out...

"I knew a Collins family from Fearrington, North Carolina. You aren't by any chance related?" Adele asked.

A sympathetic smile. "I believe not. My husband's family's from Bala Cynwyd."

"And your own?" Adele tried not to hide how crushed she might still be.

"The Santangelos? From Flushing, New York."

At least she was Christian. Although of the Roman Church.

All of them were seated, introduced, and Judge Collins fumbled through some papers on her desk before looking up at them.

"First, I want to say how sorry I am to learn the grounds of this motion, and to hear how very ill Jesse is."

Before she could get a word out, Adele was amazed to hear *him* thank the judge.

The nerve of him. She added her thanks anyway.

"I also believe that both parties present wish to do what is best for Jesse in the remaining short time he has with us." She looked down at her papers. "I've read your request, Mrs. Moody, and as a mother myself, I understand why you would wish to take such action, naturally."

As a mother herself, naturally.

"I'm less clear," the judge went on, "why it's being taken at such a late date."

She looked up at Adele, all curiosity.

"That was a question to yourself, Mrs. Moody."

"The question being?"

"Why you are making this request at such a late date?"

"It's not late at all," she said.

"According to what I've been led to understand, your son seroconverted more than five years ago and began outpatient treatment for his HIV symptoms more than two years ago." She looked over at *him*, at *them*. "Is that correct? Yes. Well, given that time frame, Mrs. Moody, today is in fact quite late."

That young fool Hugh Jr. simply sat there and gaped. But of course she'd had no idea anything had occurred five years ago, never mind two.

"Mrs. Moody?" the judge asked again.

To her complete disgust, it was *he* who spoke up. "This was the first time she found about it. Jesse wouldn't tell her. I tried to get him to tell her. It's been a standing argument between us. She only found out a few weeks ago when Jesse resigned from work."

"I see," the judge said. "I'm sorry to hear that. It must have come as a great shock to you, Mrs. Moody."

She did understand. "It was *indeed* a great shock, Your Honor."

"And as soon as you heard the news you came to your son's side."

"Well…no…I'm afraid…I…wasn't able to…"

Hugh Jr. chipped in: "Mrs. Moody has many obligations back home."

"A sick husband?" the judge offered.

"He died five years ago," Hugh Jr. said, only digging her in deeper.

"I'm sorry to hear that. Another family member ill, perhaps?"

"I had many social, voluntary organization obligations," Adele said, saving herself.

"Yes…I see."

"I had no idea my son was so ill. I told that young man myself, the other day, didn't I? How shocked and surprised I was to see how badly off my son was?"

He confirmed it. "Mrs. Moody was very shocked and surprised."

"Let's move on then," Judge Collins said. "You are contesting Mr. Henriques's medical power of attorney. Why are you doing so?"

Whatever did she mean? "I believe that is evident. I am Jesse's mother."

"Yes, and…?"

"I am his next of kin, not Mr. Henriques. He's not in any way related to Jesse."

The judge turned to him. "Mr. Henriques, what is your relationship to Jesse?"

"We've been partners for 12 years. We bought our home together a decade ago. We've signed up for the city legal partnership certificate, once the law is in effect."

"Then," the judge looked directly at her, "I don't understand what cause you have, Mrs. Moody, to overturn what appears to be a perfectly reasonable legal instrument."

What in the world was she talking about? Perfectly reasonable legal what? Adele clutched at Hugh's arm. Do something! *Do something!*

At last he spoke up. "Mrs. Moody believes that her son was coerced by Mr. Henriques into assigning him as the person holding medical power of attorney."

"Coerced?" the judge asked. "In what way?"

"Mrs. Moody believes Mr. Henriques waited until Jesse was incapable of reason before allowing this to happen and that he was under duress at the time."

She rifled through her desk looking for something.

Now the Hun betrayer spoke up. "Your honor, have you seen the shared power of attorney papers? They're dated ten years ago. Long before Jesse even knew he was infected. Does Mrs. Moody believe her son incapable of reason for the past ten years?" She handed forward a copy of something the judge looked at.

Then *he* had the gall to speak. "Your Honor, we each signed power of attorney over to each other when we bought the house together. Medical. Financial. Everything."

"That makes sense, Mr. Henriques," the judge said. "Did you hear, Mrs. Moody?"

Now it was Hugh's turn. "Mrs. Moody believes her son was under other kinds of coercion long before he was ill," he began boldly. "Possibly for the past ten years."

"During which, Your Honor," *she* interrupted, "Jesse was promoted through the ranks until he'd become an officer of a major Madison Avenue advertising firm."

"Ten years of coercion," Hugh Jr. hesitated and almost stammered as he went, "through...uh...shared...uh...sexual perversions...and...uh, possibly also, drug use."

"He fed my son drugs and seduced him," Adele said aloud. "My son would never take up with anyone like him or do any of those foul things unless he were drugged and seduced. He was raised a good Christian boy."

There. She'd said it. And now it must be clear to all.

The Hitler Youth Girl spoke up. "According to what Mr. Jesse Moody told me, Your Honor, he's been openly homosexual since the age of 16. He had numerous sexual relations with men throughout college. When his mother found out about it, she coerced him into seeing a psychiatrist. All this happened long before he met my client. Therefore, these allegations are scurrilous and," turning to Hugh Jr., "also actionable!"

"Hold on, I think we're all a little upset at the moment," the dear judge said.

She'd spoken and she wouldn't be shut up now. "This person is a pederast!"

"Jesse Moody was 25 years old when they met!"

But she had the advantage and wouldn't let it go now. "He is a pederast. He keeps a boy in his house. I spoke to him on the phone! A boy named," she found the paper, "Christopher Smith! God only knows what the poor boy's been subjected to!"

"Christopher Smith is Mr. Henriques's nephew!" the blond said.

"Thirteen years old!" Adele went on. "You can't tell me that's legal. Not even in this heathen city!"

The judge looked right at *him*. Now he was going to get it good.

"Mr. Henriques, is this true?"

"Your Honor, Mr. Moody and myself petitioned this family court three months ago to become my nephew's legal guardians. On Chris's request. And ours. We're awaiting word. He is 13. He does live with us."

"Thirteen years old," Adele cried out. "In the next bedroom to their perversion!"

"Chris has his own bedroom," *he* went on. "It's not next to ours. It's upstairs on the second floor. With his own bath and dressing area. Next to the kitchen, which is crucial for a 13-year-old."

Now the blond: "Chris's mother is a single working widow. She has a younger girl to care for. This arrangement is with her full consent."

How dare they? "It's an abomination," Adele said. "An abomination."

"In this city, in this day and age, Mrs Moody," the judge said in a tight voice, "it's an abomination when a fatherless boy of 13 with a working single mother has no one who wants him and no bedroom of his own—with or without a separate bath." She turned to the blond. "I trust that if an investigation were done, no warrants or past arrests for molestation would appear."

"He's my nephew, for chrissake!"

"No warrants or arrests for any reason would show up," the blond lied.

Incensed, Adele stood up, proudly. "You let him take the Lord's name in vain?"

"Sit down, Mrs. Moody. Sit down, all of you."

"You won't find anything even remotely wrong with my client, Your Honor," the blond had the temerity to say.

Hugh kept tugging at Adele to sit, so she subsided into her chair.

"Mrs. Moody," the Judge began. "What hospital did you wish your son to be transferred to?"

"Your Honor," both of *them* sprang to their feet, "he's in no medical condition to be moved. The doctors said—"

"Hold on, you two," the judge said. "I'm doing the talking here. Which hospital?"

Now they were getting somewhere. She tapped Hugh, and he didn't fumble much before bringing forth the information.

The judge took it. "I trust that this Doctors Hospital has full AIDS care facilities?"

"In South Carolina? Sure!" the blond piped up and was glared at by the judge.

"Doctors Hospital is the best in the state," Adele said.

"That wasn't my question. Your son is in the final stage of AIDS, Mrs. Moody. Does this hospital you want him sent to have adequate facilities to care for him?"

"I'm certain they do."

"But you don't know for a fact?" the judge asked. "You didn't call them and ask?"

"Do you ask your doctor if he is qualified?"

"My doctor is a she," the judge said. "And yes, if I required special care, I would ask if she were qualified. And if not, I would ask her to recommend someone who was."

"I have no doubt they can handle any case put before them."

"Mrs. Moody, you seem to think your son's condition is a broken foot or a tonsillectomy. It's not. Your son requires special care. Special medicine. Special knowledge. Hospice care. Do they have a hospice for the dying?"

She'd gone too far. Judge or not. "My son is not dying!"

"OK, sit down, Mrs. Moody." The judge looked them over. "I'm going to ask for an hour recess until I can straighten out a few matters. I want to run a check on any criminal record Mr. Henriques may have. I'm sorry, Mr. Henriques, the question did arise."

"It's totally irrelevant to his ability to care for Mr. Moody," the blond said.

"Even so, it did come up. Mrs. Moody, I have to speak to your hospital to find out what kind of facilities they have for your son."

The judge pressed a buzzer, and in seconds the large brown person entered and shooed them all out. *He* left the anteroom immediately. Probably to call someone to have all the torture instruments removed from their Den of Iniquity in case the police arrived. The little blond, however, remained; she stood there and shook her finger at poor Hugh Jr., berating him, telling him and her—the utter nerve of the tramp—to both watch what they said about *him* from now on. Showing her true colors, the deceitful little Jew-lover, threatening poor cowed Hugh Jr., then spinning on her heels to leave.

Adele dropped into a chair. Hugh stood and poured himself some water.

"Well, I do believe we have them on the run," she said.

Hugh Jr. didn't respond.

"I said, I do believe—"

He turned. "I heard what you said, Mrs. Moody." He sighed.

"I do believe," she went on contentedly, "that my son will be returned to me."

"Did you hear nothing that was said in that room, Mrs. Moody? He's not going to be returned to you. Not ever. Even if she rules in our favor. Your son is dying. The doctors will keep him here until he dies."

She was flabbergasted. "Surely you can't believe what you're saying?"

He looked right at her, the fool, but had the good sense not to speak. Yet she was for the first time worried. What was it Daddy Moody used to say all the time? We won the battle but lost the war. And the operation was a success but the patient died.

Hugh Jr. said, "And what if she does allow him to move? And what if they do release him from this hospital? Have you thought that through? When he dies, what do you think people will think at home?"

She was tired of his defeatism. Tired of him. "People will think what we tell them to think. As usual. They'll think he died of pneumonia. It happens every day."

"A young man? Just 40?"

"He will not die. We'll pray for him. And even if it he does, it's all for the better. It will be a moral victory!" she assured him. "Don't you see? We will have a moral victory against the perverts! That's why we must win!"

"What moral victory?" But before she could explain herself, he left the room.

The fool. The damned fool. Ruined by all his consorting with Yankees, having his own morality eroded by the constant connection. Not that his father, Hugh Butterworth Sr., had ever been that much of an attorney himself. But at least he'd toed the line; in love with Adele since the age of 12, he'd remained putty in her hands for decades, and she'd been able to play him like a piano, until he'd had the bad idea to up and die last year. Leaving her to rely upon this spiritually bankrupt heir. Ah, well! She couldn't too much complain about Hugh Jr. At least he'd done what his daddy had wanted, and even if he did live in this City of Hell, at least he'd married an acceptable young woman and raised children. Unlike her own Cross to Bear, lying a few streets over there, nothing but a skull and a few pieces of skin, a child brought onto earth for the sole purpose of denying her decency and ruining her life. Nothing but trouble from the beginning, with his contrary ways and his willfulness, just a little demon, and worst of all a demon packaged to look just like her if she had been born a boy, prettier almost. It had to have been Satan's work. And it was only due to the Black One's influence that he'd not died far sooner, trampling on the words of the Bible as he'd done for years. Still, if they were all correct about his prognosis, soon he too would be gone, and she'd be allowed to at least hold her head high when she buried him, back home, out of Grace Methodist Church, the long-suffering mother of an errant offspring, returned home to be ensconced among his forebears. She'd have to look for something new to bring back with her, as long as she was so close to all those Jewish tailors and dressmakers, who, she had to admit, certainly possessed that asset in their favor—they could make the most wonderful clothing, even the French and Italians had to stand in awe. Perhaps that black shift she'd seen advertised in the newspaper, that Anne Klein dress? Or was it Donna Karan? No matter, it would look just stunning covered by that Calvin Klein shawl. Thank the Lord he'd allowed her to more or less retain her petite figure so she might wear these lovely things. It was awfully important to make a good impression back home, no matter how sobering the occasion. Above all, she knew how important it was that she show them that the Filth could not win, not over good Christians.

Suddenly they were all being moved back into judge's chambers again. Stars! Had it been an hour already? And she hadn't even had time to wash her face, although Lord knew what this courthouse lavatory would look like, even if she was equipped with sanitary towelettes. Hugh Jr. had her by the arm and was walking her in. They sat as before. The judge had an odd look on her face; Adele couldn't tell what she meant by it.

"These are the facts," Judge Collins said, matter-of-factly, looking at Adele. "Doctors Hospital does not, Mrs.Moody, have AIDS care facilities. And the administrator I spoke to specifically asked that no AIDS patients be sent to their facility, as no one there is willing to care for, or even touch, such a patient. Furthermore, they did not even wish to know the name of the patient. Secondly," looking at *him*, "your record, Mr. Henriques, as far as I can tell in this short time is clear: no arrests, no convictions for anything. I spoke to your sister at work and she confirmed your nephew's wish to live with you. You failed to tell me that he did not get along with her...new partner. You also failed to tell me you have visited his school in a parental role. Those further helped your position here. In short, ladies and gentlemen, this court sees no compelling reason to alter this legal instrument titled "Medical Power of Attorney" signed by Jesse Moody on the 12 of July, 1982 in the State of New York, duly witnessed and notarized, assigning such power exclusively to Mr. Moody's life partner, Raymond Henriques."

She could not believe it was happening. She grasped at Hugh Jr.'s sleeve. Do something! *Do something!*

"Your Honor," Hugh Jr. blurted out, "Mrs. Moody wants the hospital to recognize her status in regard to her son."

"Meaning what?" the judge asked.

"Meaning, she wishes to be listed as next of kin."

"Next of kin, Mr. Butterworth, as you know, in this instance is a very specific term, signifying the person who holds power of attorney."

"Can't her name be added to Mr. Henriques's?" Hugh Jr. tried. "In case he can't be found?"

"He's at the hospital for hours every day," the blond said. "The first night he slept in the corridors outside Jesse's room. They've got his phone number. Why won't he be found? Your Honor, we don't like this. With all due respect, Mrs. Moody knows nothing about her son's medical condition. My client both knows his condition, and he knows and will abide by Jesse's wishes regarding care. I realize Mrs. Moody cannot be expected to know all this material on such short notice. Still, at the least, adding her name can only confuse the medical staff."

"I'm afraid they're right, Mrs. Moody," the judge said sympathetically.

It couldn't be. But perhaps she might still draw some trinket from the ashes of overwhelming defeat. "Your Honor," she began in what she hoped was a pitiful voice, "when my son was in intensive care, I could only see him five minutes at a time, every 20 minutes. But *he*—and he is not a mother—*he* could see him as long as he wished, whenever he wished. All I wish is for the same consideration."

"That does seem only fair," the judge said. "After consideration, this court has decided to petition the medical staff of the hospital. Jesse is to have Mrs. Moody's name placed on his file as someone who is to be granted full visitation rights. The final decision and the implementation will, of course, be up to the hospital, you understand, Mrs. Moody. They also have procedures. I'm afraid that's all I can do for you."

All and very little at that. "Thank you, Your Honor."

They were being pushed out of chambers again, the barbarians gleefully dashing out of the antechamber, as *he* had the infinitely poor grace to crow, "I've got to get to the hospital. I want to let Jesse know everything's going to be all right." Leaving her there with that poor specimen of a man and attorney, Hugh Butterworth Jr., who had the temerity to actually smile at her, amid the very depths of her humiliation, to try to take her arm—how dare he?—and try to move her outside the judge's antechamber, blathering about how right Adele had been, the judge had not been able to deny her full visitation rights to her son, they had achieved a moral victory after all. The idiot, didn't he realize, couldn't he see how wholly and unconditionally she had been vanquished, mortified, trod underfoot upon by this walking human garbage? Well, Hugh Jr. would know soon. They would *all* know soon, that they had chosen the wrong woman. She would live to see them destroyed, all of them, or her name wasn't Adele Vaughan Moody, née Carstairs!

nineteen

"Rags, why don't we meet you at the checkout counter?" Kathy said. "You coming with me, honey?" she asked Sable, who silently lifted her arms to be picked up. She was far too heavy for Kathy, but Ray lifted her and stood her where he could find room inside the big, already filled shopping cart. Ever since she'd discovered her medical condition, and especially since she'd begun chemotherapy, Sable's personality had changed. In weeks she'd been transformed from the fun-loving, talkative, extroverted, confident, trusting girl he'd known into one almost pathologically shy, reserved, dependent, and, above all, fearful. She'd reverted to clasping and clinging behavior he'd not seen in her since she was four years old. Where before she'd been forthright and direct, now she was whining and often spoke in what Ray termed her "baby voice." And it didn't help that she didn't look well. Always a little vain, Sable now all but disguised herself behind overlarge caps and hats and multiwrapped scarves. And no wonder. Her hair had already begun to drop out from the treatments, and her skin had dulled from its usual golden tint to a matte hue that resembled overmilked café au lait. Ray and his sister had discussed the changes. He'd criticized Kathy for pandering to her daughter. She'd told him it was only temporary, not a long-term change, brought on by shock that Sable was after all mortal, something no nine-year-old wanted to believe. Kathy insisted her "little fighter" would return in a few weeks. He was less sure; at least he didn't believe she would reappear as long as her mother kept on rewarding her infantile behavior. "And thanks, Rags, for driving us out here," Kathy added, changing the subject. "This place is so great, and I don't know how we would have done it without you and the car." She looked puzzled. "Where's Chris? He's never around when I need him."

"I thought I saw him in 'young men's clothing.' I'll get him. I want to look around anyway." Ray didn't want to be with Kathy when she was being oversolicitous of Sable.

They had driven out to the huge suburban outlet so the kids could get spring clothing at a discount without paying New York sales tax. It was a giant, impersonal mall, nothing like the cute village of the few closed-off streets of "downtown Brooklyn" where they usually shopped. It was also, Ray couldn't help notice, overwhelmingly white and middle-class in comparison. Even so, besides the money Kathy would save, this particular emporium was also amazingly wide-ranging in what it sold, from clothing to table linen, from auto parts to gardening equipment. They'd had no trouble filling a cart. Ray only hoped they could get it all into the Regal's trunk. Large as that was, he guessed some of it would have to sit in the backseat with the kids.

He'd just spotted his nephew at a rack filled with football logo T-shirts when he also noticed a sale on men's twill pants and shirts, the kind worn as uniforms, crisp chino-like material with standardized cuts in only four colors, navy, khaki, gray, and the same forest green Mike from Massapequa wore. And they were inexpensive: Maybe the line was being phased out. He checked them for imperfections and found nothing apparent. This was high-grade stuff, and at half price. The other colors looked more formal, but the navy was a handsome rich midnight blue, with double sheen ebony and cerulean, which he liked. He could always use them around the house. Why not get a shirt and trousers for himself and for Jesse? Jesse didn't have much of a wardrobe outside of his office wear. He'd look great in these; it would help him relax into his retirement once he was out of the hospital. They had Jesse's size exactly: 14-inch collar and medium sleeve, 30-inch waist with a 32-inch inseam.

Chris had been joined by and was now talking to a couple of boys his age. Both wore logo sweatshirts twice their size, oversize denims that hung several inches below their waists, revealing two inches of undershorts, and puffy running shoes, currently fashionable, which sartorially savvy Chris had so far resisted. They were laughing and punching each other's arms.

Chris introduced the two boys as school pals from Brooklyn, surprised to run into each other so far from home. Despite their gang-theme outfits, the boys were polite and well-spoken. Artie seemed Chinese or Korean, difficult to say, because he was 6'3" and built like a linebacker. Gino, smaller but more striking with his kinky hair and hazel eyes, was mulatto, some Mediterranean heritage—Greek, Syrian—mixed with African-American. "What'd you find?" Chris asked Ray, all but dismissing the others, who immediately took off.

Ray showed him the twills.

"You really going to wear these? They look like what janitors wear."

"You mean I haven't told you about my new job? Say good-bye to Mr. Gonsalves. I'm taking over Brooklyn El-Hi!" Ray joked. "What about you? I was under the impression we'd come here to get you clothes."

Chris hemmed and hawed and admitted that while he'd actually found "a coupla things," he'd decided after all that he didn't need them.

"Would you care to repeat that?" Ray said. "So I can be completely certain I do have a reason to go into cardiac arrest?"

"No, seriously, Uncle Ray, I know Mom hasn't said anything, and I realize she's got medical insurance through work, but I'm sure it doesn't cover everything. With Sable sick and all, she must have bills she's not talking about. She can't afford to pay for both of us. I can wear what I've got. Really, Uncle Ray," he protested.

My nephew, Ray thought. What a wonderful kid. Thirteen. In need of clothes, willing to sacrifice because of his sister's health problem. The Mother-in-Law from Hell ought to be here at this moment.

"Tell you what, kid," Ray put on his Groucho Marx voice, "since I didn't find what I was looking for, and since you've got a birthday coming up, why don't I spring for your stuff today? What say? Hey, kid? We'll call it even?"

"I don't know, Uncle Ray. You pay for so much already and—"

"The offer's on the table, kid. Going…going—"

"OK. OK." He put a hand up to stop Ray. "I'll show you what I found, but you don't have to get it for me."

"Going…going…" Ray threatened.

Chris turned to a revolving rack where he had placed a half dozen hangers, holding a windbreaker, two pairs of denims, and three dress shirts.

"This is too much, Uncle Ray. I only need—"

Ray grabbed the hangers from Chris, checked the prices, adding as he went. The entire load was less than $160, which meant that even before he'd decided to sacrifice, Chris had been looking for bargains. "Listen, Buckwheat," Ray teased him, "you also need underwear and socks. Ralph Lauren Polo is on sale. It's twice the price you usually pay, but the stuff lasts longer."

Chris found an empty shopping cart. Once they'd gotten underwear and socks, Chris insisted he had enough shoes. They again encountered his schoolmates at a revolving rack of logo sweatshirts, and Ray could tell from the way they talked that these were all the rage, so he made Chris try one on. Chris blushed as he modeled it, but he allowed Ray to talk him into getting one, adding that he would wash it himself. Which was to say he would place it into the washer and dryer downstairs. Ray tossed in a backstrap book bag. Chris at first protested, then accepted, and finally exchanged it for a different version, explaining, "Black's the only real color this year."

"Goethe would question that," Ray commented, which earned him the question, "Who's Gerther?"

Kathy and Sable were just finishing at one checkout counter when Ray and Chris joined the line at another. The other boys were nearby, with—Ray assumed—Gino's parents and a smaller boy who resembled Gino. As Ray had thought, the parents were handsome, the woman dark, svelte, petite, and very well-dressed; her husband bigger, more muscular, and barrel-chested in his flannel shirt and tight jeans with unbuttoned Shearling coat, a face off a Da Vinci drawing—aquiline nose, deep-set eagle eyes—and curly salt-and-pepper hair. He had working man's hands when they shook across the shopping cart aisle, and Ray would have sworn he checked out Ray's crotch, looking him over with the particular appraisal men use to assess a possible sexual partner. Maybe becoming Chris's official dad might bring unexpected advantages.

As the boys moved away from the cash registers to talk, and Ray and Gino's dad watched their merchandise being scanned, they continued a visual flirtation that Ray became more certain signaled, yes, I'm interested and yes, I know you're interested too. Not now. Not today. But sometime. A PTA meeting or… Then, as if to confirm it, once they'd paid and entered the parking lot and let the boys take over the carts and walk them to the cars, they dropped behind as if by tacit agreement. Ray said, "I don't know many parents of Chris's schoolmates. Maybe…you know…we could have a beer or coffee…?"

To his surprise, he was handed a business card: RENZO DOMITIANO, PLUMBING

Ray gave Renzo his own business card, adding, "I'm a homeowner. I might need plumbing work. Can I call on you?"

"Call me *before* you need the work," Renzo said, fanning himself with Ray's card. He had a surprisingly light voice, given his size and bulk, what Ray's high school music teacher referred to as Irish tenor. "It'll cost you less," Renzo went on. "I specialize in preventative plumbing. I check systems that are still OK. Make sure they keep working."

He said it so lasciviously, the high tenor voice adding all kinds of shades to his words, that Ray felt compelled to reply, "I've never heard of preventative plumbing."

"I'll ream your drain. I'll clean out all your pipes." It came out of him incredibly filthy, partly because of his lopsided smile and the way Renzo looked at Ray, his large hazel eyes almost gunsighting through his bushy black brows. "I think you know what I mean, Ray. I'm the kind of guy—I try again and again until everything comes out easy."

Ray became aware that he'd just popped an erection right in front of everyone—if anyone were looking. Renzo noticed, and it lopsided his smile an iota more. He didn't do a thing to hide the bulge in his own denims. In fact, he drew attention to it by hanging his big labor-chipped hands over the edge of his top denim pockets, angled suggestively toward the center. He recracked his smile on the other side of his face, and winked, "Remember, Ray, preventative plumbing is the best," before turning to his son gruffly and tossing Gino the car keys. The boys hurried to open the trunk of the big maroon Seville, and Renzo stopped. "Kids that age you got to keep on a tight leash. Don't forget to call. Gino! Tommy! Stop fooling around. Pack that trunk right or when we get home you know what you're gonna get."

Ray passed the car and called out Chris's name. He tossed his car keys for him to begin packing the Regal. He didn't know about Gino, but he was certain Chris didn't need to be on a short leash. He didn't know whether he would call Renzo. He pictured them in the partly open basement, together in the meager illumination of a hanging lightbulb, Renzo's large, scarred hands checking the overhead plumbing, while Ray's hands checked out Renzo's plumbing. Or better yet, the two of them sprawled on the master bathroom carpet, tools scattered everywhere, clothing torn from their bared midsections as they ravenously sixty-nined... And to think, six months before, Ray never would have believed a lubricious exchange between two apparently straight men, meeting for the first time surrounded by their families, in a suburban New Jersey mall in full sight of everyone would have been possible. Never mind that someone like Mr. Preventative Plumbing would be interested in Ray as a sex partner. There was something so deliciously subversive about it: so undermining to the whole all-American, God, mother, and apple pieness of it that he wondered if it wouldn't be even more fun arranging a holiday with the Domitianos—say Kathy and he and the kids on a Fourth of July picnic, with barbecue and fireworks, and while they were at Rockaway Beach or in Prospect Park, they'd let the kids take over turning ribs and franks on the grill so he and Renzo could creep into the bushes or into the dunes and tear off a fast fuck, all the while hearing children shout and play, maybe even catching a glimpse of the women, sweaters around their shoulders against a sudden summer chill, comparing cold remedies and meat loaf recipes. Now the maroon Seville was slowly driving by, headed out of the parking lot, and as it neared, Ray gave Renzo a conspiratorial wink. Now, thanks to Mike of Massapequa, Ray was cognizant of an entirely new universe of sexually active men, married and engaged, bisexual or secretly homosexual or however they might define themselves, unknown to him before, not even suspected, whom he might enjoy, and who might enjoy him. And even if he couldn't have sex with all of them, he'd at least enjoy knowing about them—a whole host of them, from fields to factories to purple mountains' majesty, from sea to shining sea.

He dropped Chris off with his mother and sister, and drove directly to the hospital. He han't seen Adele in three days, not since family court, but as he got off the elevator and turned into the corridor leading to Jesse's room, he veered right into her. Her lawyer wasn't with her; instead she was accompanied by a heavyset woman her own age, dressed a little less richly. Before Ray could come up with a greeting, Adele put up a hand, barring him.

"My son is asleep," she said. "He mustn't be bothered."

As the two moved on, Ray continued carefully so as to not to wake Jesse. But Jesse was wide awake. In fact, a nurse was with him, in the midst of a series of tests.

"I passed your mother in the hall. She said you were sleeping."

"You have to understand, she lies as easily as breathing." As he spoke, Ray realized Jesse's own breathing wasn't that easy. His words were barely audible for the wheezing and rales. This was new.

"You sound terrible." Ray sat next to him, as soon as the nurse vacated that spot. A palm on his forehead showed the fever was back. "What's going on?" he asked the nurse.

"That's what we're trying to figure out." She was checking a feed line. "What's going on, kiddo?"

"It's not like before, Ray. It's not painful like before, those sword thrusts in my back. But something's...I feel weak. I don't know why."

Ray stayed by his side a while as Jesse slowly recounted what had occurred in the six hours they'd been apart. Following last week's madness, then Adele's foolishness, Ray thought things would settle down to normal. Of course he knew, and J.K. had often reminded him, how with HIV nothing was ever normal—anything and everything could go wrong, one thing on top of another, in a matter of hours. But he'd forgotten that momentarily and had to refortify himself. Jesse wasn't in pain, which was the crucial thing. Just an unnamable discomfort. As Ray sat there, Jesse became more comfortable, spoke with more ease, leading Ray to believe that whatever occurred, Adele had been in part responsible for—if not bringing it on, then at least exacerbating it—and now with her gone Jesse was feeling better.

He wanted to talk seriously to Jesse about moving over to the next wing, dedicated only this fall into one of the so-called "family hospice" rooms, where he and Ray could be together all the time. They had applied for such a room six months back, and Ray had reminded the hospital social worker, who'd told him there might be an opening as early as tomorrow. Without saying so openly, both knew it would cut Adele's visits from several hours a day to less—she so hated Ray—perhaps send her away entirely. Either, Ray was certain, would assist Jesse's recovery. Even though Jesse had told him that since that morning at family court he and Adele had "some good conversations" and they'd "made up for lost time" and they'd even "reconciled," Ray didn't put much stock in it. He'd witnessed what a snake she could be before the judge, manipulating the truth, saying anything, leveling any charges, striking out regardless of the potential damage, ready to stoop to anything to get her way. Ray had struggled to keep from strangling the woman. He hadn't met anyone since second grade who angered him so. Liesl admitted the same, she told Ray later, but had to content herself with going after Adele's reptilian counsel, the contemptible Hugh Butterworth Jr.

Something new had seeped into Ray's consciousness since that day in judge's chambers: He'd come to understand that as long as Adele was around, Jesse would never get better. Mother and son were linked on a primitive, archaic, blood-and-bones level that could not be violated as long as both lived. Like the separate yet connected strands of a DNA helix, they complemented at the same time they antagonized each other. Difficult as it was to believe, Jesse tormented her as thoroughly as she tormented him. He'd been the only one to flagrantly defy her and, when he'd gotten away with it, to treble her mortification by disregarding her. Throughout the years, he'd been her single victorious adversary; she had to admire the depth and commitment of his opposition, even while she must see him crushed, and daily plotted his downfall. For the first time in the many years they'd been together, Ray at last understood what had remained a mystery until now: how Jesse could be so immoderately, so unrestrainedly, so effortlessly good every day, month after month, decade after decade—generous, loving, understanding, helpful, affirming, enthusiastic—not only to Ray and the kids, but to people at work, folks at his boss's Caribbean island home, seemingly everyone he encountered. Perhaps, Ray now grasped, that was possible because whatever was not good in himself Jesse managed to palm off on Adele and, in the same way that Medieval fools personified and acted out their ruler's impulsive, uncivilized attributes, so Adele—perhaps without being aware of it—had come to embody and exhibit everything not good in Jesse.

When Jesse had fallen asleep, Ray found the resident, Dr. Kumar, who was baffled by the unexpected decline in Jesse's condition but who colorfully assured Ray he was "running a bombardment of analyses to abolish any obvious culprits and to run to ground all less palpable delinquents."

He arrived home seconds after what had been a pervasively gray and overcast day cleared perversely long enough to yield a spectacular sunset, burnishing the street, house fronts, parked cars and pedestrians in Tutankhamen's bronzed antique gold. And there, brassily sitting in his driveway, was an unfamiliar, aged Plymouth Valiant. He was about park across the dropped curb, in effect blocking the Valiant from leaving, when a spot opened across the street where the lesbian couple lived, and Ray dashed to fit into it. Back at his own driveway, he was surprised to see his homeowner's parking decal hanging from the Valiant's rearview mirror. Who the...?

"I almost gave up on you."

Mike from Massapequa. At the top of the building stairs, leaning against the front door, polishing off a can of beer inside a brown paper bag. He stood and popped it, à la Larry Byrd, in a clean arc into the waste can at the next building. "I'll move it out of the way, if you want."

"It's OK." And when Mike neared, he added, "Haven't seen one of these in a while."

"A '63. My aunt had it sitting in the garage. Only 70,000 miles. Still runs fine. I figure I keep it until it's a classic and cash in." In a more suggestive voice, he added, "You gonna let me in or am I going to have to pee in the gutter?"

Mike had the same look in his eyes Renzo had at the mall. Once indoors, Mike ran to the master bath, while Ray shouted he'd be a minute, he wanted to check his phone messages.

When he reached the bedroom a few minutes later, Mike was naked in bed, on his back playing with himself. "Didn't know when you'd come, so I figured I'd start."

Fifteen minutes later Ray realized how stimulated he'd been rendered by both Renzo and Mike, when in the middle of fucking Mike reached back, grabbed Ray's head, stared into his eyes, his mouth silently working as though he were unable to utter what he meant, settling at last for "Jeeez! Man!" before he wrested his head away, bowed to the bed, at the same time thrusting into Ray's torso, presenting himself unconditionally. For the first time since they'd begun doing it, Mike came without Ray having to suck him off. Ray's own orgasm was incredibly searing and drawn out.

"No van today?" Ray at last got wind enough to ask.

"No van no more. And for a while I may not get here as often," Mike admitted. "I've been canned. Actually I quit, but my boss is setting it up to say he fired me so I can collect a few months of unemployment."

"What happened?"

"You already scoped it out. Remember when you told me the place sounded like an old boys' club and I'd never get anywhere? I don't want to talk about it." He sighed. "Anyway, I'm not worried. I've already got something lined up through my father-in-law. His brother's a bus driver for a local school. They're looking for someone who knows his way around New York to take kids on field trips. Who better? I'll drive morning and afternoon and in between. This way I'll see you, maybe even see some art."

"Sure you'll have time?"

"This old guy, Werner, told me they bring the kids into, say, the Museum of Natural History, at 11 in the morning and don't have to pick them until 2 at the earliest. It's a long lunch break."

"So I'll have a school bus in the driveway?"

"You're kidding, right? No, I'll leave the bus uptown and come by subway. Unless you get your jollies tearing off a piece in a school bus?"

Ray didn't admit to that fantasy. He was surprised, however, by how blithely Mike was taking what seemed a complete reversal of fortunes in his career. "This school bus thing, that going to pay OK?"

"Less than before. At first. But the field trip stuff is time and a half. Same

with summer school, which I intend to do. It's got pensions and health benefits. And after two years it's a solid job. This Werner's been doing it going on 20
years. He's retiring good. You know, security."

As he spoke, Ray suddenly had an idea. "You need a driver's uniform?"

"No. I'll buy clothes and have my wife sew on the decals. They'll give me
a cap."

"What color's the uniform?"

"They said they didn't care. As long as it all matches, clean and pressed."

Ray leapt out of bed and ran to the office. He came back with the bag of
clothing he'd gotten a few hours earlier, and handed the smaller ones to Mike.

"These your size?"

Mike looked at the labels. "How'd you know?"

"A guess. They were on sale. I thought I was getting them… Go on, try
them on."

Watching Mike put on first the underwear, then the midnight blue uniform, Ray experienced the kind of sublimated sex thrill he recognized from
whenever he watched Jesse get dressed. Not undressed, *dressed.* He didn't know
why, but that turned him on more. He also realized what happened when he
was shopping. He'd thought he was buying for Jesse; instead he'd been buying
for Mike. Jesse would wear old chinos or cords, not this. Assuming, that is, he
got well enough to need trousers. The two—Mike and Jesse—had similar, slender, naturally worked-out, unbulked physiques. Until now, Ray hadn't realized
how similar. J.K., of course, called it years ago. The minute Ray walked into his
apartment that summer afternoon, the first time Ray met Jesse, J.K. said,
"Sunshine! It's your lucky day. I've got a boy on the roof who is 99.44% *your
type.*" Ray avowed he had no type: He was an equal opportunity slut. But J.K.,
as always, was right. And if Jesse were 99.44% Ray's type, Mike was 99.99%.
The trouser cuffs brushed the tops of Mike's feet, the inseam was scarcely a half
inch from where it was needed, the waist and hips conformed perfectly, the shirt
bloused as though he were a store-window mannequin, the shoulders fit to a
tenth of an inch. Most sexy, with the front top two buttons undone, the deep
blue shirt exposed a faultless isosceles triangle of contrasting white tee.

"Here's your uniform," Ray said.

"Cool!"

Mike was in the bath changing into his street clothes when the phone rang
and was answered. Ray couldn't recognize the voice, and went into the office to
hear better.

At first he couldn't comprehend what he was hearing. All he knew was that it was Adele Carstairs Moody, and she sounded totally freaked out. He grabbed the receiver.

"What was that you were you saying, Mrs. Moody?"

"There you are! Thank the Lord! Ray-mond, you must come immediately. My son has a collapsed lung. The doctors say he needs intubation, but he won't hear of it."

This woman brought nothing but trouble.

"You must come immediately," she insisted. "They don't know how much longer they can keep him breathing with only a face mask. Ray-mond, you must come."

"I'll be right there!"

Mike stepped out of the bathroom and overheard his end of the exchange—and noted Ray's alarm. Hurried, Ray couldn't find his car keys, so Mike offered to drive him. When they arrived, he dropped him off at the hospital's side door. As he ascended to Jesse's floor, Ray fought an irresistible dread, trying to calm himself, steeling himself for having to deal with her, for coping with some new horror with Jesse, reminding himself to keep Jesse as the focus of everything. Even so, he couldn't help recognizing that Adele would never have dreamed of phoning if she felt she had any other option.

Dr. Kumar was no longer on duty, but a woman physician, Dr. Maistry, came out of the office when Ray reached the nurses' station. She grabbed a file, removed two X-ray photos, and held them up.

"You're looking at Jesse's lungs." She had a lovely Anglo-Indian lilt to her speech. "When nothing else seemed to be the cause, we decided to take a look. See how much smaller this side is? This sort of thing occurs with pneumonia and T.B."

"What can you do?"

"Ensure that the other lung stays uncollapsed. Otherwise," she raised a shapely eyebrow, "I've got to get a breathing tube in through his mouth. Once that's done and his breathing is stabilized, I'll be able to put him out and insert a balloon into the diaphragm of the collapsed lung. It'll act as a temporary lung until number two heals. Naturally, we'd wait ten to 12 hours for the second procedure."

Ray was conflicted. "Jesse said, and I agreed, that we would do no extraordinary procedures if his life were in danger."

"Yes, I saw the DNR written on his file. I believe this is a different matter. It's not a last-ditch maneuver. It's more of a question of his quality of life."

"But it's extremely invasive?" Ray had to be sure.

"I'd lie if I denied that. But it'll only last until the surgery's done. In case something goes wrong during the operation, we can immediately attach it to a machine."

"He specifically said he did not want to be attached to a machine that breathed for him or that pumped his heart. It's there in the file."

"In any life-threatening surgery this would be done, permission or not," she stated. "It's OR procedure, allowing the surgeon to bridge any gaps."

Out of the corner of his eye he saw Adele approach with her female companion. The way they were working their elbows as they hurried, he could tell they wouldn't be easy to shake off.

"I'll have to persuade him," Ray said. "I need a time limit for the tube."

"It's not hospital procedure to—"

"Set up the balloon-insertion surgery for tomorrow morning. I'll persuade him to give you a window of, let's say, 18 hours."

Adele hove into view. "Ray-mond," she fluted at him. "At last. You have arrived."

"It's irregular," the doctor said. "I'm not sure I have the authority to promise."

Adele had him by the arm. "Ray-mond! You must help. You must."

"Eighteen hours or nothing!" Ray insisted.

Adele wouldn't let go. "Ray-mond. We are relying upon you."

"Doctor?" Ray pressured her, hard as nails.

Dr. Maistry needed assurance. "He'll do as you ask? You're certain?"

"He'll negotiate before he does. That's why I'm negotiating now."

Adele was trying to pull him physically out of the office.

"All right. I'll set up the buccal tube insertion for 18 hours maximum."

"Put it in writing, and we'll both sign."

"Ray-mond. He shall die unless—"

"You drive a hard bargain," Dr. Maistry sighed, writing.

"He'd do the same for me." Ray allowed himself to be pulled out of the room, and watched the two women's mouths open and shut in fright and anxiety, watched their hands fly about themselves as they sketched gestures of alarm and uselessness.

"Mr. Henriques," the resident interrupted, handing him the paper. "Read."

He read it, and they both signed it. She clipped it to the outside of the file, but he insisted it be stapled on so it couldn't be lost. Once that was done, he made her apprise the nurses at the floor station what it meant. They must also tell their replacements. When they'd all read it and said they understood, Ray turned to Adele and her companion.

"Do you see what this says?" showing her the file. "DNR. *Do not* resuscitate. In the file is your son's medical power of attorney outlining under what conditions any extraordinary measures should be taken. Jesse wrote it, and I signed it, meaning I would implement it. The procedure they want is *not allowed*, the way it stands."

"But my son will die," Adele argued. "Unless it's done."

"Maybe he will die," Ray said. "And maybe he won't. The point is, the hospital is not allowed to do it, unless I say so."

"Then by all means say so."

"Since the two of us signed, Jesse also has to agree to it."

"He's too ill to agree. He's delirious. He doesn't know what's going on," she continued. "Surely you must ignore what he says."

"Didn't you hear anything Judge Collins said?" Ray said. "Jesse's wishes are the only ones that count. Not yours. Not mine. Not this doctor's. Not this lady's. Only Jesse's. Because he's so ill, I become Jesse." Before she could leap on him, Ray added, "But in this case, I'm going to agree to the tube insertion, if I can get him to agree. Doctor, you explain it to them. I'm going to see Jesse." He began down the hallway but had another thought and turned. "I'm alone in there for five minutes. If anyone comes in, anyone at all, Doctor? Mrs. Moody? I leave and we let nature take its course."

"It's...unnatural," Adele cried out.

"Doctor?"

"Yes! Go! Hurry!"

Jesse looked gaunt. He had a blue plastic face mask over his nose and mouth.

"Hey, kiddo! Guess what? You only have one lung working!"

Jesse tried to smile. Ray sat and took his hand. Jesse moved the face mask and whispered something. Ray moved his closer to hear it. "It's the beginning of the end."

"Nah! They don't seem to think so, kiddo. Just a slight reversal. Result of the pneumonia." He then went on to explain what the doctor had said. He finished, "I'll be here all the time they're doing it. Tomorrow by 8 A.M. tube's out of you."

Jesse whispered, "It's out of me whether I'm alive or dead."

That hurt. But Ray agreed, "Yes. Alive or dead."

Jesse whispered. "Are you prepared?"

Ray froze. "It's not what you think, Buster Brown." And when the golden eyes wouldn't let him go, he lied, he said yes, he was prepared.

Ten minutes later Dr. Maistry's team was in the room, dressed in scrubs, to do the procedure. Jesse insisted Ray stay and watch. Ray remained, kneeling at the side of the bed, watching as they first inserted breathing tubes deep into Jesse's nostrils, greased his lips, Vaselined his mouth, spread his lips until Ray was certain his mouth would split apart, inserted the enormous plastic tube and then plunged it down into Jesse's throat. Ray could feel it being thrust down, stage after stage, the doctor all but forcing her entire weight onto it. He could only imagine the pain and sensation of helplessness, of being tortured without respite. The plunging seemed to go on forever and to rip at his throat and insides. And all the while, Ray held Jesse's hand and talked into his ear about the Island and the boats and the catamaran rides and whatever popped into his head, as Jesse's hand clenched again and again, harder and harder, and sweat poured off his forehead and his eyes swung in their orbits, finally finding shelter inside his skull.

Ray didn't know how long it went on even after the tube was in; they seemed to have so many goddamn switches to check, gauges to turn, numbers to confirm, before Dr. Maistry's "All done!" She slowly extracted the nostril air tubes, and after a bit of a wait the tube seemed to be working. Jesse's hand was quiet again in Ray's.

He watched the resident affix a sedative bag to the overhead rack, then into Jesse's wrist attachment, noting how she avoided any possibility of eye contact with him or Jesse.

"You'll sleep in a bit, Jesse," she said. "When you wake, this will be out. Promise."

Ray repeated what she said to Jesse, then continued talking, telling him about the day, shopping in the mall, Sable, Chris, the teenagers, sexy Renzo, then Mike, all of it complete bullshit, *bullshit!*—every minute of his life compared to the betrayal that had just happened here—but that made no difference because what else could he say, talking and talking, trying to get something else inside his mind before he dropped off, until Jesse's hand went limp in his and his breathing through the plastic tube was audibly regular.

A nurse entered and confirmed that Jesse was asleep. Ray staggered to his feet.

Adele and her companion were outside the door. Their hands came at him. "God bless you, Ray-mond." The vile unctuosity of their hypocritical voices. "God bless you, Ray-mond!" He thrust them away, fighting the bile that rose to his gorge, which threatened to spill over as he ran down the hallway, slamming his way into the elevator, needing air, fresh air, *now.*

It was dark out on the street, cold and damp and deserted. Each forlorn yellow street lamp illuminated the dense night air so he could make out tiny refracted molecules of suspended precipitation. He checked his watch, 8:15, pulled up his collar against the wind's bite, trudged home through the desolate streets, trying to blank his mind, trying to think nothing at all, knowing nothing would ever rid him of the sights and sounds of the past few hours in that hospital room that played again and again before his eyes on some kind of sadistic video loop he could not put out of mind, reminding him of the torture he'd subjected Jesse to. He'd been weak! Stupid and weak! Stupid and weak and a coward! How could he? After he'd promised. How could you, Ray? The words Jesse had not said. Had not been able to say, not with that monstrous object plunged into his gullet, silencing him. And the doctor! Why didn't she tell him? How could she let him agree to it, when she of all of them knew what it would be like?

He'd arrived home and noticed the lights on upstairs, meaning Chris was there, probably watching television instead of doing his homework. Ray was halfway in the office door when he retreated, realizing he couldn't go in yet, couldn't face the boy, couldn't face himself, never mind Jesse tomorrow morning, who'd probably never want to see him again. Meaning that she'd won after all, the Monster, playing on his weaknesses like Isaac Stern on a Stradivarius. Another turn around the block didn't stop the recriminations, the anxiety, so he ended up sitting on the lowest of the steps leading to the front door, within a pool of darkness, still trying to blank his mind. He would go into the hospital tomorrow morning at 9 o'clock and he'd receive the news that Jesse had agreed to the transfer down South to Doctors Hospital. And he would deserve it, because he'd been weak, weak and stupid, a coward. He would deserve it. How could he have agreed?

"Uncle Ray?"

A small voice, a tentative hand on his back.

"Aren't you going to come in?"

Chris with a scarf around his neck, looking scared. Now you've scared the kid too, you idiot. Can't you do anything right? Why not just throw it all away, using both hands?

Inside it was warm and smelled like soup, and Chris had his homework out on the dining room table, and when Ray sat like lead at the table, Chris helped pull off his coat and gloves and fed him chicken soup he'd thoughtfully prepared for him out of a can, along with buttered wheat toast.

"Thanks. Sorry, Chris. I've just had a bear of a day."

"Uncle Jesse?"

Chris looked like he wanted to know, maybe even needed to know.

"He's not getting better, right?" Chris asked. "He had some kind of crisis today, and you had to go take care of it. That's why you're so depressed, right?" He paused. "I heard his mother on the answering machine when I got in. Is he better now?"

"Maybe. I don't know, Chris. I…" The boy looked at him, needing something from him, Ray wasn't sure what. "I did something with your Uncle Jesse, allowed a medical procedure that I'm not sure I should have allowed."

"The thing about the intubation she was talking about?"

"Yeah. It was…I can't describe how horrible."

"But he'll get better because of it," Chris tried. "Right?"

"I don't know. Maybe. In the short run. For a few days or…"

As he spoke, Ray became aware of music playing in the upstairs bedroom, where Chris had been sleeping since Jesse had been hospitalized. Tchaikovsky, no? *The Nutcracker*? Yes. It probably was on since he'd come in, but was just now getting louder as Clara and the Nutcracker finished their pas de deux and the battle with the mice began.

Chris noticed Ray listening to it and explained, "Remember the cassettes you and Uncle Jesse gave me for my tenth birthday? I read somewhere that you study better and learn more if you listen to classical music. So I put it on. Ever hear that theory?"

Ray said he had.

"I like it OK," Chris said. "It's too loud, isn't it?"

"No, it's fine. Leave it," Ray said. "It's the end of the first tableau soon anyway. That side will be over in a minute or two. Remember when we saw *The Nutcracker* at the City Center? You and me and your sister? This is the battle between the toy soldiers led by the Nutcracker against the Mouse King and his army of mice."

They listened, Chris laying his fingers atop Ray's hand spread on the table.

Here came the 12-note theme Ray remembered so well: four notes andante, pause, four more notes, maestoso, pause, four more notes, grandissimo, rising, as the victorious Nutcracker is transformed into Prince Charming before our eyes. The theme repeated, developed in tandem with Clara's motif to become a sweeping, lovely symphonic adagio that never failed to move Ray, especially as all the toys and children came out of hiding to circle the Christmas tree again in a somber little march of celebration. From the first time he'd seen and heard it, he had been knocked out by this moment in the ballet; now he realized he was breathing hard, his eyes moist.

"It's my favorite," Ray managed to get out. Chris stood and stepped behind him and put his arms around Ray, laying his cheek next to his uncle's face. "My favorite part of the whole ballet…Want to know why? It's so…juvenile…It's so…! When I was your age I used to think it was because I wanted to be like the Nutcracker, you know, transformed into someone more real, or maybe just someone more acceptable. But then I realized I didn't give a damn about that. This was my favorite piece because I identified with the little girl Clara, as I guess Tchaikovsky did, and perhaps meant us all to do. And because, well, it justified me…justified who I was and who I was becoming. It said to me, Ray, *you* too can find a Prince Charming…if you want one badly enough. It made it seem all right. And you know what, Chris? It was right. Because I *did* find a Prince Charming! I did!" he repeated as the music swelled to its ultraromantic finale. "For a while."

In the sudden silence, Ray gathered himself and looked more closely at Chris, who had not let go of him for an instant.

twenty

It was beyond irritating how very little one was told by the medical staff, despite incessant requests. Even after the desired change had been achieved, one's name scribbled atop that asinine file which appeared to command everyone's life around here as though it bore the fingerprints of the Creator Himself, instead of merely *his* name and phone number. Of course, she'd taken care to ensure that *he'd* never again dare meddle in her son's future, never again dispute and haggle, broker and bargain like one of his progenitors clad in black gabardine and carousel hat in some sharecropper's back-patch, dickering over a two-yard length of fabric. Her opportunity had presented itself the moment she was allowed to add her name and phone number to the file, thanks to Judge Collins's instructions—the number at that ghastly hotel first, that of Hugh Jr.'s office second. Finding herself completely alone at the nurses' station for a twinkling with the file, she'd accepted that moment as the Gift of the Lord it was surely meant to signify, the single indemnification for her many travails and sacrifices, then gone ahead and guaranteed *his* downfall and *her* triumph by altering the last two numbers of his listed phone number from ones to sevens—easiest thing in the world. Now only she would be reachable in case of an emergency. And no one would be the wiser. No one *had* been the wiser in the days since she'd done it, or rather in the days since she'd been forced to publicly humble herself and eat dirt in front of all of them, begging *him* to allow her boy to be intubated and thus live.

All of them, exemplified, naturally enough, in that blockhead Eva King from back home, who would have betrayed her in a second just for the tickle of being able to retail the news of her humiliation as quickly as possible, no matter that she was allegedly one's best friend in the world and totally regardless of the fact that one's own child's life had been the issue at stake, never mind the governance of it.

She'd gotten past that quite noticeably iffy moment, hadn't she though, if mostly by keeping that dolt Eva King absolutely occupied, running from hospital room to hotel, from museum to coffee shop, from pillar to post if need be, until she could barely remain upright on her two feet but must take a nap. A nap furthermore out of which she'd awakened Eva early, to be dragged to dinner, trundled to the hospital again, whisked away to a famous, long-running musical off Times Square, and then to bed and the next day's activities. By then, of course, the operation had been accomplished, the tube removed and with one's child returned to one improved, nothing but celebrations and hosannas, forget the past, look to the future.

Luckily, also by 10 o'clock in the morning, *he'd* been gone already—that little black twig of a doctor assured her by phone—having slept in the room in a cot all night. As though she gave a fig where *he* slept, as long as *he* was no longer visible when *she* arrived. Fortunately too, that dullard Eva had not managed yet to figure out even whom *he* was, or rather whom *he* claimed to be. Eva had instead accepted her explanation that *he* was a roommate, medically trained, especially knowledgeable with assorted lung diseases. The only possibly acceptable explanation for why *his* ghastly name was so unnaturally placed before hers. Then, thirdly propitious, Eva was such a total simpleton that when she'd heard *his* name she'd actually turned and asked, "Hendricks, did he say? Like Emmeline Hendricks?" To which rubbish there was only a single reasonable reply, while thanking the Lord that at least *he* wasn't dark and hunched and curve-nosed, but instead light-skinned and fair-haired and well-built and so might just as easily be a choice Hendricks as one of his own accursed people. Or rather, thanking the

Lord *and* the jot of common sense and tittle of remaining aesthetic sense that fool son of hers had retained. *He* might even, in a pinch, *pass*, as the coloreds always put it, although she'd do her damnedest to ensure that no such occasion ever need arise for *him* to do so as long as she was on God's green earth.

He was sleeping again, her dear fool angel boy. He did look like an angel, like a boy of maybe six or so, again—the very last age, she had to remind herself that he'd been malleable or in fact in any way agreeable to her. He'd been sleeping when she'd arrived this afternoon and evening and now was doing so again, after she'd dragged Eva here from dinner. Indeed, he'd been doing little but sleeping since that little transaction with the lung balloon, sleeping an immense amount. She assumed it was because sleep was the body's preferred method to promote healing. Not that it much mattered. She'd as much sit here next to his bed watching him sleep from this close, while nurses and residents infrequently entered the room to check something or other and mark it on his chart. She certainly preferred it to having him awake and possibly cantankerous.

Not that Jesse had been obstinate or contrary with her since she'd arrived in this irreligious city. Of course, one could also maintain that Jesse had not been *openly* so, relying instead on *him* to frustrate her will, as a Pasha might use a Vizier to carry out his wishes. But still it surprised her how sweet his temperament around her had become, he who had so long been headstrong and opposed. What puzzled her was that she was completely unable to determine *why* he was being sweet. Was it because he believed the End of His Days was near—even the little black strumpet said that was unlikely; these patients generally lingered another two years—and was resolved to make a virtuous final showing? Or because he simply no longer cared how he behaved around her? Either way, it suited her just fine, undeniably smoothing her way. Because, for her own part, she was dead set on spiriting him from here and getting him down South as soon as he was ready to be moved, although she had to admit she didn't as yet have an idea *how* she might do that. Hugh Jr. had been set to that particular chore, although he had hardly emerged from their last business covered in glory. And in fact it was partly *because* of his near total failure in the judge's chambers that she might continue to harry Hugh Jr., still count on him to get—at the very least—someone in his office to locate a legal loophole through which they might thwart *his* nefarious control and set her own dear boy free.

Also, she had to be candid and acknowledge that since that terrible evening, *he* had done her the minor courtesy of not being here all the time and also of being sufficiently regular in his own visitations that she might come and go at will almost as often as she wanted, without having to cross paths with him. For example, she knew he'd leave the hospital by 9 o'clock at night, ostensibly to return home to that corrupt child he undoubtedly kept chained to the wall in readiness for God only knew what perversions. Which allowed her an hour, the final hour each evening, at her son's bedside; while Eva nodded over a fashion magazine across her lap in that dingy little waiting room in the outside corridor. So while he slept, she had nothing really to do but sit here and think. At the very least, she was aware of the excellent portrait she must be painting of the Devoted Mother. That counted for something, didn't it, even among these heathen?

And in truth, she had been lately employing these slots of time to think, or rather to recollect, since recollection was one of the finer pastimes for ladies and gentlemen, about this very boy's own difficult entry into this world, herself utterly unprepared for him, startled in fact when old Dr. Lampry had told her she was going on two and a half months when she'd consulted him over a minor disagreeableness she'd been experiencing. Surprised, and despite Daddy Moody's elation, never completely reconciled to the necessity of some other person parasitically using *her* body as a method of ingress into this world, finding it if not unnatural, then at the very least debilitating and disadvantageous in too many ways to discuss. Only the last seven weeks she had carried him—high in front, which everyone agreed indicated male gender—had been in any way pleasant. It had been early spring and fortunately not too hot nor too cold: Either would have been simply unacceptable. And when her time was near, Daddy had her at the hospital well in time, and she had been sedated sufficiently to comprehend, rather than suffer through, the actual birth, although the soreness down there had lasted far longer than she'd been prepared for. Then she was home, with a registered nurse in the room adjacent the nursery, and it was May, flowers in bloom, and she had her own dear little Carstairs in miniature, small but perfect, clear-eyed and curious, a Constant Little Amazement to her, and that first year had gone swimmingly, and the next and next, him a little angel she could kiss and coax and teach to talk and walk, perfect in every way, doting upon her, the very picture, as he grew, of her own dear brother Anthony, lost before the Great War to diphtheria, in addition to being a joy and plaything for her. But then how horrible he had become suddenly, all splotch-faced and skin-blighted, gangling and ugly and bad tempered, and whose fault was that? Not hers. Not her fault that he'd turned so and then turned against her and thereafter been against her so openly. She'd never wanted that, never dreamed it might happen. Who was to blame? Unless the Lord, whom she admitted was blameless, must have afflicted the boy as a Judgment upon him and had set a Trial for her, which she had now undergone lo these 30 odd years, reaching fruition here, in this sullied hospital room in a heathen stronghold, hundreds of miles from comfort or home. Yet even her Trial would, like all things under the eye of the sun, have its completion when she brought her boy back home, where—helpless and in need of her—he would be returned to her as nearly intact as he had been when he was still worthy: clear-skinned and even-tempered, so that she might bring the Great Circle to its close and in the words of the clever old Yankee, Mr.Clemens, do good— which would satisfy some people and astonish the rest.

What was that? Out of the corner of her eye, even in her meditation, she'd caught something moving. She looked up, but no, all seemed as before. The room empty save for her and him, still asleep. It was a trick of the light perhaps. Still, it had broken her train of thought, leaving her more than a little irritated since it had been a pleasant reverie she'd been enjoying. It was nearly 10 o'clock anyway. Time to gather herself and leave for the night. She would awaken Eva, dozing out there, and…there! Again!

And now she saw exactly what it was. He'd jumped. Lying flat on the bed as he was, he'd jumped maybe a half inch from the center of himself, as though attached to an invisible wire and simply yanked up. But how could that possibly be? There it was again!

She was out of her chair and over him, checking to see if it wasn't something in his dreams, the way sleeping hounds motion with their paws and chops as though chasing after and catching prey. He did it again, and it was even more unmistakable and unnerving. So she reached over and shook him, to awaken him. She received no response at all and tried harder. Still no response, only this time the convulsion or whatever it was all but lifted him off the bed and threw him back down, no longer flat but sideways, with one arm pulled behind him, another in front, like a dropped rag doll. She still couldn't waken him, and now she was deeply frightened, deeply spooked and frightened and must do something!

"Quickly! My son! In that room over there!" She could barely get the words out to the nurse at her station.

The nurse checked her chart. "Moody, Jesse?"

"Yes, please hurry. Something's dreadfully wrong!"

The little black thing looked out her open office door. "What is it? Jesse?"

"Yes. Please come quickly. He's having some kind of conniption fit!"

She followed the resident in and Jesse was now folded back the other way, still jerking. The little black slip of a thing straightened him out, felt a pulse under his chin, checked his eyes by pushing back the lids. His pupils were way back in his head.

"He has no history of epilepsy?"

"No! Nothing like that at all."

The resident began attaching nodules from out of her side pockets to his head and connecting them to a machine. The machine went into action, a neon green EEG scan line started up. Even to Adele it looked wrong.

"What's wrong with him?" she tried. "Is he having an epileptic fit or what?"

"Out." The resident pushed her out, yelling, "Nurse! I need stat here!"

The nurse at the station and another resident ran past her into the room, closing the door on Adele. No sooner had that happened than Eva King, still rubbing sleep out of her florid face, was there by her side. "What's going on?

"Oh, Eva, dear. It's my boy. He's having convulsions. I don't know—"

The door slammed open, and the nurse ran out and to the front desk, where she grabbed what must be the file, began dialing the phone. Trying to reach *him*, to tell *him*. Not a word to her but everything to *him*.

But thanks to her, without success. The nurse hung up, hurried back to the room and went in, again barring her. This time the young male resident was sent out and began the dialing, the listening, the not being able to reach *him*. She dragged Eva over to the nurses' station for moral support and asked him what was wrong. Could she help? What could she do? Why wouldn't they tell her? She was his mother, after all: She had a right to know. Why weren't they asking her? Didn't they see her name was here on this file anyway? There! There it was! In black and white. Why were they dialing him when he was clearly not there? Off gallivanting, no doubt, not caring. While she was here, right here, on the spot, the devoted mother. Why weren't they telling her anything? Why?

He hung up, hurried back to the room, not deigning to respond to her, and a minute later the little Indian emerged, looking sober. Adele ran up to her and repeated what she'd just said to the other resident.

She was so pleased to be spoken to finally that at first she didn't understand what the little woman was saying to her, then as she repeated herself, it became clearer. Her son had suffered a series of strokes. Two aneurysms to the heart, at least three to the brain. They had given him a few shots of lidocaine to try to stabilize him, but there was no saying whether he would be stabilized. He was unconscious. In a coma. The next abdominal aneurysm would probably kill him. He was in imminent danger of dying. Mr. Henriques was not answering the phone. According to her son's files, she, the resident could do nothing further without Mr. Henriques's consent. Which, by the way, given past experience, she believed would not be forthcoming, even should they reach him, since this was exactly the kind of emergency for which the DNR had been established.

"And if you were able to resuscitate him?" Adele asked. "How would you?"

"We can attach him to heart monitor and defibrillator, to breathing machines, possibly use electrical paddles to bring him back."

"Then you must do that. *All* of that!" Adele said.

"But my instructions are precisely to do *none* of that."

"What of your Hippocratic oath? Does that mean nothing? You would let him die because of what's written on a folder?" Before the doctor could respond, she threw in, "The judge has my name added here. I'm in charge when he isn't to be reached. I say go ahead. I take all responsibility for whatever happens."

"Have you thought of exactly what could happen?" the resident asked. "You son could linger like a vegetable, not alive, not dead, for months, years even."

"I don't care. I want him to have every chance to live."

"But your son didn't want to live under those circumstances. If I do anything against his expressed wishes, I can be sued. The hospital can be sued."

"And if you let him die, I'll sue you and the hospital both!" Adele said. "I'll sue you for neglect and malpractice, and for racism and discrimination. I'll sue you for everything and anything I can think of."

The little black thing smiled at her, a toothy, self-satisfied smile. She tapped the nurse and resident. "You're both witnesses and you too," she pointed to Eva King, "that I do this against my will and because of her threats." She turned to Adele. "Fine, Mrs. Muddy," she said. "I'll do what I'm told to do. As for you, Mrs. Muddy, you have this very minute contrived for yourself an ensnaring tangle of karmic retribution from which you will require a score of lifetimes before you can ever free yourself!" She spat on the floor, just missing Adele's shoes. "Foolish woman. I *pity* you!"

Before Adele could vent her outrage, the three medical staffers had split apart, two went back into the room, the nurse to the floor station, where she immediately recited something incomprehensible over the intercom about a Dr. Blue. Adele remained in the hallway, Eva holding her hand, the silly goose. A minute later four men dressed in blue scrubs and caps exited the elevator alongside a gurney with various machines attached, shoving their way past her and Eva into the room. The nurse chose that moment to declare the floor off limits, and herded Adele and Eva back to the waiting room, saying they were in the way.

The way had become clear to Jesse. At first it had been complicated, but now it was clear. He'd been dreaming, dreaming of crossing strange landscapes, inside one of a half dozen large rolling wagons, as though part of a theater troupe or circus band, along a Daliesque panorama of melting cypresses and disturbed lakes, when suddenly he'd felt something striking and riveting in his head just above his left eye, as though a raven were pecking at it or he'd been touched with an electric cattle prod. Before he could accommodate it or even describe it to himself, it happened again, inside his left ear, and twice more in his chest, as though someone were pounding on it, perhaps trying to wake him up. He wasn't certain whether he had awakened, but the dream landscape vanished, and for a second he thought he could make out a four-foot-square portion of the hospital room, two machines, above one of them a window shade drawn, a small pot of waxy leaf begonias, but for some reason he hadn't been able to move, and soon after he'd felt the electric prod again, then everything became confusing, sort of a buzzing all around him, a general buzzing that spread and spread, just like—what was that poem he'd learned in Mr. Mazey's third grade class? yes! just like the murmur of innumerable bees in immemorial elms!

That changed, and he was aware of a great lightness, a liberation he'd never experienced. He was aware of a haziness, a vagueness all around him, everything undefined; then he realized why: He was on the ceiling, on the hospital room ceiling, all of it light blue and white, and when he sort of turned (he didn't do anything, it was the only way he could describe what he'd done to himself) he looked down. He was a little amused to see himself down there, still on the bed, looking up at himself while several people huddled around him moving quickly and jerkily doing various things—he couldn't say what—but as they all looked fairly serious about it, he was curious, if not all that interested, and anyway that sort of slightly luminescent, rainbow-colored, twisted coil he saw tethered in the air between his navel and himself on the bed looked as though it were even more stretchable, and he sensed that there was something familiar about all this—hadn't he heard of it, or read of it, or maybe seen it on TV? Yes, that was it, it was how people who'd come back from the afterlife described leaving this life. Amazing how his mind was doing this to him exactly as it had been described. Hadn't it been J.K. who'd postulated some chemical reaction in the brain, a loss of oxygen to certain blood vessels of the cerebrum, which always produced the same visual effect? Only now there was also someone calling him, a voice or voices he was familiar with, so he turned away from where he was looking, distracted, and toward the voices, confident that the cord would hold and

he was in a another place altogether, facing some large nebulously defined space, circular, almost like being an ant at the edge of a monumentally long drinking straw, and attracted to it, as it was honey-sweet and sounded lovely and felt so warm within. Then he remembered that this too had been predicted, probably yet another level of oxygen deprivation or electrochemical stimuli failing, and oh look, yes, now it was more tunnel-like, and now it was moving, swinging back and forth as though it were the eye of a tornado directly above him, with something clear at the end, and look there, inside it was a kind of cloud or mist, all white, intriguing, even if preordained, so curious really he had to see more, so he took a step forward and was propelled forward, flying

and

he found himself outside the town of Fearrington, North Carolina, at a familiar spot, indeed at the very fringe of Great Aunt Eulalie's property. It was winter outside and snowing heavily, wet thick flakes of snow that stuck to his woolen mittens and woolen coat sleeves of his outstretched hands. Yes, this was the entryway to the large farm property, barely visible, the rutted road that swung like a question mark up to the front door of her and Grand Uncle Burt Moody's big old plantation house with its various out buildings he loved to explore, and he was trudging through the snow alone along the path, but feeling fine, warm, not cold, exultant for no good reason, not at all tired, he was so very glad he wasn't tired anymore, and he knew or sensed there was family waiting on him straight ahead, at the plantation house as soon as he arrived, so he trod on more, blood-red cardinals flitting in the bare, ice-crackled upper branches of tall maples and elms that defined and lined the road, but this he couldn't recall from what those people "called back": had said on TV or in magazines, yet even so he was sure it was yet another definitive step

and

Uncle Angus Moody's station wagon appeared from a side road on an angle, little Cousin Josiah at the steering wheel waving to him, Uncle Angus clad in big old rusty-colored anorak and hunter's red-checked hat pushing the big old car which must have broken down, and wasn't that Grand Uncle Burt on the other side, and Auntie Shea? He ran to meet them as they crossed his track and made onto the road going up to the plantation house, and wasn't that his school buddy Zeb Hogwood? what was he doing here? and Daddy Moody, he couldn't believe it, Daddy Moody, as big and fat and happy as ever, and they all welcomed him as he joined them, pushing along the side of the big old Town and Country wagon, laughing and joshing like they always did, calling him

Jesse James and all, and he could already make out the plantation house a dot up ahead, and Daddy and Grand Uncle Burt said everyone was there already, Grandma and Grandpa and Grand Aunt Eulalie, and they'd have Christmas dinner with all the fixings, his favorites, Baltimore cake and persimmon pie! Snow was coming down hard now, blocking out the trees and the path and suddenly the station wagon's ignition caught and it bucked a second and they all released it out of their hands, then the back door came folding down and they all began jumping in, scrambling for room as the automobile went faster until only he was still with his feet on the ground, and Daddy reached for him and pulled at his gloved hands saying, come along, come along, boy, you don't want to miss Christmas dinner, do you?

and

he wanted to join them all so much, so very much, even though he knew what was happening to him, knew there was no way back now anymore, but that wasn't the problem, yet there was one thing holding him back, one thing, if only he could remember, and the car was going faster, he couldn't let the tail board go, had to run to stay with it, then he remembered what the one thing was, it was Ray! Ray! What about Ray? He couldn't leave Ray, could he? And Daddy Moody said, don't worry, boy, Ray'll come along too. He'll be here too in a while. And Jesse thought, but not for a long time. A long time. And Daddy Moody said, it'll be like the flicker of an eyelash in your loving mind, boy, that quick, I promise. And he knew Daddy wouldn't lie, wasn't lying now, so he let Daddy and the others pull him up, safe onto the folded-out back door of the station wagon, and the car picked up speed, and it hauled along, up into the lovely

white

dazzling

all-encompassing

snowbright

light

$*$ $*$ $*$

It was close to an hour later, and Eva was nodding again, when an older man in a white smock who looked far more like a real doctor than any of these various Indians, stepped into the dingy little waiting room, introduced himself to them, and asked if he might have a seat.

"Is my son alive?"

"Jesse's breathing. He's attached to several machines that will keep him breathing and his heart beating. But you must know that all of our best efforts were unable to completely correct the effects of the various aneurysms. Two more of them occurred during the procedures we instituted to save his life."

"What do you mean?" she asked.

"What I mean is that there's no longer any electrochemical function in his brain."

"But..." Adele tried. "He's alive?"

"He is...how do I put it?...mechanically alive. He's being kept alive by these mechanisms. Once they are removed...Would you like to see him now?"

She did. And Eva followed. She realized the minute she saw him what had happened and what now was before her. The kindly doctor showed her what the various read outs of the several machines signified. What they signified, actually, was that now she would never be able to transfer him down South, never be able to oversee any possible recovery, be by his side for any continuing illness.

"I'm terribly, terribly sorry," that dolt Eva King said, touching her arm. "But you did right. You did the Christian thing."

But all she could think to utter out of the depth of her realization was, "Of course I did the Christian thing. Of course I did right."

Ray

March 1993

twenty-one

He was inside a corridor, a hospital corridor, given the institutional mint green-tinted walls, a hospital corridor leading to double doors, connecting to another hospital corridor, this one tinged pale lilac. Uncertain what time of day it was because everything was lighted by the wan, enervated illumination typical of hospital corridors, reflecting palely off the establishment-pastel walls, but he was moving forward through them, passing one set of swinging double doors into another corridor with another pastel shade, this one salmon-colored, feebly lighted, and he was turning a corner, passing a nurses' station, into another corridor, a gruesome chartreuse, and now he could just make out, gliding through the next set of swinging double doors into yet another corridor, an occupied gurney that attracted his attention, so he hurried forward even faster, through those doors into another corridor, this one cantaloupe in color, where just that second going around the corner he could see, as he'd intuited, Jesse on that gurney, strapped down, only just able to lift his head, accelerating ahead unattended, in motion as another pair of swinging doors flew open for the gurney to hurtle through into yet another, this time pale aqua, corridor, so he hurried himself, attempting to catch the gurney as it made another crossing through yet another nurses' station, through another set of swinging doors, gaining speed, tearing through pairs of swinging double doors, careening around corridor corners, whizzing hell-bent into yet another, rose-tinged corridor, and now he could make out wailing, Jesse calling his name, and he bellowed back, told him to hang on, he was coming, as he tore through the corridors, flew around corners, whirred through yet more double swinging doors, never quite catching up, never getting more than a few feet closer, Jesse screeching for him, himself howling back that he was coming, he was coming, hold on, just hold on...

Ray woke up suddenly. He sat up fast, quickly gathered the covers about his shoulders. Around him the room was chilled, the air flat as though without oxygen, almost itself anesthetized. The early '80s digital clock on the dresser noisily shifted its cards, dark-edged with time, to announce a blanched, backlighted 6:49. Too early to get up yet, he lay back down, pulled on the German *federbed* comforter, shifted off him during sleep by his exertions, so its always unanticipated animal warmth enfolded his neck and face, leaving him thinking, *I can surrender to this radiance*, yet also aware that everything about him felt utterly forlorn.

Even the icy sheets heated up eventually between the temperature of the quilt and his body. Still, he continued to laze in the unlit room, peering sideways off the bed as though with first-time fascination at those grudging suggestions of light suffusing this side of the barely ajar window blinds, as though frozen daylight was politely disinclined to make much point of its emergence. Memories of last night at Kathy's arrived in a rush, Sable looking no better, worse perhaps, having lost more hair from chemotherapy, still babyish and listless, huddled between the two adults, insistent on remaining up long after her bedtime, drowsing there as the two of them chatted, caught up over the past two days, occasionally glancing at the TV news: ethnic riots somewhere in equatorial Africa; sullen, overequipped mercenaries in South America; the stygian aftermath of a gas explosion in suburban Manitoba; labor protests at a rain-sodden Gulf Coast port, all of it silent, hieratic, as though prerehearsed; the hijacked plane a cliché against its twilit tarmac; the overbosomed starlet's hackneyed sashay through reporters with zoom-lens hard-ons; the televangelist mechanically thumping his fist, face distorted in unanimated passion, shellacked hair a glaucous helmet reflecting overhead arc lamps like a half-hearted fireworks display; none of it new, registering anything significant, not even the words that dribbled toneless out of Kathy's exhausted lips: procedures, treatments, prognoses, medicines, possibilities; or his own equally exhausted drivel regarding Jesse's health, none of it new, unexpected, of any use.

Memories—meant to stave off the inevitable: that today was *the day.*

At last he extricated himself from bed and quickly changed into sweatshirt and pants, heavy socks, sneakers. Steam heat was just beginning to sputter through the single, well-shielded furnace riser pipe. It would still be cold upstairs. In the bathroom he passed water, then turned to the sink. Unavoidable the face in the mirror; familiar, terrifying, strange—just about all that was left now.

"The horror, Mr. Kurtz!" he intoned in a faux-Caribbean accent. "The *horror!*"

Satisfied, if not even close to amused, he opened the cabinet door and pulled out the yellow jar of Eboline, dipped his fingers deep into the gelatinous goop, and rubbed goo into his hair and scalp, wondering why he bothered with this vestige of vanity, or even if it was sensible to do it—one of Kathy's suggestions, from a coworker at the theater office where she worked—because he'd been losing his hair every day for weeks now, ever since Jesse had gone into the hospital. Well, there would be no more hair-loss mornings for him because today was the day.

The kitchen was no longer chilled yet not yet warm, more like clammy, the radiator clattering away like mad as its old porcelain filled with steam. Almost on automatic pilot, he got the coffee bags out of the freezer, mixed the caf and decaf into his grinder, ground it to the count of 45 seconds, slipped the filter in, filled it with grounds, found the bottled water, filled the Braun's reservoir, clicked all the parts back in place, turned it on, watched the red lights set. Today's *the day.* Would he be having coffee here, the way he liked it, fresh, hot, half and half, with two teaspoons of sugar, tomorrow morning? Or out of a Styrofoam container, spilling, overheated, in a jail cell?

Outside the glacial etched-glass front door, Joralemon Street was deserted and windblown, tiny cyclones of dirt and torn paper bubbling along the gutters, the sky above the townhouses a sulky pewter shot horizontally through with infected-looking blood-red as the sun unsuccessfully tried to blaze through. The double-folded newspaper was frozen in its plastic condom. No headline larger than 16 points. Slow news day. He would change that. Locally, at least.

A half hour later, despite the coffee, he was nodding again, dropping his head onto the newspaper-strewn table, totally exhausted, wondering what was wrong with him. He napped in the new warmth until startled awake by the phone ringing.

"I hope this means you slept well, Ray-mond," Liesl began.

"I can't sleep. You know that. Every night the nightmare comes once, twice, again. And when I'm awake, I see him. I fucking see him, Liesl, lying there like... I can't get the image out of my mind. You understand that's why I have to do it today?"

"Yes. Yes, of course, I understand."

He had a moment of panic. "You're not canceling on me?"

"No. But I am going to have to meet you at the hospital a little later than planned.

I've *got* to do it today," he said. "It's been two weeks already!"

"I know, but this we want, Ray-mond. I have a meeting with Collins, that same family court judge. She's going to give me a deposition on her ruling last week. If I can persuade her that Jesse's mother *intended* to defy his final wishes when she got her name put on the record, we could press felony charges."

"She'll never come back to New York to be charged," he replied listlessly.

"True, but her felony charge can only help our civil case against her and the hospital...especially in light of what you plan to do today."

"I plan to right the wrong they did," he said, unable to restrain his anger.

"I know, darling Ray-mond, I know. You have every right to right the wrong. Even so, today you also will be doing something illegal in this state. So we must keep it all in some kind of balance. You understand?"

"I understand." He was depleted. "So if not at 11, then when will you come?"

"Sometime after noon. 12:30?"

"Nurses usually come by to check on...what's left...at 12:30."

"When do they come in again?"

"Not till 2."

"Then we do it at 1 o'clock. I still have to pick up the bail bond papers and get the notarized check. They must have today's date. One o'clock, Ray-mond. I'm sorry."

"Another two hours! What's the difference?"

"Bring a paperback to read. Just in case we hit a snag," Liesl said. "It'll be a great relief, and I don't want you thinking about it afterward. I want you distracted."

"I sound so ungrateful, but you're great for doing all this."

"Remember, I loved Jesse too. Sometimes I wonder which of us is more infuriated."

Chris strolled into the kitchen, doubtless awakened, or perhaps reawakened, by Ray talking on the phone. Ray couldn't help notice that Chris had at last put on the oversize flannel pajamas he'd considered too "little kids' shit" eight weeks ago when his mother had given them to him for Christmas. He also wore the mooseskin slippers Kathy's and Ray's parents had sent, which he'd looked at once and dropped on the floor, declaring the gift "deeply lame!" Later on, in a sincere tone of voice, he'd added, "They've been living in the sticks too long, Uncle Ray. You know?"

Chris looked, if possible, even cuter half sleeping than fully awake. He shuffled to the refrigerator, opened the tallest door, and peered in for a long time.

"It's here." Ray signed off and hung up the phone, tapping the container of orange juice. Chris gazed at it totally blankly. "So's the milk and cereal," he added. "How about something hot this morning? I can concoct oatmeal. A mess of grits and possum penis?"

Chris shuffled over to the table and sat down heavily, letting Ray pour him a giant glass of juice. After he'd drunk half of it in a single chugalug, he looked a bit more alert. "You got Maypo?"

"Farina, Cream of Rice, Cream of Wheat, and oatmeal, instant and regular."

"What happened to the grits and possum…" He couldn't even say *penis.* "Whatever. Whatever's easy." Chris chugged the rest and refilled the glass.

Ray got up to prepare farina for two. Halfway through, he turned and said, "Remember, if I'm not here today when you're home, go to your mother's."

"Why can't I stay here?" Chris whined. "It's not like they're going to throw you in solitary for a month. Anyway, my homework and stuff's all here. Not there."

Chris was right. Why uproot him? Ray decided not to argue the point. When he was sitting at the table again, a steaming bowl of porridge before each of them, the boy already eating his, he found he couldn't touch the food. After a half minute he noticed Chris staring at him.

"I don't mean to be rude or anything, but you kinda look like shit."

"I'll remember this when your birthday rolls around," Ray threatened.

Chris was unfazed. "Maybe you should take some sleeping pills."

"What do you suggest? Sixty?"

"You know what I mean." Chris carefully excavated the coolest top layer off the farina and delicately slid it into his mouth.

"I've been a mess, Chris. I'm sorry. I know these few weeks have been hard on you too. But after today…" Ray found he couldn't even describe it. "I should be able to sleep better."

"Better eat up," Chris suggested, "so you can fight off the rapists in the holding cell."

"What makes you think I'd fight them off?" Ray asked, but despite that and despite Chris's odd leer, he began eating and didn't stop until his spoon was scraping the bowl.

The boy was dressed and out the door to school and Ray was still sitting at the breakfast table. As a rule he would wait until Chris had left to turn on a classical music station—in recent months keeping it low because of Jesse in the next room, even after Jesse was no longer there. He would then read the paper. He did both now, purposely turning up the volume, but the music—a late Mendelssohn string quartet—got on his nerves almost immediately, so he had to turn down the volume, and although he turned page after page of the paper, nothing held his attention. Desperate for some distraction, anything at all, even if it was something J.K. (already gone several weeks now, up to his sister's in central Massachusetts) would do, he turned to the book page and started on the crossword puzzle, well aware that he'd probably get stuck by the third clue. He'd read a dozen clues across and 10 down before he found spaces he could fill in. But he stuck at it, as the fiddle players sawed away in the background in an F-sharp minor key that kept trying to be G-sharp major and his coffee got cold and his farina turned into finely textured concrete against the sides of the Japanese porcelain. He'd managed to fill in maybe 15 blanks at various unconnected areas of the puzzle—sure sign of a puzzle whose solution would never occur—when he looked at the kitchen wall clock. It was only 8:45!

Now, more than since he'd awakened, he was aware of how much he had planned the entire day around one single action, and now that it had been postponed, he had hours and hours to somehow get through. He tossed the puzzle, simply slid it off the table and into the trash bin, cleaned up the breakfast dishes, showered and shaved, turned on the office computer he had stared at blankly for the past few weeks, for the first time in that long actually reading his list of reminders—invoices to be remailed, orders to be checked, payments from distributors to be collected and banked, catalogue and inside copy to be reedited for the Ferber disc. Two other letters required answering. He didn't know how they had found him, but two people had come forward in the past two months about keyboardists suffering from AIDS, one dead—a Russian virtuoso—the other a British *claveciniste* still barely alive—under contract with a major European label, but only for selected works. The Russian's agent, a distant cousin or something and the Brit's ex-manager or ex-boyfriend (it wasn't all that clear) had written Ray about Klavier Stuecke putting out CDs of their recordings. In theory, he knew he should be doing exactly that. Who could do it better? But for the past two weeks every time he'd gone to the computer or tried to handwrite a letter, he'd been overwhelmed and had gotten no further than "Dear Sir, thank you for your thoughtful and most intriguing note. Naturally, I've heard of the artist and admired his work…"

He had to finish the letters. But first he had to finish this business at the hospital. He stood, shut off the computer, deciding to collect and sort laundry. Partly this was due to Chris, who'd complained this morning that he was running out of socks and underwear, and if Ray didn't do something about it, Chris himself would have to—with results he could neither predict nor be responsible for. It was the kind of simple, mechanical job Ray told himself he should be able to do—could and must do.

He'd emptied two laundry bags onto the floor and already begun filling the washer with a full load of whites when he came upon a single off-white sock cleaving to the farthermost reach of the deepest corner of the bag. When he managed to untwist the material and pull it out, it revealed itself to be—unmistakable, the brand, the identifying gray Greek key motif a quarter inch from the ankle opening—one of Jesse's.

"Go *fuck* yourself!" he found himself shouting as he threw the sock into the washer and started it, correcting temperature and cycle. He'd recognized it as the last sock Jesse had worn in the house. Maybe the last he'd ever wear. "Go *fuck* yourself!" he repeated.

Now it all came back. But before it could take over, he stopped the memory film, to trudge upstairs and empty Chris's hamper, chock-full, naturally. The kid wore clothing about seven minutes before changing into something else; he had a ton of the stuff in closets and drawers. On the stairs back down to the laundry, Ray stopped and wondered, what if they changed his room again today? I'm all geared up for action, and I'll get there and they fucking changed his room again? Then what? Another *hour* before I find him?

That had been the giveaway of course. When he'd gotten to the hospital that morning at ten minutes to ten as usual and stopped at the front desk and asked for a pass to ICU. Unit 5, and she was writing it out for him when she looked up and asked, "Patient's name again?"

He told her Moody, and she'd checked her chart and said, with a little

Egyptian hieroglyph dancelike movement of her neck, "He's not there anymore. He's been moved to…" She'd searched and didn't find it and had to call the operator, who took ten minutes to locate it, at which the receptionist had smiled, saying, "No time limit on this room. You can visit as long as you like now."

That unaccountable news had elevated Ray's spirits: to think Jesse had come around after these four weeks and was suddenly doing well enough to be moved out of the ICU and into a real room, less restricted, easier care. And, since he'd ascended to floor 11, Ray only had one quandary, where the hell had they put him? Why so high? Ray hadn't even known the building had 11 floors. He'd already begun working out bringing fresh T-shirts to Jesse, maybe some books and a radio or…

The 11th floor was given over to unused offices, except for a single wing, without a nurses' station, only an unoccupied, underutilized-looking desk, not even medical offices behind it. Five patient rooms, the first two vacant. In the third…

At first Ray was merely perplexed. It seemed Jesse had been moved out of the ICU to this faraway floor, this forlorn-looking wing, yet he was still surrounded by all the trappings: intravenous tubes from three different racks, a half dozen monitoring devices, same adjustable bed, ice-pack vest upon his abdomen designed to lower fever. Then the other machine, nearly hidden behind the others, became apparent. Especially since it contained a single, convolute, striated-along-its-gyre tube, unmistakable in its thickness and in its coupling at either end—the center of the floor-set mechanism on one hand and the center of Jesse's face on the other, thrust deep down his throat, with a narrower subsidiary tube linked to a freshly opened tracheotomy slit a third of the way down his neck.

As he came to realize what the machine was for, rhythmically respiring Jesse's body, Ray stumbled against the wall. At first he thought Jesse was half asleep because his eyes were open an eighth of an inch from the bottom, until he got closer and saw that in truth Jesse was only existing because of the unnatural, mechanically fierce bellows that almost lifted his frail frame off the mattress with every periodic inhalation. It only required another horrified minute, if any further proof were needed, to see the machine doing all of Jesse's breathing. Its monitor sported a double screen, one facet reciting the heart's electromagnetic activity, regular if spaced fairly widely apart, beat by now-mechanized beat; while the brain's own electric activity was displayed on a lower screen as an unvarying, flat, green neon line.

Comprehending this, Ray cried out, "Noooooooo," and fell to his knees at the side of the bed. He'd never been in shock before and was amazed he didn't know how long he sat there, appalled, unable to keep himself from staring at Jesse's eyes moving back and forth irregularly. They seemed to insist he was alive. But it was a deceptive irregularity, involuntary, mere reflex. And there lay the bruised, livid face, the body abandoned where no one would be offended.

Rage arrived.

Fifteen minutes later he was on the first floor, elbowing his way into the social worker's office and shoving someone who'd been in there out the door, slamming it behind him, advancing upon her. He managed to scare her away from her desk, away from the phone, managed to get her against the far wall, listening but not really listening to her explanations, as he quietly said, "We agreed *not* to resuscitate. We agreed *not* to take extreme measures. We agreed *not* to do anything if he was dying. We agreed *I* would be phoned and *I* would make the final decision. It's written and signed by all parties!" Repeating the statements again and again and again, faster and louder, into her terrified face as she explained and explained and explained, until finally she saw her opening, shoved him, and ran. He quickly caught her by the arm, and she screeched a high-pitched shriek, and he actually found himself saying with quiet fury, "Don't make me do anything we'll both regret." She kind of relaxed at that and said, "It's not my fault. I wasn't there. It's not my fault. I wasn't there!" until two other women were standing in the office doorway, a security guard behind one of them, and the social worker turned to them, and said, "It's the Moody matter." Their faces of alarm changed subtly into something else—defeat, despair, he couldn't tell what exactly—but it was enough to maybe not calm him down, but at least quiet him enough to keep from doing anything reckless.

A half hour, following explanations by a hospital administrator and a hospital attorney, Ray was phoning Liesl. She'd be right there, she said. Once more, explanations of what happened were repeated to Ray. Whereupon he said, "This is *not* my phone number written on the DNR file, even though this woman," pointing to the social worker, "witnessed me writing the correct number. I was *never* told what was happening here last night. Despite our written agreement, the attending physicians chose instead to listen to someone else. I don't need my attorney here to know I'd have a viable lawsuit with potentially crippling damages, both financial and in terms of this institution's reputation. If medical power of attorneys are such a joke here—"

They protested vehemently.

"Well, you're aware of what's involved. I'm willing to let it all go, let *all* of it go, if you shut the machine off right now and let Jesse Moody die."

Three of them spoke at once, telling him that they couldn't turn off the machine now that it was attached. Hippocratic oath, etc.

Liesl arrived fairly quickly, and without any previous discussion or prompting by Ray, she said exactly the same thing: No charges or action would be filed if they turned off the machine immediately. They all answered they couldn't.

After a short while in which everyone realized the depth of their impasse, Ray and Liesl left the office, headed to the 11th floor, followed by the three women and a security guard. Liesl groaned at the sight. Distraught, she turned to the administrator. "This is *exactly* what was *not* supposed to happen. How could it?" A dozen excuses were once again proffered.

While they were in the room, Ray and Liesl silently checked how to turn off the machine. There were no buttons, no fail-safe, no lever, just a plug into an electrical outlet.

From the downstairs lounge, Liesl phoned Adele Moody's hotel and was told she'd checked out that morning, no destination provided. She then phoned Hugh Jr.'s law office and was told he was not available. She left a long message, slowly speaking so it could be copied as given, at times spelling out terms for his secretary: "felony offense," "criminal neglect," "manslaughter with interstate flight," "actionable under a dozen state and federal laws." Even so, after she'd hung up, Liesl seemed no happier.

"Well, the old bitch did it! We know that for sure. And why."

Ray foolishly asked, "Why?"

To which she'd reacted by looking at him with a pitying smile. "Because she hates you, because she hates who you are in Jesse's life. I have to check his last will and testament. Do you recall where final deposition of his remains goes?"

"What final desposition?" Ray asked. "He's—or at least *something's*—still alive there. It's not Jesse. It's—I don't know—something. But its heart still beats."

"Maybe not for long. You helped put in intravenous tubes. You must know how to take them out. When no one's around, take them out. One by one. No, wait! Listen! They won't put them back in again. That would be interfering, which they said they cannot now do. So *we* must interfere. Stop medicine. Stop nourishment. Take off the ice pack and let the fever rise. This *you* must do, Raymond. Can you do it?"

He could, and he did. Every day thereafter, when he was alone with the body, he removed a medicine or nutrient-carrying tube out of the body's hand,

and when one rack was no longer in use, he placed it far away, down the corridor, sometimes even at the elevator doors. The next day he removed something else. He was at the hospital more than before, sometimes five, six times a day, because even though there were now several court orders against Adele Moody and she could no longer even enter the building, he had to be sure she wouldn't get in and grab the body or perform some other atrocity upon it. He didn't put it past her to try. As far as the hospital was concerned, the body was in legal limbo, no one on staff would go near it or have anything to do with it. As Liesl had predicted, every IV rack Ray removed and left in the hall was taken away overnight, every impediment to death was allowed to be taken away and each remained away. Even so, *someone* had to come and wash the body, *someone* had to shave the face and clip the nails and even once trim the hair, since the body continued to exist, to endure. That became Ray's job. That became Ray's terror. Now, no matter where he was, virtually every waking hour of his life Ray saw Jesse's eyes going back and forth under their lids, the illusion of life, which he knew was false, simply reflexes, but which colored his days and haunted his nights of little or broken sleep with the persistent dream he had of chasing the uncatchable gurney.

After a week, with all other external support deleted, he realized he'd have to shut off the last and most horrible machine, the respirator.

Liesl kept saying, "No, don't do anything. Not yet. They all say the body can't endure much longer."

But it did endure. Twelve days after Adele Moody had perpetrated her outrage upon her son, Ray made his decision. And now it was 14 days later. He was set up with Liesl to do it and he was determined to do it. He would go to that deserted 11th-floor wing once more. He would wash and shave Jesse once more. He would pull the plug out of the wall. He guessed some alarm would be tripped. He was prepared to bar the door against everyone until he was certain the body had stopped breathing and could no longer be resuscitated. Then, task completed, he would let them in. He would be taken away by hospital security, arrested, driven to a local police precinct where he'd be booked and charged, and where, after the appropriate period in a holding cell, he'd be bailed out by Liesl, who planned to be nearby at every step. That was the plan, delayed for another two and a half hours. Leaving Ray to do laundry.

Figuring he might as well do it all, he was collecting dust and dishrags for a third load when he heard a strange noise from the washer. The machine seemed to be trying to lift off the laundry room floor, it was oscillating so much. He managed to shut it off, although that meant he had to first leap on and ride the erratic machine. After the electricity was taken away, it still quivered for a few more minutes. He managed to get the top hatch open, then peered in. Two sheets had become twisted together during a spin cycle and whisked every other piece of clothing into their intricate braid. He had to lift the sopping mess out, stretch it across the top of the washer, dryer, and the industrial-size sink, and try to unknot it.

In the middle of this—him drenched, underwear and socks flying in all directions, the twisted mass in his lap, around his head—the phone rang. And was picked up. From this far away he couldn't hear who was leaving a message at the other end, only that someone was and it was brief. He wrestled the muddle into the sink, tossing single pieces in, and was just getting the two offending sheets pulled apart when the phone rang again, and again he heard someone leave a message. Swearing, he managed to get the two sheets separated and back into the washer, realigned everything else inside, and turned it back on. He watched for a while, but it chugged along and didn't go lopsided again.

Soaking wet, smelling like laundry soap and bleach, he played the answering machine. The first message was from Liesl, and she sounded excited, almost breathless, She said she couldn't talk long, but would see him very shortly. He should forget the plan and go to the hospital immediately. She added that he needn't bother calling her as she was in between interviews; she'd get there as soon as she could. The second call was from someone at the hospital, a woman in the administrator's office whose name he didn't recall. She simply left her number and said to call back soon as possible. He assumed she was calling about the legal farrago they'd gotten into, and he copied down the number, planning to give it to Liesl when he saw her.

Infected by Liesl's excitement—he replayed her message—he cleaned up and changed into street clothing. Remembering to dress as though he'd spend time in a jail cell—no jewelry, slim paperback—this was now going down as planned. Almost out the door, he heard the washer shut off, ran back to move its contents into the dryer, set that going, filled the washer again with what was the bulk of Chris's clothing, wondered if it would become unbalanced again, and turned it on anyway.

He searched for an empty taxi along Joralemon Street, but none arrived until he was almost at the hospital on foot. He arrived at 11:40. Four other people were at the visitor's desk, so he had to wait. When he gave the room number, the sympathetic receptionist smiled. In minutes, he was nervously waiting for the elevator. Would Liesl be there already? If not, he'd simply continue the plan: wash and shave Jesse, then go ahead and pull the plug.

As usual, he was alone on his way to the 11th floor, and as before, it was empty when he got there. Not even a janitor. He tried not to run to Jesse's room, lest he raise suspicion before it was appropriate. At the wing, he checked the other vacant offices and rooms. Only then did he go in.

The room was empty. Stripped bare. Only the bed, minus blankets, pillows, sheets. Jesse was gone. Ray's heart did a noticeable little butterfly thing.

Stepping out of the elevator on the first floor, he ran into the social worker. "Where did you hide him?" he asked.

"I was just coming to get you. Follow me."

They went along corridor into not another room or wing, but her office. She went to her desk and speed dialed. Someone answered. The social worker said, "He's here!" and gave him the receiver.

She identified herself as the woman who'd phoned him at home. "Mr. Moody died at 10:37 this morning. If you wish to see his body, I can arrange to have it displayed in our morgue." After a pause, she added, "I'm very sorry."

He hung up the phone and felt for the chair.

The phone rang again, and the social worker answered and said, "He's here" again, and again handed it to Ray. Had they made a mistake?

No, it was Liesl. "You heard?" she asked.

"I heard," he said. How to explain the let down, now that what they had wanted so very much had happened without them doing a thing? "This is going to sound strange," he said. "But it's like he knew. Like he was watching and saw what was going on and…made sure his body died before—"

"—before we could do anything," she finished for him. "Before you could get into any trouble."

"Are we crazy?" Ray had to ask.

"It's as though he did it on purpose," she repeated.

They were silent together, then she asked if he was OK. She still had work to do with the judge. Did he want to check the body? Just to make sure it was really him? She had already looked over the will and the body was to be cremated, the ashes collected and strewn from a place on Northeastern Long Island that Ray knew of.

"The only stipulation is that you must witness the cremation," Liesl said.

"He had a morbid fear of being buried alive. He saw too many Vincent Price movies as a kid."

"You're all right with that?" she asked.

"Yeah, sure."

After she hung up, the social worker said, "I'll go with you to the morgue."

"You heard what I was planning?"

"I heard nothing," she said. "I was occupied." Then, when they were down in the basement, headed toward the morgue, she said, "I would have too."

If he'd expected comfort from seeing the body no longer attached to machines, whole, and most importantly, now completely still, it wasn't forthcoming. He signed off that indeed it was Jesse Moody of such and such address, and confirmed where the corpse was to go for cremation.

The social worker walked him up to the front door. She asked if she could call him a taxi, but he decided to walk.

Some blank ten minutes later, a thought arrived like a fist to his heart: *What do I do now?* He'd lived this past dozen years with Jesse. This past five years he'd lived for, almost *through* Jesse. *What do I do now?* was all that came into his mind. No answer.

He must have sat down on the curbstone close to the Chinese laundry, because suddenly the owner was lifting him by an elbow, pulling him into his shop. His wife was there, and they sat Ray down and gave him water, and Ray looked at them and thanked them and answered that he was better, although it was all happening as though from the far end of a gigantic telescope, them tiny and incomprehensible. When at last he stood up again to leave, he said very casually, "Oh, by the way, Mr. Moody has died. So it'll only be my things from now on. A lot less business for you. Sorry." As he left, the door chimes sang out, *What do I do now?*

At home he took off his coat and scarves, went to a seldom-used drawer, and rummaged. After a hunt he at last located the worn, embroidered silk yarmulke he hadn't worn in decades—the shawl, the phylacteries it always had taken him so long to arrange properly. He covered every mirror in the house, even the glass doors on the shelves, with sheets and blankets, then grabbed a pair of scissors and very carefully used the sharpest end to tear his shirt and trousers from top to bottom. He took the phone off the hook, then gathered ashes out of the fireplace, and scattered them over his head. He tightened the phylacteries around his arms and chest. He stood in the middle of his living room, opened the book, and tried to read the Hebrew, and when he couldn't get far, he turned to the other book, where the *Kaddish* was translated into English, and began to intone that instead, swaying like the old men swayed in temple.

Around him a universe swirled in meaningless patterns. But for hours on end, through daylight and twilight and darkness, through doors opening and Kathy and Chris coming in and leaving some time later with a bag of the boy's clothing, through hoarseness and thirst, through sleepiness, then sleeplessness, into some other state free of physical concerns, he recited the words, over and over, not as though his life depended upon them, because after all what could be so insignificant as a life? But because they must be recited, although they brought little sense of propitiation, of communication, nothing remotely like consolation, and never came close to answering the question, *What do I do now?*

twenty-two

"I've changed my mind. I can't watch!" Liesl said. "I'm a coward."

"I'll stay with you," Maurette said, once again lifting a thick yet surprisingly lightweight arm across Ray's shoulder. It seemed as though he'd barely left off touching Ray since they'd arrived an hour or so ago, as though to let go of him for even a minute would mean what? Losing him? Of course it was Ray's own fault. He'd been so out of it for the past few days. And a physical wreck when they had arrived this morning. So much so that Liesl had said, "We've got time for you to shower, you know." Hint. Hint. But he'd taken it, and now his skin felt raw, somewhat alien, his hair even more difficult to keep down than usual, his limbs as though not used in months, instead of a few days, while— the lamenting over, or at least the official period done with—he'd gone to bed, sleeping two, three days, he wasn't certain how long. He knew he would have remained there, numbed, insensate, if Liesl hadn't come by, reminding him of the appointment at the crematorium. So he'd gotten himself up and cleaned, into clothing that looked like it belonged to someone else (or rather, someone he used to know). They'd taken the Regal, Maurette driving, colossal behind the wheel but a surprisingly delicate driver—as he seemed to be gentle in all of life, despite his size and girth. Forty minutes later they were in upper Manhattan, not far from the Cloisters, which Ray had not visited since he'd first moved to the city, stepping into a startlingly cheerful edifice, bright and modern, inside and out.

They had waited barely a minute in the outer lobby before being ushered in. A good-looking young bodybuilder, with thick, gleaming jet hair and soft, almond-shaped eyes, said he would be their guide and spoke with pride of the place and how it operated; even common words assuming a lilt in his lyrical Middle Eastern accent. He'd talked directly to Liesl, had tried to hand her a small plastic baggie holding Jesse's double wedding ring—the bulky gold band and more slender white gold ring-guard with its art deco chasing. At that Liesl drew back and pushed Ray forward.

"Is it true," Ray asked, "that before cremation, you sew up the body openings?

"Indeed," their host answered, seemingly unfazed that the widow had become the widower. "So that no liquids may be released into the fire."

"I don't know if you can do it, but I was thinking maybe you could place these rings, and my own," Ray struggled to get the ring guard past his own bony knuckle, "and sew them inside his mouth."

"A very imaginative gesture," their guide responded. "Except the gold will not be reduced to ashes along with the rest, but will simply melt, even at such a high degree, and burst out of the body at some point, forming a molten pool below. So instead of several handsome rings, you'll have a fused mass of metal. Is that what you wish?"

"No. Never mind."

Their guide went on to explain that they could watch through the furnace window. The body would come in at one end upon a conveyer belt. Set in a flameproof tray, it would undergo its holocaust in full view. Once reduced to ashes, it would be moved back out. "I must warn you, because of physiological processes that take place during extreme heat, the muscles will contract, and the body will appear to move. Often the torso appears to sit up, and the arms and legs bend. It can be unsettling, even if you are prepared."

That was when Liesl decided to not watch. All three took one last look at

Jesse's corpse—livid, hideous, with eyes, mouth, and ears stitched shut, limbs shrunken at some places, bloated at others—mostly, it was explained, because it hadn't received preservation fluids, which reacted with fire. Liesl left with their guide. Maurette and Ray took up positions at the furnace's shoulder-high window.

The conveyer belt was imperfectly angled to the window so they could make out a back hatch open and the body, lying in its shallow tray, hesitantly jerk forward by degrees until it was fully within the furnace room, in three-quarters perspective to them. Jesse's white briefs had been left on: a thoughtful touch; they looked damp, probably soaked in combustible liquid. The conveyor belt stopped, and below and on either side, rows of tubelike burners were kindled in tiny, deep blue flames. After a few seconds the flames grew enormous, the color changed to red, orange, and yellow. In seconds Ray's view of Jesse was obscured by tall sheets of fire, the roar tumultuous even on his side of the window.

"This is not so terrible!" Maurette managed. Just then the body ignited at several places at once and went into motion. As predicted, as it caught fire it sat up, eventually attaining a nearly vertical position. The arms rose, the fingertips, in a subtle trembling, seemed to be testing the flames for temperature. The legs folded, rising at the knees. The head turned side to side slightly as though in time with unheard music.

"Mon Dieu! Protectez moi!" Maurette mumbled, and fell to his knees, out of sight of the spectacle. Kneeling, he made the sign of the cross over and over again, repeating his plea in an undertone, ending each signing with a thumbnail caressing his lower lip.

Although momentarily distracted by Maurette, Ray continued to study what was happening in front of him. As the flesh began to blister, the head continued to bob and flutter as though in a palsy. The combusted toes, quickly followed by the outstretched, nearly vaporized fingers, dropped off two and three at a time into the tray, followed by the blazing hands, then blackened forearms. The scalded head turned toward Ray at a seemingly impossible angle. The vanishing lips drew back in a fiery rictus that was horrifying yet familiar, reminding him of one of Jesse's overdone mock smiles. Seconds later the head was too engulfed in flame to be made out clearly: hair, eyebrows, ear tips all ablaze with individual conflagrations. The jawbone dangled insecurely; it disconnected from the left side, then from the right and finally fell. Freed of its weight, the rest of the head seemed to roll forward before itself dropping off completely, leaving the surprisingly hardy exposed tops of quickly charring vertebrae. As it landed, the skull crushed an area of already incinerated ribs, causing hundreds of sparks to fill the overoxidized air. And still the body continued to burn.

Next to him, Maurette, still on his knees, had subsided into quiet muttering, one hand gripping the seam of Ray's pants leg, as though to make sure he was still there and wouldn't get away. When Ray glanced back into the furnace, the body seemed no longer present, replaced by a few handfuls of bones, blackened and guttering, as the sheet of flames slowly relented, leaving tiny orange flickerings to erupt intermittently all over the desiccated wreckage. Another rack of burners he hadn't noticed before, this one above and parallel to the conveyor belt, now descended to within six inches of the tray, hovering over the smoldering remains. It was ignited suddenly, and 30 jets of flame shot down and played over the debris until it was little but smudged soot. Half a minute later the flames shut off. The tray's charred contents, an inch high and in no way recognizable as a person, smoked on a bit longer. The conveyor belt began with a tiny jolt to move, then continued on more smoothly. Soon the ash-covered tray trundled out the way it had come.

Ray tapped Maurette's shoulder. "It's over."

In the lobby, Liesl turned to them, anger fighting anguish evident on her face. "Her attorney has gotten a legal estop to keep us from touching the ashes."

Ray couldn't grasp what she was saying.

"He filed papers saying the old bitch was told by Jesse that she could bury the ashes back in their family plot back in Buttfuck, Carolina." She shook some papers at him. "Look!"

"Nobody buries ashes," Ray reasoned, ignoring the papers. "You keep them in an urn or you strew them. What's the point of burying ashes?"

"The point is to keep Jesse from being where he wanted to be. And to be where she wants him. Don't worry, Ray-mond. I'll handle this!"

Ray laughed. Liesl and Maurette, along with the receptionist and their guide, stared at him. He couldn't help it. He laughed again. Seeing the dismay on their faces, he tried to stop laughing but couldn't and only managed to get out through his laughter, "He's ashes! What's the goddamned difference where the ashes go?" He went on laughing. Then he couldn't stop laughing and had to sit down. When he was done, he managed to catch his breath. "I'm not hysterical. It's just…ridiculous!"

"Ridiculous or not," Liesl turned to the bodybuilder, "Mr. Moody's ashes don't leave New York state as long as I'm alive. Or you and your company will be charged with theft. You'll be arrested and sent to jail. Is that clear? And," she added, "Mr. Henriques is *not* signing papers saying you've done what you were contracted to do. Understand?"

"But we can't be paid if he doesn't sign," the guide said.

"You'll be paid. But you'll get no signature," she insisted. "That means this cremation has not yet happened. Nor has it been witnessed!"

"You're crazy," the guide insisted. "It just happened."

While the guide continued complaining, Liesl swept Maurette and Ray outside. Maurette was still looking ill, but Ray said he was feeling better, which he was: He would drive. He dropped them at Liesl's place, where Maurette got out of the car and hunkered down to the driver's side window to be face to face with Ray.

Holding onto Ray's shoulder, he said, "Don't stay here, *cher!* This city is cold and damp and nasty. Come with me to California next Monday. I need you there. You've got nothing to do here but be unhappy. There I have work for you. You will be distracted all the time—I will work you hard making the new soundtrack. You should see the recording gear they have to work with! You'll think you're in heaven. And after work, we'll eat wonderfully, every night, all on the studio. We'll take long moonlight drives through the desert and along the ocean. It will be great. You know how much I hate to travel alone. How bad I am alone? The stupid things I do? Liesl wants you to come too, you know, tell him Liesl, *cherie.* Not because she doesn't trust me, but because she knows what a big baby I am alone. Promise you'll come with me, *cher?*"

Ray promised to think about it. The thought was gone a second after he'd dropped them off, replaced by the general haze that descended after Jesse's body had died.

As he neared home, he was nonplussed to see a truck parked in the drive-way, barring entry to the garage. Could it be Mike Tedesco's? It wasn't the paint-dappled van he usually drove. Could be another company truck. Early afternoon traffic was light enough for Ray to slow down and check it out. He couldn't see anyone inside, didn't see his parking decal hanging on the center mirror. He hadn't seen Mike in some time. Because he hadn't been home—at the hospital so much—when Mike came by? Or hadn't Mike come by? He was surprised to be *so* disappointed it wasn't Mike's van. Then he was distracted by the sight of a parking space good for two hours across the street, in front of the Schnells's. Getting out of the car, he had an erection: the first in days—from just thinking of Mike.

"Sex and death," he murmured to the frosty afternoon. "Wagner got *that* right!"

Only as he had his key in the lock of his office door did Ray notice the young man settled on the stairs leading up to the front door. Dressed in a moth-eaten pea coat, bleach-discolored black denims, and decrepit ankle-high shoes, he sported a fashionable new woolen pull-down cap striped the colors of the African-American pride flag, covering his forehead to his eyebrows. No scarf or gloves: His hands were thrust deep in his frayed coat pockets. He saw Ray stop and look at him. In that second, the face the youth presented was shockingly similar to Jesse's as he'd looked years earlier: brilliant white skin, boyish features, rich chestnut hair. In another second Ray knew it was a mirage; the boy was clearly another. Still, it was weird returning home after what he'd gone through this morning to find the youth perched on the very step Jesse always sat on, waiting for Ray.

Perhaps that was why Ray's voice sounded so uncertain, even to himself, when he asked, "Can I help you?"

The youth's face registered what might have been amused puzzlement.

Ray tried again. "Were you looking for someone?"

The boy half smiled, making him look even younger. "Depends."

Ray tried again. "Were you looking for the people who live here?" He nodded toward his front door.

The youth half shrugged: totally cryptic.

Maybe he didn't understand English that well. Ray walked to the stairs. The youth stood and descended to the street. From this close, he was small, about 5'5", leaner, almost feral in how he moved. Maybe 16 years old. Seventeen. No older. He glanced toward the downstairs door. "You live there?"

"My office is there. Were you looking for me?"

The youth gave that enigmatic half smile again. "Like I said before...depends."

Ray found the boy handsome. Also somewhat repellent. The light complexion, close up, looked feverish. The finely carved nose and chin were a bit vulpine. The way the boy immediately glanced down at his body and kept looking there reminded Ray that he still had a visible erection, because his leather jacket left his lower torso exposed. "Depends upon what?" Ray asked in another uncertain tone of voice.

"All kinds of things. You live here?" he asked again. And now he was dancing back and forth on his feet. "'Cause I could really use a bathroom."

That came out of left field. How could Ray refuse? "Yeah, sure. C'mon in."

Ray guided him through the office and corridor, into the bedroom suite. He removed his coat, waiting nearby, pretending to look over his mail. When the youth came out of the bathroom, his pants were still unzipped and his pea coat was fully open, revealing a slender, hard-looking torso in a smoke-gray turtleneck. The cap was now rolled back to his hairline. More attractive than not, Ray found himself thinking.

"So I was out there, waiting for this friend," the kid began as though picking up conversation, "I don't know, 45 minutes? Freezing my ass off. You work here too?"

"The front office."

"So this friend owes me 50 bucks I loaned him, and now I need it bad. You know how it is. But he doesn't show up. I'm waiting and waiting and thinkin' he's not going to show, you know. He's gonna leave me freezing out there. But, hey, maybe it's OK if he doesn't show, since you look like you could really use a friend." He moved in close and put a hand over Ray's erection. "All you have to do is spare what my friend owes… I could be an extremely good friend to you. Believe me." He illustrated using his other hand along with the first. "I can make you really happy, you know."

The boy's eyes were beautifully set within straight brows and high cheekbones, with luxuriantly thick, dark lashes, but the irises themselves were a muddy brown. He was pretty the way starved models were pretty, with facial features suggesting he was ethnically mongrel, part Irish, part French, and something else—Magyar or Slavic. Definitely underage. Maybe even as young as Chris.

When Ray still didn't respond, the kid added in a more confidential tone, "I don't usually do oral with guys I don't know. But you're hot, and this guy," tugging Ray's erection, "seems real nice, so I might make an exception for you."

He made a motion to kneel, evidently to illustrate, when Ray understood he was being hustled. Shock was shot through with consternation—did he look that bad? Did he look like he needed it that bad? Admiration too: at the kid's nerve.

Ray helped him up. "Thanks. Despite what you think I don't…I don't…" he tried again. "What I mean is, I don't…"

The youth was suddenly defensive. "Man! You're giving out mixed signals, man, you know? With that thing staring at me! And you inviting me in!"

"You invited yourself in. You said you needed to use the bathroom."

"OK, OK. Calm down, man!" The kid was clearly annoyed at the failure of his plan. He was buttoning his pea coat, looking around for an escape route.

Ray did calm down. "Look, I'm sorry you misunderstood."

"Yeah! Yeah! Just tell me how I get outta here, OK?"

Ray showed him the way out. At the street door he said, "Wait." As the kid turned, Ray opened his wallet and took out three tens. "This is all I have. Thirty dollars."

The kid grabbed the tens. In one motion he stuffed them into his denim pockets and began again to kneel.

Surprised again, Ray reached down to raise the boy. "No. Not that. Just go!"

The kid stood up, wary, mystified, offended too. "What's the problem? I'm clean, you know. And I'm not positive or anything!"

"I didn't think you were."

"So?" Then the boy had a glimmer. "What are you? Married? Don't worry, man! I do straight guys all the time. Nobody ever finds out."

"Look," Ray tried, "why don't we just pretend your friend showed up and paid back part of what he owed you?"

The kid snickered. "There is no friend! That's a line I use to show I want money."

All at once Ray could no longer deal with the kid or the situation a second longer. "Smart! Great!" he said. He could hear the exhaustion in his voice. "Stupid me."

The kid stood another half minute, clearly unready to leave until he'd settled something for himself. Finally he brightened, obviously having thought up a satisfactory way to deal with what had just occurred. "Listen, man, what say I go for now, with this 30 and all, which I can really use...and...how about I owe you one?" He asked it with the same look of innocence Chris used to ask to go to a movie he knew he was barred from. "And the next time I see you...the very next time...I do what I can to make you happy." He illustrated with his tongue tip across his upper lip. "What do you say? We got a deal?" He held out a hand to be slapped "high five."

"Deal," Ray agreed, wearily slapping the outstretched hand.

The minute the kid was out the door, Ray had a terrifying idea: What if the kid had been dropped here, a setup, arranged by that dragon from hell and her blank-faced legal minion? What if...? He shouldn't have given the kid a cent. Now he could say anything. Ray looked out. The kid was gone. The white van too. Had he driven it here?

Twenty minutes later Ray was in his office reading chair still stewing over the incident. He was angry, depressed, tired as hell, and worse, because of the boy's come-on, now he was even hornier. Although the erection had gone down, he still was aware of his cock inside his underwear, uncomfortably aware of it, its presence, its insistence.

He found himself playing over scenarios in which the boy hadn't left but instead had stayed and blown him. Or where the boy had blown him and afterward demanded more money, and they'd begun to struggle, which had led to Ray getting the boy in a grip, down on the bed, holding him facedown where he'd angrily ripped off his pants and…

This was no good. No good at all.

Ray stood and paced. He could go out and look for him.

Right! With 30 bucks in his pocket, the kid was miles away. In Manhattan probably, scoring drugs.

Anyway, he didn't want the kid. The kid was scrawny and creepy. He had dead eyes and a hair-trigger temper. What Ray wanted, he admitted now, was Mike Tedesco. Sweet, handsome, easygoing Mike from Massapequa.

He *could* just phone him, but he'd never done that. He'd always relied on Mike coming to him. That seemed so much a part of what they had together— Mike being in charge of arriving, Ray being in charge of the sex. Could he alter it? Would Mike accept that? It was uncertain if he would even take Ray's phone call at work. He was married, remember? On the other hand, if he was so hetero at work, having a guy phone him might not signify a thing.

What the hell was the name of the new place Mike worked for? He'd written it somewhere. Where? On the back of his Day at a Glance? On his desktop blotter? Yes, there it was. The company name. But spilled coffee had smudged the number to incomprehension. Ray dialed 516 information for Long Island. There was no such bus company in Massapequa, but the operator said there was one by that name in Merrick. Where was Merrick? She said not far from Massapequa, so before he could actually consider what he was doing or stop himself, Ray went ahead and dialed that number.

It rang twice, long enough for him to begin to start to have doubts about what he was doing. He'd almost decided to hang up when a nasal female voice answered. Wrong number? No, she pronounced the company name. She must be a receptionist or secretary. Thankfully! In for a penny, in for a pound, Ray thought, so he asked to speak to Mike Tedesco. He was sure she'd tell him Mike was out on the road and he'd again doubt what he was doing, who he'd say he was if asked or if he wanted to leave a message. Make up a name? Say it was a repair job?

Instead of prying she sounded like she couldn't have cared less. "Hold on, I'll get him." Ray heard her call out in a surprisingly melodic voice, "Mi-*chael*! Tel-a-*phone*!"

Before he could hang up, another receiver was picked up. "Yeahhhh!"

"Mike?" he asked stupidly.

"Yeah-uhh!" Mike repeated.

"It's…it's Ray! You know, the guy from Brooklyn Heights."

A moment of hesitation, then, "Oh, yeah! Hey, man!"

"I know I shouldn't be calling you at work, even though you never told me not to, but it's been a while…and…I remembered the company name…and…"

Mike said nothing to help him out.

"…and anyway," Ray went on, feeling his face flush more with every absurd-sounding word as he began to sicken, knowing now this had been a big mistake-Big. Mistake. "I've missed you…and I wondered…if I could…see you soon." It was astonishingly lame. He awaited the fall of the ax.

"Soon?" Mike asked. "How soon?"

That was so stupefying, Ray blurted, "I thought…you know, now!"

He heard Mike snigger, and thought, man, I have screwed this up but good.

Instead, Mike said in an intimate tone of voice, "Missed me, huh?"

"Yeah." Ray didn't know what he was setting himself up for. "I missed you."

"And you've got that big boy all ready for me, don't you?" Mike half whispered.

"Yeah," Ray parroted his words and tone back: "Waiting and ready."

"Well, hell!" Mike sounded both confidential and intrigued. "In that case, how can I possibly say no?" He heard Mike shouting, "Tell the boss I gotta leave on an emergency." Then, more quietly, back into the receiver. "It *is* a big emergency, right?"

"*Big* emergency," Ray agreed.

"It's about noon. I should be there at 1, 1:15 at the latest."

Ray hung up the phone, went to the bedroom, fell back onto the bed, said aloud, "Well, you really pulled that out of the fire!" and immediately fell asleep.

He was struggling out of the dream when he woke up. The doorbell was ringing. Mike stood next to a shiny old mahogany Plymouth Valiant. Of course it wouldn't be the paint-spattered van any longer, Ray told himself, since he didn't work there anymore. Mike was wearing a gray variation on his usually green or navy work clothes, this one a bus-driving uniform with a car coat the same color, and a fawn scarf knotted at his throat. He had on the same funny cap with sewn-in rabbit-fur-lined earflaps tied overhead. The day's earlier promise of precipitation had been fulfilled: Fat, wet, grimy snowflakes speckled the leaden afternoon air.

"I see you've already started without me," Mike said, glancing at Ray's crotch.

Ray pulled Mike in and tore at his clothing. After a fraction of hesitation, Mike let him do whatever he wanted, without any thought of keeping their clothing separated.

It took less than 15 minutes for both to reach orgasm.

Despite an allegedly operating thermostat, the heat hadn't come on, and now that they were suddenly inactive and still naked, the chilled bedroom gave Mike's torso goose bumps. Ray drew the *federbed*, which they'd earlier kicked to the carpet in their exertions, from the foot of the bed up to cover them.

Mike snuggled drowsily into its lightweight warmth. "Don't let me fall asleep!"

Ray seized his genitals. "Minute I hear a snore, I'll squeeze."

"That might not do much," Mike said. "I'm overworked. Not sleeping well."

"Then I'll poke you where the sun don't shine."

"You already did that. That's why I'm so sleepy."

"You have a little button in there? If it's hit right, it sends you off to sleep?"

Mike turned to face him, amused by the idea. "Something like that." He looked Ray over more closely than since he'd arrived. "You haven't been sleeping much."

Ray didn't contradict him.

Mike suddenly sat up. "What's different here?" he asked, sniffing the air.

"What do you mean?"

"Not sure. Something's different."

"My...my partner's not here. The guy who was sick upstairs. But he wasn't here the last few times you were here either. He was at the hospital." Ray paused. "Otherwise, I don't know what it could be."

"That's right," Mike said, as though confirming something for himself. "But even when he wasn't upstairs, he was still somehow here. Not now."

Ray wondered whether to say it. "He died. A few days ago."

"Aw! Gee, man. I'm sorry!"

"Thanks."

"Really. That's gotta be like..." Mike couldn't finish, he felt so much.

It reminded Ray of Hamlet's lines about the player: "What's he to Hecuba? Or Hecuba to he?" Despite that, Mike's sincerity somehow allowed Ray the freedom to utter what came next, almost of its own volition, "So you sense him *not here*? Is that right?"

"Yeah, sure. Definitely."

"It's weird, but I felt him here for weeks," Ray admitted. "Even when he wasn't physically here. That's the most difficult part. After all these years, suddenly he's gone. When I was growing up, I'd hear stories about husbands and parents who were still around to their wives and children. Not him. He's *pffft!* Nothing there at all."

"People say the dead come back in dreams," Mike mused.

"I've had two dreams," Ray confided. "The quietest, dullest dreams."

"Well?" Mike prodded. "Tell me."

"You woke me from the second dream. Half an hour ago," Ray said. "In the first dream, two nights ago, Jess and I were walking along a railroad track. The sun had already set. It was peaceful, calm. We'd been strolling on different sides of the rails. We'd been speaking, but by the time the dream began we'd stopped. The sky turned colors to achieve that saturated, electric blue, and the railroad track divided. One branch curved into the trees. We kept walking, he on his side, me on mine, growing farther apart, until I couldn't see him anymore." Ray chuckled nervously. "Talk about obvious symbolism."

"Neither of you tried to cross the tracks?"

"No. Although there was nothing to stop us. All we had to do was step over. But what happened seemed, I don't know, natural, I guess. Meant to be."

"And the dream you had just before I got here?"

"Even duller. We were here, in the bedroom. I was on the bed, reading. Again it was sunset. This time it was earlier than in the other dream, because it never got dark. Golden light slatted in through the blinds. The entire room was bathed in golden light, everything golden and velvety, the walls, the bed covers, the book jacket, ourselves: We might have been butterflies or moths. While I read, he packed luggage. Getting ready to leave. We never spoke. It was understood that he was going—that was why he was packing—and that I was staying."

"You didn't argue or anything?" Mike asked.

"No. It was understood. No big deal. Like he was going away for business. Why would I argue about that?"

"Another obvious dream."

Ray agreed with a sigh. "Obvious yet odd. As though I didn't care. I did."

"Sure, you cared. But what your dream was telling you was that it was natural."

"He was only 40!" Ray snapped. "How can that be natural?"

"It can be. Natural," Mike calmly insisted. "And anticipated."

What do I do now? shrieked and shrieked through Ray's mind. *What?*

"It's weird," Ray said. "I guess I really expected to feel his presence longer. I don't know why. But I did."

"You mean like his ghost or his spirit?"

"Something! Instead of which there's...*nothing!*"

Mike stared, his face indecipherable.

Ray sat up. "This is boring, and if you stay you'll miss your return time."

"Right!" Mike threw off the covers and began to hunt for his scattered clothing. Ray did the same; both were careful to get the right underwear.

He was dressed when Mike came out of the bathroom, cleaned up, hair brushed. "I appreciate you coming and also listening to all that—"

"Hey!" Mike punched his shoulder.

"You have one minute more?" Ray asked.

Mike looked puzzled but said sure.

"I know this is crazy of me to ask, but with all that's been happening...I have to know something. Before you met me, you had experiences, right?" Seeing Mike's lack of understanding, he went on. "Sex with other guys? Fooling around with a guy when you were 12? Something like that?"

Mike smiled a little lopsidedly. "Why? You feelin' guilty about doing me?"

"No, not at all. I was just... It's stupid, but I mentioned seeing you—well not you precisely, not by name or anything like that, but a good-looking, young married guy—once when talking to an old friend, someone more experienced than me. And he said he figured I wasn't...you know, the first guy you did it with, that you'd had some previous experience...as a kid maybe? Away at camp?"

"When I was 16," Mike said, "I used to go to a gym in Hempstead. It was a workout gym for boxers. Mostly amateurs, a few professionals. I went because I was small and skinny and I wanted to defend myself. There was a guy there, 35 or so, he'd been middleweight champ for maybe three minutes about ten years before, Marine Corps. You know the type, real quiet, tough, short fuse. Terrific looking. Nice guy. Real hero to us younger guys. He took an interest in me. Started sparring with me, showing me tricks. He said I could lift weights at his place. So I went maybe...I don't know...a dozen times. Big old house. His wife was a hairdresser or manicurist. She worked Saturdays, which was when I'd go work out on his weights." Mike paused. "It was August. Hot. Sticky. So after our workout, he says we stink, let's shower. We showered together. He soaped me up and I got hard. He made me soap him up and he got hard too. He toweled me dry and blew me. After that, we'd shower and he'd blow me every time. He tried to get me to blow him. I held his joint once or twice. That was all I would do. Then some guys at the gym started saying things to my brother Vinny. So I stopped hanging around with the ex-Marine. That was it. My experience."

"Your brother told you to stop seeing the ex-Marine"

"Nah! What he did was, at the Sunday dinner table he said, 'Hey, Mike! I hear your friend so-and-so's a big fruit. You stick around with him, you're gonna end up a fruit too.' "

"And because you respected your brother you stopped—"

"I didn't respect him!" Mike flared up. "I hated him. It was because of that fucking Vinny that I had to defend myself. Because of him beating me up since I was a kid. That why I had to learn how to box! Good riddance to bad rubbish! And it's a good thing he didn't come back from the grave," he added sullenly. "I sound like a psycho, right?"

Ray put a hand on Mike's shoulder. Mike's entire body quivered with rage.

"You sound like someone who was bullied a long time."

"That's true enough," Mike spat out. Then, in a calmer tone of voice, "The weird thing, the really weird thing is, fucking Vinny was right. I am a fruit! Or halfway to becoming one. From the time I was six he called me 'cocksucker.' His worst insult was that you took it up the ass. I do both!"

"You almost sound proud of it," Ray commented.

"Kind of," Mike admitted. "I don't go around shouting it in parades, but if someone asked, I'd say so." An amused tone of voice followed. "So? Am I cool?"

"You're cool," Ray said. Cool. Handsome. Candid. Manly, he wanted to add. My ideal guy now that Jesse's gone.

At the office door Mike hesitated. "The funniest thing is, I knew I wanted to do it with guys, but I had to wait till that sonofabitch brother of mine was dead before I could do a thing. That answer your question?"

"It answers my question. Thanks for telling me."

"I had to tell someone," Mike said. "Maybe next week?"

"Great! Oh, wait," Ray suddenly heard himself say. "After next Thursday I might not be here. Business trip. Los Angeles."

"You mean that movie music stuff?" Mike asked, excitement clear in his voice.

"Exactly."

"I read in the paper that it's 75 and sunny there. Not this shit!" Mike opened the door to a dark afternoon of freshly laid snow. "Shit! It's sticking! Driving those kids is going to be a bitch!" He ran to the Valiant, unlocked and opened the door, and half turned: "You meet any movie stars, get me an autograph. To Mike. And if they ask who I am, say it's for your boyfriend. OK?"

twenty-three

"Ray? Is that *you*, Ray-mond Hen-riques?! My *God*, it is! What on *earth* is a serious person like *you* doing in a place like *this*?"

The "place" was an outdoor Franco-Greek restaurant on the Third Street Promenade in Santa Monica, one of a score of open-air eateries along the half dozen blocks of the outdoor mall, consisting of 20 tables and four times as many chairs kept in place by a knee-high wall planter filled to overflowing with what looked to be at least a score of different tea rose bushes in full bloom, even though it was early February. But then, of course, it being Southern California, everything was in bloom.

The speaker was none other than Eugenia Gershberg, or to her millions of fans, Gigi Gertz, whose recording career Ray had been instrumental in jump-starting 15 years earlier, and who now stood across the delicate pale yellow petals wearing a stylishly oversize silver-sequined silk/ramie sweater over black slacks, along with jet-tinged stockings and expensive-looking pumps. Even though she was at least in her early 40s by now, Gigi was more slender, more blond, and far more attractive than ever—even somewhat glamorous. What hadn't changed a bit, except by gaining in magnitude, was her huge, somewhat nasal voice. In fact, several people turned toward it, doubtless in recognition, which caused Gigi to slide the wraparound sunglasses back over her face.

Ray stood awkwardly for her to tilt over the bushes and buss him on two cheeks.

"I'm incognito!" she assured him, confidentially. Beyond her frosted and frizzed hairdo, Ray made out a heavyset man in matching shades and dark suit, with a battered visage, cauliflower ear, and bobbed ponytail, who could only be a bodyguard. "But we've got oodles of catching up to do. Would you mind moving inside to a quiet booth? Gratjo insists on complete privacy in public places."

"No problem," Maurette spoke up for Ray, who was still too befuddled.

Maurette called over a waiter and whispered in the young man's ear. Gigi and Gratjo meanwhile entered the restaurant some 25 feet away.

"Yes, sir. I understand completely," the waiter assured him. "Just go in and find the booth you want and we'll set you up there."

Gigi was already waiting for them in the deepest, darkest carmine-leather corner of the barely lighted restaurant. Gratjo was seated prominently at the booth in front of it, with a giant menu hiding his face. Gigi jumped up and hugged Ray.

"I don't believe it's really *you!*" she gushed. "It's been what? Five years?"

"Eight maybe," he said. "Not since the Grammys at Radio City."

"You don't mind being inside? It's all dark and dingy, but Gratjo insists."

"It's fine." They sat, and Maurette stood. "And this fellow is *not* my protection, as you might think, but instead my friend and colleague," Ray introduced Maurette, who joined them in the booth. "He's also the reason I'm in this, as you put it, *unserious* place," Ray added. "He tricked me into scoring and recording the soundtrack to his little insignificant movie, which naturally enough went on to win an award in Berlin. Now Fox is going to release it, so he's out here reediting it, and I'm here rerecording it, to update their latest sound technology and match their film stock."

Gigi's perfectly painted mouth opened in shock. "You rat!" she hit Ray's hand. "I'm stuck out in this backwoods, working my tail off making movies with the most incredible imbeciles, desperately needing someone professional to score my pictures and record them, and you have the extraordinary impudence to work for some *nobody?* No offense," she assured Maurette. "I'm being a twat to make a point to Ray, who, as I'm certain you've not failed to notice, can be a smidgen dense at times."

"No offense taken." Maurette was thrilled to be at the table with her, even to be insulted by her.

"Who knew?" Ray said. Although he very well knew Gigi had come to Hollywood years ago to make movies. But she'd already been out of his life by then; in fact, shortly after that Grammy ceremony, when she'd jumped labels.

"So you're a director?" Gigi turned all of her attention, now much mellowed, to Maurette, whose large hand she now placed in her own, caressing hands. "Maybe we can work something out. The chump they have directing is close to a hundred and thinks popular music stopped with 'Begin the Beguine.'"

Two waiters reset the table. One stood to take Gigi's order of green salad, no dressing, just a little lemon juice, and a piece of toast, nothing on it, thank you, oh, and yes, a glass of cranberry juice and don't forget Bluto in the other booth, he's with me, get him whatever he wants, no matter how excessive it seems, you're a dear, such great thighs, do you dance? I thought so, oh, and one orange, if you have nice Valencias, sliced in four, you are faboo!

"You offering Maurette a job directing your new film?" Ray asked bluntly enough. "Because if you do, I'll come and score it and record it."

Gigi's mouth hung open an excessively long time.

"These gay boys certainly don't waste their words, do they?" she suddenly said to the room in general. "Guess it comes from needing it hot, needing it hard, and needing it now. All the time." Then to Maurette, "No offense, if you're gay."

"Maurette dates Liesl. My German friend? The lawyer... Well, Gigi?"

Gigi screwed up one eye, as though peering at and evaluating a not terribly large gemstone. "Nobody railroads Diamond Lily, big boy!" She laughed at her bad impression of Mae West, then said, "You'd have to come out here. We begin preproduction in two months. Production in four. Most of it on studio sets. A few local locations. Game?"

Maurette looked at Ray. "You're serious, aren't you?"

Ray didn't know whether he was serious or not.

"You'd end up moving out here," Gigi said. "I thought I wouldn't have to, that I could come and go, but I *had* to move here. You *have* to if you want to make films. Period. And what about your lover, that cute Madison Avenue whiz? Jeremy? Joshua? Some amazingly grits-and-okra name? Would he be willing to move out here?"

Ray could feel Maurette tense up.

"Jesse won't be a problem," Ray said.

"That's what you think, buster. Believe me," Gigi began, then caught the drift and stopped herself. "What? Oh, no.! Don't tell me? Oh, Ray! Dar-ling! I'm so sor-ry! Was it...*it*? Oh, shit! And I had to go and shoot off my big mouth!"

"The change of scene will do Raymond good," Maurette said, placating her. "Besides, he likes it out here."

Gigi looked aghast. "You *like* it here? Now I *know* you're completely *farblonget* with grief." She held his hand a minute longer. In a little-girl voice she said, "It'll be fun, Ray. Remember the fun we used to have? It'll be fun, playing together again." Then she leaned over the table and kissed his forehead. Sitting down, she arranged her sweater and said in a her hard-as-nails, whiskey-laced-broad tone of voice, "Besides which, if you've *got* to be in mourning, might as well do it in a sunny warm place with lots of spending money. That's Gigi's motto. And *here, at last*, is my salad. *Look* at it! It's gor-geous. You divinely foolish waiter-slashdancer, you *told* the chef it was for *me*." she bubbled. "Did-n't you?"

"Honestly, Annabel Wilkins! It's more than a soul should have to think of," Eva King sputtered through a mouthful of ladyfingers with raspberry jam and clotted cream. Much too late, she put a hand in front of her slovenly, stained mouth and excused herself. She nearly reingratiated herself by immediately turning and asking, "And what do you think, Adele?"

Adele thought it was, suitably, the most insipid of questions about the most tedious of concepts so far brought up during this most vapid of afternoon teas she had ever allowed to be given in her west parlor. Virtually mindless, Annabel Wilkins had arrived a half hour ago, got up, not in a simple winter dress with clinging cardigan sweater like anyone normal, not even in one of those "creations" by that half-crazed octoroon woman downtown whom she usually allowed to dress her, no, but instead in what she referred to as an "Armani power suit," which made her look—not like a television anchor-woman as she preeningly supposed—but instead like an unattractively cosme-tized middle-aged man with flounced hairdo and too much hips wearing women's heels. The other four ignoramuses had, of course, just fluttered with scandalized delight, bursting with inane questions and pointless comments.

Leaving Adele to wonder if this was why she had wasted hours yesterday afternoon searching for and then along with the nearly deaf and slow-as-molasses cook, reviving this fine, old dessert, a specialty of the antebellum Carstairs family, and—she had hoped—the high point of what appeared, alas, to be what remained of local society…such as it was.

And now the old servant was unhurriedly padding her circuitous path across the Turkey carpets, around the half dozen women toward Adele, a yellow phone note aflutter in her aged, nearly white fingers, confirming that *had*, after all, been the phone ringing during the most recent bout of henlike excitement a few moments ago. Adele snatched the note. Despite the execrable handwriting, she was able to spell out the name Hugh Butterworth Jr. returning, at long last, her two phone calls from his morning.

"Can't you see I'm busy now?" she mouthed the words to the old servant. "Have him call later."

"He already done said," the servant began uttering before Adele was through speaking, "that he be out later. Right now is the onliest time he can talk to you."

"Oh, all right." She shooed her away. "Refill the ladies' coffee," she commanded too late to be heard. She excused herself to the group and marched into the foyer from where she could glance back at Annabel Wilkins, still holding court with anecdotes of her visit to Paris—outdoing on purpose Adele's own to New York, the old biddy, who did she think she was? Adele picked up the phone in the study.

"You received my letter with the copy of your son's will?" Hugh Jr. asked, sounding in a great hurry. "You'll receive the life insurance check?"

"I did, yes," she said. "Is there no way to send that damned will to court?"

"What for?" he asked. "I can find nothing wrong with it. And it gives you his $100,000 life insurance policy. You can't complain about that."

"I can and I most certainly shall complain about the will," she contradicted him. "What of my son's personal possessions? Do I receive not a single scrap?"

"I already brought that topic up with the counsel who drew up the will," Hugh began, sounding vexed with her. Lately he always sounded vexed with her, although it should by rights be the other way around. "Other counsel" was his smooth-lawyer terminology for that slut the Jew boy had succeeded in provoking against her. "Counsel said that if you had any particular item of sentimental value, that request would be scrupulously considered. Otherwise, as per terms of the will, all possessions are deemed as having been co-owned by your son, and so go to Mr. Henriques—house included."

"I wouldn't request the time of day from either of those two spawn of hell! And who in their right mind would want any part of that hovel?"

"Then that's final," Hugh said, sounding pleased. "Meanwhile your son's ashes are being held at the crematorium, with a stop order on them for 15 days. That was all I was able to legally manage," he added. "And I don't know how much longer I can keep the order alive without presenting specific evidence that your son had changed his mind and wished to be buried in the family plot."

Adele went on the offensive. "Are you saying I made that up?" she asked, knowing full well that was precisely what had occurred.

"I'm *saying* I need specific proof to continue this line of action, ma'am. A fragment of his writing, some third party who witnessed that conversation, who would swear under oath... Though it grieves me to say so, your word alone won't do doody in court. And even if it were heard, given the array of felonies and misdemeanors filed against you by the other counsel—and just yesterday also by hospital adminstration—I seriously doubt you could be anywhere near a New York State courtroom without, at the least, also having a subpoena served on you, never mind the possibility of your being arrested."

It galled her to the bone hear his words, signifying that while she may have won the battle for the soul of her boy, the war was unquestionably going to the other side. "Those ashes are what is left of my only son," she declared pitiably.

"I'm all too well aware of that, ma'am," he said coldly.

"Am I to get not one thing from this utter calamity?"

"You're getting $100,000, clear," he argued. "I'd hardly call that nothing. And candidly, ma'am, I'd recommend you not lift a finger to interfere with that will going through sans probate, or it could be months, possibly years, before you even see that money. And then only after substantially more legal fees."

"The money means diddle to me," she said grandly, lying through her teeth. But she knew he was telling the truth. "Shall they then strew my boy's remains to the wind?"

"That's what he wanted."

"It is un-Christian. It is utterly barbaric! It's *his* influence!"

"I doubt that, ma'am. Mr. Henriques's religion believes in burial of the *entire* body." But before she could comment, he added, "You understand also that judge at family court shall testify against you? She's already been deposed by other counsel."

"They're all in league against me," she moaned. And when Hugh Jr. didn't comment, she changed her tune. "Listen now, Hugh, have you given any thought to the request I made through your paralegal earlier today?"

"What request was th—" he began, then quickly said, "Oh, wait! I have it here, somewhere." Evidently searching for the message she had left. "Yes, here it is. I'm not exactly sure what this all means. Dotty wrote that you're looking for someone to do some work for you in town? Is that right? What kind of work?"

"None of your business," escaped from her before she could stop it. She hastily softened it, "It's not anything *you* need concern yourself with. What I'm looking for is a brawny man who has had need of your services in the past, if not for criminal acts, then let us say, for less-than-savory deeds." When he was still silent, she added, "Having had to come home so precipitously, I naturally left a few bits of unfinished business. I require someone to do a job for me there that I am unable to do myself. It's not anything you can do, Hugh. Believe me. It's below you." And when he still didn't answer, "You *must* know someone there who has used your services and would be eager? Not entirely a lawbreaker, you understand…someone who could use easily earned spending money."

"Do I even want to know what this is about?" Hugh asked, being less of a fool than she'd ever heard him be.

"Perhaps not, no," she admitted. "It is definitely not for someone of your importance to bother yourself with," she continued to stroke his ego. "Being so very inconsiderable a matter. In fact," she tried another tack, "you need not involve yourself whatsoever. Why not simply leave the name with your paralegal and *she'll* call me?"

"No one's going to be hurt?"

"Why, Hugh Butterworth, who do you take me for? This is Adele Moody, née Carstairs, you are speaking to. A woman present at the font during your christening."

"Because if it is…I can't be in any way connected."

"I understand completely, Hugh. Let Dotty think it's all her doing. I'll call and ask her, and thanks to you, she'll already be prepared to answer. This phone call never happened. Or," she quickly added, "was only about my poor dear son's ashes."

After a longish pause: "OK, she'll call with a name and phone number."

"Now was that so very difficult?" She'd known all along she could get him to do it. She'd never once had this much difficulty with Hugh Sr.

Adele returned to the others in excellent spirits. She even joined in a word game the sillies were playing, beaming equally at Eva King and Annabel

Wilkins, who flushed deep crimson when Adele complimented her on the Armani as she was leaving.

Once they were all dispersed and Adele was able to relax with a brown cigarillo and a small glass of sherry, the phone rang and she picked it up, copied down the name and phone number, and was told her phone call was expected. She quickly dialed.

"Yeah, hi, Mrs. Moody," he answered. "What can I do for you?"

"I don't know if you know anything about my recent loss..." Adele went on to offer a version in which she figured in the most pointedly pathetic way.

At the end of her narrative, he said, "That's all very sad. But if your son's already dead, I don't see how I can be of any help to you."

"You can be. There are things in that house that belong to me, which will never be returned to me. I would very much like them returned to me. I'm assured the place is vacant another five days, as the person who lives there is out of town, far away. I would pay well," she added. "Plus, of course, you and whomever accompanies you would be entitled to whatever else you might find."

"Such as...?"

"Televisions, computers, I don't know what else is there. I have no need for that. All I want are a few photo albums of my son, a few tiny pieces of his jewelry from when he was young. Not even valuable. Any other jewelry, besides the baubles I specifically want, you are welcome to. Naturally, because of how shabbily I've been treated, I won't at all mind how badly you leave the place. Do I make myself clear?"

"Loud and clear. There's no one home. You want it trashed and burgled. We get what you don't want. This will cost you..." He named a figure she could live with. "Just one thing, ma'am—how do I know this is on the up and up?"

"I'll wire you $200 tomorrow by noon."

"Make it 500," he said. "Now, I've got a pencil and paper here. What's the address? Name on the bell? And what exactly do you want me to find for you? Give me size, color, and identifying marks."

When they were done, he described it all back to her, the photo albums, the school pin, and the old Moody family pocketwatch she needed like she needed a hole in her head.

"It's a pleasure doing business with a lady," he concluded, gallantly.

Adele poured herself another tiny sherry and lighted another brown cigarillo. Money might not be everything in life, but as Daddy Moody always assured her, it most certainly oiled the wheels of the fastest and smoothest vehicles.

$$* \; * \; *$$

Not very glamorous, is it?" Les Brannigan asked. "This how you imagined Hollywood and Vine?"

Les—their Fox contact—Maurette, and Ray had all just stepped out of the Capitol Records building on Vine Street and strolled a few blocks downhill to the intersection. At mid afternoon it was sunny and breezy, half zipped lightweight windbreaker weather. Both vehicle and pedestrian traffic were abundant.

"You forget I used to fly out here once a year, after EMI bought Capitol," Ray said. "I've seen the area since the '70s."

They'd just signed up to make use of a second recording venue with some unusual equipment for film-sound synchronization that Maurette was eager to try out. Then it turned out that he and Les knew someone in common, whom, by chance, happened to be playing in a combo backing up a male vocalist appearing that weekend at the CineGrill. Les suggested they drop in to listen to the group warming up.

"Your rental car is where?" Les asked.

"About three blocks down Vine," Ray pointed ahead. "Where's the CineGrill?"

"Near corner of the Hollywood Roosevelt Hotel. About eight blocks down. You can just make it out from here."

"To hell with the car," Ray said. "We'll walk."

"We'll walk," Maurette agreed.

"You sure?" Les asked, looking around them along the sidewalk. "This isn't such a great neighborhood, you know."

"It doesn't look any worse than half of Manhattan."

"We'll protect you!" Maurette threw an arm over the older man's shoulder.

"No matter how close, Angelenos don't walk, unless their car's broken down," Ray explained to Maurette, disregarding Les's protestations.

Hollywood Boulevard looked like a medium-size city's Main Street that had gone gently to hell half a generation earlier as it was replaced by suburban shopping malls.

Two-story buildings of storefronts with a top floor dominated by notary public offices and *abogados* intermixed with single-story blocks accented by boarded-over movie houses and legit theatres turned into Ethiopian and Armenian Church service centers, with taller office buildings capping each corner: edifices erected in the '20s and '30s for the most part, unable to disguise their inbred art deco refinement. Discount shoe outlets vied with greasy spoons and takeout coffee shops. Lingerie emporia abutted used bookstores featuring "Film Books and Movie Memorabilia." And all were threaded through with the ubiquitious and nearly identical T-shirt, souvenir, and memento open-wall markets. Despite the masses of inelegant strollers, most dressed in previously obtained versions of what they were seeking to purchase, Ray's impression of it all was that Hollywood Boulevard wasn't utterly graceless: It wasn't even that objectionable. The swept, well-kept sidewalks with their regular patterns of stars were richly handsome. The embedded ficus trees were exuberant, well-watered, pruned, and quite green. And for every vagrant scratching his flea bites or shill concealed by visored sunglasses with an open raincoat, its inner edges stitched and studded with counterfeit Omegas and Rolexes for sale, there was something else intriguing or diverting to notice. After a while, even sensitive Les relaxed.

They were amid a melange of tourist trap "museums" and souvenir marts when a jewelry shop caught Ray's eye. Maurette had just stopped to more closely read the incredible advertisement for one venue, so Ray could take the time to peer more closely in the window with its double-shelf display of new and antique men's rings. The others towed him away, laughing, joking—about what he wasn't certain.

Not long after, they were inside the high-ceilinged CineGrill, curtained from 95% of daylight, settled at a tiny circular table, drink of choice at hand, listening to Les and Maurette's friends rehearsing.

This was the first chance he'd had to slow down in days, and as the bass player thumped, slapped, and delicately thundered his variation on the vocalist's last-sung passage, he fell back into himself for the first time this trip. Maurette had scarcely left his side or let him alone since the moment he had arrived in a limo, taking them to Kennedy Airport, days before. They shared a hotel suite, they breakfasted together, worked at Fox's sound and light studios together, lunched together, held meetings together, dined together, saw the sights together, went out to screenings and Sunset Strip music clubs together, did everything but shower and sleep together, and Ray wasn't so sure that those weren't also on Maurette's agenda. At first he'd believed what the big Canadian had told him; that he traveled poorly alone, preferring, indeed needing, another. Then he'd come to feel that was only partly true: Maurette was here to keep him distracted, occupied, so busy he wouldn't think of what awaited him back East. That was OK. He'd needed the break, needed the sun, needed the warmth, needed, above all, the change of scenery. Except with all that, those extremely rare times he did find himself alone inside his mind, he found himself trying—and too often failing—to remember Jesse: what he looked like, what he sounded like, how his body felt, how he smelled, the precise way he laughed, even the momentary rictus that had gripped his face as he bore up under some new pain. Like right now, all he could seem to come up with of Jesse was that moment in the car, Ray for once in the passenger's seat, as they drove home from the internist's office a year or so before, the new rash confirmed as a genuine symptom. Then the absolutely unprecedented look on Jesse's face, the surprising bitterness deforming his voice, as Jesse had turned to him and simply said, "*It's* started." Ray had tried to think of something to utter to counteract, to deny, but he couldn't. And a minute later Jesse had turned again, almost as though he were enjoying it, and this time he'd said it with complete conviction, "Yes, it's started!" Why? Why in hell was that flash, out of a million possibilities, the only moment he could grasp at? And with it, as though integral, hidden, an ongoing cypher, the words he'd come to hear, to fear: neon-lit, refusing to be shoved away, asking with increasing insistence, *What do I do now?*

The vocalist performed a final, silken lacing of falsetto; the coronet responded with his own modulation; the bass player thumbed a broken arpeggio; and the pianist brought it all home with a dominant chord. Scattered applause. Banter ensued between the half dozen rehearsal onlookers and the guys onstage. Good-bye hugs were peppered with wisecracks. And they were out on the street again, headed toward the rental car, to the beachfront hotel for a change of clothes, the inevitable faxed and garbled vocal messages, a night of—how long had the list grown?—things to do to distract him.

"I've been thinking, *cher*," Maurette said, his honey smell overwhelming as he enclosed Ray in his huge arm and shoulder. "You shouldn't take what Gigi said so seriously. Even with a contract, you understand, she can break out any time she wants. These film contracts! They have an escape clause on every page. It could easily all come to nothing."

"I know," Ray replied coolly.

"You know?"

"I know."

"Then why?"

"Because it's something to do. Because why not? Because it'll keep me preoccupied if I do it." And when Maurette stopped in his tracks, Ray tugged him along: "Because I figure a year being preoccupied working for her, another year being wrapped up moving out here, then maybe another year of being preoccupied looking for other work or setting up my company again while I figure out what to do with the rest of my life."

"Oh, *cher*! We weren't certain how much you knew."

"We" being Maurette and Liesl.

"I know all right," Ray shrugged. "So whatever I do makes little difference."

"But no, *cher*, it does. It *does!*"

"But no. It *doesn't*. Not really. Everything's changed now."

Les and the bassist caught up to them on the sidewalk, and Ray peeled Maurette off to let them converse. They reached the jewelry shop again. There it was.

"Why don't you go on," Ray stopped. "I want to look at something in here. I'll meet you at the car. Go!" he insisted, shoving Maurette along. "I'll only be a few minutes."

Once they were halfway down the street, he checked the display more carefully.

Maybe a dozen onyx rings, but three he especially liked and one in particular that had seized his interest before and looked as though it might be his size. He tried the door. Locked. He gazed through to the waist-high shelving, where an elderly man was hunched over, working on something, while a small Eurasian woman looked on. The store owner glanced up, flinging away the jeweler's loupe attached to a circlet of metal worn around his head to see better. He noticed Ray—pointing at the rings in the right side window—and buzzed him into the shop.

"I was interested in one of the rings," Ray explained.

"Give me a few minutes." The jeweler spoke with a European accent.

"Sure, fine. I'll look around."

The jeweler flipped the loupe back over his eye and sat down to what he'd been doing. Once more the Eurasian woman leaned over the glass counter to watch.

Even closely examining the window display, and thus looking outside, not in, Ray immediately felt a sensation of deja vu. As soon as he turned around, the illusion was consummated: that distinctive, piquant odor of precious metal polish; the evenly dim lighting offset by tiny pin spots focused upon specific gem and watch cases; the sneezy dustiness whenever anything was moved or lifted, as though the enveloping satin and black velvet wherein valuables were couched absorbed ten times as many dust motes, instantly respilling them to pattern concentric figurations in the twilight air; the perpetual hush of the spot, barely broken by the nearly inaudible tones of the superannuated Schiff Brothers, as though their merchandise was so very remarkable, the prices so immeasurable, they could only be spoken of in whispers—except of course when that muffled quiet was shattered by the nerve-jangling screech of metal against metal as it was chased, smoothed, and otherwise mutilated to make it wearable. The ambience, the layout itself with its wide central square like an apron stage surrounded by ringed tier upon tier of glass cabinets, brilliant audience stylishly settled about, rising within their satin sofas—it all corroborated that he'd been in this shop before, although he hadn't, not in this life. Still, it was so strong a sense of having already been here that he stopped and pondered how similar the place could be to the only other jewelry store he'd ever passed more than a few minutes inside.

That had been almost 30 years before, in his Illinois hometown, where he'd first glimpsed the onyx ring of his preadolescent dreams. Alfred and Frederick Schiff—gold watches, Mexican and English silver and fine gemstones, an identically sized, similarly laid-out retail store—had been located along the tonier eastern side of Shelby Avenue. It sat between Hagger's Fabric, Wool, and Sewing Shoppe—with its kaleidoscope of fabrics, massed phalanxes of yarns, protective column of cannonlike Singers in the front window—and the Fayette County Life and Fire Insurance office—venetian blinds seldom more than slitted open (to reveal a handful of paper-strewn desks and file cabinets)—fortified against the penetrating afternoon sunlight which had for decades coerced into growth, then violent overgrowth, a trio of man-high snake plants set in a mud-hued century-old Chinese egg jar decorated with pale yellow dragons, apparently tormented into helices by a neighboring agapanthus of colossal size and Hoffmanesque proportions, which if not lopped back regularly would have overtaken the office and possibly the entire downtown. All three smart establishments were fashionably across the street from the once-glittering, eternally glamorous RKO Wayne movie theatre, which he heard was now a triplex, and the Shelby Pantry, an eat-in bakery cum lunch counter, favored by local professionals, butterball matrons, and retirees lingering over the specialty extra-large lemonade.

Ray concentrated on the rings. All were handsome, and he was definitely intrigued by one in which the onyx was divided by a band of four small diamonds. Enticing as that was, it couldn't compete with the classic beauty of the simplest. Set in thick white gold with a rounded four-sided face, the darkly brilliant jet stone was nearly square, but each of its four corners had been trimmed off into a classy, unequally sided octagon, the gemstone *en cabochon*. The white gold band tapered gracefully on either side, with three notable scoring marks in decreasing width.

A clatter of doorbell roused him as the Eurasian woman exited. He turned to face the elderly jeweler, who'd slipped quietly across the shop floor. He had lifted off the loupe headpiece, revealing beneath it not dark hair, as Ray had assumed from glimpsing him in shadow before, but instead a black velvet yarmulke embroidered with purple lettering. He was dressed in gray tweed slacks, nearly colorless shoes, much laundered white dress shirt with dun tie, held in by an aged gray vest-sweater. His neatness, his small size, his doll-like features, his explicit gestures, even his unmusical voice was terribly familiar.

"Which one interested you? Ah," noting the ring Ray pointed to, "in my opinion, the most elegant." Taking Ray's right hand in his own nearly boneless, smooth-skinned fingers, he added, "Yes. It should fit. Let's take a look."

Ray pulled back that hand and instead put forth the left one, folding back all but the fourth finger, even more conspicuous because of its low band of white skin almost to the knuckle where a week ago he had taken off his wedding ring from Jesse.

"This is the best way to cover a misfortune," the jeweler commented, without a hint of emotion in his voice. "Divorce?" he asked without interest.

"Death. My..." He didn't know how to say it to an elderly Jewish man wearing a yarmulke. "I've been widowered."

"I'm sorry for your loss," the man uttered as though asking the time of day. "A little bit of moisturizer," as he added a dab of white goo, "and there it goes!" He slid the ring onto Ray's hand. "It fits well."

It felt good. Heavier, bulkier than the gold ring and its slender ring guard had been, but comforting—almost as Ray suspected it would feel.

He'd seen the price already. "Do you take plastic?"

"Visa! Mastercharge!"

At the desk, as the jeweler looked at the pages he'd just put through the stencil machine, he remarked, "I knew a Henriques on the other side of the ocean."

"Dutch?" Ray asked.

"His nationality I was never sure of. It was in a camp in England for survivors of the war. I was a kid. He was a grown man. We never spoke. He had thick red hair. Like a fire raging for a long time. I thought at first he was Irish. Later on someone said he was Sephardic. That was not so common. You know what I'm saying?"

"Sure. My father's family was Sephardic. From Portugal originally, which is where the name originated, then later from Holland, which is where they went in the 16th century after they were driven out by the Inquisition."

The old man nodded his head. "And you? You're observant?"

Asking was Ray religious: Did he observe the holy days, the Sabbath?

"Not so much anymore," Ray admitted.

"You see this face?" the old man asked. "What do you see? From where?"

"I don't know. Maybe English. Or…?"

"But gentile features, no? This is how I'm alive. My brother had the same face with a Yid nose. Right away he was *ausfuehren*, taken from me. In a day he was *tot, kaput!* Me, I lived with a well-born family. I went to gymnasium—private school. I had sentimental friendships with boys, crushes on girls. I went everywhere they went and did everything they did. I was normal. I had life. Until a few years ago, when I realized… You too! Look at you! If someone asked, I'd never think."

The machine began printing the acceptance number, distracting the jeweler. He handed it to Ray to sign.

"That watchband! It's a *bissel* deteriorated, if you don't mind my saying," the jeweler commented. And before Ray could say he'd spent enough money already today, "On me!" the old man offered. "On me. *Das geschenk.* A gift." He revolved a display of watchbands. "This row. Your choice, of course. I'd recommend cordovan. It's alligator!"

When the watchband had been prised onto the watch and the watch restrapped around Ray's wrist, and he was about to leave the shop, he turned to the jeweler and said he was thinking of moving to Los Angeles.

"Come visit."

"I will. Oh, and one thing, I wanted to say. I…I don't know how to say this, but I've escaped something horrible, like you did. Something that's killed, that's *still* killing thousands, hundreds of thousands. And like you, I'm not certain why I've escaped—it seems so unfair—while others, loved ones…wonderful, beautiful people…" He didn't know how to go on. The old man stared. "I just wondered…if you ever…?"

"Ever what? Forgave myself? No problem! Right away."

"No. Not that. If you ever forgot them…the ones who didn't make it?"

"Forgot them? I forget them every day! Every day another fades, never to be remembered."

"That's horrible."

"Maybe," the old man shrugged. "Maybe not."

An abundance of chimes and clock bells and watch alarms suddenly went off, startling and confusing Ray.

"You mean, it's not a terrible thing to forget them?" he called over the noise.

"Who knows anymore?" the jeweler yelled back. "It happens. Now I close up."

He gently pushed Ray outside and began pulling down the overhead gates. A few minutes later Ray was looking at a corrugated metal wall.

"It *is* a terrible thing to forget," he said to himself. "It is. It must be."

"...There are no monks in this land!"

He slapped the side of the downstairs door, rat-a-tat! Singing along with the CD, "...no saints in my band" Ratatat-tat! The key turned in the lock. He slipped inside...

"I be doing all I can." Rat-a-tat! He spun around in the darkness, searching for the alarm on the wall, poised to punch in the code.

"...If I die an honest man!" Rat-a-tat-tat! The alarm system there, as usual. Lighted up as it should be. But it wasn't turned on. What the...?

He tore off the headphones to look more closely without the distraction of the music. The alarm was *not* lighted up as it should be. Meaning the alarm was *not* turned on. He was sure he'd done it right last time he was here. Done it right, turned it on. Good thing he'd come back. He'd obviously screwed up last time he'd snuck in, forgot to set it, or set it wrong. That could *not* happen again tonight. When he left, he'd make sure to set it right. If Uncle Ray knew he'd been coming and going while he was in L.A. Coming when he wasn't supposed to...

He raised the headphones onto his head again, surrounding himself in the nimbus of unstoppable rhythm, the attack of the song, meanwhile locating by touch and turning on the desk lamp to its dimmest setting. This way the neighbors couldn't report they'd noticed lights on while he was away.

Now, what was it again that he needed? Oh, yeah! The library book on the NFL, which was already overdue. His gray woolen gloves to fit inside the leather pair. And the two issues of *Hustler* belonging to Kenny Rivera he'd kept hidden in Uncle Ray's storage room. Shouldn't take more than ten minutes.

He located the magazines easily, stuffing them into his book bag, between the social studies and geometry texts. Now! Gloves and library book! Up in his old bedroom. Did he dare flip the staircase lights or...? Maybe not.

Halfway up the stairs, a colossal brightness hit, momentarily blinding him. Behind it he could make out a figure!

"Who the hell are you?" asked a gruff man's voice.

He turned and doubled back down. Behind him the figure yelled, "You said no one would be here."

Two pairs of feet charged heavily down the stairs.

He had to hide. No! Had to get out.

He zigzagged, decided on the storage room. No! They'd find him! Office! No! They'd look there first. Had to get out. No time.

He slipped behind the office door, using the wing chair to wedge himself a space, and knelt down behind it.

Someone slammed the office door open. It jarred against the chair, bruising his knees. A flashlight spiraled.

"You sure you saw someone?" A second voice. From this second figure.

He held his breath, in case he could be heard breathing. His heart was thundering inside his chest so loud they had to be able to hear it. *Mommmmy! Uncle Raaaaaaaaaaaay! Help me!*

The figure was gone from the office doorway. Back in the corridor with the other one. "I don't see anyone!"

"He was right there! On the staircase as I came down."

"Fuck! We gotta find him!"

They were pissed! Pissed! He had to get out. They'd be back in a minute and when they found him…! He'd have to sprint out. Open the street door. Run like hell.

His stomach was doing flipflops, and on top of it, all of a sudden he had to take a whizz really bad. *Mommmmy! Uncle Raaaaaaaaaaaay! Please!*

He got out from behind the chair, listening at the doorway. They were in the back bedroom. They had to be burglars, right! Burglars!

Now, Chris! Go now!

He couldn't move, he was so scared.

Suddenly they were in the corridor again, at the far end, but in another few seconds they'd be here. *Move, Chris!*

He somehow made it to the street door, somehow got it unlocked and open. They were shouting. They'd seen him. They were after him. *Shit!*

He flew out onto the sidewalk. Into the traffic and lights and…

They were right behind him. He had to shout for help. Alert people. Get help.

He couldn't get a word out. He ran with all his might.

A car leapt sideways to block the next driveway. He had to stop short not to hit it. It brushed his shins. He felt something fierce dig into his shoulder, turned, saw the face contorted in murder. *Mommmmmmmy!* With all his might, he pulled free, dashed around the back of the car. Had to get across the street. *Uncle Raaaaaaaaaaaaaaay!*

He couldn't help but hear the earsplitting caterwauling of brakes that surrounded him like a million excellent loudspeakers. Stupefied, he was barely able to swing his head around in time to consider the precise significance of two pairs of huge, brilliant headlights not three feet away, before the colossal truck, slipping and shuddering like a living thing at 40 miles an hour, overwhelmed him, front bumper first slamming him in the chest, shattering the breath out of him.

twenty-four

Jesse…on what looked like an enormous bed of scrumptious, satiny, butter-colored sheets; naked, young again, healthy again, more handsomely voluptuous than he'd been since almost the first time they'd met; Jesse, in slow motion, as though awakening from a long nap, sensually stretching, arms oh-so-slowly rising, body, ah, look at it twisting, a study in sexuality, sheets beneath him furling, adorable face rising to meet his, eyes more startlingly golden than ever, skin more luscious, arms, chest, legs, more golden hued, more firm, more delectable, coming so close now that he had no choice (and why would he want it otherwise?) but to enfold those luscious limbs, delicious torso, delicate nipples to nibble on, pectorals to kiss, belly button to sink into, pubic hairs to chew, genitals to lick, inner thighs to nibble at, his tongue tip running circles around the navel, while his own body was lightly, delightfully gripped by those honey-hued legs, mellifluent arms, that indescribable breast, that heavenly face, sexual climax inexorably rising within him, if he could only get nearer, go in deeper, get nearer, go in deeper...

From somewhere, he couldn't tell exactly where, somewhere, maybe deeper within or maybe just some other place, a thought arrived, clothed in words true but also dressed in befuddlement, and with the befuddlement, panic—how could he possibly be making love to Jesse? Jesse was dead.

In the juncture following the thought he felt himself withdraw a tenth of a millimeter, and as he pulled back so very little, Jesse seemed to grip him all the closer, so in reaction, he pulled back a bit more and Jesse grasped all the more, until he felt constricted, unable to move, barely able to breathe. Panic grew to terror as he strove to break Jesse's clutch. Terror grew to frenzy as he struggled and managed to partly pull away and back, partly free himself from the incredibly strong hold.

In that instant he began to witness the golden flesh deliquesce, liquefy, dissolve and drop off arm bones and shoulder bones, ulnae and hipbones, the flesh blackening as he watched, rotting, contorting facial features as it dropped off in gobbets, unmasking the grimacing skull beneath. That only increased his dread, his abhorrence at the monstrosity that had duped him, the cadaver he had been embracing, the treacherous, deceiving ghoul that had clasped him in the guise of love. Completely revolted, he tore the putrefying flesh and rotting bones away, flinging it as far as he could, cries of loathing tore out of him, as he attempted to shake its remnants off, foul-smelling shit adhering to his fingers.

He woke up gulping at the refrigerated bedroom air.

Flicked on the light switch as though the horror were still in the room with him.

He was unable to clear the images from his mind. His heart scudded in his chest. His breath shredded him trying to get out through his lungs. Every inch of his flesh, every part of his body felt befilthed by that liquefying flesh and decomposing corpse meat. Hair stood on the back of his neck. Gooseflesh speckled his arms. Everything around him, the air itself, was clammy with putrefaction.

It was only 4:39 A.M., but he was so overwrought he couldn't bear to remain within its stench a second longer, nor stay in these contaminated pajamas. He tore them off and kicked the pile into a corner, grabbing at a heavy terry robe. He had to free himself of this defilement. In the bathroom he ran the shower blistering hot. He jumped the thermostat up to 75 degrees. Had to get this bone-deadening chill out.

The shower billowed clouds of steam. He threw himself in. Better!

He had another thought. What if it really wasn't a nightmare? Not merely some stupid *Tales From the Crypt* scenario his brain had devised? What if it actually was Jesse?

Jesse, who...what? Somehow heard? Intuited his despair? His utter desolation? And out of the goodness of his heart had somehow contrived a return, however momentarily, however fraudulently? It had been so real at the beginning. Had been so real afterward too. Was it possible? And that no matter how hard he tried, Jesse couldn't hold together the illusion?

Tell me no! Tell me that wasn't what happened. Because if it is... How I *hurled* him away! How unequivocally I drove him off!

Warmed, dressed in warm clothing, he was at last ready to inspect the bedroom. It looked fine. Not like the scene of a...? Of a what? An incubus? Isn't that what that sort of thing was called? Anyway, all trace of it was gone, the steam riser was chugging away. Where it had been clammy and repulsive before, now it was toasty, the bedroom he knew.

It *had* to have been a nightmare. *Had* to have been. The combination of what had happened with Chris last week hitting home, on top of...had to.

As he was straightening out the sheets to make the bed, he couldn't help smelling something—a scent suspended over the middle of the bed. Eau de cologne. Familiar. All over the room really. But stronger, more distinctive, directly over the bed. Had to be one of his scents. But why here? Now?

He checked back and forth between the bottles of cologne and aftershaves on his dresser top and in the bathroom cabinet. None were that scent.

"Please. Don't tell me..."

As he said the words aloud, ice gripped his entrails. He opened the other closet door, filled with Jesse's office clothes and dress suits, kept closed, as though it didn't exist, for what? Months? From before he'd gone into the hospital.

Dreading what he might learn, yet having to know, he began to sniff the line of suits, of shirts, nosing his way across the collars of oxfords and tattersalls, the shoulders of Valentino and Pierre Cardin jackets, where, among a half dozen other scents, he detected the scent. It was soaked into the shoulders, arms, back, even into the shirred silk lining of the Nino Cerruti gray-and-brown windowpane sports coat Jesse had last worn, when? At that French Baroque concert at the Met Museum's Egyptian wing, three months ago, wasn't it? Yes, the last time they'd gone out together. There it was. Unmistakable.

To substantiate it, Ray reached the top shelf, where he'd stowed cartons of

Jesse's personal effects, notions, and toiletries. He drew them down, opened each individually carved and colored bottle just enough to get a whiff. And there it was. Second one. The emerald vial of Hugo Boss.

"Jesse?"

He listened to himself calling in empty air: empty air over a vacant, messily made bed, over which a glacial chill and an inkling of a fragrance were rapidly dissipating into the slightly roasted tang of steam heat.

"Jesse, honey? Was that you?"

No answer, naturally. Even if it had been Jesse...

"Hon? Buster Brown? Because if it was, Jess, hon, I didn't mean it..."

He'd rejected Jesse so vehemently.

"I didn't mean to...do what I did, Jess...I just couldn't help it! You understand, don't you?"

Why would Jesse ever think to return...

"I didn't do it on purpose...Jess? I couldn't help myself!"

...to someone who'd only push him away again?

"I'm sorry, Jess."

Now he'd never come back. Never!

"I'm so very sorry, honey."

So that now he was more desolate than ever. By his own doing.

"I'm so very, *very* sorry!"

Ray was still huddled on the closet floor, clutching jackets and dress suits he'd wrenched off hangers, sobbing and groaning, when Liesl phoned to remind him that he was supposed to get up and drive out of state today to visit J.K. Callaway.

✳ ✳ ✳

"Carrie Fisher is coming to read to me tonight," J.K. said airily. "So you don't have to hang around here, you know."

He promptly turned to the plastic water glass on the bed tray in front of himself and splashed some shaved ice into his mouth. With the oral parasitic fungus growing unchecked, he needed to soothe his mouth every few minutes, especially after speaking.

Ray wanted to shout into J.K.'s mottled, skull-like face that he was full of shit! Carrie Fisher wasn't coming to read to him tonight! Or any *other* night!

Instead he poured more shaved ice out of the identically colored plastic lemonade pitcher on the side table into the water glass. Which, of course, J.K.

ignored. As he'd all but ignored Ray since he'd arrived here this afternoon—following a difficult, traffic-riddled, five-hour drive—content to treat him like he were some elderly, not all that intelligent attendant who'd somehow installed himself without having been asked to do so.

"This program is *très* boring!" J.K. declared. He'd insisted on turning on the 7o'clock news, then he'd scarcely paid attention to it. "Let's see my movies!" He pointed a skeletal black-and-purple-spotted hand at a stack of videos. Ray got up and began reading off the titles. He didn't know any of them. They were all full-length Japanese cartoons. *Animé*, J.K. called them, accent on the last syllable, with names like *Prince Wolfling and the Shadow Queen, Fox Girl and Her Sisters, The Return of Demo*. They'd already watched some 12 minutes of *Bad Star* when Ray had arrived, before J.K. became bored with that and demanded it be shut off so they could play cards. These days, J.K. bored easily. He was bored of movies, bored of television, bored of news, bored of gossip, bored of card games—even of simple ones like Old Maid that he could barely play, his short-term memory already so compromised—bored of reading, bored of being read to, bored of visitors, bored of his sister coming to ask if he wanted soup, bored of everything Ray suggested and anything Ray thought.

Unsurprisingly, J.K. chose to view *Bad Star* again, and wasn't in any way perturbed when it began some 12 minutes in, although he clearly had no recollection that they'd been watching it as recently as a few hours ago, constantly asking Ray in his hoarse, croaking voice who characters were who'd already been introduced.

"This is great!" J.K. enthused of a particularly colorful laser battle between the hero and a series of evil robots who kept metamorphosing into new shapes and coming up with more powerful weapons. "You ought to take this home for Chris."

I told you twice before, Ray wanted to yell into his face, Chris is dead! Three times really, since a day after he'd flown back for the funeral, when he'd told J.K. by phone that Chris had been hit by a truck on Joralemon Street. He'd thought at that time that J.K. wasn't quite so out of it. Maybe he wasn't then, it was the virus itself, eating up more brain tissue every day. Stay calm. Why blame J.K.? It wasn't his fault.

"OK, J.K. Maybe I'll bring it home for Chris."

That was when J.K. really got to him. "Ha! You said before that Chris was run down by a truck! I knew you were lying!" The last word was almost lost as he immediately began to cough, a dry hacking cough, that shuddered his entire body for the next four minutes and that required him to sit up, catch his breath, then sip at more shaved ice by way of recovery.

Luckily for them both, it was at that moment that J.K.'s sister glanced into the bedroom and announced that Carrie from down the street had arrived.

Unsure anymore what was truth and what not in this crazy room, Ray asked, as she entered, "Carrie...Fisher, is it?" shaking hands with the woman in her mid 30s.

"Fisk." She half smiled, then looked at J.K., who was smiling slyly at them as if to say to Ray, *Ha! Got you!* "So, how are you today? John Kevin?"

"Sim-ply ter-rib-ble. Come sit here. I'll tell you all about Ray. Ray's my former best friend. He lives in New York City. And you know what, Car? He's a widower! You know what that means, don't you? He's looking for love in all the wrong places! He's not bad looking either, is he? Whaddaya say?"

Carrie was immediately embarrassed and tried to get away, but was restrained by the force of J.K.'s emaciated claws, which, despite his daily weakening condition, could still grip—never mind tear—when he had a mind to, as Ray had earlier discovered when he attempted to take a magazine from J.K.

Ray decided that Carrie's arrival was a terrific opportunity to take a break. He excused himself, mumbling something about the men's room, utterly ignored by J.K., of course, who was issuing croaking oohs and aahs over something Carrie was saying. Naturally, that also led to another spasm of coughing. By then Ray was out of the suite and already in the dining room.

J.K.'s sister, Moira, drying dishes, peered out of the kitchen.

"Do you have a minute, Ray?"

"Sure. Absolutely."

"Coffee? A cocktail?"

He accepted a cup of coffee and joined her at the breakfast nook, where she had crackers and cheese for them to nibble. It was a lovely spot, this homey, warm nook, surrounded on three sides by waist-high multipaned windows, intimate even at night in the frozen heart of winter: ice-glazed snow a foot high all around them, bare tree limbs and hedge thistles rimed silver with sleet, a stone birdbath tufted white as though piled high with down pillows. Earlier, barely visible through an icy-pale blue sky, the sun had set red as a cherry—and about as small.

"Carl wants to take us to dinner."

Carl was Moira's husband, a gray-bearded, heavyset fellow, as opposite J.K. both physically and temperamentally as anyone could be.

"Don't say no," she warned Ray. "It's nothing fancy. Just the local steak house off the freeway. *And* it's the only way I'll get out of the house. He gets to go to work, but I'm pretty much stuck here all day."

"Fine, OK."

"Carl will be pleased. He loves music. I know he's got a million questions for you." She sipped her coffee, evidently rethinking something. "What I said before? About getting out of the house? You have to understand, we had no idea—*I* certainly had no idea—what we'd be dealing with when we asked John Kevin to come stay with us."

"You don't have to explain. You're doing fine."

"Really? Are we doing fine?" Her pale blue eyes—which were not J.K.'s eyes at all—peeped uncertainly out of her face, which was, in a way, J.K.'s face, though more delicate. "You're not just saying that? Because the way it looks to us, we're doing a downright terrible job."

"What you signed up for," Ray clarified, "what we all signed up for, Moira, without knowing what we were doing, is an *impossible* job. At best."

She sighed and stared out the window. "At least you knew John Kevin. You must be able to see the difference between—"

"The way he used to be and how he is now? Sure. But it was there all along. He just kept it in check before, so we didn't see what a spoiled, demanding little bitch he really is."

Moira's hands flew to her mouth, as though the words hadn't come from him but had popped out of her own mouth and now she wished they hadn't. Ray pulled her hands away. She was smiling. "You're terrible!" She laughed.

"I'm terrible," he admitted. "Who's his new girlfriend?"

"Carrie's a dear, isn't she? She's carried a torch for John Kevin ever since she met him, I don't know, maybe 15 years ago. That's how long we've been in this house. It's actually been good for both of them. Not to mention what a help she's been. If it weren't for Carrie, we couldn't—at least *I* couldn't—leave for a minute."

"Stop beating yourself up. You're doing a good job."

All humor was gone from her face, as she asked, "Am I, Ray?"

"The best possible. Under the circumstances… Anyway, it won't be long now."

"That's what the doctors say. The way he's not eating…? They don't understand how he's gone on even *this* long." She paused. "You have more experience…how long do you…?" Tears started in her eyes. "I can't believe I'm even saying this."

He shrugged. "Impossible to say. Could be…a month. More."

"That long?"

"So while he's here, he'll continue to be totally impossible," Ray attempted to sum it up. "And after…he's gone…" He choked up, couldn't continue.

Now he stared outside. Stars had emerged over roof eaves and dormers and weather-vane bronzes, brilliantly freckling the glassy black sky.

"That's why he's being extra mean to you, you know," Moira suddenly offered as though having considered it for a while. "John Kevin told me yesterday, when he knew for sure you were coming, that he was going to make certain you didn't think about your partner—Jesse, was it?—all the while you were here. He wanted you all to himself, he said… You know, John Kevin will be the first person close to me who will have died in…20 years, maybe. Both our parents are still alive."

She went on to talk about what it was like growing up the slightly younger sister of such a dominating older brother, someone so smart, so sophisticated; how he'd brought art and culture, sports and fun, music and movies, and other young people into their home, and into her life; how he'd found all the best boys to date her, including the one who'd become her husband; how he'd instructed them, entertained them, always been more to her than her mother and father put together. What an incalculable loss it would be to them all.

Carl arrived home, bringing in a bit of outdoor frigidity with himself, hugging Ray as though they were long-lost buddies, immediately fixing them strong cocktails, talking up the specials at the restaurant where they would be dining shortly.

In the midst of discussing some adventure of her eldest daughter, Moira suddenly went quiet, interrupting herself to listen more closely. "That's him. He wants something, I'm guessing. But he won't send Carrie out. That would be too easy." She took another sip of her drink and got up, wearily. "I'm supposed to read his mind and just know."

Once Moira had stepped out of the room, Carl looked up from his own drink. "Two weeks, the doctors said. Unless he starts to eat again. What do you think?"

"Dying is a lot slower and a lot harder than they show in the movies, you know."

"So I'm discovering," Carl said, without rancor.

A minor catastrophe had occurred inside the bedroom involving the pitcher of shaved ice, but it was all put to rights by the time Ray got into the room, although clearly there had been spillage. Moira had already left and Carrie had her arms filled with wet magazines and paper towels, trying to excuse herself. For a minute, before entering, Ray remained just out of J.K.'s view, looking on at her and J.K. as they banteringly interacted. The same way he and J.K. had done for so many years. For such a mousy lady, she certainly could give as well as she got.

"Gotta go?" J.K. asked perkily when he spotted Ray. Before Ray could respond, "Long drive ahead?"

"Something like that," Ray said, wondering if he ought to mention dinner with J.K.'s family. Probably not: He'd only think they were conspiring against him.

"Well, you don't have to come back," J.K. snapped.

"Why shouldn't I?"

"I'll only be worse. That's the only reason you came, isn't it? To see me? And I know you hate seeing me like this. And I hate you hating seeing me like this."

Convoluted yet accurate.

"Leave it to the women," J.K. commanded. "They can handle it better. They've been trained all their lives to handle this crap. No matter how much I shit and barf and knock over things, they're ready to manage it as though nothing happened. They're in their element with me. I give them the opportunity to become little saints… And anyway, you've had your share of shit. Enough shit for a lifetime."

"Why did you stop eating?" Ray asked.

"Don't be a jerk. You know why. Because it's painful for me to eat and…*and*, before you interrupt me, Mr. Henriques…because it'll end the whole mess a lot faster… Don't come anymore."

"I won't come anymore," Ray said.

"Don't call either. It wears me out."

Ray got closer, intending to lean over to kiss J.K. good-bye, but all at once J.K. squirmed away from him, reaching over to grab a videotape from among the mess of tapes and cassettes and books upon the quilt.

"This is my all time favorite *Animé*," he said in a voice 25 years younger, as he held out a tape box Ray couldn't read. "Chris'll love it!"

Ray took the videotape and began edging backward along the bed as J.K. rambled on about the Minor Man and Stumbo and CrackCrack, evidently characters from the movie. And so he was ga-ga once again.

As Ray was trying to slip out the door, giving a final wave good-bye, J.K. interrupted himself to hold out a woman's compact. "Hey!" He flipped it so the mirror flashed. "Want to see a monkey?"

Ray leaned forward to look, and naturally, he saw part of his own face.

"James Dean to Natalie Wood," J.K. added matter-of-factly, in his suddenly altered grown-up voice, snapping the compact shut. "*Rebel Without a Cause.* 1955. He says that to her after driving her home, following the drag race." J.K. smiled serenely, as though adding, *Ha! Got you!*

* * *

The car was cold. *Damned* cold. He should have driven it to the steak house instead of letting Carl and Moira drive him and leaving it outside to get colder. It started up right away, thankfully. But as he sat idling in their abbreviated circular driveway, the heat either blasted out, which he couldn't abide, or, when he turned it down low enough to not bother him, it trickled out, which wasn't any better. Maybe once he was on the road it would improve.

He waved again to the three of them, Carrie, Moira, and Carl, huddled inside the frosted glass entry door, then took off.

The two-lane graytop of Route 56 was empty, even at the two intersections before he reached the Massachusetts Turnpike. The car dashboard clock read 11:30. Later than he'd thought.

The six-lane blacktop turnpike was vacant.

He had wanted to take another look at J.K. That's why he'd allowed himself to be talked into going in their car and having to come back. One thing he'd learned since the epidemic had hit was that you never, *never* left things unsaid and you never, *never* didn't take the opportunity to see someone for a last time.

Carrie had been sitting out in the study when they'd arrived back, and told him J.K. had been sleeping fitfully. He'd gone in alone, and there, in the not-quite-dark dimness of the bedroom, he'd gotten to see J.K.—sleeping—once more.

Before he'd left, Ray had opened up and placed on display where J.K. would see it when he awoke, a big pop-up card of characters and scenes from *The Wizard of Oz* he'd brought, which J.K. had forgotten about. Maybe it would amuse him for a few seconds.

Where in the hell was his turnoff onto Route 84? Coming the other way, earlier in the day, he'd had no trouble finding the exit onto the turnpike. Wait, could that be it, that little sign, pointing to the Wilbur Cross and Sturbridge?

Going so fast, he'd already sped past it before it really registered that Route 84 was also the Wilbur Cross. Wake! Up! Ray! With the island in the middle of the turnpike, it would be miles before he could get back onto the other side. Wait a sec, there was a little cut in the center island coming up, with a sign that read NO U-TURN EXCEPT POLICE AND FIRE DEPARTMENT. Well, there wasn't another damn car on the whole damn road as far as he could see. He checked. No, none coming and none going either. So he slowed down, stopped, and as no one came into view yet, he performed the illegal turn. A few minutes later, he was at the turnoff ramp he'd missed from the opposite direction.

The Wilbur Cross wasn't much busier. A few cars on the other side coming north out of Sturbridge, possibly having visited the colonial Old Sturbridge Village, then he was crossing the state line south into Connecticut, and traffic was one car on the other side, and one on this side, which soon exited. Nothing else. Inside the Regal, as he'd guessed, the heat was working better, or perhaps still only seeping out, but building up. He wouldn't take off his wool beret, scarf, or gloves. He could still make out his icy breath.

Look at me, inside a refrigerated car, driving all alone through an Antarctic night. And it's so late and so cold out, I'm the only stupid sonofabitch on the road. Doesn't this typify my entire, totally fucked-up existence!

J.K. had been sprawled across the bed, looking like a starvation victim who'd been dropped from a great height. From an airplane or helicopter doorway perhaps, the way the Argentine Air Force had dropped hundreds of trussed, narcotized citizen-critics, deemed disposable. J.K'.s barely held together skin and bones seemed to have hit the bed and spread. When Ray brushed his lips against the remaining dry hair on J.K.'s right temple, the skin was hot and parched, as though from an inner conflagration.

How that man used to look.

There was a car! On the other side. Coming his way. Gone.

Kathy hadn't been able to get up the nerve herself to go identify Chris's body at the First Avenue Morgue. So he'd been delegated. What difference could it possibly make, after having seen Jesse burned to cinders before his eyes? By comparison, the teenage body was oddly pristine. Even the coroner's sewn-up crescent-moon incisions—required to corroborate internal impairment as grounds of death—looked like jaunty stabs at body decoration, something the boy might have done as a tattoo, a couple of years down the road. The chest was black and blue, of course, from the sternum on up. But the face, the face was difficult to take, the extent of destruction, the implication of the tire-tread mutilation, and worst, perhaps, the single remaining undeformed feature, the boy's left eye, wide open in complete astonishment.

What had Ray done to deserve to see that eye? Lie? Steal? Cheat? Betray? He couldn't think of anything even close.

Kathy was, of course, a mess. She'd gone back with what's-his-name. Dan, the woman-beater. Or was about to do so, Sable intimated the few minutes she'd spoken to him at Chris's lying-in at the funeral home. Sable was no better herself, although she'd undergone the complete set of chemo treatments. His and Kathy's mother, who'd flown to the city and remained at Ray's place but was gone with her daughter and granddaughter 95% of her three-day stay, had told him on the drive to the airport that she'd talked to Dad and that they were seriously thinking of taking Sable back to Illinois with them as soon as school ended. Maybe even before. He'd asked, "Is that a good idea? Kathy already thinks she's a pretty much a failure as a mother." To which his mother had pushed back her hair under her cap, and stonily staring ahead had said, "Your sister's drinking again. You know what that means. I will not allow a sick child in that environment." Two days later Kathy had asked him whether he didn't think it was the right thing to do for her to give up Sable to them. She'd already lost weight, and some of her looks, to months of her daughter's cancer. She was rail thin, infirm looking. He hadn't known how what to say to her.

What exit was that? West Willington? Sounded like a soap opera actor's name. Where in hell was West Willington?

He realized as he went past the turnoff sign that he was speeding. With no other cars on his side of the road, and very few even approaching him to compare with—everyone intelligently tucked at home in bed this freezing night—he'd unwittingly, incrementally, increased his speed from 65 and was now almost at 80. What about cop cars? In *this* weather? *This* late at night? Not likely. And luckily, he kept the Regal in good shape. It cruised easily, almost noiselessly, at 80.

Kathy didn't think Sable would make it. Those were the very words she had used. Not if she stayed with Kathy. And not if she moved to their parents'.

Up to 83 miles per hour and he didn't notice a thing.

They'd tried to piece together what had happened to Chris. Clearly, he'd been sneaking into the house when he wasn't supposed to be. After that, it got confusing. Mrs. Schnell, from across the street, believed others had sneaked in also and maybe Chris had surprised them. Of course she was always seeing burglars in the neighborhood. Even so, both she and her son reported seeing two strange men hanging around after the noise of the accident had brought everyone to their windows and front stoops. Her son was sure one of the strangers had sneaked back into Ray's house. He wasn't there when the police investigating the scene of the accident entered, guns out and cocked, on Mrs. Schnell's tip. The police found no one inside. And later on, when he himself looked, Ray hadn't been certain anything had been taken, except perhaps a few old photo albums.

The exit for Tolland. Holland with a T. Twelve o' two. Not a car on either side of the road since West Willington. Going 85 miles per hour.

A few days ago Kathy had asked, and so Ray had told her how bad J.K. had become. She'd stared at him and laughed the strangest laugh. "Then it's *not* me, after all. Or, only *partly* me!" she said, and refused to explain herself.

He didn't have to be a genius to figure out what she'd meant. It wasn't her. It was *him*! Look at the last year alone: Aunt Rose, of a heart attack. Cousin Tim in San Francisco, of AIDS. Chris. Jesse. Now J.K. Maybe Sable too. Go back five years and there were another 20 or so people he'd known. Even among family members, they were all people he'd known better, who'd been closer to him. That's what Kathy had meant.

Eighty-eight miles an hour.

Kathy was right. It was a simple equation: People he loved died.

Remember that last day in L.A.? Crossing that street in Beverly Hills? Maurette had all but walked into that huge limo turning the corner, speeding. Les Brannigan had to pull him back. Maurette had escaped by an inch. Not even a inch; he'd felt the Lincoln's side trim across his knees.

It was as though Ray was somehow responsible, wasn't it?

Ninety miles an hour.

As though Death were following Ray. Dogging his footsteps. No, closer than that. Nipping at his ankle. Like the drawing on that card in the Tarot deck Liesl had brought with her and that had come up during a reading she'd done for him, down in the Caribbean. The silly guy with the yellow tights on. The dog nipping at him.

Ninety-five miles an hour.

The speedometer went to 120. Of course it wouldn't go that fast, right? He recalled looking at the owner's manual, when he'd first gotten the Regal from his folks and reading that its top speed was actually only 110.

He couldn't remember what she'd said that Tarot card meant. Come to think of it, he didn't remember any of the reading. Only that it hadn't been a particularly bad card. Not the Ace of Spades or Death or any of the ones you always saw in movies. But he hadn't needed the cards to tell him what he already knew, did he?

And if the car really could hit 120, this probably was the right place and the right time to see, wasn't it? No one around. Good road. Visibility.

As though Death were a big black shadow of a beast, not so much biting his ankles as circling around him, coming closer and closer, snarling, growling, its foul breath steaming, fetid with putrefaction, snapping at anyone who got too close to him, taking that person down in its unforgiving jaws. But not him. Not him.

A hundred miles an hour.

As though it were wary of him. Afraid of him.

A hundred and five.

Was that true? That Death wanted him badly, but for some reason couldn't have him? And instead it contented itself with taking down anyone and everyone who even came close? Was that the way it worked?

A hundred and ten.

Sure seemed like that was the way it worked.

He could hear the roar of the engine as all six cylinders strove harder than they ever had before. The car, from the chassis up, was beginning to rattle.

That the way it works, Mr. Death? Can't *have* me! No matter how much you want?

The engine was an unceasing torrent of sound. As he inched the needle up to 112, the car began to vibrate as well.

He found himself inflated with an immense pocket of anger.

"Is that the way it works!?" he heard himself shouting

The speedometer was now at 115, 116.

"Is it me you really want?! Mister *Fuck You* Death?"

An immense lake of anger that had been roiling and boiling inside. He released one hand off the steering wheel for an instant to tear off the scarf, to rip off the beret. Found himself thrilled to absolute amazement the way the car tried in those few seconds to wrench itself out of his grip.

"You got the *hots* for Ray, don't you? You creepy motherfucker!"

A hundred and eighteen.

The damn car was shaking like anything, shaking, rattling, rolling, pitching, yawing, the engine screeching, whining.

And now fury exploded, a flaming liquid, out of his chest, out of his head.

"You...creepy...low-down...evil...hungry...piece of *shit*!"

Objects flew off the dashboard onto the seat, fluttered around his feet. Something, he didn't know what, was repeatedly striking the side of the door in the backseat. The whole damned mechanism was convulsing. But he was unstoppably furious as he pushed the gas pedal harder, hunched over the wheel, holding on, as the simplified-to-black-and-white landscape flung itself by him on either side, and the jet-black road kept shooting up at his face too fast to even see it anymore.

"You want me!" he howled into the windshield, which had become an ever moving collage of shapes and forms hurling themselves at him too quickly to be distinguished.

"Want me?" He stood up, forcing all his weight onto the gas pedal.

"Well, then come and fucking *get* me!" he exulted.

Tormented metal screeched like a dozen demons out of hell, and he screeched along as loudly, not even caring what he screamed or where he was going or how fast or anything. Not anything. Not anything at all!

Somewhere in the midst of all that, he thought he could make out a car horn dopplering off, somewhere on his right side. He thought he caught amid the maelstrom of whistling past objects, a car dropping down a ramp at him, veering off.

Another car!

There *are* no other cars. No one but me. And that *filth*, Death.

Another car, Ray! Another car trying to merge.

No. What happened to it?

No. No. He hadn't heard a crash. It must have seen him. Stopped in time.

Suddenly he was relieved. Relaxed. Slowly, he sat back down on the car seat, and slowly he released his weight from the gas pedal.

He could make out objects ahead: the black road and gray bridge crossing overhead and white snow on the center lanes and…

At 80 the car stopped shimmying. At 75 it ceased clattering. At 60 he was again calm enough to locate and put his beret back on, to note no apparent damage inside the car. He pulled onto the side of the road, slowed to a stop.

Had to catch his breath. Lord, what a ride that was! What a *fucking* ride!

He wasn't sure how long he sat inside the car with the motor turned off and the cold seeping up from between the floorboards into the front seat and all around him, only that he felt better than he had in a long time.

Something pummeling the driver's side window startled him.

A woman. Elderly. Maybe 70. Wrapped in wool. Hammering at his window. What the…?

He opened the door and she jumped back.

As he stepped out, she retreated even more. She was brandishing what looked like a rolled-up umbrella. She was small, not more than 4'9", 4'10". Tiny, really.

"What's the matter with you?" she screamed.

Who was she? What did she…?

"You nearly ran me down back there!"

Back where? What was she…?

"What…in…the…hell…is…the…matter…with…you?" she stammered.

The other car. The car he'd thought he'd seen. The one that had blown the horn. It must have been real after all. And she'd been inside it.

He tried to apologize, but nothing would come out but sounds.

"Are you drunk? Or what?" she demanded.

Again he tried. It sounded like drivel, even to him.

Now he was embarrassed. He had scared the hell out of her. She deserved an explanation, an apology, a... He flushed deeply.

"What were you doing?" she screamed. "Trying to *kill* someone?"

They both heard it when he managed to utter, "Myself. Kill myself."

Her face froze then, and so did the next words she'd prepared to say. She stared as though only now becoming aware of how dangerous he was.

She held up the umbrella as though for protection and slowly backed away. Looking over her shoulder, she ran to her car. An Escort wagon, he noted, the pale green one he'd thought he'd seen. She got in and drove off, making a wide circle around him, burning rubber to get far away, fast.

A wind arose, whipped around him, more treacherous than any he'd ever felt.

He returned to the relative warmth of the car.

Would it start up? Had he destroyed it going so fast? Because if it didn't start, and there was no one, literally no one, on this road tonight, then...?

He counted to ten and tried the ignition.

The engine turned over immediately. After a second it was purring, as though it had enjoyed the workout he'd provided.

To stop himself from thinking, he put a cassette from the glove compartment into the player and spun the volume on high.

After a few miles driving at 65, he raised his speed to 75. The road was still empty; there still weren't any cops around.

The music turned out to be a compendium of Prokofiev's greatest hits in good performances. *Love for Three Oranges. Classical Symphony. Lieutenant Kije Suite.* Selections from his ballets *Romeo and Juliet and Cinderella.* The music was rhythmic and exciting, and it kept him involved all the way into the turnoff onto Route 91, to the Merritt Parkway, to the Hutchinson, and so on.

He arrived at Joralemon Street, noting that the entire return trip, even with the increased traffic on the last three legs, had only taken two and three-quarters hours.

twenty-five

Three freckles in a row on his back. Just like that whaddayacallit? That pattern of stars? What was it called? The Little Dipper. Oh, and there was another one in the corner. And another two down in this corner. Really! Just like the...

"You find Orion's Belt on my back?" Ray asked.

"The Little Dipper, you mean?"

"Some people call it Orion's Belt. It's a constellation named after a famous ancient Greek hunter."

Constellation! That was the word he'd been looking for.

"At least that's what they call the three stars in a row," Ray explained.

Ray fell silent again, and Mike continued exploring Ray's back for more constellations. He found a scar over by his left shoulder. A little birthmark shaped like a V on his left ass cheek. He liked Ray's ass cheeks. They were solid yet not overly muscled, like some guys. He moved around on his knees now and leaned on the backs of Ray's upper thighs, trying to get a good look between his cheeks at his crack.

"Lose something?" Ray asked.

"I wanted to look at your asshole."

"Then spread them!" Ray said, and reached back with his hands to illustrate.

Ray let go and Mike spread them himself. A lot more solid, more muscled than, say, his wife Janet's. Big surprise, stupid! But steeper, and deeper too. The cheeks were pretty smooth, fuzzy yet hairless and so, really, was the area around the hole. It could have been hers—except for the muscles. Holding the cheeks apart slowly, he peered between his hands at the crack. Not much of a smell. Why was he so sure it would smell?

"Look deep enough and you'll find the lost chord," Ray said into the pillow.

"The lost what?"

"Never mind. Want to fuck me? You can get it up again, can't you?"

"It's already up!" He showed Ray. "Do I gotta, you know, wet it with my tongue and all, the way you do mine?"

"It's called rimming. And you already know the answer."

Even though it didn't smell, and even though it didn't look dirty, he couldn't. Not even if he washed it himself, he couldn't. There were just some things he couldn't bring himself to do. Not with Ray, not with Janet. Like, for instance, this kissing business. He didn't know where he'd picked it up, but he had: You could do anything with a guy—suck, up the ass, anything. But kiss him and you're queer. Stupid, wasn't it? Yet...yet...

But he sure enjoyed looking at Ray's ass. "Maybe next time."

That was their ongoing joke. How Ray always fucked him. But he always said how the next time they got together, he'd fuck Ray.

Immediately onto how after today there wouldn't *be* any next time.

Ray looked at him. But he didn't say it. Ray just put his head back in the pillow.

Then he was no longer interested in looking. He rolled over onto his stomach and looked up at the ceiling. The curtains had been taken down, and this was the first time he'd seen this bedroom in full sunlight. The walls were white. Well, not white, really, more a cream color. Christ! He really was becoming one, wasn't he? Let one of the guys hear him explain the color of the walls. What was it that friend of Danny's, Dean, had yelled at them at the AFC play-offs? When they were talking about the color of the guy's jerseys? "It's not sky blue! Or robin's egg blue! Those are gay colors! Straight colors are—blue! It's just fucking blue! Got that?"

Uptight motherfucker. Probably has a tiny pecker. Not like Ray here.

He reached over and played with it. It was already a little hard.

No curtains. No pictures on the walls. He'd liked one, the poster of the guy diving, head aimed straight down, and behind him, the pool water all in shreds of different colors. No furniture left either, except this double mattress from upstairs. The bed that used to be here had already been taken. Ray said he was going to leave this mattress. Unless Mike could use it. The two long wardrobes were empty but for a few shirts and pants on hangers. Two unzipped bags on the floor, filled with socks and underwear and… Ray would be carrying those. He was flying west tomorrow, Ray told him, as soon as he'd arrived today and looked around at how stripped down the place was. He guessed Ray must have told him before he was going, and he'd just forgotten it. What a *chitrool* he was, forgetting that. Good thing he'd had the urge to come today. All the furniture and stuff had already been packed into one of those extra-long semi rigs a few days ago; it was already on its way cross-country.

"Do you remember what I told you about being with guys?" Ray asked.

"Don't get fucked unless he wears a rubber."

"No matter…?" Ray prompted.

"No matter what he says." Mike sat up. "*You* never used one."

"I should have. I apologize."

"But you didn't. So how do you expect—"

"I'd just been tested a week before I saw you. I knew I was negative."

"And negative's good, right?" Mike tried to recall what Ray had said.

"Not generally. But for this, yes, negative is good."

"But it's OK to suck, right?" Mike said, and quickly amended, "Unless I've had dental work recently. Or if I have a sore in my mouth. Or he has a sore on his dick." Mike illustrated with a tongue-tip swipe at Ray's dick head. He wouldn't suck it, of course, now that it had been inside him. No matter how much Ray washed it. Another one of those stupid things he couldn't get over.

"Ex-cellent!" Ray said. "Oh, and after you've been blowing someone, try to gargle with mouthwash. And…?" he prompted him.

"If there's no mouthwash, gargle with scotch or bourbon or vodka."

"…because the alcohol will kill germs. Just follow those rules and…"

He only half listened. Wonder what Ray would say if he knew he'd already had sex with other guys? Three other guys since he'd met Ray. But one, especially, one who looked promising. More than just regular, actually promising. When Ray was in L.A., he'd gotten horny and gone to visit Shirley, the middle-aged woman he'd told Ray about who lived two blocks away. He'd been buzzed into the building, but when he got up to the third floor, she hadn't answered. The next door had opened, and this guy had looked out. Big guy, dressed in those colorful swirly kind of pants like pajama bottoms and a yellow ribbed guinea T-shirt that showed how big his shoulders and arms were, how worked out the guy was. Thick, dark red hair, almost like a helmet. Blue eyes. Light blue. Probably even—fuck you, Dean!—probably even robin's egg blue. Nice-looking, although not a pretty boy. Definitely not the kind of guy who'd model. Not great skin on his face, around his chin and cheeks, as though he'd had really bad acne when he was a kid. Long nose, like Ray here. Wide mouth with nice lips. But the guy was so fucking...sexy, he'd just stood staring at him with a bone on. What a *chitrool* he'd been!

"You keep playing with that," Ray warned, "something's going to happen."

"Like what?"

"You *know* what."

The guy had said Shirley wasn't home. He must have hit the wrong bell to get in. Then the guy asked was she his mother. Shit! His mother! He'd said, no, just a friend. And the guy said why was he holding his dick like that? Did he need to piss? He'd looked down and sure enough, he was actually holding his dick. What a double *chitrool*! Embarrassed, he said, yeah, he hadda go, and the guy said, well come on in, and he had, and gone into the bathroom, where it stayed too hard for him to piss, and after a few minutes the guy came into the bathroom and took hold of it and said he could fix that, and he went down on him and he was getting so hot that he pushed the guy's head away, and he knelt down to where the guy was sitting on the toilet and his dick was already out, also a diamond cutter and not small either, so he didn't hesitate. One thing had led to another, and he'd gone back twice now, and each time this guy, Donal— like Donald, but without the "d"—he'd told him it was a Scot's name—each time, this stud Donal had been hotter and better and...

"I'm giving you one last warning," Ray said, "then I'm going to turn you over..."

He turned over and looked invitingly back at Ray.

Instantly Ray was on top of him, kissing his shoulders and neck, reinserting himself, which wasn't difficult as he was already relaxed from being screwed ten minutes before, and excited. It would be Ray's last time with him. Let him have seconds.

It was nice too, feeling Ray going in and out. Kind of a massage, he guessed. Ray had already explained to him that it *was* a massage, of some little organ inside his ass called the prostate gland, which only guys had, not women, which was why guys enjoyed getting screwed more than most women did. That sure was true in his case. And it was true that the few times he'd tried it with Janet, she'd pushed him out, wouldn't let him continue. Well, hey, as his old boss used to say, "It's one of the perks!" Of being a guy.

Ray told him all kinds of useful shit he'd never heard before. He'd miss him.

Too bad about Ray's luck lately. He thought *he'd* had a bad run for a coupla years, what with Janet being sick all the time and Christy's hypoglycemia, and having to leave the shop and go to work driving a school bus. But that was nothing compared to Ray, what with losing his partner and his nephew and now his best friend was dying, and his niece having that kids' cancer and all. He could understand why Ray would want to get the hell out of here and try his luck on the other coast. Who wouldn't?

Shame about the kid getting run down. Although there he'd benefited. A few weeks after it happened, he'd dropped by and Ray had screwed him, as usual. Only this time Ray had asked if his boys could use some of the kid's things? Could they? What a haul that turned out to be: inline skates, ice skates, portable CD player, Sega game system, book bag, couple of new pairs of shoes, all kinds of clothing. Oversize of course, but Mike Jr. would be there soon enough, if not Darryl. Musta been a few thousands of dollars worth. Good thing he'd emptied the trunk of the car a few days before. Between the trunk and the backseat and the passenger seat, the trusty little Valiant had been packed full. He'd showed it all to Janet, and she'd put aside a few of the items that looked new—basketball, new baseball bat, knee guards, looseleaves—in the garage, hidden, saying they would be for the boys' birthdays and for Christmas. She was so smart. He would've never thought of that. And of course, he could never have afforded it. Not on what he made. He'd told Janet a coworker's kid died, and the parents wanted the stuff out of the house. "God, Mike! How awful," she'd said, a hand to her chest, a tear dampening her cheek. He could see her thinking what if that happened to her kids, especially Christy.

Ray hadn't talked about his boy. And the photo of the two kids he used to see on the dresser was taken down by then, so he couldn't remember what the boy had looked like. Must be tough for a guy who has no kids himself to lose one that close. It wasn't as if he'd go out and make another anytime soon.

Poor fuckin' Ray.

But at least Ray was moving to sunny California. And landing himself a fancy job in the movie industry. He was going to be working with Gigi Gertz, again, who he'd helped make a singing star…*maybe* working with Gigi, Ray had said. Maybe helping to score Hollywood movies, he'd said. Downplaying it. Being modest. As usual. One thing him and that guy Donal had in common. How they both downplayed how important they were. Unlike his friends, especially that loudmouth Dean! But Donal? Last time he was at his place, after they'd done it and Donal was in the john, he'd scoped the bookcase and there were five books by him. Five fucking books he'd written! Also in French and

German editions. Jeez! Imagine being smart enough to write five books, books people wanted to read around the world? He'd teased Donal into telling him about the books, what they were about and all, and Donal's eyes had looked anywhere but at him as he'd spoke, downplaying it, modest. Guy wasn't 40 yet!

Ah, that was beginning to feel really good. Ray sure knew how to screw. Good thing he'd met this guy Donal, because he was sure going to miss Ray.

Wonder how it was that both of them looked alike? Donal and Ray? Well, not alike if you did it point by point. But similar. That was the word. He'd heard some woman psychologist on the radio talking about how men always looked for the same kind of sex partner. She'd been talking about women. But it was true about men too. At least for him. She'd said they were often like people from your past. Maybe from when you were two or three years old. Who could that have been for him? Who was the guy who'd turned him on when he was standing in a crib, going goo goo and wetting his diaper? He knew it wasn't his dad or any uncle. Friend of the family? Whoever, he must of made some impression.

The way Ray was moving now, doing that kind of butter-churning thing, meant he was close to coming. Yeah, there he was nibbling on the nape of his neck, which he was crazy about, then nibbling farther down and nudging his cheek, like some big old horse. Big old horse dick on him, churning his butter but good. Who was the guy who used to say, "I don't mind getting screwed. It's the way he pants down my neck, bothers me"? You could tell *he* never got plowed. Because that was one of the best parts, once Ray no longer had control of himself but started going crazy with coming, how he kissed you and hugged you and said things, not even words, weird little grunts and groans.

Jeeter. That was who. Friend of Vinny. Tall skinny motherfucka with big teeth. Dressed like a Seventh Avenue pimp in those shiny shirts with big buttons. Jerk. Whatever happened to Jeeter? Wasn't he upriver for stealing cars? Then maybe he *was* getting plowed now.

"Mike? Mike?" It was like Ray was asking him questions. He wasn't. Or checking that it really was him getting screwed. No, all that meant was Ray was just getting ready to come. And now he had him, had him good, and it was like Ray was trying to dissolve them into one body instead of two, which was what he liked best and so he tried too, wrapping his legs around Ray and pulling Ray's arms together close in front, and letting Ray to try reach his mouth to kiss him, though he wouldn't, and pulling his dick inside, gripping it harder, really pulling him in. "Mike? Mike?" Yeah, baby. Yeah, Ray. Yeah, man, it's Mike all right you got here, and jeez, this was a big come, he could feel himself being fucked in half. Jeez! Ray! He'd be squirming on that bus seat later.

Sweating, panting, Ray slowly pulled out. The little wet pop it made. Ray fell over on the bed. A minute later Ray reached for his dick.

"Give me a few seconds, Mike." Really heaving. What a workout. Ray wouldn't forget this afternoon soon. "And I'll blow you."

Except he'd already come. Look at it, all over his stomach, all stuck in his hair there. Jeez! That had been a good one.

"I already came." He showed him, grabbing Ray's hand and squishing it in.

Ray came closer to him, nestling from behind, so they were like two spoons in a kitchen drawer. "So I got it right! Now that I'm leaving!" Ray groaned.

"You mean because we came together?"

"That, and because I made you come."

It was stupid, he knew, but he had to know. "You and that guy who died? Your partner? When you screwed, he came without you blowing him all the time?"

"Not all the time. A lot. More later on than earlier."

Ray's voice got all sad. He'd seen the photos of the guy, and he was all right looking, but kind of skinny, kind of like a teenager, even as a grown-up, even at...what had he been? Forty? Made you wonder what the hell Ray was seeing when he looked at him, huh? Still, if they'd had this kind of sex a lot, it'd be worth it, skinny or not. He'd have to let Donal know he knew how this could work. Get him to try.

Ray was hugging him from behind. "Can't believe I'm letting you go."

"You gotta be kidding. All those terrific-looking guys I see on TV and in the movies out there in Venice Beach and all?"

"Ah! They only have sex with each other. Won't even look at me."

"And you're going anyway?"

He felt Ray shrug behind him. No answer for a long time. Then, "Can I tell you something, Mike?"

Uh-oh. He hoped it wasn't something mooshy.

"Something I once did? Something...well, that I'm not proud of?"

He rotated himself in Ray's arms. He wanted to look at his face, to see Ray's eyes as he told him. "Something bad?"

"Yeah, something pretty bad."

"Sure. Tell me."

"It was, I don't know, some years ago," Ray said. "I was in Manhattan, at Sheridan Square in the West Village. I'd met a pal for lunch, and afterward I decided to walk around and window shop. I met this kid, I don't know, maybe

21, 22, young. Not badly dressed. Not shabby or anything. Beautiful! Body. Face. Eyes. Just…couldn't take my eyes off him. He comes up to me and says do I want to go home with him? I almost collapse. He lives on the East Side, he tells me. We'll take a cab. And by the way, he likes to get high first. Do I smoke? I say yeah, and he says he's temporarily out of it, but he knows a place to get it. I say I don't have much cash on me, and he says there's a bank machine. So I take out $30, and we grab a taxi and go across town. All the while he's rubbing my thigh, and I'm thinking, this is going to be so hot. The cab stops at this street! It looked like a war zone to me. Burnt-up cars on the street. Empty tenements. Lots filled with all kinds of garbage. A few skanky-looking people loitering. The kid already had my cash and he paid the driver, and we walk into this tenement doorway and he says I better stay down there while he goes upstairs to cop the smoke. So I'm downstairs, I don't know, it seemed like an hour. Probably it was only 15, 20 minutes. I go outside and the whole building looks vacated. No window glass. Nothing. I'm just about to tell myself that I've been had, I've been ripped off, when he comes out the front door. I go over to him and he's high as a kite. Not on smoke either. He's used my money to buy himself heroin at some shooting gallery up there. And now he's flying. Doesn't know who I am, or where he is. And doesn't care."

"What did you do?"

"I guess I was supposed to be so disgusted that I say oh, fuck it and take off. Or maybe I'd hit him. Beat him up. He didn't care if I did. He was so high."

"But you didn't?"

"What I did was I pulled him back inside the building. Grabbed him by the shirt, and pulled him into one of those empty rooms with bare floors. I found one with I don't know what it was, some kind of beanbag chair or something like that. I pushed him down on it, and I took his pants off, and I screwed him. Rats running around. People screaming in the building. I even heard gunshots. Did I care? No! I just fucked him as hard as I could. Then I got up and left him there, his bare ass hung over the damn thing. I zipped up and I left. Walked five or six blocks looking for a cab. Couldn't find one. What cabbie in his right mind would go anywhere near there? Found a subway station and went home."

"You paid for it. Might as well take what you paid for. No?"

Ray put a finger up to his lips. "You're saying it *wasn't* bad?"

"The whole thing was bad, Ray. It was fucked from the beginning!"

"I know that, Mike, and that's what bugs me."

"And what? You never saw him again?"

"I wish. Two, three months later I'm in Sheridan Square, and there he is, hustling some other guy. He didn't remember me. Didn't notice me. But I grabbed the other guy before he took his money out of the ATM and told him the kid was planning to use it for junk. I'm sure five minutes after I left, the kid got someone else to do it."

Fucking Ray. Leave it to him! "So this is like, a fable? A riddle?"

"No. No. Don't you see? It was something I could never deal with. Something I was totally unprepared to deal with. Despite all my education and thinking things through. Despite all my experience "

"I get it! So…it's the same now. With your partner and best buddy and nephew and the little girl all sick and dying and dead. Only this time you're doing it the other way? Right? Instead of fucking the guy who just fucked you over, you're saying no. Instead you're backing down and taking off." Whaddayacallit? He was fishing. "Taking the high road. Right?"

Ray looked at him and didn't say anything for a long time, until he was beginning to wonder if he'd gotten it wrong. But when Ray finally answered, so slowly, so thoughtfully, he knew different. "Is that what I'm doing, Mike? Trying another way?"

Ray was so serious about it, so gloomy, he had to laugh.

"Sure it is, Ray. It'll all work out. You'll see. You know what? I predict you'll even find some younger guy who's looking for a good screwing."

When Ray still didn't answer, he added, "*Maybe* someone as good looking as me!"

"I appreciate your saying that, Mike. Really I do."

"I'm not just saying it. I mean it."

"But it's not all that likely," Ray said.

"Why not?"

"Because now, after all I've gone through, I'm damaged. I'm damaged goods. It's going to be a long time before I'm good for anyone else. Guys pick up on that kind of thing, you know. You've picked it up already. I can tell."

He started to deny it, but Ray was right. Being here today, he *had* picked it up.

"Chances are," Ray went on, "even if I did stay in New York, you and me…we'd end up seeing less and less of each other. You'd start seeing other guys."

Fucking Ray was psychic.

"I still don't get it. What do guys pick up?"

"That they have no possible future with me, Mike. Even a butch guy like yourself." Ray punched his shoulder, man to man. "Married, with children…you want to feel there's some possible future, even if you choose to never go for it."

It was just then that he noticed the alarm clock on the floor. Shit! Had to get his ass back uptown to the bus. Kids would be leaving the museum precisely at 2 o'clock.

Dressed, at the door, the familiar office door, the office empty, not an oom pah pah poster on the wall, not a CD on a shelf, bare, he grabbed Ray by the neck for a hug.

Ray was still in his fucking Calvin Klein jockeys. Still looked sad. He would never forget what Ray had said back there. How does a guy live with that? Jeez!

That was probably why he reached over and kissed Ray on the lips. And because Ray was surprised by that, he decided to go all the way and even slipped Ray a little tongue.

It wasn't so bad. He didn't feel more queer doing it. And it cheered Ray up. "I'll come visit you in L.A."

It was only as he was skipping every other concrete step down into the subway station that he realized he hadn't taken the new address. And here was his train uptown.

Not that he'd ever go to L.A. Or if he did go, ever look Ray up. Even so… What a *chitrool* he was!

twenty-six

Two hunting horns leapfrogged each other in dotted notes, clambering cheerfully toward their predestined E-flat major culmination. Only to be suddenly barred by scrambling violins, furiously *scordatura*. They in turn were superseded, silenced in fact, by the *whump* of a viola *da gamba*, giving way to the dilatory tinkling of the clavier, leaving just enough room for the horns to again interecede, issuing a plangently intertwined, rising plea, soon joined by violas, violins, twittering oboes, all settling into a massive, only conditionally concordant, yet totally Telemannic, cadence.

Ray shut off the portable CD player on his lap but left the earphones in place. Through their charcoal-colored foam he could make out the ongoing muffled roar of the airplane's interior. Outside the 1011's window at his left shoulder, clouds ranged in pale puffy continents as far as he could see. Only looking straight down through them could one still make out hints of mountains, suggestions of lakes. Eye level and above was an immense dome of pale blue. Dead ahead, visible around the in-bent metal gleam of the cockpit, the sun hung, glowing orange, a beacon.

He'd been listening to the even-tempered Baroque prodigy since he'd sat down. And it had brought him luck. No one had claimed the seat next to his. He spread out there now: CD player, Liszt biography he was determined to finish, *New York Times* folded vertically to provide a platform for his crossword puzzle, plastic bottle of water.

A stewardess was at his right side, offering magazines he ignored, handing him a menu, wondering if he'd like a cocktail, complimentary champagne. He pointed to the items he'd have: tri-tip beef, *pomme de terres* Alice, Caesar salad, half bottle of Chateau d'Yqem, lemon chiffon mousse. She lifted a plastic-wrapped pair of earphones for the onboard movie, but he shook his head; he'd use his own.

Jesse still had frequent-flyer miles, which he'd inherited, and he had some himself. He'd converted them into a first-class ticket. Below him somewhere, perhaps already in the fertile black dirt of central Illinois not far from where his parents lived, his household goods were trussed up, speeding toward Southern California. Following them, attached via metal harness, the Buick Regal he'd at the last moment relented and decided to keep. He'd need a car on the coast, anyway. He could always trade it in for another. Meanwhile, a rental coupe awaited to take him and his few bags to the garden-enclosed semidetached duplex Maurette had found not far from the beach and the Pacific yet within easy driving distance to the sound studio they would be using; not to mention near Fox, and even closer to MGM-Sony's Culver City studio, where—and hadn't Jesse predicted something like this?—Gigi allegedly hung on tenterhooks for his arrival. He'd told everyone he'd arrive two days later, giving himself free time to hang around. The furniture and car might not arrive for another week.

He could see it all fairly clearly—his future. Not that he'd absolutely determined yet to have a future. He'd give himself one more year to reach that decision. But if a future did happen, he'd already resolved there would be no more of the insane recent drama; nor, despite the locale and even the industry he was flying into the center of, would there be any illusions at all about it being in any way illustrious, or even satisfying. He'd already had his life, and he'd already lived it to its fullest. He'd already had love, and like Shakespeare's Moor, he'd perhaps loved not very wisely and far too well. Still, he had made of it what he'd been able to, given the circumstances. He'd passed the last few weeks as objectively as possible, assessing his gains and considering his losses. A sort of balance had been found. He was certain he'd reached a point where nothing in his future could ever again cause him to leap in the air in pure joy. And he expected nothing could again leave him sunken to the floor amid shredded clothing, head doused in ashes, incanting antediluvian litanies he wasn't sure he believed in. From now on, it would be an excess of moderation.

In the row ahead, they were speaking again, the British actress and the American actor. He'd noticed her as soon as she'd boarded. Tiny, catlike, with a blunt little cat face and catlike rounded nose, dressed in black, save for the oversize tree-brown leather bomber jacket. He'd seen her Off-Broadway years ago, in a revival of a smart '60s farce. She'd made a name in British TV. Must be over 40 by now, but a girl's body, girl's gestures. Hadn't he'd read somewhere she was bringing Sophocles to Broadway? She must be meeting film people. The actor, a decade younger, nearly twice her size, with aquiline nose and a sweep of golden hair—Hollywood Hair, poor J.K. Callaway would have called it—he'd also seen, playing a featured role in some TV army drama five years back. Perhaps he played other roles onstage. As the actor passed her row as he headed to his own seat, she'd reached out tentative fingers to scratch his chinos at the knee. He'd looked down, beamed surprise, lifted her out of her seat in a huge embrace, set her down, then sat himself down in the adjoining seat. She curled herself up into his big body, even during takeoff, the two of them, talking, holding hands, catching up.

Now the actor was speaking, saying how he always took this 4:15 flight whenever he was returning to the West Coast. It took off late enough to get plenty done in New York, and landed just after sunset, so you had the whole night in L.A. In fact, he added, he and his friends called it The Sunset Flight. Look, he pointed it out to her, you could see the sun straight ahead. Not only that, but because of the speed at which they flew and because they were headed west, crossing three time zones, you could see the sun just ahead for most of the flight. Only when the plane began to make its descent into LAX would the sun set. If they were lucky, it would be eternal twilight, all the way across.

First their cocktails, then his chilled flute of champagne arrived. It was tart and bubbly and surprisingly fine. Then the meal, also quite good. He switched to a Chet Baker CD as dinner music, and replaced the headphones. When the demi of Bordeaux was gone and the soiled dinnerware removed, he nestled in the seat to view the movie, but it couldn't hold his interest. Once or twice he lifted the plane window shade, and stared out at the more or less endless gold prairie of clouds.

A tiny face, looking out a not quite oval window, one of 22 identical windows per side, sparkling like priceless stones, studding the tapered metallic cylinder of the aircraft, itself a gleaming spindle gliding high above a majestic meadow of multihued cirrocumuli stretching on all sides in celestial tones, the little glittering needle aimed dead ahead, as if drawn by invisible wire directly into the long, infinitely slow, somewhat cold, red-golden glow of a ray of mid March, 5:15 in the evening light.